THE CHOICE

ISBN-13: 978-1998775569

Give feedback on the book at:
lorhainneeckhart@hotmail.com

Twitter: @LEckhart
Facebook: AuthorLorhainneEckhart

Printed in the U.S.A

THE CHOICE

WALK THE RIGHT ROAD
BOOK 1

LORHAINNE ECKHART

WALK THE RIGHT ROAD

"There was not a human emotion I did not go through while reading this book. I will forewarn you, you will need a box of tissues and a punching bag while reading this dynamic tale."

ROMANCE JUNKIES

"I loved every single book in this collection. I loved Eckhart's writing style and her ability to develop a cohesive story line around strong characters is refreshing! I am looking forward to reading more of her books."

REVIEWER CHERYL

"Lorhainne Eckhart is a master storyteller and this collection is a steal. It includes all of the books in Walk the Right Road Series."

JRA

The Choice: One Woman. Two Men. And A choice that could kill her.

Lost and Found: 'A 2013 Reader's Favorite Award Winner': A hit and run. A deserted country road. A parents worst nightmare.

Merkaba, A Novella: Everyone thought he was dead and that's exactly how he needs it to stay. Until one day he stumbles across a mysterious dark haired beauty. Only, there is nothing average or ordinary about this secretive woman, and she knows exactly what and who he is.

Bounty: *Some pasts are best forgotten.* Most cops have a past. A past, they can speak of. A past, they can share, but not for Diane.

Blown Away: The Final Chapter: Imagine that the man who's been the source of all your misery shows up on your doorstep. Imagine this man wants your forgiveness for every bad thing he's done to you and your friends. Would you believe him?

He Came Back: One woman's haunting journey when her husband returns home and everything she thought she knew about their life together has suddenly changed.

What would you do for someone you loved?

—*"The Choice will leave you questioning your own morals and motivations and leave you asking others what they would do in that same situation. This is a genre-bending novel that will surprise you"*

REVIEWER, JRA

—*"From the Pacific Northwest to New Orleans, with its rich Cajun heritage, dialect, food...and voodoo, comes this spellbinder from Ms Eckhart."*

REVIEWER, ELYSABETH

—*"This book has everything I love. Romance, suspense, action and spiritual life struggles. Loved it! Kept me on my toes. The author creates characters that the readers either love or hate or a little, of both."*

REVIEWER, TINA MARIE

One Woman...

Marcie is crazy in love with Dan who has been using her and
promising his love in return. And she'll do anything for him, which is
fast becoming a one way ticket to trouble. But in a freak accident she
loses her memory landing in the path of sexy DEA Agent Sam Carre.

Two Men...

For DEA Agent Sam Carre when this attractive stranger lands in his
path he just can't resist helping her, even though he's haunted by a past
that gives him no peace. But as the sparks fly so do questions of what
she's really involved in.

And a choice that could kill her...

This complex case pushes them both to explain the unexplainable
bringing them face to face with generations-old evil and a haunting
question. Sam's forced to make a choice: walk away from the attraction
connecting them or risk losing everything.

TWO WOLVES

One evening, an old Cherokee told his grandson about a battle that goes on inside people.
He said, "My son, the battle is between two 'wolves' inside us all.
One is Evil. It is fear, anger, envy, jealousy, sorrow, regret, greed, arrogance, self-pity, guilt, resentment, inferiority, lies, false pride, superiority, competition, and ego.
The other is Good. It is joy, peace, love, hope, serenity, humility, friendship, respect, sharing, kindness, benevolence, empathy, generosity, truth, compassion, and faith."
The grandson thought about it for a minute and then asked his grandfather, "Which wolf wins?"
The old Cherokee simply replied,
"The one you feed."

~Author unknown~

PROLOGUE

It was too quiet. Unnaturally quiet.

The sort of unusual quiet that happens right after a big storm rips through. But there hadn't been one—a storm, that is. This was just another sunny day, exactly like hundreds of other brisk autumn Fridays on this off-the-grid, rustic island of Las Seta in the Pacific Northwest.

DEA Agent Sam Carre squinted from the blazing sun that brightened the calm, blue sky as he walked out of the shade. From the edge of the old-growth forest, he glanced back into the heavy foliage to where he'd separated from his partner, Diane, two hundred yards back, along the hidden fence line.

This island was an absolute crown jewel to any logging company, but a nightmare for Sam's team. It provided too many hideouts, the wrong kind—the dangerous kind—along with the perfect cover for marijuana agriculture.

Sam popped on his dark glasses and cut around three parked cars. He snagged his black jeans on some thorny bushes as he hurried toward the six solid, sure-footed male agents in front of the wrought-iron gate protecting Lance Silver's secure estate.

"Nobody goes until I say so." Sam kept his authoritative voice even and his charming grin hidden as he thought about slapping steel cuffs around Lance Silver's wrists. Tonight they'd celebrate, because today they finally had all the proof they needed to bust Silver and lock him up for life. He was a dangerous and connected man who had, until now, controlled the highway of drugs flowing down the west coast and across the country, with deep ties into South America.

"What's taking Diane so long? Can she even make it over the fence?" Agent Donaldson, a junior member on the team, pulled his ball cap over his prematurely balding head. He stood with Agents Craig, Daniels, Green, Mercer, and Winters. They were suited up in their Kevlar vests and dark glasses, weapons holstered and ready to go.

Sam cursed under his breath. Donaldson was pushing it again. It'd only been five minutes since Sam's partner, Diane Larsen, climbed the security fencing, leading four agents, two of them women, into the forest behind the house. And this was after she'd disarmed the wire triggering the alarm. Sam wasn't in the mood to argue with the young agent who liked to challenge Diane's authority. He undermined everything she did, which was absolute crap. Diane, the only woman on this team with a leadership role, worked ten times harder than any of these guys. She was kind hearted and respectful—yet capable of kicking ass when she had to. She'd been a rock for Sam when he needed a supportive friend to help him keep his head together. But since she'd fallen apart at the field office—the news her dad had died after accidentally mixing up his meds had hit her hard—she'd been getting all kinds of grief, especially from Donaldson. One incident, just one time, and it was all these tough-ass pricks could remember.

Sam moved away from the gate and back into the shaded forest to see if he could spot Diane.

"That kid's really vying for Diane's spot," said Agent Green as he dogged Sam's heels. He resembled a middle child, always trying to fit in, his round baby cheeks a contrast to his quarterback shoulders.

"Yeah, well, he ain't going to get it." Sam crouched down. "Can't see anything."

Green chuckled softly. "These damn renegades love this, off the grid, wilderness. It's the perfect hideout. Nothing but a bunch of hippies, musicians, and artists live here." Green spat on the ground a few inches from Sam's black boots.

"Hard for those families raising kids here, you'd think. No electricity, no stores." Sam breathed in the clean air.

"Sam, we're inside," Diane's low, silky voice whispered over the radio.

"Let's go, let's go." Sam signaled the six men with him.

Mercer stepped forward to cut the padlock with heavy bolt cutters. It broke, and he yanked the chain and tossed it to the ground. He and Green flung open the double gates. Sam jumped into the passenger side of the first car, and Donaldson climbed behind the wheel. As he slammed the door shut, Donaldson floored it. Craig, Daniels, and Winters followed in the two cars behind him, whipping up a trail of dust. Green and Mercer raced behind on foot.

Two hundred feet up the long, narrow driveway, the two-story estate house appeared magically out of the secluded forest. It rivaled any mansion from the Old South, with a fancy porch, woodwork, and gardens on all sides. Nothing moved; not even a curtain shielding the floor-to-ceiling glass windows. Lance Silver had people, a lot of them. The place should have been buzzing right about now. Sam pulled the warrant from under his Kevlar vest. He flicked the holster of his Glock and ran his fingers through his short brown hair. His gut warned him that something was wrong. Where was everyone? They shouldn't have been able to drive in without creating mayhem. This had been too easy —and too easy meant a problem. "Shit!"

Sam pressed his hand to his earpiece. "Keep your heads up, eyes open. Something's not right here." As a seasoned cop, Sam had learned, the hard way, to see and analyze things others didn't notice. It was a coping mechanism that had become his mode of survival, especially after what happened to Elise. They pulled closer to the front door. He felt the downward slide of something he couldn't put his finger on, but Sam knew—something was off.

Donaldson slammed the brakes and skidded to a stop at the front door. Sam placed his hand on the dashboard before jerking open his door and jumping out into a cloud of dust. Donaldson bounded over the hood and raced Sam up the stone stairs. Craig and Daniels hurried around the side of the house. Winters, Green, and Mercer flanked Sam.

Donaldson banged on the door. "DEA, open up."

Nothing, no response, and Sam really listened. By now, they should have heard footsteps, some kind of rustling from inside.

Beads of sweat covered Donaldson's face, and he appeared to vibrate, as if he itched to kick open the door.

"Open it." Sam stepped to the side, holding up his gun. Craig took the other side. Donaldson pulled up his knee and kicked hard with the heel of his black boot over the dead bolt, letting out a rough *oomph*. The doorframe splintered as the mahogany door crashed open.

"DEA, we have a warrant," Sam called. His adrenaline was pumping as he aimed his weapon and went in. Everything went into slow motion. Details stood out. In his peripheral vision, Sam caught a glimpse of the shining black steel of a gun and nearly crapped in his pants. It took a second to register that it was his gun, his image, in a floor to ceiling wall mirror. It filled both sides of the massive front hall. "Christ almighty," he muttered before gripping his weapon and shouting to the others: "We're in. Green, Winters, check the basement. Donaldson, upstairs." His gut twisted tightly as he struggled to listen. Where was the scrambling, the shouting, something—anything to break this chilly silence? "DEA, show yourself," Sam shouted again, clearing the front hall and the sunken living room, through an open archway to a huge chef's kitchen; which was extremely neat and tidy. Not even a measly cup had been left sitting on the counter.

Floor-to-ceiling windows filled every room. He could see Diane and the four agents out back behind the solar panels as they searched the outbuildings. Sam frowned and leaned against the double-pane glass door. This massive house was silent except for his agents, who were scouring every room.

Winters' deep voice grated through Sam's earpiece: "Basement's clear."

Everyone checked in. The garage, the greenhouse, all empty. This upscale, state of-the art, energy-efficient estate had been abandoned. Not even the caretaker remained.

"Sam, there's no marijuana. There's no equipment," Diane said through his earpiece.

Beads of sweat popped out on Sam's forehead. Beneath his Kevlar vest, his snug T-shirt stuck to his well-sculpted back. The radio buzzed with furious updates from their twelve-man team on the mainland, which included the Sequim sheriff's detachment, the Coast Guard, Interpol, and the DEA. This had been a simultaneous sweep of all Lance Silver's property, both here on Las Seta and in the underground truck trailer at his compound across the water in rural Gardiner, Washington. All empty.

Sam pressed his microphone close to his mouth. "Diane, where are you?" He slid open the glass kitchen door and walked onto the massive stone patio overlooking the pond and the luscious, well-tended rose garden. He slumped against the patio door and tried to rub away the pulsating pain between his eyebrows. Since this investigation started, he'd begun to experience a sudden sensitivity to light and sound. It could be gone in several hours, but the usual warning had been there for the last few days—a blue aura in his peripheral vision, black spots. But he ignored it; told himself it was the stress of running, what had started out as, an independent investigation by the DEA but had escalated into an international task force targeting the marijuana grow-ops running rampant on the isolated islands in the Pacific Northwest.

World-renowned high-grade marijuana was being shipped and traded for cocaine and guns. This was big time, a major business and an international problem that law enforcement had yet to defuse—as if they could.

"What's wrong?"

He never heard Diane approach. Her words stretched out long and loud. It took forever for his senses to override the roaring in his ears. His blood began to pound through his body, pulling him deeper into throbbing misery.

"Here, take this."

He opened his eyes when Diane tapped out three pills from a small bottle. He didn't question it. He just swallowed. There wasn't much Sam wouldn't take from his trusted friend. Diane was a woman of medium height and build, compact and tough, with tan short-cropped hair; the type of woman who didn't distract a man with flirtatious curves. But she was the kind of partner who'd do the gritty groundwork while keeping her partner focused, which was what she had done on the boat ride over this morning; ignoring Agent Donaldson's crude jibes, and guzzling coffee with Sam.

"If you don't pull it together, some woman on this team's going to fulfill her dream and have you bedded and nursed before we can wrap this up."

Whatever she gave him took the edge off the pain, which would have otherwise been blinding.

"Eat this." She tossed him an energy bar. He didn't argue, ripping open the foil wrap with his teeth and chewing the gritty bar.

"He knew we were coming," he said.

"Click off your radio, Sam."

He ripped the headset from his ear. "You know we followed the letter of the law to make sure this scumbag didn't get off on some technicality. All those stakeouts—we did our homework, Diane. We know who the little guys are; every fucking one of them on the street. We have video footage and rock-solid evidence that the drugs were here!" Sam pounded the fleshy part of his fist against the smooth fir siding.

"Agent Carre, you better get in here and see this," Donaldson beckoned quite arrogantly, undermining his superior, Diane, by not addressing her.

Diane, one to always hold her emotions close and rarely show what she thought, tilted one eyebrow up as her face hardened. This prick was deliberately pushing her buttons and deserved a one-on-one ass kicking. Personally, Sam would have liked to plant his foot far up that kid's ass by now, except this was Diane's fight, and if she wanted those guys to respect her, Sam couldn't fight it for her.

Sam and Diane followed Donaldson down a long hall, which resembled an art gallery, to Lance Silver's study in the solar glass wing. Green, Mercer, Winters, and Craig looked up, but only Winters— a big, dark Irish and African-American guy with long, fuzzy hair— would honestly look at Sam. The tension multiplied when the other tough guys turned away slightly, crossing their arms and glancing awkwardly at Lance Silver's palatial mahogany desk. All of its drawers hung open.

"We found this in the top drawer of the desk." Donaldson appeared to own the room when he picked up a crisp yellow piece of paper from the cluttered desk and passed it to Sam.

Diane peered closer, her head never topping Sam's shoulder.

His vision cleared. Bold black letters spelled out his name. He didn't miss how still the room had become. He could feel the heat from every agent while they waited for Sam to explain, but then Diane ripped the note from his hands and stepped in front of him.

"What the hell is this, some kind of game?" she snapped.

No one answered.

Sam was ready to clear out. When he replaced his headset, he could hear his boss, Dexter, shouting over the radio, bypassing Sam as he spoke directly to Diane. Diane pressed her hand to her ear to listen.

"I want your asses back here now," Dexter said. "We got a problem. A tip was called into the Sequim sheriff's detachment telling us to check Sam's locker at Ocean's gun club. The tipster said we would find a key to Lance Silver's estate and implied that my golden boy is on Lance's payroll."

Sam looked up so fast that his head spun. Dizzy, he stepped back and leaned against the mahogany bookcase. "What the hell? That's bullshit."

Dexter yelled, "There's a chopper en route to get you now. Two deputies from the Sequim detachment just opened your locker, and they found a key, along with five pounds of marijuana."

Sam's blood chilled. The bad feeling he had earlier had just become a clear epiphany. He could almost see that suave, tight-assed bachelor, Lance Silver, laughing at him. Instead of Silver going to jail, all this shit flying around had landed hard right on top of Sam. Not only did he look like the leak in Lance Silver's back pocket, but there was also doubt of Sam's true allegiance painted on the faces of the agents surrounding him. He could feel their censure.

Amazing how quickly they turned. They thought he had tipped Silver off about the raid. Pissed and completely furious, Sam gazed hard at all of the turncoats until each one stepped back. He wasn't about to dignify this with a response, not after how hard he had worked to nail that bastard, following every lead the other agents missed or brushed off. Sam hadn't missed a thing—he lived for this investigation. He had breathed life into it and lost sleep because of it. Those guys should have known that, out of anyone, Sam wouldn't be the one to betray this team. He ground his lips together so hard that they trembled. He felt as if the rug had been ripped right out from under him, and he was positive that he could hear a toilet flushing six months of steady, solid work away. How could this have happened again? Why was he such a target?

Well, for one, this was Las Seta, an unpoliced, reclusive island, part of the San Juan Islands in the Pacific Northwest. History alone should have warned him this job wouldn't be easy. The explorers and adventurers who had claimed this island over a hundred years before landed there quite by accident, for one reason or another. Whether hiding or running from something, they had all insisted on a land free from politics and civilized order. Families and clans remained year after year, protecting each other, and, staying true to tradition, they followed their own way of doing things. So, while Sam hunted Lance Silver; Lance Silver and the island of Las Seta had changed the rules of the game and ambushed Sam.

CHAPTER 1

"Get on the plane. It'll be fine. I've got your tickets and passport taken care of. We practiced this. You know what you need to do." Dan McKenzie was broad shouldered, with an exquisitely lean body and mesmerizing hazel eyes perfectly situated on his lightly freckled, aristocratic face. His nose was a little too large, with a small bump at the bridge where he'd broken it, at the end of his brother's fist, as a child. He also had a firm mouth that she knew, all too well, could set her soul on fire. He was quite the package, with a magical face that could belong to some fairy-tale hero and all that unruly reddish hair, which he trimmed himself. He was a fine specimen of a man, standing nearly a foot over Marcie's average height, with well-sculpted hands that knew how to touch a woman.

"I thought you were coming with me and we'd finally have time away together?" Marcie's soft voice trembled. Her heart sank. This wasn't what she expected. What was he doing? This was supposed to be their time to rekindle their love—time to lift off whatever had been oppressing him. She needed him so much but felt him slipping through her fingers like dry grains of sand, while she struggled to hold on.

Dan leaned back, his hazel eyes dark and sober, as he crossed his arms over his chest. How could she convince him to come with her? She had so much fire and passion for him, that it tugged a cord deep inside her.

What was it about him? He was dressed so casually, in a T-shirt and blue jeans, but the man could wear a grain sack and would still look good. He wasn't handsome, but he was pretty. Unfortunately, even letting her down didn't shake the mega chemistry that attracted her to him. It made her want him more. Just looking at him, she wondered if Zeus himself had been the image Dan was cut from. He had long, solid arms; a tight, firm ass; and long, lanky, well-muscled legs that she knew, all too well, intertwined nicely with hers. And those lips—man, she loved to kiss them, as had scads of other women. After all, the man was a magnet for women; like honey is to bees. He said, time and again, that women were always landing in his lap. He could have had anyone he wanted, so why had he chosen her?

"Can't, Marcie. I'm too busy, you know that. I have faith in you. You can do this." Before Dan could turn away and open his door, she reached over and grabbed his wrist. He leaned over the middle console separating the bucket seats, but hardness tightened his muscles like a brick wall between them as she held on.

"I love you." Panicked, she felt some part of him slip away. His body, his eyes, everything about him seemed to take a step back from her, as if he were holding some part of himself in a secret location and had forgotten to tell her. He hovered a few inches away, gazing out the front window, resting his other arm over the steering wheel. He didn't once try to pull his arm away from her grasp.

"I don't understand what's going on. We were so close, and you've been pulling away—bit by bit."

Dan glanced over in a way that told her his patience was thin. "Marcie…"

She placed her hand over his mouth. "Dan, please, I don't know what to do. I feel you pushing me away. You ask me to babysit your marijuana plants, but I don't see you anymore. Then you ask me to go to New Orleans, which I thought was a trip for us. Now, I'm going alone. Why are you pushing me away?" Shaking, she couldn't bear the thought of losing him. He no longer looked at her with that deep, magical spark that said she was important to him—that they were connected at a cellular level as soul mates. That had been after Granny died, when she'd felt so alone on Las Seta. After she met him at the farmers market, he said he fondly remembered her from high school, and they had spent hours talking. Every week after that, he showed up at the market, where she sold her herbs, to see her. He connected with her on a level no one else ever had. He understood how different she was. She felt things from other people, their emotions, and she had a love for nature and felt the need to protect the environment—to respect Mother Earth. What excited Marcie, and still did, was his ability to pick up warning vibes, just like she could.

Each time she saw him, his radiant smile shook up the butterflies in her heart. He would tell her that he planned to be near her each and every day. In the beginning, it seemed like he couldn't get enough of her. He made her feel special before she fell, head over heels, in love with him.

He caressed her cheek with his warm hand and then tucked her heaps of rich, wavy brown hair behind her ears. "You need to stop. I'm not pushing you away. I'll be here when you get back. You and me, Marcie—I'm still interested. I have a lot on my plate right now. You're it to me. You got in when no one else ever has." He pressed his hand against his heart. "Come on. Your plane's leaving." The next instant, his eyes softened, and that slightly crooked smile he flashed did what it always did—it sucked her right back in to where she believed she could somehow grasp some tiny morsel of caring from him.

Dan popped open his car door and stepped out. He didn't come around to her side to open hers. She knew he wouldn't. He didn't do all that mushy stuff. She told herself it didn't matter, and she smiled away the hurt that stung beyond belief. He carried a lot of pain from a hungry childhood; forced to eat out of garbage cans after his father walked out, leaving his mother to raise and feed him and his five brothers and sisters alone. Marcie supposed that was what had shaped him into who he was, and why, at times, he became distant; unable to be the perfect man. He needed love and lots of it. Then he'd stop making her feel less of a woman—then he'd genuinely love her, or so she told herself. After all, in her entire life, all she ever wanted was to be loved deeply, as every woman had a right to.

Marcie climbed out of his early model Olds. He pulled out a backpack and handed her two tickets, along with her passport. She flicked open the passport and frowned at the name.

"It's fine, Marcie. With what you're doing—you don't use your real name."

"What if I get caught?" she whispered when alarm turned to nausea in the pit of her stomach.

"Come here, give me a hug." Just like that, she was in his arms. His tall, lean body pressed against hers. His wide-palmed hands, with the fingers of a carpenter, slid firmly up her back. His voice whispered like silky rum: "I love you, too."

When she let go, he held tighter, so she slid her hands back around his neck and nearly wept from their connection and from what he couldn't say with words. When he finally let go, she felt foolish for doubting him and offered an honest, dimple-creased smile.

"Go, Marcie. Your plane leaves in fifteen minutes."

So she did, all the while grasping some artificial hope that she remained, very much, Dan's one and only.

Her cellphone buzzed while she hurried through the enormous Sea-Tac Airport, bustling with travelers. She glanced down at the number that flashed across the screen. "Ah, crap," she said, but she answered it anyway. "Sally, I'm in a hurry. I can't talk right now."

"I've sat by the sidelines for too long, Marcie. As one of your granny's oldest friends, and your teacher, I'm going to speak."

Marcie glanced upward for help while hurrying toward the ticket counter. "Sally, let me call you back in a few hours." Some lines she wouldn't cross, and one would be to disrespect Sally and hang up.

"No, girl, you listen to me. You think I don't know what you're doing? You're crossing over to something dark, and it's going to kill you. There are dark entities around you, and I've been fighting, for over a year, to keep them away, but you keep letting them in. Walk away from him. Whatever you're doing, wherever you're going, don't do it, girl. I don't know if I'll be able to keep saving you. Come home, back to Las Seta. Let me finish teaching you. You've only just started."

She stopped at a bench before the ticket agent, blew out a breath, scooped back her hair, and then rested the backpack on the cushioned seat. She could almost picture Sally, the short, plump, white-haired and very English good little witch, with her wheezy voice, standing in front of her. Instead of a cat, she had a fluffy golden retriever. Instead of a black cape, she wore a white or cream sweater over her shoulders.

"You mean Dan, the fantastic man I've been asking for my entire life? I think you're confused, Sally. I'm just going on a trip. There's nothing for you to worry about." Marcie knew she had let the old woman down. She could feel her hurt in the soft sigh on the other end of the phone.

"Marcie, girl, I love you. You don't know what that guy is. You can't believe anything he tells you. You know you've never healed from that cesspool into which you were born. Your granny, my best friend, yanked you from your no-good parents when you were twelve, but you're still a magnet for that abuse. You've been snared good; caught in a trap. You don't understand. This guy's a wizard. He came into this world with dark entities attached to him. His karma came with him. He knows how to get past your weak aura. You're vulnerable, and you see him how he wants you to—not how he really is. Please, I'm begging you, if you go and do what I think you're doing for him; I may not be able to help you."

The last call for her flight was announced.

"Shit, I've got to go, Sally. I promise I'll call you." Marcie hung up and slid her cellphone in the front pocket of her backpack. "I'm sorry, Sally. Please forgive me."

For a second, uncertainty made her pause. After all, Sally was the wisest woman she knew. She'd always been brutally honest—she'd always been right with whatever she shared with Marcie, and she never spoke lightly. In fact, Sally wouldn't go out on a limb like this, unless there was a dire need. That stoked a chill up Marcie's spine, but just as quickly, an image of Dan flashed in her mind, along with the ultimate love she felt for him.

"She doesn't know him like I do. She doesn't understand how badly he's been hurt. She's wrong this time," she whispered under her breath, convincing herself that the nagging hesitation was merely

Sally's doubt. She shrugged the nylon backpack over her shoulder, well aware that what she carried, if caught, could put her in prison for years to come. But she wouldn't get caught. Dan had promised her that the package of bud would never be detected by security; and, right now, she needed to trust and believe in her red-haired prince with the dreamy hazel eyes. So, she ran, stuffing her burning confliction away in the same hidden place that she'd buried the heartache and rejection of growing up with an alcoholic mother, who had drowned her sorrows and been drunk by noon, and a father who flaunted all of his dirty secrets, including how much he liked young girls.

CHAPTER 2

Marcie trailed the other passengers off flight 918 into the main terminal of the New Orleans airport. Her eyes were lowered, shutting out everyone around her. She strode at a steady clip, dressed in her favorite Levi's, the jeans that attracted a man's eye to her rounded bottom. Her tan blouse shimmered over her pert, shapely breasts; the size a guy could fit nicely into the palms of his hands. She rubbed her forehead, reminding herself that she had no need to paint her face as other ladies chose to. Marcie rarely shed the healthy glow from her days spent outdoors, but that was where her comfort ended. She claimed a spot in the middle of the pack, behind a wide lady sporting a navy suit, doing her damnedest to blend in.

How low have you sunk? Marcie cut off the cruel, persistent voice prodding her conscience. During the cramped four-hour flight from Seattle, her face had heated each time her toe touched the backpack she'd stuffed under the seat in front of her. She'd refused a drink, but her tightly wound nerves could have used a stiff shot. Instead, she'd suffered in misery, wondering how she'd made it this far. Dan told her it'd be easy—so far, so good.

She needed to shake off her anxiety to enjoy her first visit to this vibrant city, one she'd dreamed of experiencing for years. New Orleans was famous for its mouth-watering cuisine, jazz musicians, and Creole culture. Marcie was, more than a little, intrigued with the voodoo legends that had sparked the imaginations of many a writer, with the unexplained chills and the auras in graveyards and buildings; this was the most spellbinding haunted city. Marcie remained determined to experience all of it firsthand.

How much farther? The drop-off had to be close.

Heaviness weighed down her heart when Dan's face entered her thoughts again. If only he'd come, this trip would have been perfect. She knew he'd share her excitement for the gifts and mysterious secrets New Orleans was famous for. But he hadn't come, and this wasn't the first, or even the second, time he'd gone off and left her alone.

This roller coaster of emotions, one that she experienced only with him, had now left her on the downswing, as was usual when distanced from Dan. She shook her stubborn head to get him out of her thoughts. He wasn't here, but he had a way of slipping in to disrupt her peace of mind at least twenty or thirty times a day. He was an addiction that consumed her, making her want to do anything for him, and she did. But the one thing she wouldn't do was give him Granny's place on Las Seta.

Her days had shifted down a steady slope of turmoil—just so she could have him in her life. This was crazy.

Nevertheless, there were boundaries, and, right now, she knew deep down that she needed to establish them. She could no longer ignore the volatility of this relationship, nor how she had willingly gotten on the plane for him. "Let it go, let it go," she whispered under her breath, keeping her head down while walking with the other passengers through the terminal.

Her heart pounded in excitement when she rounded the bend. She could see the silver luggage conveyance contraption and the back wall of baggage claim. Was anyone watching? She needed to look closer but feared being too obvious. *Think of something else … Emeril's restaurant!* She gave herself a discreet high five, and a weight lifted inside her. For the first time since leaving Seattle, she felt lighter. Should she call Dan? *No.* Why did he continue to slip into her head?

Almost done. Peace, blessed peace, blossomed in her heart. Marcie offered thanks to her angels for guiding her safely through.

She glanced at a magical, jazz mural exploding with vibrant color. It drew her into the rhythm and music that pulsed to life in the vivacity of the art. Marcie loved art, but then, she had grown up around the artists who sojourned on Las Seta.

Overhead, a saucy Cajun lilt announced incoming and outgoing flights, and it melted the tension in her stomach a little more.

Then everything went into slow motion. One moment, she clutched the black and red knapsack over one shoulder, and the next, she felt a cut, a snag and a pull at the same time that a large, rough hand shoved her. Unable to stop the momentum and regain footing, she went down in a hazy blur. Her ears roared. Her blood pounded through her veins. She felt nothing when she smacked her head on the hard concrete floor.

Her ears rang and her vision blurred. She struggled to focus on the maze of faces wreaking havoc on her overloaded senses, but she couldn't think. As she pushed herself up, she started to sway to some indistinguishable hum buzzing in her head. She shifted her bottom on the cool floor and balanced on a shaky arm to keep from tipping over.

What happened? She couldn't think. The downy hairs on the back of her neck spiked with icy unease, adding to her discomfort. Something remained vaguely out of reach, an ache. When it hit, it became a ripe sting burning the side of her head. She couldn't understand what she was looking at—her hand, and it was streaked with blood.

Voices, sounds, chaos existed in slow motion, like a puzzle in her brain. A strong hand grabbed her shoulder. Another touched the side of her face. At first, she gazed unseeing, then blinked. A crowd gathered close behind the rough, unshaven face of a stranger who resembled a fallen angel. He peered into her eyes. His full, firm lips moved, but she couldn't make sense of the rumbling sound. He turned away. This time, she heard his smooth, smoky voice shout out to the crowd of bodies behind him.

What was it about this man with his shabby, light hair? Even his intense blue eyes appeared tired, with lines of life that deepened his godlike appearance. Did she know him? There was something familiar about him. She wanted to trust him.

"Ouch." She flinched when he touched her head. Her brain blanked out. "There's blood on my hand." She hadn't meant to speak, but her voice cleared away the fog and piercing ring buzzing in her ears.

"Your head's bleeding. You've got a big gash. It's going to need some stitches. What's your name, sugar?"

She liked the honeyed richness in his voice, except something worried her, and she didn't know why. "Marcie, ah … what happened?"

"Don't you remember?" He watched her again in a way that made her want to reach out and touch him. He seemed nice. She liked him. Maybe it was his husky southern drawl, or maybe the concern this good-looking stranger had showered over her.

Marcie reached up to touch her head. The stranger quickly grabbed her hand.

"No, Marcie, don't touch."

"Oh."

He pressed something against her head, bringing on a wave of dizziness. She wanted to lie down and close her eyes, but when the room tilted out of control, she grabbed his shirt instead.

CHAPTER 3

Sam Carre pressed a napkin to the oozing cut on Marcie's forehead. Her face turned a pasty white, and she grabbed his shirt. He knew that look. She was about to pass out.

"Marcie, sweet thing, take a breath and look at me. You going to be sick?" She said nothing. Her arms shook as she held tight. "Marcie, come on. How you doing? I need you to answer me."

Slowly, her cornflower blue eyes met his. They appeared dazed, confused, and, for a moment, unseeing. "I'm dizzy."

He pushed back her long, curly locks. Each strand was like silk against his fingers, and all that full, wavy hair enhanced the plump roundness of her cheeks. He looked around to see if someone claimed her. No one stepped forward.

He lifted the soaked napkin and studied the gash on the left side of her forehead. Blood seeped and dripped in a steady stream over her brow. Sam glanced up when an elderly woman dangled a linen scarf in front of him.

A large, mocha-skinned, out of shape security guard pushed through the crowd. His name tag said "Stoffer," and he leaned into Sam's space. "Wow, that's a gusher. She sure knocked it good. So what happened here?"

His colorful manners snapped Sam back like a time warp.

"Snatch and grab. Kid took off, got her bag and sent her for a tumble. Did anyone call an ambulance?"

"Hmm, ambulance is coming," Stoffer replied roughly. He squinted his dark eyes to get a better look and then shook his head. Grimacing, he glanced at Sam and leaned closer with his hands balanced on his knees. "She with you?"

"Nope, just on my way home."

"Lucky guy." He patted Sam on the shoulder and then stepped back to reach for the radio fastened to his belt. He uttered something incoherent into it and wandered off.

Sam forgot his own misery when he focused on Marcie. It felt good, in this whole convoluted mess called life, to help someone else. When had he last done that?

"My name's Sam. Where'd you come from, Marcie?"

Her face shifted through a mirage of emotions, as if struggling with the simple question. Long, dark lashes and pale eyelids blinked when she glanced up to the left over his shoulder.

Sam followed her dreamy gaze but saw nothing except a bunch of gawkers with luggage passing by. Marcie stiffened; her eyes widened, and color infused her cheeks. Did she know someone? Should he jump up and ask the crowd if anyone knew her? Before he could, her arms trembled again.

"Are you looking for someone? Is there someone with you?"

Her eyes leapt to his, startled like a deer. He'd seen that wild-eyed plea many times on victim's faces. Maybe she knew her attacker. This was a complication; one he didn't need in his screwed-up life.

A gurney squeaked behind him.

"Move aside." Stoffer waved his hands, shooing back the crowd.

The pretty lady tightened her hold on his cotton shirt. Sam held her shoulders. "Calm down. It's going to be all right."

She was such a small woman, with curves in all the right places; a body the right man could scoop up with one arm to protect from whatever frightened her. Her mouth gaped wide. She tried to speak. She gasped for breath once, twice, until her sweet, clear voice pulled him further to her plight. "I don't know.... I can't remember."

Sam blinked. Holy shit, what a long response time.

She had a strong grip for a woman with such tiny, delicate hands. She wasn't going to let go. Sam swore under his breath because he was no more able to leave her, at this moment, to fend for herself than he could a wounded puppy. "Ah, shit."

Sam rubbed her hands to calm her down and then pried them gently away. "It's okay. The paramedics are here, and they need to have a look at you." Sam didn't wait for a reply. Instead, he stepped back, allowing the paramedics room to move in.

Sam turned and eyeballed the throng of travelers. *Who did she see?* That fear in her eyes—it must be someone. With a cold eye, he scanned the area, looking for anyone who paid that extra bit of attention, but nothing unusual stood out. Or maybe it was just him—maybe he needed to stop at the first bar for a shot of whiskey. Could he trust his instincts? He didn't know anymore.

"Well, well, look what the cat drug in." Sam swung around toward the familiar husky drawl.

A tall, charismatic Cajun made his way through the crowds, looking a little worn and rough around the edges. Jesse Crawford was an old friend, rival, and a detective with the New Orleans Police Department. He was dressed the same way Sam remembered: a cheap, rumpled blue suit, spotted red and white tie, and a faded white dress shirt. His nose was long and slightly crooked from where Sam had planted his fist six years ago when he'd ended their friendship because of Elise. Jesse looked older. The tired, craggy lines had deepened around his eyes and mouth, a result of the long, underpaid hours of being a cop.

"Jesse, what the hell are you doing here?" He reached out and gripped Jesse's large proffered hand, squeezing tight and sizing up his old friend. Did he remember the scandal, the hard feelings? Of course he did, except now was not the time.

Jesse returned the grip, squeezing harder. It was bone crushing, and Sam nearly winced. Determined, though, he held tight, a mocking game they'd played for years. When he let go, he tried to be inconspicuous as he flexed his fingers.

"Going soft, are you, up north with all those yanks?" He then leaned around Sam to get a look at Marcie, her head now bandaged, being loaded onto a stretcher. "Didn't know you were back. It's been a long time."

"Yeah, I thought it was time to come home for a bit."

Jesse said nothing, but there was something in the way he watched Sam. Maybe he knew why Sam had come back. After all, they shared a childhood bond; two local vagrants from broken, abusive homes growing up together. Or maybe Sam was just paranoid, being back in this city. This place was tinged with too many memories, both good and bad.

Jesse turned away when Stoffer tapped him on the shoulder. Sam shoved his hands in his faded blue jean pockets and debated whether now would be a good time to slip away. He craned his neck, looking for the door, when those damn memories invaded his head.

How many times had Jesse swallowed his pride and reached out to him? He had never trusted Elise. He loved Sam. It was why he had told Sam, when he married Elise, that she was trouble. But Sam wouldn't listen, and now a fresh wave of pain punched a hole right through him. But he did what he always did. He shoved the ache back in the dark pit it came from.

"Sam, are you listening?" He blinked. Jesse was in his face again. "Got a call, purse snatching and assault. The powers that be get a little nervous when things happen in our airport." His friend frowned, shaking his head in mock dismay. "Don't tell me you're mixed up in this?"

"It wasn't a purse. Try backpack. My lucky day—I was behind her when she got tossed."

"Big, strong, good-looking guy like you, women are still jumping in your lap. Amazing." Jesse's invisible green horns of envy flashed.

Sam stepped back and chanced a glimpse at Marcie.

"You get a good look at the guy, did ya?" Jesse's sharp gaze missed nothing. He took a step into Sam's space, eyes level and pinning him to the spot.

Sam blamed his obsessed, scattered focus for the reason he didn't zero in on the tall, lanky kid before he'd taken Marcie down. The thief had operated with speed and skill. He was definitely a pro. Pissed at the young thug, Sam struggled to remember where he'd come from. *Ah, that's right.* He'd slid in behind the lady, cut the straps of her bag, and knocked her down before bolting; only to be swallowed up in the crowds. It was the perfect snatch and grab.

Street-smart instincts had kicked in when Sam started after the kid, but he had stopped cold when Marcie's head smacked the ground. He looked back at Jesse and then over to the door when he realized his name would be on the police report.

Jesse's crooked smile widened as he appeared to read Sam's mind. "Trying to sneak away, are ya?"

Sam snarled before he could mask his reaction. He shuffled his feet and then crossed his arms. He really needed to get out of here. He used his six-foot-one height and his solid build to tower over Jesse.

"Sam, come on. I know you're trying to get out of here, but you've got to help me out."

Sam sighed when he looked back at the girl. "Not much of a look. Tall, lanky kid sidled up to her. Blue jeans, gray T-shirt, grungy brown baseball cap, picture of sea lions on the side. Dark kid, maybe six feet with a gold earring in his right ear." Had time stood still?

"Don't miss much, do you? What he have for breakfast?"

Sam cocked his head and narrowed his eyes. "Fuck you, asshole."

Jesse chuckled.

"Excuse me, sir. The lady's asking for you." A slightly balding, short paramedic, whose name tag said "Wesley," spoke softly. "We're ready to go."

Sam looked with ease over Wesley's head. Marcie appeared stricken, with doe-like eyes. She needed a friendly face.

"We need to get her checked out. She's going to need a couple of stitches for sure, and they're going to want to do a head CT for her possible memory loss and confusion."

Sam moved beside Marcie. She reached for his hand, and he winked and watched her face soften with relief. He warmed a little in his belly, feeling like a gallant knight who'd saved the damsel in distress, until he caught Jesse's sharp eye watching the entire exchange suspiciously.

"Memory loss… What're you saying, she has amnesia?" Jesse stepped forward and spoke directly to Wesley.

"She's confused. Not unexpected with head injuries. The doc will look her over."

Marcie clung to Sam with both hands now. *She's scared.* God help him, but he was stung by a piercing drive to protect her. He didn't want, or need, this complication right now. He had his own problems to deal with.

"I don't want to go to any hospital."

"Marcie, it's not a choice. You need stitches, and the doc needs to have a look at you."

"Will you come with me?" she pleaded, her eyes desperate.

"Sure." He slammed his teeth together. *Digging yourself in further. That was your last chance to slip away, you idiot.* He closed his eyes to stifle the irritating voice, except those smooth, tangy words poked him again. *You just couldn't mind your own business and walk away. Good boy.* Whose voice was that? It sounded like Mama Reine, the large black woman who was his surrogate mother—a loving woman who had sheltered both him and Jesse during the worst time of their childhood. Great, now he heard other people's voices. Maybe, while at the hospital, he should have his head examined.

When he looked down, Marcie gazed up at him with something akin to worship. Swimming in those cornflower blue pools had him sunk. What made it worse, when her panic faded and she eased her hold, was the way she watched him with no pretense, no games. She'd hooked him as her lifeline.

If, in fact, she had lost her memory, she'd just emotionally latched on to him as the first and only familiar person. *What have you taken on, boy?*

CHAPTER 4

Other than going and getting stinking drunk, what else did Sam have to do? So he, along with Jesse, trailed the paramedics. Stoffer and three airport security guards cleared a path for the gurney through the swarm of travelers.

Sam grumbled when they passed the luggage conveyor. He should stop and grab his bag. That would be easier than the corporate hoops he'd have to jump through to reclaim it later. Instead, what did he do? He followed, shoving his hands in his pockets while being escorted out the sliding glass doors to the parked ambulance.

Jesse dogged Sam, his raspy chuckle grating in Sam's ear. "So, explain to me again how you don't know the lady, yet here you are, holding her hand, escorting this pretty young thing to the hospital."

Sam ground his jaw together before firing back at Jesse. "Is it absolutely beyond you to step in and help someone who needs it? She's alone. I'll go with her to the hospital. Then I'm leaving. It's called chivalry, asshole." He hoped it'd send him withering away. It had worked on the young agents he worked with, but now he remembered that with Jesse, it only added fuel to the fire, and he'd use it to dig deeper.

"Helping someone, sure, I've done it. But the two of you? Nah, there's something more. Come on, you and this pretty young miss, you know each other? You two have chemistry. Come on, tell Jesse everything."

Okay, that last remark was too much. Sam whirled around, raised his hand, and jammed his index finger against Jesse's chest with a hard thump.

"Keep your hands down, and don't do that again," Jesse snapped. "Did you forget where we are?"

That was a decent pail of ice water thrown on him. It doused his fiery temper in an instant. *Wake up, boy, and look where you are.* Words in his head jolted him when he saw the hundreds of people surrounding them, eyes aglow and fascinated, fixed solely upon him. Another scandal—*pile it on.* That was the warning he'd heard. It would be something he couldn't afford, so instead, he uttered in a low growl, "You stupid ass, fuck off." Sam flinched when Jesse smacked him in a brotherly way in the middle of his back and then let out a boisterous whoop of laughter. This time, he shrugged Jesse off with nothing more than a warning scowl while the paramedics loaded Marcie in the ambulance.

"You always did have a way with words," Jesse said. "Now get in."

SAM MADE A PLAN AS HE FOLLOWED THE GURNEY TO A CUBICLE IN THE emergency room. Get her settled, see she was looked after, and then leave. Two nurses, a doctor, and the two paramedics assisted Marcie onto the bed.

Sam leaned in to say goodbye but was asked to step aside when Marcie was questioned, poked, and prodded by nurses and interns. Three butterfly strips were taped across the bloody contusion along the front of her hairline. Then, after the standard blood test, they whisked her upstairs for a head CT. Again he was told to wait, so he crossed his arms and waited. He expected to be dismissed to the waiting area, but instead, a pretty, blond intern on staff questioned him.

"How long has she been confused?"

"I guess since she hit her head."

"Can you tell me how she hit her head?"

"She was robbed and pushed. She went down hard and smacked her head on the concrete."

"Are you family?"

"No, I don't know her. I was just behind her in the airport."

"Is there any family we can contact?"

"I don't know. Hey, Jesse, was there any ID in her pockets?"

Jesse wandered in from the nurse's station. "Nothing. Suppose if she doesn't remember anything, we can get her picture up on the news."

A tall, lanky orderly wheeled Marcie back in and helped her into bed.

"Listen, is it common for someone to lose their memory from banging their head?"

The intern was busy scratching notes onto Marcie's chart, but when she looked up with twinkling light brown eyes, she gave Sam a pleasing smile. "Not necessarily. We're only seeing symptoms of a mild head injury. I've seen nothing that makes me believe this is anything permanent." The Barbie-doll intern wore blue scrubs. She wiggled her rounded bottom a little extra as she wandered over to Marcie and shone her pen light in Marcie's eyes.

Sam shared an amused glance with Jesse, and both pointed at the other.

"Her pupils are normal and reactive. There's been no vomiting. She's sitting with relative ease. Do you have a headache, hon?"

Marcie glanced up at Sam first before answering. "No, not overly bad."

"Very good. Your speech sounds clear, and I like your eye contact."

The intern stepped closer to Sam. "I don't see anything leading me to believe this is more than a mild concussion. Memory loss can happen, but I've rarely seen it. Sometimes it can be an underlying psychological condition. I'll ask the psychiatrist on call to do a psychological workup. Other than that, if the head CT comes back normal, she probably just needs a few days of rest. Her memory should return."

Sam watched the worry build up in Marcie's shoulders. She

hunched forward and played with a piece of lint on her blue hospital gown before looking helplessly at him. "I still don't remember who I am or why I was at the airport."

Sam was disturbed to see this vulnerability. He didn't quite know what he'd do if everything familiar disappeared from his memory. Of course, he was embarrassed by the response hovering on his dry lips. *Say goodbye. Wish her well. Hell, leave your number just in case she needs something.* He shook his head. No, he couldn't be that cruel.

"Marcie, do you remember what the guy who stole your purse looked like?" Jesse crossed his arms.

"Jesse, I'm pretty sure it was a backpack," Sam said. That had been Jesse's way to trap her, but Sam, too tired to play games, interrupted. He wanted this done.

"Yes, Sam. Good thing you're here, or we'd never get to the bottom of this," Jesse snapped.

Marcie's eyes darted between the two of them. "I didn't see anyone, and I don't know what I had. The only thing I remember is seeing my hand covered in blood and you stopping to help me." Her hand flattened, palm up, in a powerful gesture toward Sam. "I'm pretty sure my name's Marcie. I don't know my last name. I don't know how I got to the airport or how I ended up with my head cracked open. And I don't even know if anyone's looking for me."

The intern patted her hand. "I'm going to have the psychiatrist come by and have a chat with you."

"Is that going to help me get my memory back and provide any of these answers?" Marcie asked. Sam liked that spark of personality.

"It's too soon to tell, but psychiatrists can decipher all kinds of things going on in someone's head that we can't see." The intern smiled warmly at Sam, ignoring Jesse, who stood off to the side. Then she deliberately placed her back to Marcie, glancing down at Sam's ring finger. "You know, there's really nothing more you can do here, and I get off in an hour. Any chance you'd like to grab a coffee?"

Jesse chuckled from the corner, reminding Sam of how easily women flocked to him, but it was the bright tears sparkling in Marcie's hurt eyes that sliced open Sam's gut.

"Ah, no." Sam moved to stand by Marcie, annoyed by emotions he didn't care to explore waging war inside of him. "Listen, what happens after all these tests are done? Are you going to admit her?"

The intern's suggestive smile vanished. Her spine stiffened. "Most likely, she'll be released. We're overcrowded as it is. There are no beds."

This time Jesse stepped up. "Oh, come on. Are you telling me you'd throw out a woman who can't remember who she is? Where's she supposed to go?"

The nice perky intern vanished before Sam's eyes. She crossed her tanned arms in front of her. "Oh, come on, Detective. That's not fair to put on me. We've got no beds. You know how bad it is for county cases. She's got no insurance, right?"

"If my memory's gone, how would I know if I had insurance?" Everyone looked down at Marcie, who seemed very aware.

"Maybe we can get you to one of those women's shelters for tonight."

How thoughtful of Jesse. But Sam knew how bad some of those places could be, and that was if you were lucky enough to find a bed. "Look," he said, "I haven't been home in a while. My place has been closed up, but there's a bed for you to sleep in tonight, and tomorrow, we'll come up with a new plan."

Marcie said nothing, though she gave a weak nod, appearing to consider the idea. "Just for tonight, then. I really don't want to put you out."

Now he felt bad for having tried to sneak away earlier. She seemed genuinely nice, which was a far cry from the criminal element he usually encountered. At least he'd have one more night of sobriety. Maybe tomorrow he'd get a chance to wallow in misery.

CHAPTER 5

Marcie's head CT came back negative for any serious head trauma. The psychiatrist assessed Marcie briefly and said there was no clinical explanation for her memory loss. He suspected her memory could easily return in a few days, but if it didn't return in a few weeks, he suggested she explore it further with a neurologist.

Jesse drove Sam and Marcie back to Sam's small apartment in the French Quarter. Instead of going right home, Jesse accepted Sam's invitation to come up.

"Let me open some windows." Sam slid open the balcony door. An instant breeze stirred the musty air.

Marcie leaned against a bare wall, crossing her arms over her blood-splattered shirt. She looked around the simple box room. Every dingy wall remained free of pictures or adornments. This place was merely four walls and humble furnishings.

"How long's it been since you were here last?" Jesse had a heavy rhythmic walk, swaying his shoulders with each step, wandering the plain apartment kitchen as he spoke. He had a tanned, slightly scarred face; mysterious, dark eyes; cropped, curly hair, and a wide mouth, which smiled on command to shamelessly flash a gleaming silver tooth.

Jesse appeared distracted and distant, pulling open the fridge and then the old, scratched cupboards as if inspecting the unmaintained unit's condition.

"Over six months. Don't know why I keep the place. Guess I can't figure out what to do with everything. So I keep paying the rent." Sam fiddled with an old clock sitting on a cluttered desk in what Marcie supposed was part of the living room. The way he smoothed his hand over the brass cover and then pulled his fingers back as if burned, she realized some emotional link kept him here.

"You've got no food. Do you want me to make a run to the market for you?" Jesse's concern appeared brotherly, as if he were playing the familiar role of watching over Sam. He swaggered over to Sam, hiking up his baggy pants just under his heavy beer belly.

"That would be great. Grab us some burgers too." Sam pulled out a worn wallet and fingered out a handful of bills, mashing them into Jesse's hand. "And don't forget the beer." Something passed between the men; hesitation, awkwardness.

Jesse didn't linger. He turned and shuffled to the door. He stopped when his hand turned the knob and gave a look of kind consideration to Marcie. "Do you need anything, Marcie?"

She blinked and moved away from the wall. This compassion, for some reason, pulled a little in her heart. It was foolish, really, but it meant something. She darted a quick glance at Sam. He, too, looked thoughtfully. "Thank you. I don't know what I need."

Sam flushed and firmed his lips as he stalked across the room like a man secure on his feet. He handed more bills to Jesse. "Get her a new shirt, toothbrush, some essentials. I don't know what else. You have a wife."

"So did you. Don't mean I know what she needs nor pay any mind to what she buys." Jesse tucked the money in his pocket and went out the door. "I'll do my best."

Sam patted Jesse's back. "Thanks, Jesse." Jesse left, and Sam rested his palm against the closed door, watching Marcie with his mesmerizing blue eyes.

"Let me get your room done up for you." He continued on into the only bedroom, walking slower, putting his lean linebacker body into each step. He filled the doorway when he passed through it, and she was glad he didn't see the dreamy clouds that came into her eyes.

He was so much the shabby, fallen angel, confident, oozing with integrity, and quite the package. She lingered in the doorway, watching while he pulled bedding from a cupboard and made the double bed.

"Why didn't you go for coffee with that doctor when she asked you?" Marcie instantly colored, wishing she could take back the words.

He froze while hunched over to tuck the sheet under the mattress and then slowly turned his head toward her.

Marcie shuffled her feet. "I'm sorry, it's none of my business. I just … you took me in; you don't know me—and you didn't turn your back on me. You were concerned for me. You turned her down flat without even considering it."

He flicked the top sheet over the mattress and folded stiff hospital corners. His nostrils flared as he breathed deeply. "Only creeps do that, sugar. It's not even a consideration, in my mind, to act that way when I'm with another woman who's flat-out hurt." He arranged a blanket on the bed and plumped a pillow. "Bathroom's around the corner if you want to get cleaned up before Jesse's back with dinner." Sam directed her with a nod.

"Would you mind if I had a quick bath?"

"Not at all. I'll get you a towel."

Marcie followed Sam. He pulled a towel from the linen cupboard and placed it on the worn, chipped counter in the apartment-style bathroom. He paused for a moment. Sadness lurked in his eyes when he touched a hairbrush, lying neatly assembled with cream, lotion, shampoo, and assorted makeup. He closed his eyes tightly as if blocking out some painful emotion waging war inside of him. "Use whatever stuff you need here." He didn't tarry but crossed over the threshold and pulled the door closed.

Marcie didn't know what to make of this, but she remembered the comment Jesse had made before he left. Sam used to have a wife. If so, were these things hers, and what had happened to her?

CHAPTER 6

J esse returned shortly after Marcie finished with a quick bath. Her mind was full of questions regarding Sam's wife, because it was obvious that she remained a ghost in this apartment and still had a prominent place in his life.

Jesse dumped three plastic bags on the kitchen counter, and Sam put away enough food to keep them fed for a few days. Burgers and greasy fries tempted Marcie's stomach, which grumbled from the savory aroma.

They gathered around the living room coffee table, downing burgers, fries, and soda. Well, the soda was for Marcie; Sam and Jesse opted for beer.

"Drinking on the job, or are you off shift?"

Jesse took a deep swig from a bottle of beer. "You've been away too long. You know things are done a little different down here. Besides, it's just one." Jesse belched. "Oh, pardon me, ma'am."

Marcie offered a shy smile and shoved more fries into her mouth.

"So what're you doing back, Sam? Last I heard, you were running some high-profile case, nailing some big-time drug dealer."

Sam said nothing but leaned back and downed the rest of his beer.

Jesse frowned, deep lines cutting around his eyes. Sam got up and helped himself to another beer from the fridge.

"You know, ever since we were boys and I found you with that busted lip your daddy gave you, I knew that when you clammed up this tight, something bad had happened. You'd get moody, didn't want to talk. You haven't changed," Jesse said.

"What the fuck? Are you my shrink now?"

Marcie bit into her burger while her heart kicked up a bit, watching with large eyes, first Jesse and then Sam. So Sam was a cop, too.

"Marcie, you're looking kind of pale." Sam wandered back, sinking down into the worn, narrow couch.

"I'm fine, just hungry." To prove it, she took another bite of her burger, wondering why she felt so unsettled.

"I noticed you still got her things everywhere. She's been gone for two years. Don't you think it's time you got rid of everything?" Jesse leaned back in the soft easy chair, nursing his beer. "It's been six years, Sam, since you busted my nose for sticking it into your business. Don't you think it's time we cleared the air?"

Sam splayed his hands in acquiescence, spilling a few drops of beer on the brown, dingy cushion.

"I shouldn't have called her a lying piece of whore trash before you married her," Jesse said.

Sam's gaze darted over to him, and Marcie wondered for a moment if he'd follow. Positive she must look agog, she shrank back, trying to make herself invisible. So Sam's wife hadn't been a nice lady. Now she really wondered what happened to her.

"Look," Jesse jabbed an extended index finger toward Sam, "we grew up together through the worst of times. Your, piece-of-shit daddy, using you and your mama as punching bags, and mine was no better. How many days and nights did you and me camp out at Mama's, talking up our dreams? Then in comes Elise, some perky, blond bombshell of a teen, with a black eye and major attitude. Never knew why Mama Reine let her come around."

"Why? Because Mama was a saint of a woman who opened up her home to all us local beggars every and any time we needed a safe place to hide." Sam leaned forward and whispered the last part: "She said every child deserved a chance. But it was still our own choice how we wanted to turn out."

"But you tumbled head over heels in love with her, just a kid tailing her like a love-starved mangy puppy. She was wild, and what she did, she always did for Elise. No one else mattered, whether you'll admit it or not. How many times did she lie to you? She would show up wearing some fancy trinket only a rich man could afford, always said she found it or that it was given to her. Don't even try to deny it. You know as well as I do that she'd steal anything not nailed down." Jesse leaned forward and dumped his empty bottle on the table.

"Why do we have to rehash this? She's dead, okay?"

Marcie froze and stared down at her plastic cup. His wife was a thief, a whore, and she was dead. She didn't know what to say, so she firmed her lips tight and hoped one of them would break the silence.

"Marcie, if you're tired, just leave all this mess and turn in. I threw one of my shirts on the bed for you to sleep in." Sam jumped up and hastily grabbed the remnants and packaging from their feast, stuffing it all in a plastic bag. "Jesse, you mind dumping this in the trash on your way out?"

Jesse hefted his stocky frame out of the burgundy chair. "Marcie, good night to you. I'll come by in the morning and see about finding out who you are."

"Thank you, Jesse, for dinner. You've been very thoughtful. I appreciate it," she said.

His soft, dark eyes swam with a considerate emotion before he winked. Then he moved past Sam, taking the garbage with him.

Marcie climbed into bed. She could hear Sam tinkering with something and knew he planned to sleep on the lumpy couch. She didn't know how long she lay there, mystified by the strange, sexy man who had taken her in. To learn, second-hand, that his wife wasn't nice touched some part of her she couldn't explain.

She should have been devastated, not knowing who she was and where she came from, as that knowledge seemed to be stuck behind an impenetrable brick wall, but she wasn't. She struggled past the slight ache in her head to understand why. Finally, after much deliberation and no answers, she relaxed into a dream state. It was another time but a familiar place.

"The house is burning!"

Marcie bolted upright and smacked her head on the RV's low vinyl ceiling. Someone pounded the door. She jolted awake, instant alarm hammering in her chest—boom, boom. Her wide eyes scanned the dim confines of Dan's second-hand fifth wheel, parked on his newly acquired rural property.

She jumped down from the top bunk, landing hard. In a flash, she pulled on day-old clothes and shoved the door with so much force that the metal frame smacked the side of the trailer. She leaped down and bolted to the old house, which was already engulfed in flames. Heat pushed her back as angry fire burst skyward. Richard drove the yellow loader, and Dan maneuvered the compact excavator. Both pushed in an opposite wall, and to anyone else, their actions resembled two desperate men trying to contain a fire. Marcie feared judgment day was battering her with unruly wings. Alarmed, she closed her eyes and listened to the wail of high-pitched sirens, louder and closing in.

"Hurry!" Marcie ran closer and cupped her hands around her mouth, but angry sparks blocked her way.

"Get the hell back," Richard shouted. Gears ground, and he reversed the loader.

All four walls collapsed. There was so little time. Flames shrieked in fury, consuming what was left. Two fire trucks, sirens screaming, arrived, followed by three sheriff's cruisers. Lights flashed in unison against the backdrop of rippling flames. All authorities were here and closing in, covered in protective gear, assuming full control. They shouted, "Shut it down now!" over and over—angry words barked at Richard and Dan to get them to pull back.

Hoses were pulled out, connected and hooked to a standpipe at the front corner of the property, every maneuver synchronized. Two more red fire trucks pulled in, Discovery Bay *written on their sides.*

Marcie couldn't keep track; there were too many people—too many lights. Richard and Dan refused to stop. It was too much for her eyes. She didn't know where to look: the heat, the sparks, the overwhelming smoke and surrounding darkness. "Oh my God."

Two firefighters climbed up on the moving equipment and forcibly shut them down. The sheriff arrived, angry—shouting, waving his powerful authority.

Three abandoned cars in front of the house were scorched. One by one, windshields exploded from the heat. A uniformed deputy grabbed her arm, holding tight when she tried to move away. The sheriff and another deputy cornered Richard and Dan. Dan locked his hazel eyes on her. She instinctively knew the unspoken words he was sending her: Shut up. Say nothing.

An agitated volunteer approached the deputy, who let go of Marcie and turned away. A white flash drew Marcie's attention. She peered behind her in the dark and glimpsed a strange woman in front of the RV. She stood horribly unnatural. A breeze kicked up, waving her long blond hair in an odd rhythm. The woman smiled in a way that was cold, mischievous, and vaguely familiar. The woman's hand seemed to reach right into Marcie's heart and squeeze. She'd never get used to that sudden chill.

"Who are you?" Marcie couldn't breathe. The air was stuck somewhere beneath her stomach; she choked. This sultry, kickass woman didn't answer. She just aimed her index finger and thumb like a loaded gun, a direct line of fire, straight at Marcie. The eerie sound of metal grinding jarred the marrow inside her bones. Then the strange woman laughed a deep, throaty chuckle, tossed her head back, and strode around the trailer to the old woodshed, hidden in plain sight.

Panic licked the back of her throat. She didn't know how she moved. All she knew was that no one could go near the shed. Heat closed around them. She became deaf to everything but the drumbeats filling her head. Shivering and haunted by nothing but darkness, the padlocked wooden shed, and a crazy, dead woman, Marcie felt very much alone.

Marcie bolted upright. Out of breath, she gasped for air. Her chest hurt, and a vise-like pressure from her pounding heart wouldn't ease even a little. She pressed her hand to her heart. Dizziness blurred her vision until one by one, her sense of body and awareness returned to the pinching ache of her swollen gash, taped on her forehead.

Pots clattered, and she breathed in the fragrant aroma of sizzling bacon. She slid her legs over the side of the bed in this strange, cramped room. Marcie gazed at her pale, bare legs as awkwardness hit hard. She dropped her pounding head into her hands, covering her face. There was nothing but a big blank in her memory, although she remembered her handsome knight and the dark, disheveled detective who cared so deeply for Sam that he had risked their friendship by speaking truthfully about Sam's dead wife. A thick, dark fog of nothingness hid every memory before the airport floor and the blood on her hand.

She touched her soiled clothes, dumped in a heap at the end of the bed, and wondered if she was decent enough to leave the room and say good morning. She slid off the bed. Sam's large T-shirt slid down to mid-thigh.

Her head hurt after her dream-filled, restless sleep. She padded barefoot across the cool wooden floor into the kitchen.

"You're up. How'd you sleep?"

Marcie stood in the doorway of his open kitchen. "In fits, really. I'm not sure...." She trailed off when the room took a sick, slow spin. Before she could stagger and lean against the wall, Sam raced across the room and scooped her into his arms.

"Whoa, whoa, girl; you need to lie down. I'll get you back to the doctor." He deposited her on the sofa as if she weighed nothing more than a feather. "Lie there." He pulled a knitted blanket over her. "Look at me. You got a headache?" He examined her eyes the same intent way the intern had done the night before.

"I'm good, sorry. I don't know what happened. I think I kind of got up too fast. I didn't sleep that well, and..."

"And what? Come on, what were you going to say? Finish it—don't leave me hanging out there, sugar." He sat in front of her on the cluttered coffee table, scattering beer bottles. He ignored the mess even when they clanked on the floor.

Her face heated when he aimed those magnificent blue eyes at her.

He coughed to bring her back to his world. Had she been ogling him? Flustered, she dropped her eyes, confused by the need for him that was growing inside her. Her dream blazed clearer, and so did the implication of something being not quite right. Fear, guilt, and worry spiked up the heated connection between them. She studied her clasped hands before looking back up. "I don't know what to say."

"You remember who you are, where you come from, something?"

Marcie lowered her eyes again and shook her head, saturated by a ridiculous instinctive response to deny. She couldn't meet his intense, honorable eyes. She felt cornered, unable to tell him about her dream, because she knew, deep in some private, secret hollow, that her dream was a very real memory.

Drenched by a miserable guilt, she felt warm when she glanced up. Sam watched her with grim eyes—eyes that slipped into the soul, searching for secrets, lies, and, she supposed, how a person ticked. *What did he see?*

He grew silent and seemed to pull all his feelings back inside, behind a heavy armor, right before he stood and walked away. She couldn't stop her hands from trembling, so she squeezed them and slowly sat up. The unsteady breath she'd been holding escaped, sounding a little too much like relief.

"Just remember something, Marcie—I know when people are lying to me."

Tiny beads of sweat drenched her forehead. Thick knots tightened her already anxious stomach, and Sam didn't look back.

CHAPTER 7

After breakfast, Marcie carted the Walmart clothes Jesse had picked up for her, the night before, into the bathroom. She climbed into the hot shower and scrubbed her head a little harder than she needed to, but she was mad—mad at herself for not coming clean about the dream. What was the big deal? Well, she already knew the answer. Listening to Jesse talk last night about Elise and how untrustworthy she had been, there was something about Sam, in his quiet confliction, that made Marcie want his respect. She didn't want to be like Elise.

After she dressed in the pale shirt and khaki shorts that were a size too big, she wandered out to Sam.

She found him on the balcony in the bright sun, barefoot, wearing blue jeans and a clean white T-shirt. He appeared lost in another world, a deep thinker who leaned over the railing, staring into the street. The wind fluttered the sheer curtains, beckoning her forward, so she stepped closer to the lively chatter drifting in from outside. Marcie clenched her damp hands and then relaxed, releasing a slow, measured breath. One step closer, almost there. The floor creaked on the threshold of the small balcony, and Sam turned and leaned against the black iron rail. He crossed his strong arms. He said nothing, but his hardened eyes reflected suspicion.

"I lied," she said.

"I know."

Marcie stood so close that she could feel his warm breath whisk over the top of her head. She licked her bottom lip, sucking in a breath for courage. The breeze whipped up her damp hair. *Don't be scared.* "I don't know if it was real...." A sharp knock at the door hurled her insides a little closer to the edge. Frustrated, she let her head drop toward her chest. How could she confess with this unwelcome interruption?

"That's got to be Jesse." Sam brushed past Marcie, his heavy steps echoing down the hall.

Marcie claimed Sam's spot leaning over the rail, taking in the beautiful view from this second-floor apartment. The vibrant energy from the colorful crowds of people on the street below rose up and connected with her. For a moment, she was pulled into the flamboyant revelry, like a powerful magnet intercepting a rainbow of emotions from all the people on the street: joy, lust, anger, jealousy, being hurried.

"Oh my God—what the hell?" She jumped back. Her whole body stung as she trembled. Flustered, she pressed her hands flat against the white stucco, flooded by some instinct to breathe. Her mind stilled. She sucked in another deep breath, and the tightness twisting up her stomach eased. "I must be going crazy." Spooked, she remained plastered against the wall.

"Marcie."

She jumped as if a fist had jabbed her heart and slammed shut some secret door inside.

"You okay? What are you doing? You talking to someone?" Sam reached out and grasped her elbow, a gentle touch filled with tender concern.

"Yes, no—sorry, just some weirdness, that's all." Nervous flutters began inside her chest. He was so good looking, and those solid, tanned arms of his—a girl could get lost in them. His closeness became too much. She needed to look away, so she stalled and tucked her unruly damp hair behind her ears to shake off Sam's amazing intensity, a gaze like the depths of the ocean weaving its way into her heart.

"What?" Sam moved closer.

"This is going to sound nuts, but I got scared. I leaned over the balcony and suddenly I was in all those people's heads, picking up what they were feeling." She shut her eyes and refused to look at him. "See? I told you. It even sounds crazy to me. Maybe I'm going crazy," she rambled, and he stopped her by gently tucking a stray strand of hair behind her ear. Her eyes popped open. His touch stirred some lovely, odd feelings inside her. The way he looked at her made her feel as if what she had said wasn't so crazy—not to him.

"Jesse's here," he said.

She must have been staring like a fool, because he coughed to break the spell and held out his large hand. When she placed hers into his, it was like a soft wing stroking her skin, tipping her belly with a faint thrill while she allowed him to lead her inside.

A large canvas bag lay heaped on the scratchy beige sofa, a crumpled airline tag dangling from the strap. The kind dark-skinned detective was wearing the same rumpled blue suit, but with a clean light blue shirt and striped tie. He eyed her now with a look that had Marcie taking a step back. *Something's happened. He doesn't trust me.*

"Jesse retrieved my bag from the airport," Sam explained.

Jesse shrugged his bulky shoulders and loosened his sloppy blue tie, but his hard eyes remained glued on her. "It was the least I could do for an old friend. Funny thing though, Marcie; I couldn't find yours."

Her stomach twisted. "I don't understand?"

"Come on, Jesse. It's more than possible the airline lost the luggage," Sam said.

"Sure it is. They do it all the time. Why, just last year they sent mine and the missus' to Florence. Always wanted to go there. At least my bags got to go." He chuckled at his dry attempt at humor, except Marcie couldn't shake off the implied distrust. He looked at her with the same hardness he had used when speaking of Elise the night before, and that worried her.

"Don't forget the backpack, Jesse. Maybe it was her only piece of luggage."

"Okay, maybe. But then, what woman carries only an itty-bitty backpack with all her things for a trip? None I've met. But hey, there's always a first."

Hearing Jesse's assumption raised questions she hadn't thought of. She paused, confused, looking at her pale hands and her long, slender fingers. She had really tried to clear the muddled darkness clouding her past, except it made her anxious. At the same time, though, her loss of memory filled her with an unexpected blissful peace.

"So what do you suppose was so valuable in that backpack you were carrying?"

Sam cocked his head and frowned. He took a step toward Jesse. "Now, what are you implying?"

"I'm not implying anything. Just asked a question, is all."

Sam looked Marcie square in the eye and then exchanged another scrutinizing glance with Jesse, as if trying to piece together a puzzle.

Okay, now would be a good time for her memory to return. She pressed her fingers to her head and struggled to pull the backpack in question out of thin air. Just as quickly, she felt an urgent need to backpedal. "I don't remember having a backpack, even though I was told I had one." She stumbled for words and some tangible explanation, but even she had to admit something was off. She didn't want to remember, or maybe it was that damn dream. She couldn't shake it—or maybe Sam didn't believe her. *Once a liar, always a liar.* Steamy heat rose in her cheeks from the obtrusive voice that squeaked in her head. Now she really wanted to hide. Instead, she stared at her bare toes and the dingy hardwood floor.

"What about the passenger manifest, and all the planes arriving at that time?" Sam paced and circled his hand in the air for emphasis.

Jesse cast his rough gaze at Marcie. "We know from security footage that you came off Sam's flight, but I couldn't find a Marcie listed on the manifest. Why's that, you suppose?"

Marcie didn't know what to say, she was dumbfounded. The floor softened beneath her feet, while a spiraling sensation rippled through her. Disconcerted, she searched out to Sam for help, but he too narrowed his now accusatory eyes.

"Oh, no, I swear I don't remember." *Just confess.* The pressure became too much. Her throat closed up, and her lip trembled when bubbled tears flowed with a noisy sob. She scrunched her eyes shut to block out all doubts. She couldn't suck back the cry no matter how hard she tried.

"Oh, no, woman crying. Sam, I don't do the crying girl thing. Do something."

"Shut up," Sam muttered.

Marcie clenched her trembling hands.

"Marcie, stop. Come on." Sam touched her, except she could tell by his hesitant, distant, awkward squeeze—an obligatory touch—that he'd pulled inside himself. *Why bother?* It was such an affront that she was mortified and took a step back, and Sam's hand fell away.

She clutched her hands under her chin and tried to see Sam through the film of tears that coated her swollen eyes. "Sam, I don't remember. I know I lied when I didn't tell you about the dream. I'm positive it was a memory, and you knew. But I think I did something really bad, and I don't know what it was. Maybe I don't want to know. I don't want to be a bad person. Please help me."

"What dream? She did something—Sam, what the hell's going on?"

"Marcie, come sit down." He grabbed his bag and tossed the canvas tote so that it landed with a heavy clunk on the floor, just missing Jesse's foot.

"Hey, watch it," Jesse said.

Sam slung his arm around Marcie's shoulder, being kind again as he settled her on the sofa. He hunkered down across from her on the now cleared coffee table. His long legs encased hers, and he leaned in and rubbed her arms. How could he be so nice? He should have tossed her out.

Jesse cleared his gruff throat. "Look, Marcie, I just don't want to see my man here tromped on again by another deceitful woman, and there's something about you; with no luggage, robbed in a crowded, busy airport for your backpack—it leaves me with a lot of questions."

Sam wiped his hand across his forehead. "Mother of God, will you stop, Jesse? I'm not a kid anymore, and I somehow don't think Marcie's here to rob me blind," Sam snapped with pure annoyance. "Did you find out anything useful?"

Jesse held up both palms in surrender. "I'm telling you the passenger log doesn't list a Marcie or Marcia or anything similar. So I still don't know who she is."

"Maybe Marcie's a nickname. Have you thought of that? Can't you get her face up on the news and see if anyone recognizes her?" Sam sounded pissed.

Marcie jumped up when an icy shiver raced up from the center of her belly. Her face lost all color. The room swayed. This time, Marcie knew she was going to faint. Her vision tunneled. Sam's firm hand on her back sat her down and pushed her head between her knees.

"Take a deep breath. If you feel like you're going to puke, let me know. Jesse, grab me that bucket under the sink. Come on, hurry."

CHAPTER 8

Sam loved Jesse like a brother, even after the angry rift that had torn their friendship apart; Elise—his first love—his wife. Maybe that was why he understood how Jesse could assume the worst about Marcie, why he had questioned the backpack.

Marcie was in the bathroom, attempting to compose herself. Water trickled from the bathroom tap, squeaking through old pipes, cutting through the silence. Jesse impatiently drummed his fingers on the checkered kitchen counter.

"Sam, what the fuck was that about a dream, and what did she lie about? She did something wrong? This whole thing isn't sitting right in my gut. Could you fill me in?" Jesse lowered his agitated voice.

Sam pushed aside the scattered papers on the corner desk in the cluttered living room. "I don't know. She's freaked out about something and was about to tell me when you showed up."

Jesse crossed his arms and firmed his full lips. "Please don't tell me you've been fooled by yet another pretty face?"

Sam turned away from his cleaning spree and leaned his hip against the half wall separating the living room from the kitchen. "She's not Elise, and I think you know that. Elise was street smart, savvy...."

Jesse cut him off with a grunt. "Elise hopped in and out of the back of cars with any guy who'd offer her a free ride. Then she'd empty their wallets. She was a player. She'd steal anything she could flip for money. She planned to go into a store to take. She had no morals. Did you forget her first abortion at fifteen, a second at seventeen? And you, you dumbass, took her and paid for each one; even though neither was yours."

Sam's eyes glazed over with a frosty, distant hurt. He gritted his teeth, shook his head. "Why are you doing this? Why now?"

Jesse shuffled closer to Sam. "Don't you think it tore my heart out to watch you twisted around her finger? You couldn't see what she was doing. She went from one guy to the next, and you were always sitting by the sidelines. What'd you promise her so she'd marry you?"

Grief and anger waged an ugly war inside of Sam. He glared at Jesse, then snapped, "I dared her, because I knew it was the only way she would. Are you happy now?"

Jesse didn't touch him, but his gruff voice softened. "I was never happy watching the way you were ripped apart from the back forty. I knew you loved her, and maybe she loved you, too, as much as she could. But she was never honest with you, and that I can't forgive her for."

The floor squeaked behind Sam. "Good God, woman, you scared me. How long you been standing there?"

"Long enough. Jesse, I hope to God I'm not dishonest. Just the thought…"

"Marcie, Jesse isn't saying that."

She stepped closer to Sam. "Well, actually, Sam, Jesse's trying to protect you from being hurt and deceived by another woman. He's watching your back. Friends don't come any better than that." She crossed her arms. "I'm thinking I did something. I don't know what's going on, but I seem to be picking up on feelings and stuff…." Her hand shook when she paused. "I have a feeling I may be listed under a different name."

"And what name might that be?" Jesse responded.

Sam ran his hand up and down the back of his head, pacing in a circle over by the balcony.

Marcie shrugged, seeming like a frightened child. "I don't know. It's just a feeling I have."

"Jesse, you should be able to find out from security at Sea-Tac airport."

"That'll take time—time my boss ain't gonna give me. This morning, he told me to wrap it up, no chance of catching the thug who robbed her. He don't give a rat's ass about her lost memory." Jesse firmed his lips and looked down with a mix of distant concern, maybe trying to decide if Marcie could be trusted. "I'll ask Dev in airport security to contact them for me. He can find out."

"Actually, Jesse, I'd like to see the security video. Any chance you could get me in to watch it?" Sam asked.

"Why?" Jesse puffed out his chest and crossed his arms

"Just a hunch I want to follow up on. Humor me, please."

Jesse merely grunted while keeping his hard, dark eyes focused on Sam. "Let me guess; you're not about to share this hunch."

Sam paused before a faint boyish grin lit up his striking face. He slowly shook his head.

Jesse threw his hands up in the air. "Let me see what I can do."

"Last night, I had a hard time sleeping. At one point, I fell into a dream. Except I think it was a memory of something I did or was part of." Marcie faced Sam.

Jesse wandered out of the kitchen and leaned against Sam's cluttered desk.

"It was real, Sam. I swear, and this will sound crazy, that it was a cover-up of something. I was staying on this large rural property in a trailer. There were two guys I knew there, Richard and Dan." Her eyes widened. "I don't know where that came from. I don't remember anything about them."

"But you know their names?"

She shrugged and glanced at Sam and then Jesse with an irritated, helpless look. Sam moved back beside Jesse and leaned against the half wall, struck by Marcie's natural beauty, which flowed all around her. The soft skin at the bridge of her pert little nose wrinkled while she concentrated. He blinked to get back on track.

"There were other trailers, campers on this vacant land. Dirt piles, cleared lots like a new housing development. The house burning was old and rundown. I don't know why I know that." Her eyes widened. "The weird part was this old wood shed behind a fifth wheel trailer. There was something about the padlocked door and closed-up windows. I can't explain it, but it felt as if we were hiding something. I was afraid of being caught, as if it was my responsibility to keep everyone away. This last part is going to sound weird. A woman appears: blond, gorgeous, and very much dead. She laughed and mocked firing a gun with her hand, like kids do, except I heard the distinct chambering and shots of a real gun. It was pointed right at me. Then she wandered around the RV to the shed, and I panicked. No one was supposed to go back there."

Marcie moved behind the sofa, dropped her head into her hands. Long strands of gorgeous, damp, wavy hair fell like a curtain over her face. Sam crossed his arms. His head screamed to distance himself. She was involved in something, all right, if this dream was real—if she was telling the truth. Except, why would she incriminate herself?

"Marcie, let's back up. What were they trying to cover up?"

Marcie brushed her hair back with her fingers. "I don't know. First, it was something about the old house. They needed to make sure everything burned. And I knew it, because I screamed at them to hurry. They kept going even when the fire guys tried to shut them down."

"You're talking about arson there, girl. Were you involved?"

Tears pooled and glistened in her vivid blue eyes. She pursed her trembling lips as if refusing to allow one tear to fall. "I don't know. That's what scares me. What if I did something wrong?" Her thickened voice cracked.

Weird didn't begin to explain this story. On the surface, Sam realized that now would be the time to walk away. If he was smart, he would. But he wasn't—smart, that is, with this whole convoluted mess with Marcie. He was doing his best to bring logic to this tale, except her story reminded him of his strange and mysterious training grounds, Terrebonne Parish, where he had grown up and learned to trust his instincts, stifling his logical mind's need to explain the unexplainable. So why stop now? Well, for one, her dream wasn't reality, and reality was where he chose to live.

So why did he feel this need to protect her? Maybe it was her genuine honesty and fear and the fact that she needed him. When was the last time someone had really needed him? If he were candid with himself, he'd admit Elise never did. It had been the other way around.

Sam walked over to her and traced the soft contour of her plump cheek and the outline of her chin, all in a gentle caress that invoked a deep longing dead center in his gut. Her chin wobbled. He could see the hurt in her eyes. It only added to the massive puzzle he found himself entangled in. What was it about this fiery, patient, sweet girl that made him want more? Instincts, not his head, had him opening his arms, and Marcie walked right into them.

His arms closed around her. She shivered and fisted her hands in his shirt.

"What do I do now, Sam?" Her warm breath whispered against his chest as she spoke.

Sam rested his chin on top of her head, torn by duty as a federal officer and bound by a strange connection to Marcie, a link that he clearly understood could jeopardize his career if, in fact, she was involved in something illegal. Except his inner voice, which had saved him time and again from past adversity, was warning him to put aside his black and white sense of duty, and he didn't know why.

Jesse cleared his throat and looked away before he gallantly left the room.

"One step at a time, Marcie, and first things first. We need to find out who you are."

CHAPTER 9

Jesse, true to his word, arranged with airport security for Sam to watch the surveillance video. Jesse planned to meet them there, but, first, he needed to check in with his captain. He had a heavy caseload, and not a lot of priority was to be given to a woman robbed. Apparently, those had been his boss' exact words first thing this morning.

Marcie, tired from her restless sleep, lay on the sofa, bunching the blanket under her head while Sam walked Jesse out. She told herself she'd rest her eyes a moment, except she allowed her mind to still, breathing deeply until an image of a golden autumn forest appeared as she flew over, dusk settling in. Lower now, moving through golden leaves, until a large owl, with great wings and feathers, perched on a thick oak branch. She instinctively recognized it as a symbol of death and renewal.

The scene changed, flashing to full dark, and this time she raced down the center of a dirt and gravel road. A full moon and shining stars blazed in the northern sky. Scattered distant lights from nearby rural properties provided a beacon out of the surrounding darkness. Smoky shadows poked her fears and then deepened into the alders trailing both sides of the road. Overwhelming terror gripped her heart right before an awful, anxious hum sizzled up her spine. She was late and needed to hurry.

Jogging shorts and a T-shirt were no protection from the cold air pinching her bare skin. She ran on, faster, steadily gaining a solid rhythm until her chest burned. She had to stop, slow down, but she couldn't. Her nerves, her senses, were cranked as if the devil himself was biting at her heels. She was in trouble, and she damn near jumped out of her skin when she caught sight of a golden-haired man illuminated under a sparse country streetlight twenty feet in front of her. She blinked. Where had he come from? Her heart jerked and slammed against her ribcage when she dug her heels in and stopped.

The man wore a baby blue down jacket. She took a step farther away, circling around him, drawn back by an obsessive need to look closer. Golden threads were woven through his wavy hair. Something about him dumped a simultaneous wave of fear and peace through her. How was that possible? She felt unthreatened by his powerful, kind stance—yet she was terrified. His hands remained deep in his jacket pockets, an observer standing guard. Her mind worked overtime. Dark thoughts swirled faster than she could register. If I turn and run, can he catch me?

He spoke, but his lips didn't move. "I came to see how you are, if you're all right."

"I'm fine. Go away."

"No, Marcie, I won't go. I was sent to help you."

"Who are you? Who sent you?"

He opened his hand. A field of daisies appeared in front of her. "A new cycle awaits you. I'm your guide. You're on the wrong path, Marcie. You've turned your back on what's right, but there's still time. You'll soon need to make a choice. Listen and follow where your angels and I take you. Listen, do as we say."

"What's your name?"

"My name's Jerome Standford. I'm watching over you. Powerful prayers from your teacher were heard."

He didn't move, but she did, running again, faster, harder, around the corner. She glanced over her shoulder and froze. The light was now gone, and so was he.

A hand squeezed her arm, and her feet and stomach plummeted in a fifty-foot free-fall. A deep, frigid scream broke through the icy darkness. *Who's there?* Wide eyed, she gasped as the sun—the room—and Sam hovered over her.

"You okay? Another dream?"

Another dream, all right, one she wasn't ready to share.

She sat up, sinking into the small foam cushion. Her vague memory had ebbed now, somewhere between the illusionary dream state and reality. Beside her, the seat dipped. Sam allowed no space between them as he rubbed her shoulder and then her back. She dropped her head into her hands. What the hell was that? Who was her teacher? Okay, she was spooked big time, but she still wasn't going to share this with Sam, not yet.

"Marcie?" He gently lifted her long, wavy hair over her shoulder.

"I don't want to talk about it because it's just plain weird and makes no sense."

He dropped his hand and stood up.

She craned her neck. "I'm not lying or holding some memory back. I just need to digest this bizarre thing. Can you let me do that?"

"Fair enough. We need to go now anyway. Jesse's arranged for us to see the security video."

It was a short drive in Sam's blue Camaro and a hurried walk through the newly tiled airport to the security offices at the rear of the terminal. A pale, balding security guard buzzed Sam and Marcie in through a secured white door, which led down a long, sterile hall to a small windowless room. Professional equipment filled the austere, square office. Marcie sat in a dark blue armless chair. Sam's cell phone rang, so he strode outside the heavy steel door to answer it. Bright lighting danced off scads of monitors that captured intrusive scenes of people bustling through the airport.

Marcie twiddled her thumbs and wondered what it would be like to be cuffed. Those damn doubts and a sick vibe hummed in her belly. Her lost memory had to be filled with something scandalous and illegal. She felt as if her life was spinning out of control in a direction she couldn't handle. So really, was it any wonder she expected the worst? Could they arrest her for something she couldn't remember?

Sam clapped his hands together when he reappeared. "That was Jesse. He got tied up. He'll get here as soon as he can."

He didn't so much as glance at Marcie; instead, Sam shook the hand of the tall, dark-skinned man with linebacker shoulders and lady-killer dimples. He wore a diamond-studded earring and a well-fitting navy suit. When packaged together with his, off-the-charts, charisma… *Wow.*

"Marcie, this is Dev Hamilton, head of security.

His eyes held some familiarity with her circumstances, along with well-bred compassion. He gave her a sweet touch when he took her hand and asked, "How's your head, darling?"

Mesmerized, she touched her forehead. "It's fine."

He smiled so brilliantly that Marcie warmed from inside out. Then he winked. *He's flirting with me.* Her jaw loosened, and she didn't know if she was incensed because of Sam or flattered. Wisdom won out. She slid her chair closer to Sam, and Dev's attention left her when he leaned down and worked the computer, bringing up the video footage.

"Jesse and I've gone through this a couple times, but I'll let you have a look before he gets here."

Marcie clasped her shaking hands and leaned closer to the screen. Passengers disembarked from an American Airlines flight. Single file, they hustled down a narrow walkway, entering the main terminal. It was watching herself move that twisted her heart. There she was with a backpack draped over one shoulder, swinging the other arm, striding behind a woman wearing a dark pantsuit. What had she been thinking at that moment? For the life of her, she couldn't remember. She looked confident but kept dropping her head, rounding her shoulders and looking down. Why? She glanced left, to baggage claim, just before a tall man slid in behind her, cutting the strap of her black and red knapsack, snatching it away—all in the blink of an eye. Although she'd swear that was her, she remembered none of it.

"I have to say, after watching this footage a few times, questions have been raised in my mind. One, and the most vital, is that I'm absolutely intrigued and dying to know what was in your backpack, because something's not quite right. It smells like you were up to no good there, darling," Sam said.

Why didn't he shove a knife in her heart? It would be kinder than this ugly censure, which pounded self-scorn deeper into every cell of her body. Except he was right, even she had to admit none of this boded well. But whatever had happened to diplomacy? She glanced at Sam, but his eyes remained glued to the replayed image on screen.

"Whoa, baby, look at that right there." Sam rose out of his chair, pointing at the frozen footage. "He was waiting for you."

CHAPTER 10

"Marcie, you okay, babe?" Sam squatted in front of her. His strong, comforting hands smoothed over her shoulders. Maybe he thought she'd pass out. Maybe she would. The bile rose in her throat, and the room swayed as if she were now sailing over rough seas.

"Lean over, head between your knees." He pushed her head down, his fingers sinking deeper into the firm flesh of her back.

"What just happened? I'm okay now." She gripped the chair arms and sat up. None of this made sense, and both men were studying her as if she were some weak, hysterical woman. That made her blood boil —because she wasn't. For some reason, she couldn't stand to be viewed that way.

"What happened? You turned as green as the moss on a live oak." Dev hovered behind Sam, and Sam stayed right in front of her.

"If either one of you looks at me one more time like that, I swear I'll…" She didn't know what she'd do. Those were hurt words spouted in anger because she doubted herself, and to top it off, she felt violated in a way she couldn't explain.

"You'll what? Come on, Marcie, we're not your enemies here. We're the ones trying to get some answers."

She wanted to cry and wished she could, except something inside of her wouldn't allow that pathetic despair to surface.

"Can we watch this again? I want to show you what I saw," Sam snapped, and Dev shuffled his awkward stance, pretending to ignore them in the tiny space they found themselves crammed in.

Marcie swallowed the lump jammed in her throat, peering awkwardly at Sam. "Yeah, sure."

Sam returned to the high-backed leather chair, and Marcie scooted beside him, leaning closer to the monitor. Dev replayed the video.

"Okay, freeze. Start right here, and look at the guy in the ball cap by the gift shop." Sam traced the tall, lanky kid's movement with his finger across the screen. "See there? Now watch how he sees Marcie and follows in behind that other older couple. Whoa, wait a second. Did you see that?" Sam shot a swift glance at Dev.

"Yeah, man, that's Reggie. He's a baggage claim supervisor."

Stunned, Marcie was afraid to breathe as she watched Reggie, an overweight, white-haired, middle-aged man dressed in dark blue pants and a white shirt, walk past the dark, sure-footed kid and pass something with his left hand. Delivered with such smooth control, it'd be easy to miss. Next, the dark kid stuffed what he had been handed into his baggy pants pocket and sidled up behind Marcie. One hand grabbed the strap of her knapsack; the other flicked open a switchblade and sliced through the black strap. He shoved Marcie hard, and she fell forward onto her knees before smacking her head on the unforgiving tile.

Her head stung just watching the recap. Sam and Dev faced her again. Were they worried she'd pass out? Or maybe it was her reaction. Was she a victim or somehow involved with her attacker? No one could say for sure. Even she wasn't naive enough to deny something was at play.

"You okay, babe?" Even with his gruff, scratchy appearance, Sam destroyed all doubts she had of his credibility. He wouldn't toss her to the wolves—he wouldn't abandon her, and he wouldn't sneak away, and that meant more to her than she could explain. Instead of being comforted by this revelation, she was rattled.

"Marcie, you okay?"

She tried to force a smile past the rising lump stuck in her throat. She failed miserably. "Yeah, sure, just peachy."

"Is that the beginning of some attitude I'm sensing? Under the circumstances, Marcie, I'll cut you some slack. But watch it."

Why couldn't she say thank you? Sam stood between Marcie and Dev and leaned in closer to the screen. What was he looking for? *The eyes can fool you. Look deeper for your answer. Not all may be as it appears.* Her heart beat faster. She looked at both men, trying to figure out what was going on.

"Dev, what's the story on Reggie?" Marcie couldn't see Dev's face; Sam pulled his chair in closer and sat, then he swiveled the chair around, blocking her view of Dev. She felt hidden, protected.

"Come on, Dev, what gives? This guy smuggling contraband or is it something else?"

"Look, Sam, I can't say. Just know we have our eye on him. But I'm curious about something. See here in the video, you, right behind your girl before she goes down, watching her. And even when she falls, you pause, but you don't go after the kid who robbed her. Why's that?"

"What the hell are you talking about? I just got off the plane after busting my butt for months on an operation that was fucked up. I was tired, and there was a whole bunch of people around. I'm not the only one walking behind her." Sam waved his hands in the air, making no attempt to lower his voice. Marcie could tell by the way Sam bunched his shoulders that he was well on his way to being in a piss-poor mood. She wondered if Dev was deliberately provoking him.

Dev crossed his arms and rolled his solid shoulders back. His full mouth tightened so his lips resembled a thin line. "Take a look from my perspective. You walk away from some big undercover operation with the DEA after marijuana's found stashed in your locker, and from what I understand, it wasn't a small amount. That was after a tip was phoned into the Sheriff. You claim it was planted." Dev shrugged his shoulders. His sparkling eyes steeled to something hard and accusing. "So, Sam, how would it look to you that you just happened to be right behind some babe in my airport who's probably carrying something suspicious. Add in the one guy who works here, who we suspect is involved in smuggling contraband, and he just happens to pass something to a guy who takes what she has—coincidence? I'm sure you'll agree there's no such thing. You have quite a history, Sam, not all of it good."

"Whoa, whoa, Jesus Murphy, where are you getting all this bullshit?" Sam stood right in Dev's face, flexing his fists, his back ramrod straight, as if getting ready to take on a street thug.

"Back off, Sam. I just happened to find out from Seattle PD when I sent a copy of this video segment to help your girl here find out who she is. Someone recognized you, and the detective I spoke with was quite free with his information. Apparently, you're a hot topic this month."

Uneasy tension rippled. "Time to go, Marcie."

She had no time to respond. Sam snatched her hand and pulled her up behind him, hustling her out the door. His arm slid around her shoulder and propelled her forward, one step from a jog. Her sandals flopped on the tile floor down the narrow corridor as she struggled to keep up.

"Sam, what's going on? What was that about drugs in your locker? I knew you were a cop, but I didn't know… Hey, wait a second. Why'd he imply you were following me? Sam, slow down." This was all wrong. Sam wasn't supposed to be in trouble. It was her—all her. And that awful man, Dev, was trying to turn all this on Sam. "Sam, what's going on? Why won't you answer me?"

Sam pushed open the security door, taking them into the main terminal. "Marcie, we need to get out of here now. Don't say anything else until we're in the car."

She caught a glimpse of his hard jaw. He looked around, maybe not conspicuously, but he watched for someone or something as he rushed her along. This wasn't good.

They were almost at the exit when two uniformed officers marched through the busy sliding glass door. Sam steered her into a crowded tour group and squeezed out the bank of doors a few yards away. Another NOPD car pulled to the curb behind a line of cabs. Sam propelled her into a lineup of travelers waiting for cabs and then crossed over to the parking garage.

"Keep walking. Don't look around," Sam said. Marcie clutched his arm with both hands before she tripped while trying to keep up. He hurried her to the passenger side of his Camaro, opened the door, and pushed her in. "Put on your seatbelt."

Her hand trembled while she buckled up. Sam yanked open his heavy door and gunned the engine before his door had closed, backing out so fast that Marcie jolted in her seat. The tires squealed when Sam shifted gears. The speed with which he accelerated pinned Marcie back against the soft leather. She gripped the hard vinyl dashboard and stared through the thick windshield. Sam weaved in and around slower vehicles.

"Sam, you're scaring me. What's going on?" And she was scared. It wasn't just the questions surrounding what Marcie carried. Speculation about Sam's own character and his link to drugs had been dumped right in the middle of this. *A dirty cop*. Wasn't that what Dev had implied? This wasn't reasonable, and only now did the implication sink in. His cheek twitched. He held his emotions so tight. His furious glance sliced a hole in her heart. Was she supposed to know the answer?

"Sam, spill it. What's going on? What did Dev say about drugs in your locker, and why did we have to leave so fast?"

He focused on the road, continuing to swerve in and out of traffic. "Let's start with one of your answers, darling. I suspect the police are interested in talking to you. And two, just so we're clear, sweetheart, for some reason, I think you may be right. You're involved in something. The guy on the video expected you, and I suspect the plan changed and you weren't consulted. My guess, whatever you stashed in your backpack, these guys knew about it and were waiting. If it was drugs or other contraband, how the hell did you get it past security? And three, I'd bet my last dollar you're a mule, darling. Just so we're clear, I'm no drug dealer. Those drugs were planted in my locker. How Dev even found out about that…" He yanked the wheel so hard that Marcie's shoulder bumped the door. Sam cut off a minivan, and the driver responded by blasting his horn.

Sam's lips thinned. He was furious. "I was set up. But you weren't, and I sure as hell wasn't following you for your backpack."

"I believe you. So why'd Dev imply you were somehow involved with trafficking marijuana? He didn't come right out and say the words, Sam, but just the same, he suggested you're a dirty cop." She could see she had struck a nerve by the way his hard eyes fired back at her. "Don't get mad at me. I'm just trying to find out what's going on."

Sam shut down. His face could've been made of stone, for all the emotion it showed. She may have lost her memory, but she was no fool when someone held on to something. Why wouldn't he talk? What had really happened?

"Shit. Hang on. We've got a tail."

Marcie whipped her head around, searching out her side window at the hundreds of cars all fighting their way down this crowded side street. "Where?"

"Two cars back, beat-up four-door piece of shit only an underpaid NOPD detective would drive." Sam turned right and then left down an alley and right again on a busy side road. He weaved in and out of traffic and finally slowed from his erratic speed, blending in with a single line of traffic. Harsh lines deepened around the focus in his eyes, which were divided between the rearview mirror and the road in front of them.

"Did you lose them?"

"Maybe." Beads of sweat popped out on his forehead. His hard gaze was glued to the rearview mirror as if it were their only guide to safety. Sam's cell phone buzzed from his shirt pocket. "Carre here," he said. What an odd way to answer. Her stomach gave a little tug when she realized she didn't know his last name. "Jesse, give me twenty minutes and I'll be there."

Sam clicked off his cellphone and fumbled it back in his pocket.

"Where are we going?" Their eyes met briefly, but for the life of her, she didn't know what he was thinking.

"To meet Jesse."

What she did pickup in his brooding silence was some need to ponder the situation quietly. She supposed that was what he did now, as he circled two city blocks three times before reaching the turnoff to Algiers. Her gut burned, and she told her head now would be a good time to bring back her unwanted memory, release all those dirty secrets. At least it could help Sam. Then she'd know for sure if Sam was right. Had she been carrying drugs? She prayed it wasn't true, except that deep down, her gut pinched, screaming its ugly accusation. *Guilty!*

The car lurched and snapped Marcie's wandering mind back. Her seatbelt dug deep into her shoulder when Sam yanked the wheel, a sharp right at a turnoff across the four-lane steel bridge. He pulled up alongside a lone dark sedan in a deserted dirt and gravel lot. Average rundown houses were scattered in the distance.

Car doors squealed open and clattered shut. The crunch of gravel and muffled voices met behind the car. Marcie didn't wait for an invitation. She pulled the inside handle and leaned her shoulder into the heavy door, giving a good shove. The hinges creaked. Marcie stepped out and joined Sam and Jesse.

"Thanks for meeting me."

"It's starting to get a little hot. What the hell's going on, Sam? Derek, my captain, your former boss, has gone ballistic. And Dev called, told me you took off. He also said a couple of uniforms showed up and took Reggie in for questioning. And get this—Derek's now overseeing the interrogation because you're back in town and just happened to be behind this mystery girl when she was robbed. This is all crashing in on you, and Derek's really pushing your connection with Marcie. He suspects you two are transporting drugs together. Why the hell didn't you tell me a sack of marijuana was found in your locker up north?" He didn't give Sam any opportunity to respond. He paced his heavy body back and forth, kicking up dirt. "You know Derek's got it in for you, and I don't like the direction this is heading. Did you know her up north?" Jesse jammed his stubby finger in the air at Marcie.

"I didn't know her. She was attacked and robbed. I stopped to help. There's nothing more. You know me, how could you even think…"

"How could I think? You should have told me about the weed,

especially when we knew she was up to no good. Yes, I'm your friend, and as your friend, I've watched your back over and over, every time you did some lone ranger stupid-ass move, always because of a woman. It's just that before, it used to be Elise."

"The drugs weren't mine. For six months, I … we … my team investigated one of the most powerful drug dealers on the west coast; a guy by the name of Lance Silver. This is the big time. He's no little guy. He's got houses across this country and down into South America, connections all over the world. He's the largest marijuana grower in the Pacific Northwest, if not the country. Our team was big. We had everybody investigating this guy, and I put everything into nailing that bastard. He trades marijuana for guns and cocaine. I don't know how he did it, but he got someone on our team to act as his informant. He knew we were coming, because when we showed up pounding on his door with our warrants—all the marijuana was gone. He must've had quite the team working all night to move the amount of stuff he had. And we knew it had been there. We have informants too, but, suddenly, no one saw anything. His marijuana hadn't even been cut the day before. How's it possible to clean up that quickly? The marijuana in my locker was planted. Don't you think it was pretty convenient that during our raid, an anonymous call just happened to go into the Sequim detachment to check my locker at the gun club?"

"So what happened? You're suspended, under investigation...which is it?"

Marcie knew her mouth was agog. Her mind spun, trying to make sense of what Jesse said. And that name, Lance Silver, churned butterflies and fired chills inside her stomach. Why did it sound so familiar?

Sam leaned against the back of his car and rapped his knuckles on the trunk. "I left."

"What do you mean, you left?"

Sam crossed his arms and shrugged.

"You just walked away, said nothing. You're kidding, right?"

Sam didn't answer.

"Are you under investigation for the drugs in your locker?"

"I don't think so. I was pissed off. I threw my badge on my boss' desk and walked out."

"You quit, or did he ask for your badge? I want the whole story, Sam. Christ almighty, is the DEA looking for you?" Jesse ripped off his tie and tossed it through the open window of his beat-up, brown Olds. He was so livid she could see veins bulging on the side of his neck.

"Look, I'm not under investigation. My boss knew I had been set up. So did my partner, Diane. I was angry about how Lance Silver had screwed me. I wanted a break, that's all."

"So why'd you turn your badge in?"

This time, raw emotion flooded Sam, and he shut his eyes. When he opened them, a hint of pink colored his face. He took a hard, deep breath and then honestly faced his friend. "I wasn't planning on going back."

Jesse must have recognized something in his expression, because he grabbed Sam's shoulder and shook hard. "You fucking idiot. You're planning to take care of it yourself, maybe looking to do some kind of vigilante justice, handle the problem the cops can't. Huh? Yeah, I know I'm right."

"I'm not going to let him get away with what he did to Elise."

"Elise! What the hell does any of this have to do with her?"

Sam scrubbed his hands down his face as if trying to wipe away a layer of skin. Then he looked upward and closed his grief-stricken eyes. "Elise was investigating some smuggling ring of guns and drugs flowing down from the north. For months, this case with the ATF distracted her. After she was killed, I found notes in one of her home files about the case, including a mention about Leon, Mama Reine's grandson—how he distributed for this broker in New Orleans, receiving this endless supply of marijuana and guns. She didn't come right out and say in her notes that it was Lance Silver, but with the leads and stakeouts I've done since I went up north; I know, in my bones, he's the guy."

"Sam, where are you getting this? Elise was killed by Della, Leon's mama; a grief-stricken woman who wanted simple justice after Elise killed her baby boy when she apparently tried to bust him on illegal possession of firearms and drugs."

The way Jesse said it, even Marcie knew there was something he wasn't telling.

"What are you saying? That the shooting wasn't justifiable?" Sam snapped.

Jesse stalked two steps toward Sam and then stopped. "Maybe it's time this all came out. You've been angry with me for years, even cut our friendship, because I couldn't get you to wise up. Elise may have joined the academy before you and I, but her motives were not to help those in need and make this city a safer place. She wanted things. I don't know what. Even her ATF team members started to wise up to her. She was no team player. And that so-called case with Leon and a smuggling ring up north, she wasn't working on anything like that with her team. I checked. Forensics didn't jive with what she said happened in the shooting, either."

"That's absolute bullshit. What the hell are you doing?" Bitterness cracked Sam's voice.

"I'm not saying this to hurt you. I was watching her on the side, too, and so was someone on her team. Too many times, drugs, guns, and even evidence went missing from a few of their big busts. They knew someone on the team was dirty."

"She wasn't dirty. Not Elise." The fierceness with which Sam eyeballed Jesse had Marcie taking a step back. She wondered if Sam would hurt Jesse. But then he shook his head and ground his teeth before looking away.

"Don't you remember that, after Della killed her, all those rumors popped up that you and Elise were on the take? And Della, I talked to her. That poor woman was so wracked with grief. She swore to me that she knew Elise was dirty and that she used her connection to Mama Reine to seduce Leon into the dirty world of drugs. She said Elise was the broker, and Elise killed Leon because he wanted out."

"Leon was just a scared kid selling Lance Silver's drugs. Elise wasn't..." Sam knocked Jesse's hands away when he tried to touch him. "I don't want to talk about this anymore, Jesse. I want to know what's going on with Derek. Why's he pushing my connection?"

"Because he believes, like I do, that Elise was a dirty cop, except he won't believe you knew nothing about what she was doing. You were married to her. It's called guilt by association," Jesse snapped. "Sam, you made a hobby out of studying people telling lies and figuring out how they tick. The NOPD homicide department knew this about you. And yet you couldn't see what Elise was doing. I think deep down you did, but you'd never admit it. Didn't you ever question where she got her money? Those fancy clothes she bought, the sports car, all on a cop's salary. Come on. You had to know she was up to something. She had money stashed somewhere. She would have kept her own accounts, and I'd bet anything, that you still don't know where they are."

Marcie stood off to the side and breathed softly. She tried to make herself nonexistent. More than anything, she believed, at this moment, that she had become an albatross around this amazing man's neck. Sam had taken her in, stood by her, and still hadn't turned his back. Why?

"Come on, Sam. You want to fix it. You look at this whole circumstantial mess through Derek's eyes, and if you're honest, you'll see it ain't all that far of a stretch." Jesse held his large, fisted hand up. "One, mystery girl carries a backpack that's stolen, but the security footage shows Reggie and the kid are waiting for her." Jesse raised a finger. "Two, they expected her. Three, Reggie's been under investigation for a while, which I just found out, for his suspected role in transporting drugs. Four, you happen to be right behind mystery girl, right after your own case crashes around you and a knapsack full of marijuana's discovered in your locker. Five, you've taken Marcie, a virtual stranger, in like long-lost kin, and we know she transported something." Jesse held his outstretched hand high to make his point. "Add to all of this, Elise's sketchy past of being a dirty cop; a dirty cop you were married to at the time." Jesse dropped his hand and took a step back. "This may not play out well for you, my friend."

Jesse shed his dark, rumpled sports coat and tossed it through the open window of his sedan. Sweat stained the underarms of his blue dress shirt. His dark glasses obscured his telltale eyes, constantly showing the question that Marcie was thinking.

"What's Derek saying now?" Sam asked.

"That you may be involved with whatever went down at the

airport with mystery girl, that you're part of a smuggling ring bringing marijuana down from up north, and Reggie's working for you. And the Elise thing—Derek's reopened the file."

Goosebumps chilled Marcie's warm skin. This was her fault, what was happening to Sam, even though it had been started by another woman; a destructive, dishonest woman. But was she any better? She couldn't do this to Sam. It wasn't right.

Sam paced back and forth. Gravel crunched beneath his feet as he ran his hand up and over the back of his head, refusing to look her way. Marcie sensed a pile of pretty heavy shit heaping up from a dark past, his and hers, filled with secrets and lies. What a mess.

"You thought about calling your boss? If you're not under investigation, you get him to back you up. Help get this heat off you."

"Not yet. You said you got something for me."

Jesse shook his head. "You amaze me. That ego of yours makes you think you're untouchable. You refuse to ask for help. Why do you always have to do things the hard way?" Jesse didn't wait for a response. He reached in the open passenger window of the front seat and pulled out a manila envelope. He waved the tan envelope like an alluring red blanket in the air. "Look, these are just facts." Jesse faced Marcie with a shadow of speculation. "You sure you want to read this in front of her? I'd bet my bottom dollar that whatever she's neck deep in, you want no part of."

Don't push. She heard it. She knew it. But she didn't listen. "I have a right to know, so, both of you, please don't treat me like some mindless ditz," she said. "And, Jesse, I know you're concerned for Sam. I am, too, but don't ever speak through me like that again."

"Whoa, Marcie, back off. Jesse's put his butt on the line for whatever shenanigans you're involved in, and whatever trouble it is, my generosity's been rewarded by being dragged right in the middle of it. So cool your mouth, girl," he snapped, driving the knife a little deeper in her heart.

"Let's all get a grip, okay?" Jesse's radio buzzed with static. "Shit." He gave the police scanner a hasty look before stepping toward the car.

Sam pulled a few papers from the envelope. He walked while he read and then stopped cold about twenty feet away, turning to Marcie. His sharp eyes were filled with accusation.

To be viewed with such contempt shredded her heart a little more. *What did I do?* Would Sam finally turn his back and walk away?

Tension appeared to vibrate across his wide shoulders. "Who are you?"

Her stomach twisted. *What was in the file?* "Sam, you know as much as I do. I don't know. Please don't look at me like that."

Jesse stepped forward, maybe to block the potential explosion he expected from Sam.

Sam ignored him. He waved the papers in the air and firmed his stance. "It appears you produced a passport at check-in under the name Lisa Francis. The birth date matches no records we can find. Is this an error?" Sam shrugged. "We can't check because the passport's no longer in your possession. So let's say it was lifted along with the knapsack. This is the question of the day: What was in the knapsack, Marcie, Lisa Francis, or whatever your name is?"

"I'm supposed to bring you both in. Derek wants to talk to you and Marcie," Jesse said.

Heaviness surrounded her. Everything at stake began to snowball into something completely beyond her control.

Sam stuffed the papers back in the large envelope. "Does Derek know about the passport and the name on it?"

"He does now, Sam. He too finds it weird she remembers her first name as being Marcie, but this passport, we know it's a forgery. There's no way I can hide that kind of information." Jesse offered a helpless shrug and turned his head away to face the noisy traffic. He shook his head before facing Sam again. "You know the political game Derek likes to play. Right now, he's making it sound as if you're on the run with Marcie. He's spiking it up, making himself look the martyr. He's spouting off now with the argument that if he'd known about the passport from the get-go, he'd have taken Marcie then and planted your ass in a holding cell."

"Shit, what next?" Sam wiped a rough palm across his forehead and walked in a wide circle.

"Well, actually, Sam, it gets better."

Sam froze.

"Derek's alluding to a connection between the missing drugs on your island adventure with the Feds, the marijuana found stashed in your locker, mystery girl's mishap at New Orleans airport, and her missing backpack. Because of your connection to Elise, the ATF and NOPD's suspicion that she was on the take, he's tying a whole shitload of circumstantial crap against you. He's building a case that maybe Elise wasn't investigating any northern smuggling ring on her own, but you and she were actually part of it before she was killed. You and I know fools have been put away on less."

"I'm not working for Lance Silver. I was set up. That marijuana was planted in my locker. I'm not under investigation. You talk to my boss; he'll tell you." Sam loomed in front of Jesse, and this time Marcie did step back.

"I don't need to talk to your boss to know the truth," Jesse said. But you need to know this; Derek's going to spin his own tale on this and bypass the Feds. This is a different jurisdiction. Read between the lines, my friend. Call your boss. Get him to pull you in. You need his help. He can make it go away. You know the Feds down here have always proven their ability to take down dirty cops in New Orleans. The tale Derek's spinning, they'll see it as it is; corrupt and bad policing by a politically motivated captain who's good at making an innocent man look guilty." His frustrated words spewed. Any fool could see the common sense Jesse tried desperately to hammer into Sam.

Sam hurried to his car and pulled open the door. "You haven't seen us, Jesse. I'll call you later."

"Fuck, Sam. You're digging yourself in deeper. Cut her loose. You're putting me in a tough spot. You know, as well as I, how serious this is. The drugs, especially this airport stuff… Ever since 9/11, airport security's been jammed up tight. Didn't you notice today that airport security's at level orange? Come on, Sam. With the possibility of a false passport and questions about what she transported; this is bad. You know this. This could get ugly real quick. Use your head and think."

Sam slammed his door shut and stalked toward Jesse. "That's exactly what I'm doing, and you know why. I have way too many eyes on me, all this speculation and a whole lot of questionable crap. No, I need to handle this my way."

The potential of this snowballing into a nightmare was unavoidable. Jesse plainly cared deeply. Marcie could see how he fought to convince Sam to make a clean break and walk away. And he was right. He should leave her.

"This is my fault, Sam," she said. "I don't understand any of this or why you've been dragged into the middle of it. You were there for me and took me in. I'm grateful for it. I don't know what to do. Maybe I should just go with Jesse. At least then, your name will be cleared. You don't deserve to be treated this way." Her voice shook and her eyes burned, and she wept deep inside, needing to give him this way out. At the same time, she prayed he wouldn't take it. When had she begun to need him so?

"Don't play the martyr. That's exactly what you don't do down here. You can't remember anything, or do you suddenly remember? Which is it?" He crossed his solid arms, confronting her, attitude and all.

"No, Sam, I don't. I wish I did. Then maybe we'd have our answers."

"Careful what you wish for, Marcie. You may not want to know."

He had her there. She stuck out her jaw over the sting of his words. He was a crack shot, and he'd hit his mark.

Jesse's police scanner sizzled to life when a voice demanded his whereabouts. All three heads focused in on the dispatcher's lilt as if she were a viper ready to strike.

"Tell them you haven't seen me, that I blew you off." Sam took another step toward Jesse. His white shirt clung to his damp back, showing off his well-sculpted muscles. "I know I'm asking a lot, but we go way back, and you know I'm not involved in this. You and I both know nothing in this investigation is being done by the book." Jesse ground his teeth. Beads of sweat popped out above his brow. He reached in the open window and switched off the radio.

"Get going now. I haven't seen ya. Just don't forget a lot of the guys down here believe there's something more. Remember, Sam, you're the one who left." His nostrils flared before he climbed in his sedan and fired it up.

Sam leaned in Jesse's open window. "One more thing. Find out where all this heat's coming from, and why now?"

"The heat's coming, Sam, and so's the time to clear the past. You've put it off too long. There's one of your answers. You should have stayed and shown them you weren't on the take. You made yourself look guilty when you took off and joined the Feds. To anyone who doesn't know you, that's how it seems. If you're guilty, you run."

CHAPTER 11

A storm brewed amid the lingering dust trailing Jesse's sedan. Sam pulled onto the highway but went in the opposite direction, toward the storm and heavy gray clouds rumbling in the distant sky.

Sam needed another shower. He'd yet to acclimatize to being home. Each time he stepped outside, sweat glazed every inch of him. To make it worse, Jesse's last words had opened the congealed wound that hadn't quite healed. Sam had to admit Jesse was right. To anyone else, his leaving town would appear as if he'd run, but that hadn't been why he left. Now every censure he'd brushed off whispered through his mind. Those icy stares at his back, each caustic hint anytime an investigation went sour. Had he slipped up?

What made it worse were the friends of friends and distant acquaintances within the NOPD, even the Feds, who believed they knew the truth. But, in fact, each had been led on by nothing more than mere gossip, circumstantial evidence, and the fact that Sam made an excellent scapegoat, all because he refused to stay and clear his name after Elise died.

"Sam, what was Jesse talking about?"

Trapped in his head, he stared through the dusty windshield, and, for a moment, Sam forgot where he was. Tired and disillusioned, he didn't want to answer, so he ignored Marcie and kept driving, except after a few minutes, his conscience cut through his pity party. This wasn't her fault. What a coward, unable to face her mirage of innocence that looked him square in the eye.

He dropped one hand from the steering wheel and rested it on the stick shift. "Three years ago, I joined the DEA task force and left New Orleans."

"So what did Jesse mean when he said you made yourself look guilty?"

He didn't want to discuss his past, not with anyone. On his last homicide investigation, he had logged cocaine and marijuana into evidence, but after a forged requisition, in his name, the drugs had vanished. The next painful day, during the inquiry, his world shattered. Elise had been killed. What followed were malicious accusations, one of them being that he was on the take. All that turmoil was packaged neatly into a past that continued to haunt him. He still wasn't any more clear on what had actually played out. Grief had a way of clouding your judgment and hiding the bigger picture. Who had been motivated to set him up? He had to admit, Jesse was partly right; he had made himself look guilty when he packed a suitcase of essentials and jumped on a plane to Seattle. But the entire truth was that, for Sam, running away hadn't just been a matter of vengeance— he had needed to escape the gut-wrenching pain.

"Someone forged my signature on a requisition, and drugs disappeared. I was investigated and cleared. It was a bad forgery," he said.

Marcie furrowed her brows. "And they already suspected your wife of doing the same thing with the ATF? No, I can see that wouldn't look good. I can also see why being with me is making it really bad for you."

He couldn't respond honestly. This situation wasn't entirely her making. He had walked away from too many things. Why was it up to him to clear his name? He already knew the answer. That was how the world ticked—guilty until proven innocent.

Trees thickened on both sides of the busy highway as Sam drove deeper into bayou country.

"Sam, where are we going?"

His eyes remained glued to the road. "Some place where we can lie low for a bit, just until I can figure some things out. You'll be safe."

Sam drove cautiously, not fast enough to be pulled over and not slow enough to attract attention. Alert and silent, he continued to glance in the rearview mirror, his full lips pursed in a manner that gave nothing away.

A ROAD SIGN ANNOUNCED GRAND ISLE RIGHT BEFORE THEY CROSSED OVER the wide-open Caminada Bridge. Marcie shivered in the damp heat, hit by an unexplainable sense of déjà vu along with a strange yet familiar sense of coming home.

They drove through downtown Grand Isle, past a few restaurants and gas stations. When Sam turned down a narrow winding road guiding them to a middle section of the island, Marcie was swept up in the majestic beauty of the old, towering, windswept oak trees and oleanders that seemed to grow around each rustic Creole cottage.

Then, out of nowhere, they passed downed trees and vacant lots that looked more like a war zone; piles of busted wood and rotted foundations.

Sam slowed and turned right down a long dirt driveway surrounded by massive oaks leading up to an old clapboard cottage, completely secluded. He parked in front of old, weathered plank steps that led up to a screened-in front porch. Sam climbed out of the Camaro and shoved the door closed. Holding his head high, he walked around the front of the car. He pulled in his broad shoulders, deep in thought and contemplation. Sam opened her door and held out his hand. He was an enigma, and Marcie couldn't understand the jerk in her belly and why her heart flipped by such a simple gesture.

A self-conscious wave passed over her. She felt sticky, dirty, and just plain gross. She longed for a bath filled with scented lavender oil, surrounded by white candles. The peaceful thought faded instantly when she stood in front of the tiny run-down cottage with boarded up windows. Sam pressed his hand into the small of her back, urging her up the rickety steps to the screen door.

"I haven't been back in a while. As you can see, I'm one of the lucky ones. Not much damage to mine after Katrina swept through. Many places were condemned, abandoned, or torn down; no way to save them. We passed those along the coast and some inland, too."

Marcie ducked under his arm and stepped cautiously across a creaky, unpainted porch. Sam wasn't as careful. He squeezed around Marcie and tried to open the heavy oak door, but a secured lock held. For some reason, he seemed satisfied and bent over with a pick, inserting a silver prong in the lock. He had a strong focus. His tongue slipped out the side of his mouth. The lock clicked. Sam grinned.

"Forgot my key. If you recall, we left in a hurry. Voilà. In you go, madam." He pushed open the door and gestured her in with the sweep of his hand.

The sparse cottage consisted of furnishings from the sixties, maybe earlier. Marcie walked into a tiny, square box-style kitchen with a small, banged-up second-hand dining table and two rickety wood chairs shoved against the wall behind the door.

Sam removed plywood from each window, allowing the late-day sun to infiltrate the quaint cottage. Against the back wall of the rustic kitchen, a set of steep stairs led up to a door. Marcie wandered up the narrow stairs. Something about the attic urged her to open the door, so she turned the small ivory doorknob, but nothing happened. A turn-of-the-century brass lock appeared implanted in the wood frame above the doorknob. She couldn't tell if it was stuck or locked.

"You got a key to open this door?"

"What are you doing up there?" Sam stood at the bottom of the stairs.

"I'm curious, Sam. What's up here?"

"I don't know, probably a bunch of junk." He turned his back, clearly not interested, and pulled open the ancient rounded fridge door. A pungent stench quickly filled the room. Sam gagged.

Marcie trotted down the stairs, waving her hand in the air to disperse the offensive odor.

"Shit, that stupid ass," Sam said.

Marcie's stomach heaved, so she breathed through her mouth.

"I pay a guy who lives in Jefferson Parish to look after the place. Comes out here every now and then to fish, hang out, mainly to get away from his wife. He left his food." Sam let out a restless sigh. "I need to go to the store. I'm hungry." He shoved the fridge door closed. "Do you think you'll be okay till I get back?"

"I'll be just fine. Go on now." Marcie smiled until she realized he expected her to clean the fridge. Her smile faded.

Sam started to say something and then stopped while he walked across the old hardwood floor straight toward her. "Come here. I need you to stay out of sight. Don't go out, and keep the door closed. Bolt it after I leave, and don't open it for anyone, not until you hear my voice. Understand?"

"Yes, sir."

Strong hands touched her shoulders and slid down her bare arms before he turned away. "I'll try to hurry."

Marcie followed, still tingling from his touch. After she bolted the door, she leaned her back against the rough wood, listening to the Camaro's rumble as Sam revved the engine and drove away. She wondered for a moment where his head was. He'd been so angry earlier. He blamed her for this mess. Yet here he was, touching her in such a possessive way. *He cares for you.*

She closed her eyes to block out the voice, letting out a sigh while she wandered back to the steep stairs. Something about that door urged her to find a way in. She felt the words in her head more than she heard them. *Up here, open the door.* She glanced behind her, downright spooked. She heard nothing now, but when she peeked at that attic door, she knew she needed to find a way in.

There were three tiny drawers in the bare-bones kitchen. Marcie yanked open each one, rummaging through old utensils and junk until she found a long metal prong. "A chicken skewer, that'll work." She bounded up the rough wooden steps. "Okay, so this is easy, right?" She turned the glass knob and pressed the metal prong in the lock and jiggled. Then, somehow, she fumbled her grip and stabbed herself with the pointy skewer in the soft pad at the base of her thumb. The shiny metal landed with a clang and clattered down three stairs. "Damn, damn. Shit, that hurts." She cradled her throbbing hand while blood oozed out of a small round puncture, splattering the top step. Her energy zapped, she picked up the skewer and hunkered down the stairs, where she rinsed her burning wound under a huge single tap in the oversized porcelain sink.

"Now how am I supposed to open the door?"

———

Sam knocked and waited with a plastic bag filled with dinner and groceries. Marcie's soft padded footsteps approached. The bolt clanked when she slid it open. Sam sniffed at the fragrant tang of vinegar. The fridge door was propped open by a white plastic jug. She'd been busy.

"What did you do with all the crap in the fridge?"

She walked ahead of him and knelt down on her bare knees, picking up a rag on the bottom shelf, sticking her head in the rounded fridge. He couldn't help appreciating the wiggle of her bottom and the way it made a simple pair of shorts drive him to the point that he wanted to give her derriere an intimate and friendly squeeze. "I threw all of it in a garbage bag I found in the cupboard and dumped it in the can around back."

His blood heated as he set down the groceries on the small wooden table. "Dammit, Marcie, what'd I tell you? Didn't I say to stay out of sight and not open the door to anyone?"

She froze, tossing the silky mane of endless hair tumbling over her shoulders, and then stood up, blinking. She clutched a pathetic checkered rag and tilted her chin in a determined way, keeping her words even and very matter of fact. "But I didn't open the door to anyone, and I made sure no one saw me. I was careful. I looked around both ways before I went out. There was no one around."

He wanted to throw his hands up and yell, but instead he stomped to the door, jerked it open, and flung the screen door wide until it smacked the outside wall with an echoing thud, rocking ancient, rusty hinges. Did he feel better? *No.*

CHAPTER 12

The wind whipped around his dark, tousled hair. The familiar man was filled with a powerful hate as he gripped the steering wheel of a rusty brown Mustang convertible. In a flash, the scene changed to a man and a woman standing at the edge of a steep mountain road with a bare fir tree and unbarricaded cliff beside them. The tall blond man had his arm around the despairing, curvy woman. Their heads were lowered, standing before a simple cross. Jerome flashed in front of her, arms crossed over his broad chest, his golden hair whipping in the wind. "Go to the attic, Marcie. You'll find some answers there."

Marcie bolted upright. Beads of sweat danced over her chilled skin. Her breath shook, and she struggled in the surrounding darkness to shake loose the dreamlike state—that memory. And Jerome—Jesus, what was he trying to show her?

A faint light illuminated a yellow rectangle into the room from the open door. Marcie crept out of bed wearing just her long beige shirt. She could hear Sam talking, so she followed his deep voice to where he stood by the dim window, his cell phone pressed to his ear, listening.

He disconnected without turning around and slipped the phone in the back pocket of his blue jeans. He didn't acknowledge her or turn around. He leaned his arm upon the chipped window frame, staring out into the darkness. "What're you doing up?"

Obviously, he'd heard her. She should have realized she couldn't sneak up on him. His words were clipped. He must still have been mad.

Dinner had been tense, quiet, and lonely. The hamburgers had tasted like sawdust when she tried to swallow past the lump in her throat. He had so many quirks in his personality. Sam pulled into himself when he was irritated, as if he replayed whatever bothered him over and over in his mind.

His response to anything she asked had been either a grunt or a curt one-word answer. Her traitorous thoughts shifted. Maybe he couldn't stand being in the same room with her—maybe he'd had enough and questioned his wisdom in helping a virtual stranger. This must be the end. Yes, he'd turn her in and walk away. At dinner, she'd been unable to bear that thought, so she excused herself, pushing her full plate away, saying she was tired and escaping to the only bedroom. She didn't know how long she had lain in bed with a burning ache ripping a hole in her heart before finally drifting off. Now all she wanted to do was cry as she stood before Sam in a skimpy shirt with bare legs in this tiny, cluttered sitting room connected to the kitchen.

"Are you turning me in?" Marcie didn't mean to say it aloud.

"Dammit, Marcie, is that what you thought?" he snapped, jamming his fingers through his wavy hair. "You don't get it, do you?" He paced and then turned toward her, hesitating a second before closing the gap between them. He cradled her shoulders with his large, firm hands. "Look at me. You can't be taking chances like you did. When I say stay in, don't open the door to anyone, that means don't take the stinking garbage out, nothing!"

She blinked. "Are you telling me you've been angry all night because I took the garbage out? And that phone call had nothing to do with turning me in?"

His eyebrows furrowed, and his strong, stubborn jaw tightened. "Fuck, Marcie, what kind of asshole do you take me for?" It was obvious from the weary lines on his face that he hadn't slept.

With a shaky hand, she skimmed over the dark hair on his chin; two days without shaving. "You confuse me."

Sam dimmed in front of her when tears glazed her eyes. He softened his tone. "I was talking to my partner, Diane, in Gardiner."

Her scalp tingled, and her face warmed with excitement. Then the worry dashed away all her hope like a splash of ice-cold water. This was help for him. Or was it something else?

"Can I ask you something, Sam?" He looked so tired. How much sleep had he gotten since watching over her?

"Sure."

"Is Diane your girlfriend?"

His eyes widened in what could only be explained as shock. "Ah, no, she's a very good friend and my partner on the task force. Why would you ask that?"

She knew why. It was the way he spoke of her. But it was also a deep distrust that rose out of some hurt part of her heart—jealousy—and she didn't quite care for it. So she said nothing and merely shrugged. "What about Elise, some of the things Jesse said: Are they true?"

He turned away and stared vacantly out the window. She wondered if he'd answer. When he finally did, his baritone voice was gruff.

"We grew up together. Jesse was right. I loved her since we were kids. I suppose I did follow her around like a fool. She was as screwed up as all of us. There was this woman named Mama Reine. She provided a home for all us local vagrants. When I met Jesse, he took me to her after my daddy knocked me around. She patched me up, told me to come back anytime. She did that for every lost kid who showed up on her doorstep. That was where I met Elise, an unlikely sort. She stumbled in and crashed there often. I think she stole from Mama, too. Of course, Mama knew, but she said the Lord had provided everything she ever needed.

"Elise pulled herself together and entered the academy before Jesse and I. She was scooped up by the ATF not long after. I wanted her, with all her tough take-no-bullshit attitude. I tried to be her knight and save her. Stupid, huh? We survived Katrina. Lost our home, most of our belongings. She took it hard. I found us an apartment and salvaged what I could. But then she started keeping long hours, became secretive, more so than usual. I thought it was some big case she was working on. We never talked about our cases. So I didn't push.

"When she killed Leon, she told me he had pulled a gun when she tried to arrest him. I didn't know what to think. He was Mama Reine's grandson. He'd been in trouble since he was a kid, mixed up in gangs, always something. Then, the next day, while Elise was at an outdoor café, Della followed her, walked right up to her, put a gun to her head, and pulled the trigger." Sam wouldn't look at her. He rested his forehead against his arm and placed himself against the chipped window frame.

Marcie couldn't imagine a man who loved a woman so much he'd do anything to fix things for her, to love her so much that he would wear blinders.

"I holed up here in this cottage for a long time after, drinking. Then the rumors started—Elise and I were on the take. I didn't try to fight it. Instead, I went back to the apartment and searched through everything of hers. I found a file she kept that outlined some guy in the Pacific Northwest who shipped marijuana, guns, and cocaine; some big-time operator she was keeping an eye on. Then I found a note. Leon worked for the broker here who was this big dealer's contact. That was when an offer came from the DEA to join them and a new task force they were assembling, out of the Seattle office, to target all the marijuana grow-ops running rampant on the isolated islands in the Pacific Northwest. And I jumped on it, knowing this was my ticket to finding the grower responsible for killing my wife. If she hadn't been investigating that smuggling ring, she never would have come across Leon. This chain of events would never have happened. Three lives destroyed: Elise, Leon, and Della.

"Six months ago, our task force went international. We had the Sequim Sheriff's Department, the Coast Guard, and Interpol. It was a lot of bodies, which upped the chances of someone on the team being an informant. With a high-profile investigation, the leads, the stakeouts; each day we got a little closer to establishing rock-solid evidence on the largest marijuana smuggling ring operated by, this big drug lord, Lance Silver. This guy's almost untouchable—and he screwed me by turning the tables. A knapsack of marijuana was discovered in my locker after an anonymous tip was called into the Sequim detachment at, exactly, the same time we were raiding his deserted estate on the island of Las Seta."

Lance Silver… just hearing that name again triggered something familiar; except Marcie couldn't pull that elusive thread from her memory. Even at the name of the island, her stomach gave a little pang, but why?

Headlights flashed, and Sam jumped back. "Stupid, careless, do you see what you do to me?" he muttered under his breath as he peered out the side of the window, tracking a car when it pulled up and parked behind his Camaro. He seemed to relax for a minute before grabbing the blue shirt dangling over a shabby, orange easy chair and pulling it on. Marcie couldn't see who it was, and Sam didn't waste any time hurrying to the door. Each porch step creaked under the weight of an unknown intruder.

Marcie held her breath. Her heart slammed against her ribcage.

"Get in the bedroom and stay there." Sam whispered the order.

His gun was drawn. An unmistakable click pierced the silence when Sam removed the safety. *Where'd he get the gun?* She didn't argue but backed away, fighting cold panic while slipping quietly into the bedroom. A heavy hitch in her breath echoed, she was sure, through every room in the cottage. It was too late to close the door. She couldn't remember if the hinges squeaked. She needed something to use as a weapon, only the darkness made it impossible to see. She bumped the nightstand, rattling an old-fashioned wind-up clock. She grabbed it and held the loud ticking against her chest while she slid behind the door. Marcie could see only a sliver of light. The front door squeaked, and in a blurred flash, a wild tussle ensued, followed by a muffled curse.

Marcie struggled to see, but the kitchen's dim light was blocked by a large man's shadowy outline. His determined footsteps were approaching fast. She could taste the fear in her mouth, briny and sour, as her heart rose higher and thumped erratically in her ears. *What happened to Sam? Was he hurt?* With both hands, Marcie gripped the alarm clock, raising it high over her head. She held her breath when a large man stepped into the room. She didn't think. She reacted, bringing the clock down hard, aiming for the back of his head, only he quickly whirled around, knocking the clock from her grasp. It sailed, landing with a shattered clang across the room.

"What the hell, Marcie?" Sam. Her Sam, incensed, tired, and he smelled so good. Her fear transformed to overwhelming relief when she fell into him. She looped her arms around his neck and cried—a real, messy, tears-flowing, nose-running cry.

"Hey, hey, what's this? It's okay." He rubbed her back and tightened his comforting hold. Marcie burrowed her face into his strong chest when hit by an aftershock of what had transpired. Her body trembled. He wasn't injured, so it must have been the other guy.

"It's okay. You're safe."

"I thought you were hurt, that it was the bad guy coming in here." She felt the rumble deep in his chest before his thunderous laugh burst out.

"The bad guy, Marcie?"

He chuckled in a way that sent her emotions tumbling. She planted both palms on his chest and tried to back away, only his powerful arms held on while sliding teasingly down her curvy waist, as if appreciating all the curves of her slim, womanly body.

"Sam! What about the bad guy?" She pointed when he wouldn't let go. Sam reached for her hand and dragged her out of the bedroom to the open front door. He flicked on the dim porch light, and there was Jesse, sprawled on his stomach, cursing while he stirred and struggled to push himself up.

"Sam, did you hit him? He's hurt."

"It was dark. I didn't know it was Jesse. Don't worry, he'll be fine." Sam released her hand and squatted down beside Jesse to help him up.

"You asshole, what the hell did you hit me for?" Sam guided Jesse to one of the old kitchen chairs. The chair creaked when Jesse sat. He winced as he leaned back, pressing his hand to the back of his head. "Shit, I think I'm bleeding."

"Oh, stop your damn whining, will you? You're not bleeding. And just what the hell are you doing here? I asked you to call me—hey, wait a second. How'd you find me, anyway?"

The look that passed between them was brotherly. Marcie couldn't help feeling left out.

"Calling you after I'm telling the cap'n I don't know where you are would not be smart, since, I'm sure, my calls are now being monitored. Besides, this is where you came the last time you hid out. You may want to ask yourself how many others know about this place."

Hide out, when was this? Marcie watched raw emotions dig in around Sam's eyes. She wanted to ask, but she didn't.

"Okay, okay, I get your point. So what'd you find out?"

"There's a lot of heat right now on this whole situation surrounding you and the girl. Derek's quite the hothead, and he's really pumping up your involvement, another notch in his belt to look really good with the commissioner. They've interrogated Reggie about his role in the missing backpack, except he clammed up and demanded a lawyer. And his lawyer pointed out we got nothing since the video's not solid evidence of a crime. As a matter of fact, the video shows clearly that Reggie didn't take the backpack, and as far as passing something to the guy who robbed Marcie, the lawyer said that'll be hard to prove. The video doesn't show what was passed. Also, we're not allowed to talk to her client again unless she's present, and she warned us that next time we had better have real evidence. We had no choice. He's been cut loose."

Sam shut his eyes and tilted his head up.

"Sam, we got a tail on him. You and I both know whatever he's part of, he's only the little guy. What I'm worried about is Derek's tunnel vision in wanting to see you go down for all this. He doesn't give a shit about Reggie. It's you he's trying to pin this on, as if you're this big connected guy overseeing some smuggling racket from up north. Derek's determined to talk to Marcie. He's convinced Reggie and Marcie are mules. And the only reason she's with you is so you can keep her quiet. He even ordered one of the detectives to go through all baggage claim security footage to see if you or Marcie appear at other times. But then guess what happened? Local Feds shut him down and are now claiming jurisdiction at the airport. They even yanked all the security videos Derek confiscated."

"Well, this is getting better and better."

"It actually does get better. Derek put an APB out on you and Marcie. Even went to your boss, implying you're a dirty cop and a drug dealer. But then a funny thing happened. Apparently, your boss didn't share his suspicion, indicating this is the first time you've been back in New Orleans in over six months. He shut Derek down, said he won't even consider the notion unless credible, solid evidence is produced.

"Then before I got here, this amazing woman by the name of Diane Larsen called me, said she's your partner. Well-organized lady pulled out all the stops. She's responsible for sending the Feds to get Derek off your back. It's nice for me to hear she's watching your backside."

Sam shrugged. "She has integrity, an anomaly on our team, and works damn hard to make sure we follow the letter of the law so scumbags won't get off on a technicality. I don't have to prove my innocence to her. She knows me. She's a good friend."

"Yeah, I figured that much. She's about ready to hop on a plane, come down here and save your ass. Help clear up this mess with Marcie—clear your name."

Just listening to the woman's name sparked another wave of jealousy. Sam said they weren't involved, but they sounded really close.

"Sam, if Derek keeps pushing, you and I both know evidence could suddenly appear against you. And then the Feds won't have a choice; you'll be dragged into this investigation, your career gone, your freedom, too. Is that what you want?" Jesse said.

Marcie couldn't believe what she was hearing. She waited for Sam to say something, anything, but he'd clammed up. The hard lines in his face turned to granite.

"Look, Sam, just let Derek talk to Marcie. Don't piss him off any more than you already have. If you give him something, he might back off on you."

"Why does he want to talk to me? I don't remember anything." Marcie crossed her arms over her braless chest.

"Well, see, that's the thing. He doesn't believe it." Jesse shuffled over to the sink and splashed cool water over his face, dunking his head under the rusty tap.

"Sam, maybe I should just talk to him and tell him I don't know anything," Marcie said. "I'm sure if I explain, it'll clear this whole thing up. Maybe then Derek will leave you alone."

Sam gave her a look as if she had sprouted a second head.

"Okay, maybe not," she said.

"Marcie, that's a very honest gesture, but it's also very naive and dangerous. Jesse here wants me to throw you to the wolves to save my own skin. And no, Jesse, I won't do that. Marcie doesn't know who she's dealing with. You aren't talking to Derek or any cop right now. These guys are trained to twist your words. You wouldn't stand a chance. Derek's not looking to find the right guilty party. He wants to close this and doesn't care who takes the fall, just as long as he looks good to the brass. They'd have you confessing to crimes without any clarity from your lost memory. I wouldn't be able to get you out, Marcie."

Sam grabbed a tin percolator from the back burner of the stove. He tossed Jesse a dishtowel and then shoved him aside to fill the coffee pot with water, sprinkling in ground coffee and setting it to boil. Jesse dried his face. Both men continued as if she wasn't there.

"You want coffee, Jesse?"

"Sure, and then I need to head back before Derek decides to put out an APB on me, too."

Didn't they realize she stood beside them? Even with this lapse in memory, Marcie knew she had a voice, yet she said nothing.

Sam was being high handed and protective, and, honestly, she liked it. Jesse, what could she say? He was Sam's friend.

Jesse cocked his head toward Marcie, a purely chauvinistic motion. "You sure she didn't get her memory back, even a little?"

Both men studied her. Marcie felt her cheeks burn from being thrust into the hot seat, her integrity constantly in question. She directed her response solely to Sam. "No, the girl didn't get her memory back." Her voice mocked an imitation of Jesse's southern drawl. "And please stop talking around me as if I'm not in the room."

Jesse flashed a wide smile. His deep, raspy laugh shook his soft belly. Marcie wasn't sure if this was humor or another insult, so she glared, and, in a childlike retreat, turned and walked over to the stove, pouring herself a cup of coffee.

Sam reached around her and grabbed a second mug on a plastic rack above the stove. He poured a cup and handed it to Jesse.

"Thanks."

Marcie felt heaviness expand the room. For a moment, nothing was said. Sam and Jesse exchanged some shared knowledge.

"You're not going to let me take Marcie, are you?" Jesse said.

"No, Jesse, I'm not. There are too many pieces missing in this puzzle. Look at her. She wouldn't stand a chance with Derek. I need to find answers first."

"I better get going. Call me, especially if mystery girl here remembers what she was really doing. Oh, and thanks for putting me in touch with Diane. At least now I know who to call to make sure you stay out of trouble." Jesse blew on the hot coffee and took a couple swigs before setting the mug on the table.

"Ma'am." Jesse's dark eyes cut deep into her heart, a warning she understood—don't mess with my boy. Then he gave Sam a friendly slap on the shoulder. "Watch your back."

Sam followed Jesse and locked the door behind him. Irritation steeped the standoff on opposite sides of the room. Marcie dumped her coffee out and listened to the gurgling idle of Jesse's car. Tension burned in the silence, magnified by her soft breath and the intensity of Sam's mutinous glare.

What a childish game. But Sam caved first, with a heavy sigh. He walked right up to her and rested his palms on her shoulders, sliding them down her slender arms, a gentle caress, and then he leaned his forehead against hers. "Don't get so pissed off. Jesse's put his neck on the line."

She touched the tobacco-colored, two-day growth shadowing his face. On any other man, it would look disheveled, but not Sam. It only accentuated his full lips, which looked like they were made for kissing a woman and knew how to do it right. He was a stretch. The top of her head only reached his chin. His blue eyes darkened as he slid both hands to her waist.

"He loves you, and he's trying to protect you from being hurt by me," Marcie said.

He framed her face, combing his fingers through her long, wavy hair. "He pisses you off."

"Yes, but I respect him. And, in an odd way, he gives me peace, knowing he's one person watching your back."

Boy, did he look good; that wavy, sandy blond hair, those magnetic blue eyes that sparkled when they connected with her, not to mention his well-defined shoulders, strong, solid. A girl could really lean into him. She wrapped her arms around his neck as if he was the only steady thing that could anchor her.

"Your heart's pounding—I can feel it." He pressed his hand against her heart. She blinked when he leaned in. So close now, his warm breath teased her.

"Ah, I…" She couldn't speak, not from fear but because she was spellbound by this fiery tug of attraction and something more—a rightness, as if they were meant to be together.

She made the move unconsciously, or did they both move? Their lips touched, brushed lightly, as his feathered across hers. His hand slid like magic under her shirt, caressing her bare skin, shifting up, skimming her navel to tease her slender curves. It was an unchoreographed play from a storybook. The dance of his fingers lifted and glided under the swell of her breast.

"Sam, what's happening?" She trailed off, a pathetic attempt to get him to stop, which no doubt was exactly what she didn't want him to do.

"I want to see all of you and this amazing body of yours." His breath whispered across her wanting lips.

Her breath caught, quaked and escaped. "Don't stop." The sensuous words tumbled out; filled with desire. She covered his cheeks with her palms, feeling the close connection and sensing the gaze of his hard bedroom eyes. She opened herself completely to him.

He slipped the shirt over her head and then let his gaze run over her naked body. He trailed his hands up from her waist and cupped her breasts. Her breath caught, held, and then released when her knees started to weaken. He lifted her in his arms as if she weighed nothing and carried her to the side of the bed, kneeling over her.

"The light," she said.

"It can stay on. I want to see all of you."

He pulled off his shirt and shed the rest of his clothes. His hands were hard as iron one moment, then soft as cotton the next. She wrapped her slender legs around his waist. Maybe it was his passion, his skill, that had her opening herself willingly to him. No, the truth was, she wanted all he'd offer. She balanced in between bits and pieces of tortuous sensation as he trailed tender nips down her shoulder, over her plump, full breast, trapping and gentling her nipple between his teeth. Pleasure rushed into her so fast she nearly panicked. This was trust, an absolute surrender that she knew, on some level, she'd given to no other.

"Oh, Sam, Sam." She said it with a moan as he drove himself into her, pressing her thighs wide. Fast and hurried, he took on a desperate pace as he rocked within her, leading her to a place hovering on the edge of some sheer rock face, becoming her choice to let go and glory in the abyss. He pushed deeper. Their tongues entwined, retreated, touched and teased. It was fevered and fast, flesh against flesh, nothing pretty and dainty, when she sobbed his name. She tightened, building up, higher, faster, and shattering the veil-thin wall separating her from him. But it was his hoarse shout, followed by a fiery magic, that bound them together.

CHAPTER 13

Her first surprise came when she opened her eyes to bright sunlight already filling the small room. She'd had no dreams and felt relatively rested. The second surprise was Sam's firm hand keeping her anchored to him on the edge of the small double bed, saving her from tumbling out while he lay sprawled in the center.

After all, it was considerate of him to make sure she stayed there instead of falling out and landing on her head. When she tried to wiggle her way out, he tightened his hold, pulling her back against him, and she realized then that not all of him was asleep.

"Sam, time to get up. I'm hungry."

He answered her with merely a grunt and slid his hand up to cover her breast. Then he lifted her leg and showed her how awake he was. "Me too, so you can lie here while I feed my hunger."

Later, as they shared a shower and then dressed with easy intimacy, she had a vision of how it could be with them. Easy mornings spent loving and cuddling together could easily slip into routine, but one built on commitment. Something cracked inside of her heart, as if that dream was something she'd never deemed herself worthy of.

"I've got to go out. I'll be gone a couple hours, so bolt the door behind me. Don't let anyone in, and don't go out." He pulled her from those fairytale thoughts, dropping a fast kiss on her brooding lips before walking out of the bedroom.

"Sam, I tried to get in the attic last night when you were out, but the door's locked. Do you think you could open it before you go?"

He paused and faced her as if contemplating what to say. Did he expect her to sit quietly and do nothing while he was gone? She reached up to touch the tiny nick on his chin from shaving that morning, but he grabbed her hand when he noticed the scabbed-over puncture.

"What did you do to your hand?"

"I tried to pick the lock on the attic door and cut myself."

"What the hell did you use, a knife?"

"No, I found a chicken skewer in the drawer and I tried to pick the lock. But it wouldn't work."

His mouth fell open.

"Well, you made it look really easy," she said.

"There's antiseptic in the kitchen." The old wood floor squeaked when he stomped to the kitchen and yanked open the cupboard door, taking out a brown bottle of hydrogen peroxide. "Use it, Marcie, or I'll do it for you. The last thing we need right now is to be red flagged while sitting in an emergency room because you've got an infection."

She viewed the bottle as poison, already feeling the ripe sting even before she poured it over the wound. "Fine, but what about the door? Can you open it? Please."

"Why do you want to go up there? It's dusty, dirty, and filled with a bunch of old junk."

"Please, Sam. There's something about the attic, call it intuition, but I can't shake this voice, like an angel telling me there's something up there I'm supposed to see." She closed her eyes. "You think I'm nuts, don't you?" She opened her eyes to a man who wasn't watching her with horror but was intrigued. She stumbled a bit. "You don't think I'm crazy?"

He raised his eyebrows. "No, but if your angels are guiding you to some buried treasure stashed up there, remember, it's mine."

She laughed when a bit of lightness filled her heart and pranced behind him up the steep steps. This time she watched closely while he bent with a pick he pulled from his brown leather wallet. She breathed in a distinct piney scent from his soap, which overpowered the musty shirt. He smelled good—really good—and that was a very real problem, which distracted her. She licked her lips and drew his eyes to her.

"Watch yourself, girl, or you'll be in heaps of trouble before I go." Then the door was pushed open. Light streamed in from the small corner window. Dust and cobwebs lingered over boxes and old furniture piled up in the cramped eight-by-ten space.

Sam went in first. "Stay there until I know this old floor's safe to walk on. I don't remember when I last came up here, if ever."

He shoved boxes over and appeared to study the old plank floor while he ran a hand over the buckled hardwood by the only corner window.

"What're you looking for?"

"Rot, cracked boards where the floor's not stable."

"Sam, where did all this stuff come from?"

"It's always been here. This was my granddaddy's place. He willed it to me. It's been in the family for generations. I guess he liked to save things. I didn't know him. A lawyer found me. Apparently, my real daddy died before I was born. Joseph Carre, who I thought was my daddy, turned out to be just a stepfather. Always wondered why he hated me." He moved toward her but remained distant with a vague light in his eyes. *Must be a lot on his mind.* He stopped and lifted her chin with his finger.

"Happy hunting, and remember to keep the door locked."

She cut him off before he could finish. "Don't answer the door, do not go outside for any reason, stay in the house like a good little girl and make no noise."

Sam looked skyward, as if searching for help, from some unseen force, and then squeezed past her. "Marcie, get down here and lock the door behind me. Then clean your hand before you start rummaging through junk."

Oops, I guess he's punchy, too. Instead of arguing, she followed him down and bolted the door. She listened to his tires grind in the dirt as he pulled away. Peace washed over her. Just being here with him had changed things between them. They were closer. She couldn't explain why.

Marcie wandered to the sink and eyed the bottle of peroxide. She had promised, so she didn't think it to death. She unscrewed the white cap, held her hand over the sink, and dumped a small amount of fizzy liquid over the wound. She shook off the miserable sting before putting away the bottle and racing upstairs.

Dusty cardboard boxes and wooden crates were stacked against the wall. Some were labeled, others left bare. Old furniture was mixed among the boxes, stacked and draped with yellow, dusty sheets. Marcie batted at the cobwebs.

She breathed in dust and coughed before making her way over to the small corner window. She turned a rusty old latch and tried to lift, but the window was stuck. She had to make a choice; put up with the stuffy air or abandon the search.

Marcie moved closer to the door. At least it wasn't as bad there. The first box had the name Benjamin Reynolds written in thick black ink on the side. Intrigued, she opened it. Inside were stacks of old photos, a football jersey, and an old high school yearbook from 1960. At the bottom of the box was a yellowed newspaper clipping of a tragic accident. A front-page photo featured both the dark-haired man who had driven the car in her dream and the same cliff on the mountainside. A crushing energy tightened in her stomach and spiraled like a funnel cloud. She had read the news story depicting an overtired driver losing control and driving off a cliff, leaving behind his young bride. A friend of Benjamin Reynolds' had been quoted in the story: *Ben was struggling with some personal issues and had come to him for support. He said he tried to help, that Ben felt overwhelmed by his new responsibilities.* The friend, Joseph Carre, was photographed escorting Benjamin's young wife to the funeral. This man and woman were the same two who had been in her dream, standing at a roadside grave marker. This was plain weird. This was Sam's real father, but what she picked up in her gut when she looked at the clipping was a terrible feeling that the crash was no accident. Sam's real daddy had gone off that road, and she suspected Joseph Carre was responsible.

She repacked the box and moved on to the next carton, clearing space as she re-stacked the boxes she'd rummaged in against the wall behind her. By the time Marcie had rifled through a dozen boxes filled with junk and trinkets, she was bored and considered packing it in. She pushed a heavy box against the wall but soon discovered it hid an old wooden chest. "Now, how did I miss you?"

Something about the chest drove the beat of her heart up. Without warning, something rustled. Her stomach bottomed out, and she instantly flattened her hand over her chest. "Probably a damn rodent. Just breathe." Marcie trembled while looking around in the shadows, willing the noise to happen again while at the same time fearing that it would.

Marcie tried to lift the lid, but it was stuck. She had to get down on her knees and lean in. It creaked when it finally gave. Small boxes, paper bags, and tons of old photos filled this deep chest, but it was no fun looking at a stranger's photos, so she continued digging until she touched a bulky tissue-wrapped package. Marcie carefully pulled back the crisp tissue to find an old creamy lace wedding gown. Under the dress were cream-colored leather boots with a slight heel and a hook and eye closure. They were nice but had to have been uncomfortable.

She reached to the bottom and touched a rectangular parcel. Lifting the package, Marcie was mesmerized by the curved handwriting on the old brown paper until she saw the name: *Mrs. Jerome Standford.* "Holy shit," she whispered.

CHAPTER 14

"Who's there?" she called, jumping as a warm tingle shot so hard and fast up her spine that, for a moment, she thought it'd blow off the top of her head. Beads of sweat popped out above her brow. The air chilled, and for some inexplicable reason she'd swear that time appeared to shift and merge; there was no here, now, or yesterday. A broad sense of something else or some deep presence pressed up her spine. Her first instinct prompted her to hide, which spurred this unknown terror. She swallowed hard and then peeked around the stack of boxes where she hid. "Hello, anyone there?" Nothing moved. "Well, did you expect a ghost to answer? Forget that thought." She waved her hand in the air to swoosh those words away.

Truth was, she was damn scared, and in order to ease the fear, she crouched down, squeezing in between the box and chest, wrapping her arms around her knees. She started to examine the paper-wrapped bundle, turning it over and then removing the knotted string. *Breathe in, blow out.* She tried to still the shaking in her hands. "So my dream's real, and Jerome's dead, and he's in my dreams—this is crazy." She turned over the package. "This is something addressed to Jerome's wife. How can this be possible?"

She wanted to analyze and reason but stopped herself. "Don't try to figure it out. Jerome, is there some hidden message here for me?" She looked up as if waiting for his golden image to appear. But she was grateful when he didn't. She opened the paper package; several letters fell into her lap, tied together with a delicate pink satin ribbon, faded and worn from time. Each letter was addressed to Mrs. Jerome Standford, Grand Isle. She sighed before carefully opening the first letter.

OCTOBER *12, 1814*

My Darling Isabel,

I love you and can't wait to be home with you. I am so happy about the babe and promise to be home long before he's born. I cannot tell you where we are, but Master Jean gathered many fine staples for our friends and those in need. They will not eliminate the hardship, but it will be enough to see us through.

We were greeted by his old friend, the colonel. Master Jean has warned me to watch him and his crew when they come about. Although friends he calls them, he also does not trust them.

The colonel has mentioned many a time that he would sell his mother's soul for a plantation like Jean's. He's in it for the money, not to help others. He continues to feed Jean information on where enemy cargo ships are expected to be. It seems almost too good to be true. The man makes me uneasy. But I promise, love, this will be the last time. This run will set our future, and today, I'll tell Master Jean. I promise to be with you when you have the babe. I miss you and dream of you each night.

Your loving husband, Jerome

MARCIE READ IT AGAIN AND STUDIED HIS WORDS. WHERE HE WAS, IT WAS another lifetime. Why had this name appeared to her? She lifted up the paper package when a folded picture slipped out from behind. The bold inscription on the back read: *Jerome and Isabel, our blessed day.*

Marcie studied the man and the woman in the timeless, austere pose. The resemblance to the golden-haired man in her dream that night under the glowing light was astounding. As she looked closer, so was the resemblance to Sam. Jerome's hair was long and tied back in this photo, but the features of his face, jaw, and broad forehead were unmistakable. He was dressed as a gentleman in a tuxedo jacket, riding breeches and hessians. Isabel's face in the photo was faded, as if it had been gripped between someone's fingers repeatedly. She wore an antique lace wedding gown. Jerome's hand rested upon her shoulder, a familiar pose for that period in time.

"How'd you get buried way back there?" Sam said.

Marcie's stomach dropped when his growling voice rushed her headfirst back to the present. She placed her hand over her chest to calm the wild beating. "Jeez, Sam, you scared me. Didn't your mama ever teach you not to sneak up on a lady?"

The way he smiled made it seem as if he'd figured things out. "But you forget that in cop school, that's exactly what they teach us. So how'd you get in there, sugar?"

"I just kept moving boxes until I was here. Sam, wait until you see what I found. Come here."

Sam shuffled boxes and crouched to where she sat cross-legged on the floor. Marcie handed him the picture.

"Turn it over. See the name?"

Sam frowned. "It's an old picture. Where'd you find it? Cool." He handed it back with absolutely no interest.

"Sam, read this" She held up the packet of letters. Sam took all the letters, including the one she had read.

His lips moved as he whispered over each word. "Wow, interesting history." Sam handed the letter back.

"Who do these letters belong to?"

Sam walked toward the stairs. "I don't know for sure, probably some distant relative. I didn't know my granddaddy, so all this is a mystery. But as a former detective, don't people usually stash all their old family photos and trinkets in the attic?"

"Good investigating, Sam. Do you mind if I keep these letters to read?"

"No, go ahead. I bought you some clothes and picked up lunch. I'm hungry, so let's eat." Sam extended his hand and helped Marcie up. "So did you discover any treasures in all your digging up here?"

Marcie appreciated his broad shoulders, all of him, really, while he moved ahead of her down the stairs. She clutched the packet of letters as if a window from another time had burst open and handed them to her. "Sometimes treasures come in a way we least expect," she answered.

After lunch while Sam spoke on the phone, first with Jesse and then Diane; Marcie hefted out the letters and curled up in an old easy chair in the sitting room, a tiny alcove off the kitchen. She opened the next letter, wondering why Jerome wanted her to see these. What was he trying to tell her?

DECEMBER 5, 1814

My Darling,

Navigating the waters of Barataria Bay, we expected to be home some time ago. Please don't lose faith. We ran into some trouble. There was a supply ship waiting where we were told, but they were prepared for us, and out of nowhere, the Spanish fleet joined them, coming down hard upon us. It was a bloody fight. We were betrayed. There's a traitor among us. Master Jean has assembled a small team to discover who it is. He'll be dealt with harshly. We lost many good men in the fight, and the ship sustained some damage, but we narrowly escaped. We have to lie low for a while and have stashed ourselves in Master Jean's stronghold. I expect this letter to find you safely. I do not know when it will reach you but have given it to a kind captain of a local supply ship. I pray every day I will be home with you, my loving wife, before the babe comes. Keep safe, be strong, and keep loving thoughts of me as I dream of holding you once again in my arms.

Your loving husband, Jerome

MARCIE'S HEART FELT HEAVY WITH JEROME'S DESPAIR AND HIS DESIRE TO BE with the woman he loved. She glanced at Sam while he paced through the kitchen and bedroom, talking on his cell phone. Marcie sighed. She opened the next letter, dated several months later.

• • •

My dearest love, please do not forget me. I dream about you every night and long to hold you in my arms. The pain and emptiness I feel at this moment tears my heart out. I'm in the brig and have been wrongly convicted of treason. Evidence was planted in my bunk, letters to the Spanish, describing in detail our holds and the location of Jean's stronghold. My dear friend has turned his back on me, and his look of contempt for me is damning for this perceived betrayal. I swear to you, my love, I did not do this. I'm trying not to lose faith, but I fear that by day's end, I'll be dead. There's still a traitor on board. I do not know who it is. Somehow, I suspect the colonel's connected. My love, tell our babe every day how his papa loved him. I do not even know if it's a boy or girl. My greatest fear is never holding my child. Keep safe, my love, and know my last thoughts were always of you.

I will love you always. Jerome

THE WORDS BLURRED. MARCIE'S CHEST BURNED FROM THE UNSPEAKABLE torment that Jerome must have felt in having his life and love wrenched away.

A soft touch on her shoulder nearly sent her through the roof. She allowed Sam to pull her into his arms.

"What happened? I heard you crying."

Marcie shook her head, the emptiness of a lost love embedded like a solid rock deep inside her. "They killed him. He was set up."

"Who killed him? What are you talking about? Who was killed?" He sat her down and knelt beside her. Marcie sniffled while he held her hands.

"There, in the letter." She pulled her hand from his and picked the letter up from the rickety paint-splattered side table.

Sam took it from her, his face a mirage of questions "Oh… okay." He put the letter down and wandered away with only a vague flicker of interest. "What happened in that letter was over one hundred and fifty years ago. A tragedy, sure, but nothing I can fix or do anything about. Besides, we need to go." He tossed her a plastic bag.

"What's this?"

"Your new clothes. We leave in fifteen minutes."

Sam whistled as he strode into the kitchen. So much was going on inside of her. She couldn't separate one feeling from another, feelings that were refusing to allow her to be happy: doubts, anxiety, pity, and the fact that she was losing control of who she was; all mixed up with the fear that she was falling for Sam big time, all because he dictated, took charge, looked after things for her, and protected her. She felt inadequate, which made her furious, because out of all of this, somehow he'd stolen her heart. Marcie stomped into the bedroom, afraid of the lighthearted giddiness fluttering through her heart. She viewed this unknown element with such distrust that a familiar misery leaked out from some secret compartment locked deep inside her.

<hr>

SAM CHOKED ON HIS COFFEE WHEN HE HEARD THE DOOR SLAM. HE KNEW she was mad but couldn't help the devil in him, who enjoyed getting a rise out of her. He couldn't figure out why he was drawn to her. He barely knew her but couldn't keep his hands off her. She was trouble, in an honest sort of way—a way he couldn't explain. He told himself that if he was smart, he'd have walked away; but some feeling he couldn't shake had him believing, as was the case with his own circumstances, that she, too, may have been a pawn for someone else's gain. He knew the criminal element darkened some people, and no part of that greed or manipulation filled her. If he were honest with himself, he'd admit he had already lived with that. Deep down, he had always suspected Elise had her hand in some pot, skimming off the top; except, he loved her so much that he had thought he could change her. The icing on the cake was that Marcie had more fire and passion knotting him up than any woman he had ever met—even Elise. An inner war waging inside had him bouncing back and forth between anger, honest-to-goodness chivalry, needing Marcie, and just plain lust.

Then guilt washed over him. He closed his eyes to block out her face when Elise crept into his thoughts again. He refused to be sucked into that despair. He had to let her go.

Marcie was different. She piqued his interest, and he craved being with her in a way he had never experienced before. Right now, it had thrown him a curve ball he wasn't sure he wanted. He shook off this craziness. Still, for some reason he couldn't explain, he had a burning need to keep her with him. She was now his lover, his friend; and what did he know about her past? Nothing, but his gut and heart urged him not to walk away.

Marcie erupted from the bathroom five minutes later. She shimmered in her red cotton sundress, with her miles of hair hanging past her shoulders, and it punched up his heart a few notches. *Wow.* It was the only word his brain could produce. Thin spaghetti straps enhanced her lovely breasts, and the soft cotton fell loosely from her waist to mid-thigh, magnifying her curvaceous body. Alarmed, he realized his mistake. She now stood out.

"Thanks for the dress. It's beautiful." He turned away and poured her a cup of coffee.

"I like my women wearing a dress," he said. When he handed her the steamy mug, a harsh glare greeted him.

Where the hell did that come from?

Then his cell phone buzzed on the table. "Good timing." He reached for the gifted reprieve when Marcie gave him her stiff back and sauntered into the bedroom.

This was an emotional roller coaster. His nerves were stretched thin, and he had no desire to traipse after her and smooth over ruffled feathers. He had to deal with things—more important things. Didn't she get that?

"Sam here." Now he was pissed, too.

"Whoa, bad time?"

"No, Jesse, we're about to leave. What's up?"

"Lots. Derek figured out where you are. Time to move it."

"Thanks for the heads up."

Sam disconnected and stuffed his cell phone in his back pocket. "Marcie, hustle your butt. We're leaving now."

Sam rushed Marcie out the door. A warm wind rustled her hair from the Camaro's open window. Sam hurried across the bridge on Highway One to Lafourche Bayou.

"Sam, where are we going?"

He met the fire still brimming in her eyes, then put his focus back on the road. "We're going to see a friend of mine, Mama Reine. She lives outside Thibodaux." He pointed out her side window. "Those are sugar cane fields. Ever seen one?"

SHE SHOOK HER HEAD AT THE STATELY VIEW OF MOSS-LADEN OAKS AND sugar cane fields filled with an active labor force. Several dark bodies were at work in the field. A chill swept outward from some part in her center. *There's no happiness alive within these people. Maybe times have changed, but also not.* What she watched reeked of despondency, drudgery, and dictatorship, which had manifested itself and become stronger over time.

"Sam, what's going on with us? I'm scared. I need to say that much."

Sam reached over and squeezed her hand. "It's going to be okay, Marcie." But with the way he said it, she wondered if he truly believed it.

"Tell me about Mama Reine. She sounds like an amazing woman, taking kids in and living way out here."

He let out a heavy sigh. "She is. I guess you can say Mama Reine was kind of a surrogate mother and father to me. My own parents sucked. My daddy grew up in violence, so that was all he knew, how to be mean. And that was what we got. I guess you learn from what you see. Anyway, he used to smack Mama around, threw her down the stairs. I was just a little kid. I'd hide and watch, and she'd always make excuses for not leaving. 'He's a good provider.' 'He meant nothing by it.' Or even better, 'I made him angry.' How many women say that, Marcie, huh? Tell me. Then he started in on me until I was big enough that he couldn't push me around.

"Mama Reine provided us local vagrants with a safe place to come. If we were hungry, she'd feed us. If we were hurt, she'd patch us up. She did weird stuff, too, like always having a line drawn in the dirt outside her front door so no one bad or with evil intent could cross. We'd always be safe, and to a little kid, that's a slice of heaven."

Marcie frowned at his comment. "Line? What do you mean, a line? I don't understand."

Sam laughed. "One of her many superstitions. It's a line in the dirt with red clay, like she cast a spell of protection. Some folks out here lay them in front of their doorways, but you need to believe in them for it to work." The last part he whispered, spiking an icy shiver up her spine. Sam averted his gaze, but not before she saw generations of hurt transform his face. Once again, he had shut her out.

He slowed the car right before a narrow dirt driveway appeared, like a magical trail, among thick, moss-laden oaks. Sam turned. The car jolted over ruts and potholes. An old wood cabin emerged, weather worn and raised on stilts. Sam parked beside an old rickety shed. He leaned his head back and let out a heavy sigh, pulling a thick wall around him as if drowning alone in some private hell he wouldn't let go of. Then he climbed out without a word or a glance, clutching his keys and slamming his door. He didn't come around for her. He walked away, self-absorbed, and she felt abandoned and discarded—a woman of no importance, triggering a flood of memories, filled with hurt, pain, and everything she'd forgotten. The locked door hiding her past suddenly flew open, and it was time to accept what she'd done.

She remembered Dan and how self-centered he could be, how he kept her at arm's length despite what she willingly did for him. From the fire in her first dream, the memories of him were packed with hurt, wanting, desire, degradation and lust—memories of their time together as lovers, but only when he was playing. His charm and charisma exuded a powerful need to be surrounded by people—lots of people. His gifted ability to transfer his entire focus in an instant to her, with those whiskey-colored eyes, became an addiction. Even now, she felt a familiar tug inside of her, a connection to his magical presence, that left her obsessed with a fiery need to be his one and only; to please him, to help him, to do anything for him, except the outcome was always the same. Their past had been saturated with pain, hurt and scandal; never the fairytale she dreamed.

She closed her eyes when bitter nausea burned in the pit of her stomach. The bile climbed. Each hazy blank filled, one by one, until her keen awareness acknowledged one thing—what she'd experienced the past few days had been a blessed gift.

A lone tear weaved a path down her damp cheek. She understood, now, the difference between lust and love. She was worthy of being loved—worthy of honest caring given by a real man, an honorable man. Sam oozed respect in his role toward women. She'd honestly never experienced this before. Dumbstruck, she wondered if she'd have seen the gift in Sam before her memory loss. Probably not. Now what she feared more than anything was her weakness. Had Dan snared her so far into his treacherous web that she'd lost any chance for happiness with a man who could be her everything? She was faced with a choice that only she could make—to continue on this path of destruction or walk the right road.

She opened her door and climbed out into the stifling humidity, closing her eyes and lifting her face into the bright sunlight. Marcie followed the rough dirt path to the rickety front steps with a rough, narrow railing hammered together with two by fours. Marcie clutched the green cloth bag Sam had bought her, filled with her clothes and Jerome's letters. The warm air was so damp and heavy that she found it hard to breathe. She grabbed the railing with a trembling hand and forced herself to climb until she stood, shaking, outside a torn mesh screen door.

"Well, I's been waiting for ya. Come on in," came a voice from inside the house.

Marcie pulled on the broken handle dangling by one screw. Rusty hinges protested with an angry squeal. Small bones dangled from a string and caught in her hair when she passed over the threshold.

"Chicken bones, to keep the bad spirits out."

Sam shrugged as he leaned against the light brown paneled wall. His whole body, his spirit, appeared coiled so tightly that she was positive he'd snap if she dared to touch him. It had to be ghosts of painful memories: Elise, Della, and Leon. There was so much someone needed to atone for, but who?

"Step in here so I can have a look at ya."

Marcie shuffled past Sam, still hurt by the rebuff that had triggered her unwanted memories. She swallowed her fear when she faced him. "You left me out there, why?" she said.

He knitted his brows. Something harsh faded from the confusion outlining his face, but he said nothing.

Marcie faced a large woman wearing a sleeveless blue housedress, rocking in her chair. When she smiled, her aged, dark, spotted skin creased like worn leather. She was the image of a sightless old gypsy woman, with the way she watched Marcie with those unseeing eyes. Marcie was positive this woman could tap into her very soul and rip open each vile secret she'd hidden. She swallowed hard. Her weak knees threatened to give out.

"Spirits talk, they share. You listening there, girl?" The white covering her eyes was indicative of her long-since diminished eyesight in this world. How did she look after herself?

"Marcie, this is Mama Reine. Mama, meet Marcie," Sam said.

The old woman with bony knees had crammed her plump body into an old rocker, with not an inch to spare. Bunions on her crooked toes peeked out through the tops of worn dark sandals.

"It's nice to meet you, ma'am." Marcie stepped closer to shake Mama's hand but teetered back a step. Feeling foolish, she yanked her hand back. Marcie glimpsed a bookshelf behind the rocker, jammed with photos. Mismatched frames, wood, silver, brass and gold, were filled with faces of children, adults, families, graduations and weddings. One stuck out like a sore thumb amid all the colorful, unfamiliar faces. The gorgeous dead woman from her dream, a ghost she had really seen, was wrapped in the arms of Sam as he gazed adoringly at her in a way that said, *You're everything to me.* The younger Sam sported a mustache and spotted red bandana tied around his head. He was leaning against his Harley, his wife tucked safely in his arms. The woman was a knockout. Her long, blond hair swung free and loose with the same radiant smile that had beckoned in Marcie's dream, and it hurt Marcie to see how much he loved her.

"You ache just looking at that photo? Don't deny it now, girl. Any fool can feel the air spark when you two are in a room together. You want his love so much it damn near kills you. But that's all you've ever wanted." Mama pursed her fat lips. "I may be old, but I remember what it's like to want nothing more than to be loved by the right man. That'd be Elise in the photo. But you already know that."

"The first night here, I dreamed of her." Marcie pointed her finger as if Mama could see.

"What kind of games are you playing?" Sam snapped. His words hurled daggers at her heart. "You don't—whoa, stop. How do you know Elise? And don't you dare give me any more bullshit about a dream. That's not real."

"Oh, hush up, you," Mama said. "What do you know about what's real and what's an illusion? Get your lady a chair, and you'd best listen this time. She knows some, not everything, though."

Tears burned from the ache Marcie felt in that moment. He didn't understand, and he didn't move. Sam stood there declaring mutiny, his Adam's apple bobbing up and down. His face contorted with a crimson hurt, exposing the depth of his despair. Somehow, Marcie knew Sam felt responsible for Elise having killed Leon and for Della, Leon's mama, serving life in prison for her role in this tragedy; shooting Elise in a fit of grief out of some sense of misguided justice. Of course, he couldn't help but take this on. It was how he was made.

"You don't understand, my boy. She's not to blame. Go 'n collect yourself. The girl will stay here."

There was kindness in the rude, harsh commands. Those sightless eyes saw more than a person with twenty-twenty vision, right into the soul of the man. She jumped when the screen door clattered. The rusted hinges wobbled as they fought to remain rooted in the rotted wood.

"Pull up a chair so I can see you," Mama said.

Marcie dragged over a straight-backed chair by the door.

"I knew you were coming. Elise told me."

"Ah." A chilling tingle pinched Marcie's skin. She knew the room was full. She remembered that her granny and her teacher, Sally, had also seen through the veil. Angels and spirits surrounded each person, and they could hear messages sent from the other side.

"Open your eyes, child. Don't be afraid."

"I didn't know she was his." Marcie's unsteady voice broke when panic of her unknown future rose.

"Their time's over, so, let it go." Mama was so matter of fact. But these feelings weren't so black and white, not when Marcie was drowning in them.

"Girl, do you remember now? You were walking the wrong road, but you know that now. You don't know it yet, but you were sent to him."

"No I wasn't. I was delivering something for a friend."

The old woman's face tightened. Her angry glare reached out and snagged Marcie's heart. "Oh, no, don't you lie to me. I see and know what you had with you. You've been the broker, a mule, carrying drugs to destroy some poor kid's future. Fate intervened and stopped you. Right now, you have a choice to make. You and I both know what happens if you don't pick right.

"You were born with the sight, but you abused it. Everything you did for that guy, you believed it was the only way he'd love you. Haven't you learned yet? That ain't love. You even believed he was the one you'd been asking for—your soul mate. Be careful what you ask for. He's a lesson you needed to learn. You were together before, in another life. Soul mates isn't always who you should be with. Understand the difference.

"You just want to be loved. That's all you've ever wanted. You turned away from your teacher too early. You're vulnerable, and you didn't listen to your angels, guides, and the good spirits around you. They warned you about him. I do understand why you didn't hear. You'd lost the one person who centered you.

"Marcie, we all need a teacher when we're learning how to channel the spirits and talking to the other side. You can't do it alone. That's how you end up targeted by darkness. And you were an easy target, swept up in the lies of a predator. He had you right where he wanted. The only way to break his hold was to give you a taste of freedom; and you got it when you hit your head."

Shame warmed Marcie's face, and she knew that wasn't the old woman's intent. Tears spilled and dripped onto her lap.

"You need to tell Sam everything," Mama said.

"I can't."

"You need to tell him. You need to trust him and have enough faith in him, or there'll be no change." Mama said nothing more, leaning back and rocking. She raised her bony hand at the pictures behind her, where Marcie saw the dark teenage boy with dreadlocks. A shiver slid up her spine when she looked at his eyes, eyes that held secrets along with hurt, anger, and greed, appearing to slither down into nothingness. She knew those lost eyes were the same as those plastered on wanted posters, filled with darkness, exposing a dangerous thug, someone not to be trusted.

"That's Leon, my grandson. That was taken the year Katrina ripped through. He was lost to us then. We saw it. His mama did, too. And my son, well—he did poorly by that boy's mama. He's still out there wandering, just another lost, angry black man, trying to find his way. He could see nothing, let alone the gift God gave him. Enough." She swept her hand out in front of her face.

Marcie saw regret in Mama's loss with her son and grandson.

"Della, that's her up there at the top with a lively spark. Leon was five in that picture. He had hope then, until the city got hold of him. And Elise killed him. You afraid to ask what your part is?"

Caught off guard, Marcie jerked her head back to Mama.

"It's time to pay the piper, girl. Your friends brought the drugs. Leon worked for your guy down here, the same one you were delivering to."

"Mama, I didn't know the guy. This is the first time I've carried marijuana."

"Maybe so, but your man's been grooming you for this. He has plans for you."

Hot color flamed Marcie's cheeks. Her mouth dropped open, unable to hammer down the betrayal she felt at that moment. "He's been grooming me? He told me…" She couldn't finish. Her voice broke when a horrible ache ripped through her heart.

"He told you all kinds of things. But they were always lies, lies, and more lies. Deep down, you already know this. When you throw a stone in the water, your actions cast off a whole chain of events. Remember, whatever you do, always do it out of love, and harm none."

"Elise killed Leon," Marcie said. "I heard Jesse say she was a dirty cop and that shooting Leon may not have been justifiable."

"Elise was always a troubled girl. She fit in good with many of the dirty cops around here." Mama grimaced bitterly. She never broke rhythm as she rocked in her old wooden chair, back and forth. "You'd best call Sam in."

Marcie's rubbery legs trembled. She gripped the back of her chair, pausing a moment to gather strength, before doing the old woman's bidding. She pressed open the squeaky door.

Sam leaned against the rail at the bottom of the stairs, smoking a cigarette. He flicked the butt in the dirt, exhaling, and their eyes met. When did he start smoking? There were many secrets between them.

"She wants you to come in."

He started up, one by one. His heavy footsteps rattled the unsteady stairs. He froze in front of her, studying her with such an odd expression. He stepped inside and searched out his dead wife's photo, but Marcie couldn't make sense of what he was feeling.

"Her memory's returned." Mama raised her chin when she spoke to Sam, and he swiveled his head around so fast that his caustic look burned into Marcie.

"Why didn't you let me tell him first?" Marcie said.

"Don't you get prissy now, girl."

"Mama, did Jesse stop here, tell you about Marcie losing her memory?"

"I saw the boy, but I knowed she was a coming. Spirit told me." She flicked her aged, spotted hand at Marcie. "You find the letters?"

Beads of icy perspiration erupted down her back at exactly the same moment goose bumps spiked her tender skin. Marcie swallowed, unable to speak.

"What letters?" Sam was genuinely confused.

Mama grinned, a crooked smile showing her aged, chipped teeth. "Why, boy, the ones in your attic that your girl here found. She was supposed to find them."

The cryptic messages were beginning to unnerve Sam, and Marcie, too. He paced back and forth in front of the door, his hands shoved roughly through his damp wavy hair, leaving it sticking up in clumps.

"What kind of bullshit are you selling me?" he snapped.

"You watch your mouth, boy. You ain't too big to get your mouth washed out with soap."

Marcie gaped at the mental image of Mama washing out the tough guy's mouth.

The scowl on Sam's face was priceless. "Crazy old woman," he muttered.

"Pay him no mind," Mama said. "Did you read the letters, child?"

The stifling emotions in the room scraped like claws in Marcie's stomach. "It broke my heart. They framed him, and they killed him."

"Oh no, girl, you didn't read all of them or you'd know. Old Jerome lingered a long while, rotting in the Cabildo. He was set up, same as Sam, by the same dark entities close to him. They can be a friend, family, or acquaintance, and they know what they're doing. They got one agenda, to destroy you, and I know you know this." She pointed to Sam, and he frowned.

"Old woman, you're making no sense. What happened to that guy was over a hundred and fifty years ago. It's got nothing to do with now. You're confused."

"Oh! I don't think so, boy. Everything has to do with now. You don't know how the universe works. Jerome was your great, great, great granddaddy, but he's Marcie's guide now. Sit on down here." Mama stilled. Her face softened as she tilted her head.

"Mama?" Marcie asked.

She didn't answer for the longest time. She stared through Marcie, nodding, completely pulled into whatever spirit surrounded her. "Hmm." Then she blinked. "Jerome's with you now, behind you. He wants you to know his story, what happened to him."

She continued: "He was a lieutenant under that old pirate, Lafitte. He made his home on Grand Isle. He was right hand to Jean and Pierre. They flew the flag of Cartagena, attacking as many Spanish ships as possible. The ships they raped at sea were mostly Spanish ships. They harvested boundless booty, furniture, clothing, the latest silks, crinolines, dinnerware, wines, cheeses and medicines, even slaves.

"Jerome was independent and loyal to Jean, even when Jean established his Village of Lafitte on Grand Terre. Jerome stayed on

Grand Isle. His beautiful wife, Isabel, waited for him in the home he built. Jerome maintained he was a privateer like Jean, but unlike the others, he kept his independence. Jerome chose when to join one of Jean's raids. Jerome didn't trust everyone. Most of the crew were simple fishermen. There were a few who did whatever it took to get close to Jean. Jerome was smart and kept an eye out.

"When the British paid a visit to Lafitte to bribe him into betraying the American government, Jean refused and dispatched two missives, one to the governor, the other to Andrew Jackson. Instead of accepting his help, they attacked him on his island in Grand Terre.

"Of course, Jean and his people scrambled and regrouped on the last island on Bayou Lafourche, sixty miles west of the temple. Those close to him warned him of a traitor among them. When suspicion was pointed at Jerome, his quarters were searched onboard his Ladybird, and a missive was found detailing where Jean Lafitte and his crew could be found.

"Jerome, of course, denied this, but Jean was too angry; he wouldn't listen. Everyone who knew Jean understood his laws were strict. In anger, he sentenced Jerome to hang, only Jerome didn't. Instead, while locked away in the hold, one of his lieutenants got him out. But it was a trick. The lieutenant was the traitor, and he turned Jerome over into the hands of a bounty hunter. Jerome woke up in the Cabildo. The price on his head collected, and he was left to rot. He never did get out, but he guided you to those letters, and he came in your dreams. He's one of your guides, Marcie.

"Your teacher asked the universe for help for you, and he's been sent. He put you in Sam's path because you two are supposed to be together. The one who betrayed you and him is the same enemy. It's time for justice to be served. This enemy has come back in a different skin. It's not a person, and it doesn't go to the same place you and I go when we're done here on this earth. He's after you now, Sam. It's your turn. He's following the sins of the father, and he's gone after each generation of Jerome's descendants. Only Jerome never knew why he did it. Darkness doesn't need a reason. The only way for a dark entity to grow stronger and survive is to destroy anything good. You need to bring his hold, his power, to an end. Your girl there knows him, too."

Mama rested her head against the high back rocker, humming *Amazing Grace.* "It's about a repented slave catcher. He wrote it. He found religion. He saw the light," she explained.

Marcie looked up at Sam, still mesmerized by the woman's voice, her speech, how it had changed. Did Sam hear it, too? She noticed how he stiffened his jaw.

"Who's this dark entity—this person you're talking about?" he asked.

She smiled wide, exposing three missing teeth. "Go back up north, where you both came from. You already know him without me telling you, Marcie. It's your guy. And don't forget he's smart. He knows things—he knows how to manipulate magic for his benefit. Protect yourself—both of you.

"And Sam, best watch your back when you return, and ask yourself what you walked away from. Something was found on you, planted. Remember when you go back and meet up with the darkness, and you will, that it flows in the blood, except it's still a choice. You always have a choice."

"You make no sense, old woman, all your carrying on," Sam said.

Marcie shivered, feeling a slithering reptilian darkness surround her, knowing it was attached to those who sought out that vile hatred. A dark image of her dysfunctional family surfaced—her mother, father, brother. Sometimes darkness soared like poison down through the line.

"Don't you fear those hooks thrown at you. If you feed fear, you give it power. I know you know this, girl. You make sure he listens; that's why you're here." Mama pointed her finger at Marcie. "Don't be ashamed. What's done is done. You need to start trusting the voice inside yourself. Bring back hope and faith. Keep those ugly cords from cutting him. You and I both know who I'm talking about."

Dan.

"Heal those holes inside you and bring back the innocence he stripped away. Go back to your lessons, to your teacher. Remember something—piracy's still piracy. It's not much different from what Jerome did then to what you did, too. Everything happens for a reason. You're right in the middle of a battle. You chose to be one of the players, Marcie, and to go with that guy—to do his bidding, until

Jerome stepped in. Stay strong, and do not allow his hooks back into you. That tall man, the one you thought you had, he's not of this world. There's nothing right about him. The light doesn't touch him, and his darkness would have killed you. He still may. You need to watch your back. He got Jerome, and Sam's next. You'd best get on and look after your man. He knows, even if he won't say—he knows."

This made no sense, but anxiety kneaded every part of her. Dan was just a man—a man she had fallen head over heels in love with. How could he be connected to Jerome, to Sam?

She closed her eyes to block out Dan's image. He was poison to her peace of mind.

Mama started humming again, staring right through Marcie. Nausea rumbled again. Marcie'd had enough and needed air. She stumbled across the plank floor and held on to the doorframe, assaulted by a burning wave of dizziness. The bile churned in her stomach. Sam's hand pressed awkwardly against her back. Marcie pushed the screen door open and hurried down the stairs, vomiting in the dirt.

Sam hovered beside her, lifting her hair back from her face while she gagged and shook. Her throat burned. Her eyes watered, and her knees were weak.

"I'll get you some water." She had no energy to reply, let alone look up. Sam helped her sit on the bottom step. She rested her head against the railing. The air stirred when he hurried back up the shaky steps. Marcie trembled even though beads of sweat rolled down her back. She wanted nothing more than to close her eyes and sleep, except she couldn't, because dread rose out of the unknown, the fear of what was still to come and the truth she needed to share.

CHAPTER 15

"So, do you mind telling me about your long-lost memory? Oh, yeah, and how about when you planned to tell me?"

Marcie placed the empty glass on the weathered stair beside her, letting out a heavy sigh. "When we pulled in here, you ignored me in the most hurtful way, as if I was of no importance, and what it did was open a door up here." She tapped her finger on her head. "I started to remember every bad, vile, disgusting thing in my life, along with what I had done."

He crossed his arms and leaned back against the narrow handrail.

"You may wish you'd never met me, and I expect you'll turn your back on me once you know what I've done," she said. She looked down at her trembling pale hands. "It's not a bad drug. Everyone smoked the stuff in high school. That's what I told myself. We grow the best in the Pacific Northwest, high-grade marijuana."

He didn't laugh at her flippant remark. Instead, he covered his hands over his face and scrubbed them over his five o'clock shadow.

"I'm sorry, Sam."

He dropped his hands. His gaze smoldered with disgust, as if this was the first time he truly saw her. She hurt everywhere, but she kept going. Sam deserved better.

"Dan was our leader. I think I did it because I fell in love with him. I didn't search it out, nor would I ever do this myself. It's not who I am. Right after Granny died, I met Dan at one of the local farmers markets. I hadn't seen him since high school. He took me out and came to visit me. We clicked. He listened to me while I mourned. He understood me in a way no one else could. He shared my same love of earth-based spirituality. He said he got vibes, too, just like me. But it was something more about him, this powerful charm. The air buzzed with electricity anytime he was around. And when he wasn't…" She shut her eyes; she couldn't finish.

Her voice weakened when she spoke again. "Then one day he showed me his pot plants; the ones he grew for friends. There weren't that many. Next, I was watering them because he forgot or didn't have time. I never stopped to think how he slid me in there. All of a sudden, I watered all the time. I became the sitter. Dan became busy with other things. And I started to worry he'd leave me. I told myself that if I did this for him, maybe he'd love me just a little, maybe he'd spend more time with me; maybe this would make him so happy he'd finally commit to me. Then I thought I could change him. After all, what he was doing wasn't so bad."

Sam studied her with such horror that she thought he'd leave her sitting on the rickety step and drive away.

"But make no mistake, Sam, I chose to follow him. Mama was right, no matter what. It's always your choice. I was obsessed with loving him, so much that I'd do anything for him. Isn't that what you do for someone you love?"

"Marcie…"

She could tell he didn't want to hear this. "Sam, stop. Please let me finish so you can understand every bad, horrible thing about me and why I did it."

He rested one foot on the stair above her, circling his hand in the air for her to continue. "By all means, Marcie. Oh, but first, what's your real name?" He was angry and hurt; any whisper of trust that had existed between them was now destroyed.

"My name is Marcienda Dawn Hollis, Marcie for short." A hint of peace followed, even with the burden of what she'd done. "We grew pot. Do you want the exact type, all those gory details? Why not? The last batch was northern lights." She didn't wait for him to reply. "Doesn't matter, does it? But it was just marijuana."

"Okay, stop right there, Marcie. Growing contraband for distribution and trafficking is a major criminal offense. You're a drug dealer! What I do is put people like you in prison."

"Sam, I'm not a drug dealer. We grew marijuana for friends. It's just weed, Sam. It's not a bad drug...." She felt the wind go out of her sails as Dan's own soapbox came out of her mouth. *What's the big deal, Marcie? It's just weed.* "You're right, Sam. I was a drug dealer. Dan moved me to his property, where he had the plants in an old wood shed. That was where it started. I looked after the weed he grew for himself and his friends. And yes, they paid him. I got a cut for babysitting. Dan's a very good teacher. He actually did nothing after he taught me how to grow and cultivate. But that's what he does. He's a busy man, building houses. This is just a sideline. He'd tell me what to do, and I took all the risk—willingly. He always had a scheme or big idea to make money. And I hung on every word and idea, loving him. Doing anything I could for him." *Not everything.*

"Then he wanted to go bigger. He said there'd be a big payoff. And I followed. I set up all the outdoor gardens, found isolated, well-hidden spots near a good water source. It's been a long, hot summer, almost as if he knew it would be. We have thirty gardens, and last I checked, we only lost three that someone cleared out." Gritty degradation swept over her. Could she see through the mirage now? *Yes.*

"Marketing's done by a friend of Dan's. Her name's Sandra." Even repeating her name filled Marcie's mouth with a bitter and acidic aftertaste. "There's something about her I hate. Dan would defend her. She had the contacts; but then, she grew up in a family of professional growers outside Sequim. She knew the buyers, and I didn't. And you know what, Sam? Right now, I'm grateful for that. Sandra's really good with drugs. It came naturally to her. She had indoor grow shows of her own. She has a nasty, mean streak, except with Dan. To him, she's sweet as pie. She'd lie, cheat and steal from her own sister, but never in front of Dan. Why's that, Sam?"

"Marcie, I'm not interested in childish catfights. I want to know everything you were doing, who you sold to, who the buyers are. Oh, and let's start with the million-dollar question: What was in your backpack?"

"My backpack was filled with marijuana, the bud from indoor crops Sandra harvested. I was to take it to baggage claim and leave it. There'd be an identical backpack sitting there. I'd leave mine and take the other. Dan told me where to go. Apparently, I was meeting Sandra's contact. I wasn't given a name." The click of a double cross enlightened an agonizing truth.

"You were transporting. Do you have any idea how long you'll go to prison here? And, in Louisiana, baby, it ain't no picnic. Oh, and Reggie? You tell me, right now, how he's involved. Let's go with the obvious. Isn't he your contact?" Sam paced in front of her, slamming a concrete wall between them. No way could she touch him, let alone reason with him. This was all business.

"Sam, I swear I didn't know Reggie. I didn't know any of the contacts, and I have a sick feeling I may have been set up."

"Oh, no way are you going to play that card now."

She touched his arm, but he shrugged her off. The look on his face ripped her heart open. He was visibly repulsed. He blurred in front of her as she fought the tears burning her eyes. "Sam, please listen. Dan was pushing me out. He became more secretive—especially after the fire." Memories flowed faster than she could explain.

"Fire? What the hell, Marcie?"

"I already told you about my dream the first night here. Dan was involved in so many things, but everything was tied to drugs. After the house burned, all I did was look after the outdoor crops. Dan changed things, started working and meeting with Sandra secretly. I thought he was ending things with me, and then he surprised me with a trip to New Orleans. At first, I thought he had planned a holiday for us, but I was wrong. It was nothing more than a trip to deliver a sample of Sandra's bud. At the airport, he surprised me. Suddenly I was going alone, and it was me who was supposed to exchange the backpack for an identical one—one that'd be at baggage claim. I willingly got on that plane for him. But, Sam, I swear I didn't know Reggie or the guy who stole my backpack. Either they ripped me off, and that was their plan all along, or maybe Dan had a different plan."

Sam pushed away from the stairs. He crossed his solid arms, guarding his emotions to the point that his face seemed made of stone. "What was in the backpack you were supposed to pick up?"

"I don't know, and I didn't ask. Honestly, Sam, I didn't want to know."

He tilted his head. She could see how he struggled with her story. "My guess, you're picking up cocaine. If you're caught, you'd take the fall. This guy's slick. So tell me, how many trips have you made?"

A tear fell. "This was the first one. I've never done this before."

His eyes narrowed, stripping away what was left of her shaky dignity. "Let's start with where you're from and where this little operation is located."

"Gardiner, Washington. That's where Dan's properties are."

"And this is where you live?"

"Well, actually, no."

He leaned closer.

"I live on Las Seta, a small island off the coast in the San Juans," she said.

"That's where my last bust was. You doing something there?"

"Sam, that's my home, Granny's place. I would never grow there, no matter how much Dan pressured me. That's a line I wouldn't cross."

He didn't respond. What he did was study her with a weird can't-quite-figure-you-out expression, and it wasn't in a good way. "You still haven't told me who you sold to and who Dan's buyers are."

Marcie shook her head. "Sam, whether you believe me or not, I don't know. I wasn't in the loop. Dan told me once there were things I didn't need to know. Who he sold to, or planned to sell to, that was a game between Dan and Sandra. All I know is he's a middle guy growing and selling to someone bigger. I suspect a family connection through Sandra."

"Come on, Marcie. You expect me to believe you were that naive and had no idea who he sold to?"

"I knew the friends he grew for before he went big—before Sandra started growing at his other rural property deep in Gardiner."

"Where in Gardiner?"

"On a five-acre parcel close to the state park where he's got several illegal houses. That's where Sandra lives and where she grows. What I carried in my backpack was a small sample from her indoor crop, ready after three months. There's a lot more, but I have no idea where the rest went. I suspect he may be growing somewhere else, involved with someone else. It's what he does. He's secretive and always on the lookout for new prey."

"What are you talking about?"

"I could be wrong, Sam. I suspect Dan may have lured another woman to grow for him somewhere else."

"But you don't know for sure?"

"Call it a vibe, one I wouldn't have admitted before today."

He gave a harsh nod while he appeared to digest all this information. "That's quite the entrepreneurial operation. You said he has several illegal homes on an isolated acreage, most likely for growing. Obviously, it would have to be one of the more secluded Gardiner properties. Then add in the possibility of another woman growing for him, with you doing his outdoor gardens. Wow, this guy's good. Could he be involved in a larger operation, maybe heroin, cocaine, weapons?"

Marcie wondered the same thing; always fearing that whatever Sandra and Dan were up to was bigger and more dangerous than she knew. "I don't know, Sam. I can honestly tell you Dan's ability to scheme and manifest greed and destruction is amazing. There's probably something bigger going on, and he'd do it behind my back. That's who he is. No loyalty to anyone."

"You're in love with him. You're his girlfriend." Sam leaned viciously toward her.

"No, I'm not. I may have thought I was, but I'm nothing more than a pawn in his pocket, someone he can feed off of and then toss away when he's done." A flicker of panic licked the back of her throat. "You'd never treat me that way, ever. You've never used a woman, have you? You were honest with me. You opened your arms to me and not once did you have some sick motive to be kind to me just to get something out of it. I don't know how to handle that. I've never had that from a man. I didn't know it was possible.

"When I banged my head, I had no memory, no burning link to that sick, destructive love for him. And you stuck in here." She thumped her hand over her heart. "I've spent two days in your life, sharing your hurt. You're an honest, loving man; and you've just turned my entire world upside down, showing me that how I've lived, and what I thought was love, isn't even close. It's as if I woke up on the other side of a river. The bridge is down, and I'm watching Dan, objectively, for the first time, seeing him and what I'm doing for him. It's sick, twisted...." She felt violated and knew she alone was responsible.

"What about the false passport, Marcie?"

She rubbed her throbbing temples. "The morning I left, Dan gave me the airline ticket and passport. I had no idea he had arranged it. My original passport photo was on the forged document with the name Lisa Francis. I don't know how he got his hands on my original passport, and I didn't ask."

"He stole your passport and created a forged one, which you willingly used for air travel? That's a federal offense. What gets me, Marcie, is that you don't need to produce a passport for travel within the United States. So why'd you use it?"

She closed her eyes, remembering that moment vividly. She didn't dwell on it because she believed he loved her, and she needed to have faith in him. *With what you're doing, you don't use your real name.*

"The truth, Sam, is that I chose to listen to him, thinking he wouldn't allow any harm to come to me, and maybe this was his way of caring—of watching my back. So yes, I produced the passport. And he was right. No one questioned the validity. It was a great forgery, and I didn't question how he had done it."

"This guy's more connected than I think you realize. Or maybe you do? Is this a game, Marcie? Gain my sympathy. Get me to help you. Maybe that's all your convenient memory loss is." He turned away from her, stomping and kicking up the dirt, facing the swampy vegetation of the bayou. Then he froze and circled back. His hardness cut right into her soul with the way he slowly stalked toward her.

"You working for Lance Silver by any chance, maybe trying to finish me off; make sure I'm nailed as being the head of some northern smuggling ring? Is this his plan, send you in, have someone assault you and fake a memory loss? Because you know my weakness; I'll stop and help. Then you slither your way into my life and fuck it up even more. Was that your plan, Marcie; plant more weed in my apartment, call the cops, make a deal? You've already got Derek thinking I'm part of your ring."

Her eyes widened in horror. "How could you think such horrible things? No, God, no! I would never do that to you. I don't work for Lance. I know him from the island. Everyone who lives there does. But I'm not stupid enough to get involved with the likes of him. He's a powerful man. You live on Las Seta, you learn to look the other way. Bad things go on all around us, Sam, all the time. You pick your battles, and, I can honestly tell you, he's one I'd never take on."

He raised both hands. "Stop, stop, I don't want to hear any more. You tell me right now, Marcie, why I shouldn't call Jesse and let him hand you over to Derek. Maybe it's time I got smart and walked away."

She shook so hard her voice trembled. She wrapped her arms around her bent knees. "I've put you in an impossible situation. You're a federal officer. You have every right to turn me over. You have your own problems, which were made worse when you took me in. I can't, and won't, make excuses for what I did. I don't have the right to ask you to help me. I just don't want to go back and be that same person. I feel something so strong for you it hurts. So maybe you *should* walk away." She couldn't see him through the rain of tears streaming from her eyes. Her nose was plugged and started to drip. Her bag, where was her bag? She used the back of her hand to wipe her nose.

"Ah, Christ Jesus, Marcie." She heard him run, a car door open, slam shut, and his feet pounding the dirt as he hurried back. "Take this." He shoved a box of Kleenex in her hand.

"Thank you," she croaked, grabbing a handful of tissue. She blew her nose.

His voice softened, and he swore under his breath. "Well, baby, guess where we're going? Back to where we started."

CHAPTER 16

"How soon do I need to be at the airfield?" Sam asked into his phone. He leaned against the hood of his car and watched Marcie through the front window. She looked like a lost child gazing out the passenger side. He had to fight the urge to go over and hug her.

"The FBI jet's two hours out," Diane answered over the line. "Go to the New Orleans Lakefront Airport. I already spoke with Jesse. He's going to meet you there. Two FBI agents from the New Orleans field office will be there as well. They've handled all the paperwork." Diane let out a sigh on the other end of the telephone. "Sam, are you sure about bringing Marcie back? I mean, really, how good's your judgment right now? You could turn her over to the Feds down there, let them work a deal with her. You could walk away."

Sam ground his teeth. He was irritated, downright tired, and didn't want to hear one more person tell him to walk away. With his warm hand, he squeezed his cell phone. What a bloody mess. What he saw through his windshield was someone he refused to abandon. This trouble wasn't entirely her own doing, but for now, until he could make sense of his jumbled emotions, she was coming with him.

"No. She stays with me. Did you run what I asked past Dexter? Marcie's a material witness and will help with our case."

"You really want her to walk away scot-free?" Diane was like a dog with a bone. She wouldn't let him change the subject. But then she grunted a noise he knew was disgust at about the same time that he heard what sounded like a shoe banging the wall. "Forget it, you pigheaded…" She stopped and let out a huff of air. "Dexter has a lot of faith in you. I gave him a sugarcoated version of your story. He believes Marcie's coming with you as she has firsthand knowledge of the local grow-ops—where they are, and can help bring down a major player who's tied to Lance Silver."

"He didn't ask too many questions about how I met Marcie and the problems down here?"

"Sam, if you're asking whether he knows she transported an illegal substance—the answer's no. But then, no one does but you, me, Jesse, and Marcie. For now, until we have a plan on how to nail Lance Silver, let's keep it that way. One more thing; because of the leak on our team, Dexter's agreed to let us handle this investigation for now."

Sam felt hope teeter within every muscle of his body; positive the tide was about to change and that he now stood on the threshold of something that could alter his whole world. But for good or bad, he didn't yet know.

"See you tonight," he said. He disconnected and watched Marcie clutching her bulky bag, staring at him through the thick glass like a wide-eyed baby doe. She'd allowed him to decide, for her, what happened next—no lies and no games. What was this need for her growing inside of him? As he shut his eyes, he couldn't shut off his heart. When had he started wanting more?

"Bad idea," he mumbled to himself before climbing in the car.

"All set?" She held her head high, ready to face the piper with a pink, blotchy face and swollen, red-rimmed eyes.

He started the engine and merged back onto the highway. "Jesse's meeting us at the airport. My partner's arranged for our flight back on the FBI jet. There won't be any problems."

Her voice was barely above a whisper. "I'm not worried when you take care of things."

Sam looked over, but she'd already turned away.

An hour later, Sam pulled into the small New Orleans airfield where private charters flew in and out. Jesse waited alone in a small gray pickup truck. He popped open his door and climbed out wearing blue jeans and a black T-shirt.

"Can't be department issued; it's too nice. When did you start driving a truck?" Sam asked.

"My wife wanted it. She thought we could use it to haul things."

Sam squinted. This was the first time in years that he'd seen Jesse dressed in something other than a suit. Jesse lifted a small carry-on bag from the back of the truck.

"Going somewhere?" Sam asked. The sharp blast of a small jet engine provided enough distraction that they went unnoticed. The passenger door of Sam's car popped open, and Jesse watched Sam and then allowed his eyes to linger on Marcie. Her stride faltered. Then she tightened her mouth before moving toward them.

"You think I'm going to allow you to dig yourself into any more trouble?" Jesse asked. "I'm going with you."

"What about your wife, the department? You can just take off?"

Jesse's smile deepened. His silver tooth gleamed in the rays of the setting sun. "I've got so much vacation time banked that I told my cap'n now's a good time to use some up. And my wife's a good lady, more than fine with me helping a friend."

Sam didn't know what to say. A lump jammed his throat. "Thanks, Jesse...." Sam stopped and squinted. He'd always had a hard time sharing his feelings.

"It's what friends do. Listen, we'd better get going. Plane should be here." Jesse took a couple steps toward Marcie. "You got your memory back. I hope, for your sake, you told Sam everything. No tricks, no lies, Marcie."

Her face softened, but she held her head high. "I'm not standing here making excuses for what I did, for what I've done, Jesse. I haven't lied, not once, nor will I. I'll do what I can to stop Dan and bring an end to his madness, his stronghold. I need to make up for the wrong I've done. But more importantly, Sam's name needs to be cleared."

"I hope you mean that, Marcie." Jesse watched her thoughtfully, as if trying to decipher the truth.

"So, this Dan, he's partners with Lance Silver, the guy you've been after, Sam?"

Marcie remained in their circle but isolated herself a few steps away. Sam could see the hurt that stiffened her spine.

"I'm pretty sure this Dan McKenzie's in Lance Silver's back pocket. He sounds too big to be some little guy," he answered.

Marcie spoke softly. "I know Lance from the island, but at a distance. I can honestly tell you that, if Dan has some connection with him, I know nothing about it. I don't know who all of Dan's contacts or buyers were. Thankfully, I was kept out of that loop." Marcie shook her head. "You two need to know that Lance Silver's not a man you mess around with."

There was something in her eyes that Sam hadn't seen before, an awareness that whatever they were about to walk into could have consequences harsher than any they could imagine.

CHAPTER 17

The small FBI jet flew them directly to the Port Townsend airfield in Washington State.

Diane Larsen stood at the gate, wearing blue jeans, hiking boots, and a faded jean jacket. A ball cap was pulled over, from what Marcie could tell, a mouse-brown boyish haircut. She wore dark shades, and her jaw worked a piece of gum. To Marcie, it seemed this was her way of pondering something in her head—good Lord, another deep thinker.

Marcie stood off to the side while both Jesse and Sam bonded with Diane with handshakes and pats on the back. Marcie held her cloth bag in front of her and shivered in the cool night air. She still wore the vibrant sundress Sam had bought her, making her grossly underdressed for the Pacific Northwest coastline, where fall temperatures hovered around fifty degrees overnight.

When Sam introduced Marcie, Diane studied her with not so much as a flicker of emotion. Her throat squeezed shut. Marcie realized that this hard woman loved Sam, not so much in the way lovers do but with the closeness good friends shared. So Marcie didn't try to win her over. This woman wouldn't be swayed by any nice, frilly words.

Marcie followed obediently, climbing in the backseat of Diane's dark blue Toyota SUV. Sam rode shotgun, and Jesse slid in beside Marcie. She never asked where they were going. They wove their way onto the isolated highway toward Gardiner. She felt some sense of balance nurture her inner self when they drove on, immersed in the old-growth forest surrounding the land. This rural, preserved area of the Pacific Northwest was a crown jewel; land the logging companies had yet to rape. There was power here in the trees, bushes, and branches that reached out and hid secrets and life deep in the forest. Even developers hadn't yet taken over and built row after row of housing.

What the county hadn't preserved, state park land did, with tough environmental guidelines, leaving miles and miles of vast forest and mountain ranges protected and unpopulated. Living on the west coast, with her love for the land, Marcie understood the importance of keeping a healthy ecosystem intact. She knew this part of the Olympic Peninsula well. After all, it was where she had planted her outdoor marijuana gardens for Dan.

Diane turned down an isolated, well-treed driveway hiding a lovely cedar A-frame house.

"Nice place, Diane. How many acres you have here?" Jesse asked. Marcie enjoyed seeing the property through his eyes.

"Ten acres."

"Wow, is this whole property treed?"

Diane chuckled. "Yes, I like my trees and my privacy. I think you'll find most of the properties around here are heavily forested." Diane led them into her home: three bedrooms, two bathrooms, and a river rock fireplace, cozy and comfortable.

It was late. Marcie was tired and cold. She needed time to regroup. Diane handed her a worn beige sweater. She must have seen her shiver.

"Thank you," Marcie said. "If you don't mind, I'd like to sit out back for a bit."

Sam and Jesse exchanged a meaningful glance. Diane extended the flat of her hand toward the sliding glass door in the kitchen leading onto the back deck. Diane, Sam, and Jesse sat around the kitchen table. A large plate-glass window looked over the massive back deck. Marcie felt the heat from Sam's gaze when she walked out and sat in a cozy Adirondack chair. She wrapped her arms around her stomach, and only then did she allow herself to reflect over the circle of events. The sun drifted low, sprinkling vast orange and yellow light over the horizon.

She didn't realize how far her thoughts had drifted until she heard the mechanical purr of the truck and a vehicle pulling away.

"Mind if I join you?" Diane didn't wait for a response before sitting beside Marcie in a second chair. Diane was what Marcie would have called big boned, with her compact, tidy body. Once Marcie had cut past the deep protective role Diane had appointed herself with, as friend to Sam, Diane came across as an honest woman, in her early thirties, with a boyish, fit-in-with-the-guys, haircut.

"So…" Marcie couldn't finish. She didn't know what to ask—what to say.

"Sam told me how you met." Diane studied her in a way similar to how Sam did when he was in cop mode. Except, with Diane, it was kinder.

"Where's Sam?"

"He's meeting with Agent Dexter, our boss. Jesse went with him. Listen, Marcie, we need some questions answered, and we decided it'd be best if I spoke with you."

Her heart sank a little more. Maybe this was Sam's way of saying he was done with her. She couldn't blame him, really, but it didn't stop the ache that throbbed inside her chest. On top of that, she was exhausted by all this traveling, the attack, her memory loss. She just didn't feel well. This left her vulnerable and nowhere near the top of her game.

"You look kind of pale, Marcie. You feel okay?"

"I just need some sleep, I think. What do you want to know?" She forced a smile to break the sympathy that had surfaced in Diane's big, round, hazel eyes.

"We need to know about the people involved, where you're growing, inside and out, who the buyers are, all about Dan McKenzie and his connection to Lance Silver. That would be a start for now."

"Well, why not ask for the sun and the moon?"

Diane frowned in reply.

"Sorry, that wasn't fair. I already told Sam all of this."

"You need to tell me, Marcie. I'm sorry, but I'll probably keep asking the same questions over and over."

The air around them flickered with distrust. A lot needed to be established between them; ground rules at the very least. Marcie closed her eyes to block out the disgrace that wouldn't go away. "Dan has two plots of land in Jefferson County. One he owns by himself not far from here. The other's a rural zoned, commercial property right off the highway in Gardiner. He bought that one with a partner, Richard.

"The commercial property's been cleared to build houses. Dan has this dream of being a big-time contractor and developer. He lives in his fifth wheel on that property along with a few other RVs belonging to friends, all parked around a really old, wooden outbuilding. Inside the large shed is where Dan grew over eight hundred marijuana plants, which I babysat for him. Richard wasn't involved in the marijuana part of it. He's Dan's partner in the housing development. We need to leave him out of this."

"Marcie, this is how it works. You're going to tell us names and work with us. Then we're going to investigate. We need background on everyone. Maybe you don't realize that there's a secret life a lot of people seem to have." The tension thickened the air between them. Diane was a strong woman whose will and determination couldn't be swayed.

"Diane, the people you want are Dan and Sandra. I know Sam keeps talking about Lance Silver, but I don't know what Lance is doing, and I have no idea about his connection to Dan, but Sandra might. All the buyers are her contacts. You have to know, too, that Sandra makes me uneasy. Her energy's so low, and she's dangerous. She grew up in a family of growers from outside Sequim. I'm pretty sure that's how her dad made all his money. When Dan wanted to go big, he discussed and planned with Sandra. She hired the trimmers. There's always this unknown thing between them, as if they're up to something new. They've got their hands in other pots, literally. I just don't know all the details, and it's only a feeling I have here." She patted her stomach.

"Dan's first property, the one he owns himself, was subdivided a few years ago and he built a bunch of illegal homes on it," she continued. "I'm pretty sure he did it just to say 'Screw you' to the powers that be. Also, how many can he use as a grow-op? They're isolated, private, and no one's watching. Dan knows wiring better than most electricians do. Also, by stealing hydro power for all the lights; I assure you, he won't get caught. Sandra lives in one of the illegal dwellings he'd built onto his shop. They started growing inside his shop first and then in one of the houses after he kicked out a young family he'd rented to."

"Are you aware that Dan McKenzie's currently under investigation for arson along with his partner, Richard McCafferty?" Diane didn't give her time to respond. "What do you know about the fire and the house we suspect they burned down?"

Marcie's face tingled when heat spiraled up her cheeks. She swallowed hard, still remembering how her dream and reality meshed together as one. She closed her eyes, then opened them to face Diane's own intensified look. Smart lady, she already knew.

"Yeah, um, look, Richard's a good friend. I don't know who started that fire."

"Okay, Marcie, why don't we start with you telling me what you do know?"

Marcie closed her eyes, wishing Sam were here. She didn't feel well, and she had her own questions regarding the fire. She'd suspected Dan had been growing marijuana in the basement of the house. "I was asleep and woke up when someone banged on the RV's door. Dan was gone, and I hurried outside. The house, at the front of the twelve-acre parcel, was completely consumed in flames. Dan drove his excavator, pushing the walls of the house down into the fire. Richard was in a loader and yelled at me to get back. The first fire truck pulled in, except by then, the roof and walls had collapsed. There was nothing to save. That was when I saw Sam's dead wife, Elise, and, yes, I do see dead people sometimes." She didn't look at Diane. Instead, she gazed into the shadowed forest.

She continued: "It was freaky when she laughed at me. Then she pointed her hand and finger at me, as if it were a gun, and pulled the trigger. I heard the sound and the clink of metal, but there was no gun. It was just her hand. Then she disappeared behind the RV, where the shed was."

"What kind of bullshit are you trying to pass off?"

Marcie jumped when she heard Sam's voice. Diane turned to the sliding glass door. Jesse stood off to the side behind Sam. The smirk on Jesse's face, Marcie would swear, was one of pure amusement.

"Sam, I didn't know you were back. It's not bullshit. I really saw her. And, unfortunately, I do see dead people. Sometimes I can read someone's aura and see things that are going to happen."

She faced Diane and stopped cold. Every sensation in her ceased and focused in on this one moment. Time stood still as warmth brushed over her from head to toe. Over Diane's shoulder, she was drawn into a hue of orange, an image she didn't try to analyze. Every cell in her body lived within this one moment. She had no idea of time. It didn't exist. Sam appeared in front of her, shaking her arm, calling her, but the sound was muffled. She blinked, and her head bobbed as if she'd woken from a dead sleep. She gazed at him, weak and confused, and then faced Diane, blinking until her focus returned.

"You need to be careful tonight when you're out," Marcie said. "On the street, there'll be a vagrant sleeping in a doorway. He's going to have a knife. He'll be quick and aim for your stomach." She looked past Diane and then stood up, freezing cold. Bile climbed and burned the back of her throat. She pressed her clammy hand to cover her mouth, stumbling past Sam and Jesse to the bathroom, off of the kitchen, where she threw up.

CHAPTER 18

Marcie woke with a start when a shadow moved beside the bed. When she tried to sit up, Sam gently touched her shoulder.

"Don't get up. I didn't mean to wake you."

The mattress dipped with Sam's weight when he sat on the edge of the queen-size bed. She tried to fight the comfort his presence had brought. She wanted to touch him, except his anger and hurtful words had become a wall between them. "If you didn't want to wake me, why're you in here? I think you pretty much made it clear you can't stand to be around me." Ouch. Her words were cutting, but she didn't care right now. She was hurt and angry and bothered by what she had seen around Diane. It had left her shaken; zapping away her energy, and was one of a few images from the trance that had stayed with her.

"I guess I had that coming."

Marcie glanced at the open window. The curtains parted, fluttering from the cool night breeze. The moon's bright silhouette exposed some depth in the way Sam watched her, and that confused her.

"Diane called," he said. "Something happened tonight."

Alarmed, her whole body tightened; and she bolted upright, turning on the bedside lamp. "Is she all right?"

He leaned closer. "Diane was called into the Sequim detachment to consult on a case right after you went to bed. She stopped for coffee with Jeff Stillwell, Sequim's sheriff, in downtown Port Townsend. A vagrant was sleeping in the doorway of the bank next door. They woke him to move him out of there, but the guy pulled a knife and aimed for Diane's stomach. She stepped back, and Jeff…" Sam turned his head, clearly shaken.

Marcie reached out and touched his forearm.

"The homeless guy stabbed Jeff below his right kidney," Sam said.

Marcie touched his solid forearms now with both hands. She could see his fear.

"You knew, but how?" he asked.

Maybe he was ready to hear her answer: "Sam, I saw it."

"What do you mean, you saw it? What, are you like some psychic, who has a crystal ball, or something? I don't understand."

Marcie could hear the frustration in his words. Instead of responding immediately, she took a deep breath and pictured herself connected to the earth with white light surrounding her. "I pick up on people's feelings around me. Quite often, I have a hard time being in a room with a lot of people. It drains me, all of those conflicting emotions. Sometimes I get pulled into another time by Spirit, a trance, where there's no time. Sometimes the image in my head from a trance doesn't stay with me long, but Diane's did. I don't know why. I don't get them often, but the after effects… I get so cold. With Diane, I saw it in her aura, playing over her shoulder like a movie scene."

"So you're some kind of psychic, a witch, like Mama?" He shook his head.

Marcie could see how he struggled with the intangible unknown. Who wouldn't? "I don't like titles, Sam, and to be labeled a witch is dangerous and archaic. It wasn't that long ago you were burned at the stake if someone called you a witch. That fear still lingers. I'm spiritual, Sam. I developed my gifts through protecting and honoring Mother Earth. Everyone has the ability to tap into Spirit. It all depends on whether you allow the gift to develop. Don't get me wrong; some people come into this world with their veils thinned, bringing magic with them. Do you understand what I'm trying to say?"

"Maybe."

"Everyone's ability's different. I've learned to trust the feelings I get. If I'm confused, I've learned to ask for help from my guides, angels, Spirit. It's not that I hear them speaking; I feel it, see it with all my senses. I see in the spaces between instead of seeing the physical object or person. Sometimes it's a trick to fool me, and the trick's to know the good from the bad; like the good, peaceful feeling deep in my tummy. My granny taught me to read tarot cards, but they're just a tool. My mom's convinced they're a tool of the Devil, and so is this gift we have. As a kid, I believed her. I was so freaked out that I prayed it'd disappear."

"But with Diane, it didn't play out exactly the way you said."

"A warning's sometimes all you need so that it doesn't happen. I warned her. You said she pulled back." Marcie shrugged. Sam turned away. She suspected he was spooked. "It's simple, Sam. She listened. Are you scared?"

"What do you see in me, Marcie?"

"I can't read you right now. For some reason, you're blocked to me; the same way I don't always know what's happening with me. We're too close, or were. What are we now, Sam?"

He didn't respond. Instead, he got up off the bed and left.

———

The next morning, Sam paced the large, airy kitchen, with its light oak cabinets, moss-green walls, and west-facing windows. Sam's stomach was so twisted in knots he couldn't sit still, so he kept busy, first making coffee, now eggs and toast.

Jesse sat at the light oak table. He pushed back a potted aloe vera from the center and rifled through the morning paper. Sam knew he was keeping one eye on him. "If you start washing the floor, I'm leaving," Jesse said.

Sam froze behind the long counter.

Jesse held up his splayed hands. "I'm just saying you're making me nervous with all your prancing about. You should be used to all the weirdness and the psychic spirit babble. You saw enough of it around Mama."

The front door clicked open and then closed. Diane walked into her well-organized kitchen and stood on the other side of the counter. Sam studied Diane from where he cooked eggs over the propane burner. Marcie must have decided that now was a good time to show herself, as she appeared wearing the shorts and T-shirt Jesse had bought her in New Orleans.

Diane stared at Marcie. "Hello." That was all she said before disappearing down the hallway, where the walls were painted a soft green, decorated with family photos and soft white trim, to her bedroom at the end of the hall. The door clicked closed, and a few moments later, the shower popped on. The whole house felt on edge, as if a spark would erupt at any moment. Or maybe it was just Sam.

Marcie wandered barefoot over the pale tile floor. She claimed one of two ceramic butterfly mugs perched upside down before the stainless steel coffee maker. She poured herself a black coffee and then slid open the sliding door, wandering outside into the sunshine with the packet of ancient letters from Sam's attic.

Jesse refilled his coffee, adding cream and sugar and then dumping the spoon into the double stainless steel sink. "Sam, let's focus on the case. As your boss said to you last night, obviously Lance Silver's onto you, so you need to be smart, keep your head together, and stay cool. This is your last shot to bring him down. Try something different. Focus on Dan McKenzie and his connection with Lance. Didn't Diane say he'd been on the sheriff's and DEA's watch lists for some time? You guys have a big list, don't you, of who's growing weed and who you need to watch?"

"We do, and Dan McKenzie's on there, but I never figured him for the big time." Sam pulled a file from a small stack on the counter. He flipped it open. "According to these notes, word on the street is that, at one time, he grew for himself and his friends, but he's upped the ante. It's rumored he's into other things, and one of them could be trading marijuana for cocaine."

What bothered Sam more was what he had found out the night before from Dexter. Dan McKenzie had women running things for him. One looked after his outdoor crops. Another babysat the indoor crops in the houses he owned. He'd never put it together until now.

"Jesse, in that file we got from Dexter, the notes about Dan McKenzie, isn't there some mention of one of his women being connected?"

Jesse snatched up all the files and carried them to the kitchen table. He sat back down and then rifled through the top file. "You think that's the broad Marcie's talking about. What's her name—Sandra? Didn't Marcie say she grew up in a family of growers? You'd definitely know all the big-time contacts, wouldn't you?"

"Could be. What bothers me, though, is how this guy surrounds himself with women, not dumb women, but smart, educated women. How do you think he manages to get them to take all the risks for him?"

Jesse licked his finger as he turned over another page. "Probably the same way a woman wraps a man around her finger and gets him to ignore all her lies and unredeemable behavior."

Sam tossed a checkered dishtowel at Jesse. "Are you ever going to let it go about Elise?"

"Only when you finally wake up and stop painting her as a saint and admit she was up to no good. Face it. You saw stars and not the truth with her."

"Let's focus on this case. What are the chances Dan McKenzie was supplying Lance Silver?"

"I think that's where we need Marcie."

"Yeah, but I'm worried about how deep she's really in and whether there's more to her role than what she told me." Sam held up his palm when Jesse opened his mouth to speak. "Don't even go there, Jesse. She's not Elise."

Sam dished up eggs and buttered toast. He passed Jesse a plate and then carried his breakfast with Marcie's outside to the back deck, where she sat cross legged, reading one of the letters.

"Eggs are ready."

She accepted the plate with a distracted smile. "Thanks. Sam, look at this." She handed him a dated photo of a small boy. The inscription on the back said *Jemmie on Grand Terre*, no date.

He flipped it over to look at the photo and scrawled inscription on the back again. "No date, interesting kid." He handed the photo back and sat beside Marcie in the cedar Adirondack chair. Her eyes smoldered when he looked back over. "What?"

Marcie held up a second picture. "Sam, the boy's picture was stuck behind this one. It says it's a picture of the manor house on Grand Terre. In the letter, it refers to this as being new; after the US attacked Grand Terre, destroying Jean's encampment. This is a picture of a new plantation. On the back, look at what it says: 'Isabel, Jemmie, and Rand, Grand Terre.' I'm positive this Isabel is Jerome's wife, and Jemmie is Jerome's child. I feel chilled when I look at the man beside her."

"Marcie, for one, it's fall, so this time of year it's cool in the morning, and two, he's her new husband. She moved on. Maybe he wasn't very nice, but women did what they had to in those days. Now put those letters away. We have more important things to talk about than someone's interesting history."

With one hand, she bundled the letters and pictures and put them beside her on the plastic end table. "I need to go back to my home on Las Seta. I need some clean clothes. There's a charter service out of Port Townsend I can take. He usually schedules for ten or eleven in the morning." Not even a flicker of doubt dawned on her face. She wasn't asking. Where had this determination come from?

"Marcie, you're not going anywhere. I'll get you what you need here."

"No, Sam. We're taking Marcie right now to Las Seta. I'll rent a boat at the Sequim marina," Diane said.

They both turned to see her standing in the open doorway. Her pale, apple-blossom cheeks appeared ghostlike. Her damp hair stuck up on one side. She must have tried to sleep but couldn't.

Marcie rose out of her chair and walked right up to Diane. She still held her plate of eggs, but she placed her other hand with an apparent genuine soft care on Diane's forearm. "Diane, are you okay?"

What struck Sam was that some closeness seemed to pass between them. Suddenly, he was the odd man out. He didn't expect this, not from Diane. She was his pit bull, and she watched his back. What they did next really threw him. They both went inside without saying a word. Sam followed with his empty plate. If anything, he needed to find out what was going on and had to regain control.

"Diane," he called to her, but he stopped cold in his tracks when he stepped into the kitchen. What he saw took the wind completely from any hope he had of regaining authority. Jesse was washing dishes in the double sink, looking miserably uncomfortable. His eyes directed Sam to where both women stood in the middle of the kitchen, by a potted fern. Marcie had her arms wrapped around Diane, hugging her.

Diane pulled away, as if she had suddenly pulled it together "Let's get going. We've got a lot to do and a lot to talk about. One of them being the connection and open file on Dan McKenzie and his partner, Richard, and how they're connected to Lance Silver." Diane clapped her hands. "Let's go. Sam, Marcie, Jesse, I'll drive."

Sam held his plate and watched a spurt of determination rise in both women. They slipped on their shoes. Marcie pulled on her borrowed brown sweater, and Diane grabbed a black windbreaker from the closet. Both went out the front door.

"Let's go, hoss," Jesse said, grabbing his tan jacket off the back of the Windsor chair and following the two women. They left the door open for him, but Sam knew that if he didn't go now, they'd most likely leave him behind.

CHAPTER 19

Sam was silent the entire way across the channel. It was impossible to have a conversation on the small cruiser Diane had rented. The crossing today was hit by a southeaster, which made the ride unbearably rough. The warm, bright sun illuminated a soft, blue sky. Frothy waves were a petulant white as they swelled and rolled up and over, rocking Marcie's already shaky stomach. She held tight to the vinyl seat with one hand and the bulk of her hair back with the other, struck by Sam's brooding silence across from her. A brisk wind flapped his jean jacket back and forth and bulked up his dark blue shirt even though he'd tucked it into his well-fitting jeans. His short, wavy hair blew every which way. What had the potential to be a bad hair day didn't diminish what a good-looking man he was.

But even through this wild ride, Marcie could feel that the pull home, to her rustic island, seemed to restore something vital that had depleted long ago.

"Marcie, are you listening?"

She leapt when Diane rested a tender hand on her shoulder. Sam jumped onto the narrow wooden dock at Starry Bay and secured the boat in between a small steel rowboat and a wood cutter painted a vibrant red and scripted with the name *The Mirage*.

"Sorry, I just realized how good it feels to be home." Marcie took a deep, cleansing breath. Life was so pure and clean here. No hydroelectric power—no paved roads, just a simple, honest respect for the land. Each step on this reclusive, isolated island held a mystical energy. Marcie would swear any unsuspecting soul could reap the magical spark exuding from this place—well, from some parts, anyway. This island was ten miles long from south to north, heavily forested and primitive. It was a land filled with family secrets and clans who'd arrived and stayed, year after year. This island afforded privacy, and no questions were ever asked; an unwritten code by those who live here—stay out of your neighbor's business.

"Where to, Marcie? You have a car, or do we walk?"

Marcie stepped over the side of the boat, onto the dock. There were lots of boats tied to the U-shaped dock, possibly thirty cruisers, sailboats, and dinghies. There must have been a few dozen people milling around the dock, wandering the rocky shore, and scattered up the hill.

"My truck's parked up the hill, next to the hotel." Sam, Jesse, and Diane followed Marcie up the gangplank and across the bridge leading to a dirt hill where a horde of vehicles were parked side by side on a road that disappeared behind the small, ten-room, Las Seta hotel. Marcie swung her arms, amazed by a sense of lightness making each step effortless. The twisted knots and confusion that Marcie had felt, because of Dan, began to dissolve. At the same time, the constant pang of wanting Dan and the obsessive need to see and be around him, having him control her every move, had all but vanished. She closed her eyes for a moment, eternally grateful for that one blessing.

Sam stopped her halfway up by pressing a gentle hand on her arm. "What's wrong?"

She searched his beautiful, light eyes. Something softened in the way he watched her. She reached out and caressed his unshaven cheek, and she was filled with such gratitude, in that moment, for Sam that she knew it for certain when the words popped out. "I love you."

But he said nothing. His hand loosened its hold, and he stumbled back a step.

Every bit of peace inside her fled, so Marcie turned and walked away. What had she expected him to say? Well, something. Anything caring would've been nice. She fought back the unwelcome sting of tears.

"Here it is." She struggled to focus on something else. She pointed to her older Toyota land cruiser, parked among the dozens and dozens of beat-up cars left by residents who caught the passenger-only ferry off the island. Marcie didn't miss the way Sam, Diane, and Jesse glanced at each other. Of course, they'd heard what she said to Sam. She hadn't been thinking before she spoke, let alone looking around to see who was listening.

She forced herself to look away, to smile at some of the residents, to keep going. She yanked open her driver's door. The hinges let out an angry squeal on her rusted-out SUV. A musty odor from the dark vinyl interior greeted her. She rolled down the driver's window, hopped in, and reached for the ignition. The keys were dangling right there where she'd left them. Marcie cranked the engine of the rusty beige SUV, and it started on the first try, although a little rough and rumbly. "Yeah, baby."

Marcie glanced over her shoulder and froze when Sam loomed over her from the passenger side.

"Turn it off," he said.

She stared at the fire that appeared to flicker to life in his ocean blue eyes.

"Turn off the truck, I said." This time, he didn't wait. He leaned over and turned it off, confiscating her keys.

She glanced out the window, into the back, but there was no sign of Diane and Jesse. She closed her eyes and ordered herself to take two deep breaths. "Where are Jesse and Diane?" She looked around Sam, unable to shake the hurt and anger.

"They're in that cute little store behind the hotel. I told them to give us some privacy. I have some things to say to you." He sounded really mad.

"What do you want to say? I said what I feel, Sam, and I didn't say it lightly." She slapped her palm against her chest. "I'm sorry the words slipped out. It hurts and confuses me that you mean so much to me. I opened up my heart in front of your friends, and you tromped on it."

"Knock it off. I did not. You can't just say those words...." He swept his hand in a circle while he struggled with some emotion tripping up his tongue.

"I love you. You mean those three words?"

His hand dropped, and his face hardened. "Marcie, you could have knocked me off the dock into the icy water and it would've been less of a shock. You can't just say things like that so casually and hit me out of the blue and expect me to smile and say 'That's nice.' This is serious." He was getting louder. A few heads turned from locals who hung around the store. A couple stepped closer and peered curiously through Sam's grungy window.

"Sam, it's how I feel. I've been honest with you about every fuck-up I've made, but you're not one of them."

His large hands were rough and callused. They showed his character. He dug in—worked hard, didn't slack off. It was those hands that touched her chin kindly when she looked away and turned her back to him.

"Don't turn away from me," he said. "I too have some things to say. You've turned my whole life upside down. I don't know what the hell it was about you that made me want to protect you when I should've walked away. I still don't. Do you think I'd do it for just anyone? I have strong feelings for you. I don't know what they are, and if you think I'm going to let you brood away because I didn't react the way you expected me to, you're sadly mistaken. I do things my way, not yours. That includes how I feel about you. You mean more to me than I want you to. And, baby, I'm still furious at you for the lines you've crossed. You've broken the law."

The flash in his eyes when he shoved his hand roughly through his hair should've been warning enough of the depth of his feelings. "You need to back off, Marcie, till I figure some things out. And get this into that stubborn head of yours—if you hurt, so do I. With the trouble you're in, at this point, I still don't know how deep it is or if I can get you out. And, Marcie, so help me, if you've lied to me or you've withheld anything..." He gritted his teeth as he turned away in his angry rant, unable to finish, but not before she glimpsed a sheen of tears gloss over his vulnerable blue eyes.

Her hand trembled as it covered her mouth and butterflies overtook her stomach. She was afraid to touch him. He didn't hate her. He cared, but trust was essential. If she wasn't completely forthcoming, he'd turn and walk away for good. She'd much rather endure a sledgehammer in her gut then suffer that wrath.

"Understood, Sam."

He wiped his face with his hand. She glimpsed Diane and Jesse standing at an awkward distance, ten feet away, pretending not to notice all the sparks flying between them.

He rolled down his window. "Diane, Jesse, get in. Let's go." He shoved the keys back in the ignition.

Marcie started the truck while Diane and Jesse climbed in. Jesse crammed in behind Marcie, his knees pressed up against her seat back. His head, like Sam's, almost touched the roof. Marcie drove east down Ferry Road. A trail of dust followed, taking them to the center of the thickly forested island to the only T intersection. Marcie turned right.

"So you always leave your keys in the ignition?" Sam asked. The icy tension between them melted a little more.

"Pretty much. That way I know where they are."

"Aren't you afraid someone's going to take your truck?"

"Like who? We all know each other here. Where's it going to go? It can't leave the island. If someone took it, everyone here would know. It'd be easy enough to go and get it." She could feel his eyes burning into her as if he was trying to wrap his head around living in a place where you didn't carry the same worries as the rest of the world. When she came around the next bend, half a dozen cars were parked, blocking the narrow gravel road. Nine people loitered, drinking beer. "Oh, a road party."

"What the hell is that?" Sam said.

Marcie stopped behind the green truck. There was no squeezing past. Sam scowled. She saw his whole body tense as he grabbed hold of the rusty handle and wrenched the door open.

CHAPTER 20

Marcie grabbed Sam's arm before he could bolt out the door and play cop, shutting down this party, which would humiliate her with the locals. "Sam, please don't. That's not how it's done here." She could feel his heart racing. "Sam, please."

He pulled away and climbed out. Marcie slid her bum around on the black vinyl and stared at Diane. "It's what happens here. Sometimes it goes on for days and no one can get by. It's life here, and it's harmless."

Diane only grunted as she climbed out. Jesse followed, frowning and shaking his head.

"Jesse, please help me. Get Sam to stop. I have to live here with these people."

"Hey, Marcie! Didn't know you were back. Wow, what happened to your head?" Betty, a chunky woman in her fifties, decked out in her trademark eighties retro-pink, satin shorts and faded yellow shirt, walked past Jesse and hugged Marcie.

"I fell. It's nothing, really. Good to see you, Betty."

Marcie recognized all the familiar faces of the laid-back local partiers, who were always looking for a good time. Unfortunately, this summed up the extent of their ambition. She declined several offers for a beer, and it wasn't until she chatted over some good times, and rehashed the latest gossip, that she spied Sam and Jesse. Both faced hippie Bob as he regaled them animatedly with some broad tale, his beer sloshing out of the can each time he flapped his arms. His long white hair and matching beard rustled in the wind.

Somehow, Diane had managed to convince the drivers of three cars parked on the left-hand side to move so that only one lane was blocked. In less than an hour, Marcie, Sam, Diane, and Jesse were able to squeak by and continue on their way.

"So is that a common thing, starting a party in the middle of your only main road on the island, drinking and then getting back in your car loaded? Completely illegal, Marcie, just in case you missed that part of the law."

"Sam, I'm not going to argue the laws of the state with you. I guarantee that I won't win. I'm also not condoning their behavior, but I'm not willing to judge them either." The air sizzled between them, and there was nothing but icy silence from Jesse and Diane in the back.

Around the next bend, Marcie passed a three-by-five cookie shack, hammered together with plywood, with a peaked, cedar roof. There were several on the island at various spots along the main road, all owned by locals and loaded with fresh garden vegetables. Peggy, an elderly, plump lady wearing a floppy straw hat, waved Marcie down while holding a bunch of carrots. Marcie stopped and leaned her elbow out the open window.

"Oh, Marcie, you're back. Are you going home?"

"On my way now." The truck rumbled while she pressed the brake.

Peggy waved her wrinkled hand high in the air. "Well, you go on, then. I'll be right over to see you."

Marcie waved her hand out the window and pulled away. Sam's eyes scalded her again.

"Interesting lady."

"Who, Peggy? She's awesome."

Sam offered a mere grunt in reply.

"So what was that little hut about? What kind of stuff's being sold?" Diane leaned forward, grabbing the back of Marcie's seat.

"That's what we call a cookie shack. If you live here, you have to be self-sufficient and grow your own food. People sell their extra vegetables, fruit. Some even sell baking. Those cookie shacks are filled daily with whatever the owner of the property has available to sell. It's an honor system. Price is listed, and people leave the money in a can."

"Let me guess—nobody worries about getting ripped off," Sam said.

"Not by locals."

Sam was apparently not familiar with the workings of a small community. Man, had she missed this place.

Around the next tree-lined bend, one of the island lakes magically appeared. Marcie turned down a rough dirt driveway that sloped at a gentle incline, surrounded by thick fir trees opening into a clearing with a quaint log home, which appeared deserted. No dog, no chickens, just thirty acres of birds, nature, arbutus, fir, and juniper trees overlooking Mirror Lake, with a clear blue sky and warm sun—simply a slice of heaven.

"Here we are, home sweet home." Through fresh eyes, she could see the magic of this place. The front porch listed. The overhang leaned heavily on one side, and Marcie glowed at this magnificent, peaceful sight. "Watch the top step. The front board's cracked. Jesse, Sam, with your weight, you'll probably go right through it."

Time stood still. That special feeling you get when you return home staggered Marcie until she wanted nothing more than to curl up and cry. Shaking and a little misty eyed, she opened the front door. It was the same—but different, as if she could now appreciate the beauty of this place. She loved the large, square kitchen with the fir log walls. The corner wood stove, a small, modern propane fridge and stove, and her granny's nicked oak table filled the center of the room.

"You always leave your door unlocked?"

Marcie wiped her eyes, so lost in thought that she didn't realize Sam stood right behind her. Before she could respond, a car rumbled down the driveway. Marcie wandered back outside. Peggy, in her spry, eighty-eight-year-old body, climbed out of a rusted, brown Hyundai, making a beeline straight for Marcie, wearing blue, polyester pants, a short-sleeved, striped shirt, and sturdy, beige shoes, similar to what nurses wore. She was an image in her floppy, straw hat, with a long, yellow scarf draped over the top and tied under her chin.

"What happened to your head?" Peggy asked. She retained the southern accent from her youth. Years ago, when someone on the island had commented on it, she articulated, in a very matter-of-fact way, that to lose it was to shake her roots, and that she wouldn't do.

"I fell and hit my head, but it's fine."

"You need to be more careful. Put some lavender oil around that cut, you'll be healed in no time, and without a scar. You'll still be pretty as a picture. Now listen, the reason I'm here is as part of the first responders. Old Mike Stuckey took a fall off his boat onto the dock and broke a vertebra in his back. He's flat out for a while. When I went over there, he had nothing for food in that camper he's living in. I opened the fridge, and he's been using it as a safe," Peggy continued dramatically, splaying her hands wide to enunciate each point.

Marcie felt the screws tighten in her stomach when she realized the interest Diane, Sam, and Jesse projected. Her back was hot, and she stood center stage.

"Now, I've managed to line up enough volunteers for the next five days, till Sunday, anyway, to cook his meals. He's out of everything—even his pot. Rob's graciously offered him a bottle of rum and a bag of pot, but I told Rob he needed to monitor it so that he doesn't mix them and overdo the rum. Sandy's going to feed the cat. And to top it off, when I was there, Mike asked for a six-pack of beer, but I told him I'd chill it at my place and only take him two a day...that's enough."

Sam's arms were crossed as he sidled closer to Marcie. His face tightened, and if she didn't know him so well, she'd be shaking in her boots. They had to be thinking the worst. She wanted to stop Peggy, but she gave up and closed her eyes, trying to rub away the worry lines between her brows.

She could hear shuffling in the dirt. Diane and Jesse stepped forward. That was when Peggy's head shot up, her face agog, as she darted her head first to Diane, and then Jesse, before landing straight on Sam. She scrunched her lips together and stepped closer to Sam, peering through her outdated thick glasses.

"Who're you? Are you Marcie's boyfriend?" She gave him no time to respond. "You got yourself a new man? Finally saw the light and kicked out that no-good scoundrel you been dogging around."

"Peggy, this is Sam, and that's Diane and Jesse." Her hand trembled. She was worried about how they read Peggy. Not well, obviously, by the way they each appeared to slip into their own cop modes. None of them showed a flicker of emotion. She wanted to yell at Peggy, *Stop talking! They think you're a drug dealer!*

"These are my… Sam, what are we, anyway?" This time she passed him the ball before her throat jammed up.

He stood stone faced, giving nothing away by his shadowed, tight eyes. "We're involved." His arms remained crossed in front of him.

"Hmm, well, sonny, I guess that'd be another word for sleeping together, boyfriend, girlfriend, shacked up. Afraid I've heard it all in the thirty-six years I was a schoolteacher down south. Makes no difference to me. Just treat her right. She's a good girl. Any fool paying attention can see sparks zapping back and forth between you two. Now, listen, Marcie, I'm here to ask you what can you do for old Mike." Peggy could throw anyone, in a second, with the way she changed the subject. And she spoke so dramatically, with the way she used her hands to speak fluently as much as with the way the words flowed from her mouth.

"I won't be staying, so I can't do anything for him," Marcie answered. Then she remembered: "I'll give him some essential oils and herbs that should speed up the healing. It'll help with the pain some so that he's not popping pills, and, at the same time, it'll clear his head. And, Peggy, he really shouldn't be smoking pot; especially when he's flat out. It's bad for the digestion."

"Ah, Marcie, I missed you, girl. Just give me what you can." Peggy's voice echoed across the property as Marcie slipped inside the cottage.

Marcie kept her distilled oils and herbs in a small, hand-carved cupboard, which hung beside the kitchen window. She'd grabbed a small bottle of each when a shiver raced up her spine, prickling the hairs on the back of her neck. She jumped, wondering if someone had followed her in. "Geez, what the hell?" There was no one there. She squeezed the bottles in her hand and hurried out.

Sam turned to her as the screen rattled. She saw Peggy taking the opportunity to size Sam up while conversing with Diane and Jesse quite intimately.

Marcie caught only the tail end of the conversation. She was on a rant about the government's atrocities and a black military chopper that had shown up a few weeks ago, landing on the Millers' acreage. The cops had rappelled down their lines. "What do they think? One call from the Millers and we all know they're here. Oh, and, Marcie, I forgot to tell you; next Saturday's the annual Las Seta awards, and old Mervin Phelps is up for the slowest driver on the island. Do you know he actually broke ten miles an hour, his top speed, just last week in his shiny, red Escort?"

"Wow, he's speeding. I'll be sorry to miss it. Is it at the Fireman's Ball?"

"Yes, and the emcee will be our esteemed Lance Silver."

"Lance Silver, you don't say? Hey, Marcie, I think we should go. It'll be fun. What do you think? Diane, Jesse—bring some friends?" It was the first time Sam had said anything spontaneous since Peggy arrived.

"You know Lance? He's quite the entrepreneur, you know. He just hauled over a big combine on that new barge of his. Says he's going to be a wheat farmer now. Here on Las Seta; can you imagine? He's such a grower." Peggy leaned back, allowing a deep rumbling laugh to flow out of her.

"Here you go, Peggy." Marcie handed her both bottles. "Now tell Mike to use just a teaspoon of this herb. Make it into a tea. The oil—drop it on his shoulders and spine."

Peggy plopped both bottles into the bulky canvas bag looped over her arm. "Why don't I hold on to this herb and send it round with each one whose turn it is to feed Mike? They can make the tea for him. Now, listen, Marcie; is this guy here going to treat you right and give you the respect you deserve? Or is he just using you for sex?"

Sam choked beside her. Diane actually snickered under her breath, and she thought Jesse was going to pass out from laughing so hard. And Peggy, well, she beamed in mischief.

"Well, you're a big girl, Marcie. This time, use that head God gave you. You're still young enough to get it right. Make your granny proud." Then she hugged Marcie and climbed in her car with a huge wave before backing up in a giant circle and roaring up the driveway.

She'd never told Sam what she did, selling her herbs and oils as a natural healer. She'd need to clarify a lot after Peggy's visit. On top of that, she realized he might have the wrong impression about the island folks.

"Interesting lady. What's this first responders society of hers all about? Supplying illegal substances?"

"It's about looking after your neighbors, Sam. When someone's in trouble, this is what a community's supposed to do. Step in and help. She's not a drug dealer. She's a fabulous lady who was the first to show up on my doorstep when Granny died. She helped me, made things easier for me in my grief. She handled the arrangements. And that's another thing I'd like to do before we go. I'd like to go and visit Gran's grave and make sure it's being tended, though I've no doubt, that with my neighbors here, it's being cared for diligently."

"Nice speech, Marcie. How many people here, on this island, are growing marijuana? And let's start with the herb you supplied her, and, this Rob, who's supplying a bag of dope to the injured guy."

Diane and Jesse flanked Sam, their arms crossed. Okay, this wasn't good. They had the wrong impression.

"I grew the herbs in my garden. It's what I do, Sam, for a living. Granny was a healer, and she taught me. I grow oregano, sage, thyme, lavender, peppermint. You know, all those things you buy in the store. Well, they have natural healing properties. I grow and sell them. I don't take drugs, legal or illegal ones. The herb I gave Peggy is ground up peppermint leaves. It helps digestion. The pot from Rob… I think you already know, Sam. There are people on this island who grow marijuana for their own use. That's all Rob does. He's not a dealer. Feel free to look around this property, but you'll find no marijuana plants here."

Marcie didn't wait for a reply. She went back inside, bumped by an uneasy vibe that escalated as she stepped through the doorway. She kept moving farther into the cottage, through the wooden archway dividing the kitchen and cozy front room. She paused before the wide picture window in this once comfortable, easy space filled with an overstuffed sofa and cozy furnishings; her inside place to meditate. She stepped around a side table and ran her hand over the packed, four-shelf bookcase; once again nauseated by an uneasy feeling. She moved down the short, dark hallway with light pine, finished walls and touched the cross, the only adornment outside her granny's room; one of the two tiny bedrooms across from each other. Both bedrooms contained a small closet, a double bed, and a dresser. The bathroom at the end of the hall was small but modern, a new addition added to the cottage ten years before. The original loo, as her granny so fondly called it, was an old outhouse out back, one that Marcie still used to this day.

She pushed her bedroom door open, and the knots in her stomach tightened. Something wasn't right, but what? Her gut ached when she realized her peaceful, tranquil space had been invaded.

"Marcie."

She started. Sam stood behind her.

"You okay?"

She shook her head. "I don't know. Something's wrong. I think someone was in here." Her voice trembled.

Sam brushed past Marcie into her cozy bedroom, with walls of muted lavender adorned with a dream weaver above the bed, framed sketches of a wolf, bear, and eagle mounted on the walls, and a small plate-glass window. He scrutinized everything the way a cop does. "Anything missing? Come on, Marcie. Look around you. Has anything been moved?" His tone turned all business, demanding, but at the same time it helped her focus.

She scanned her room from the doorway. On her neat pine dresser was a small hand-carved jewelry box. A small kerosene lamp sat on her bedside table. Her grandmother's patchwork quilt covered the double bed. "No, no, I don't think anything's moved. It's just a feeling that someone was in my room. Can't you feel it? You know, when you go into someone's house, or someone comes around you who's not a good person, and you get that icky, heeby-jeeby feeling? And then you feel your hair prickling up the back of your neck because there's something dark about them?" She jammed her fingers through her hair. How could she get him to understand? "That feeling's a warning, and I'm getting it here now." Her hand shook as she rubbed her stomach. "Whoever was here left that ick behind. This isn't a good person." Marcie waved her hands in the air, trying to send it away.

"I'll look around outside," Diane said. Marcie hadn't realized the other woman was hovering behind her. She left, and for the first time, Marcie wasn't hiding the spiritual side of herself. This was who she was.

Jesse searched her granny's dark, windowless room. "Marcie, where's the light?"

"You'll have to light the kerosene lamp in the kitchen. There's no electricity here."

"Leave it, Jesse. Go help Diane look around outside," Sam said. Then he was beside her, holding her arm, being ever so much her knight in shining armor.

"You believe me?" Astonishment filled her heart with a sense of unfamiliar wholeness, and yet, it scared the hell out of her. The caring in his eyes instantly switched over to watchful protection. No man had ever looked at her that way. He didn't need to say the words now; she already knew. She wanted so badly to be held by him, except his wary distrust was like an old, miserable dog between them. It'd be the hardest thing she ever did, but now she knew there was a chance, after all, to shake the doubt, to repair what she'd done.

He squeezed her arm, not hard. In a way, it was safe for him to touch her. Granny had always said that her place, her land, was magical, and all who set foot on it with good intentions would heal.

Sam led her back to the kitchen. She closed her eyes and breathed deep. The murky, invasive feeling wasn't as strong here.

"Nothing outside. It's pretty dry, so I can't see any tracks. The long grass is trampled out back. Oh, and I saw your sheep." Diane was fast and thorough. Jesse tromped in behind her.

"Not mine, believe it or not. There're feral sheep on this island. They turn up when you least expect it," Marcie explained.

Sam rested his hands on her shoulders in a familiar way. "If someone was here—they're long gone. Maybe you should think about locking your door."

She needed to think of something else, so she pulled away. "I'm going to put some coffee on. Can we stay a while? I want to get some things in order here before I pack some clothes."

Sam rummaged through her tincture cupboard. She knew what he looked for. "Just so you know, Sam, I don't smoke marijuana. I don't have any, never did. You should find a good supply of oregano for colds and flu, along with thyme, sage, and peppermint. All legal, last I checked. But since you don't trust me, please search the entire cabin."

His hand stilled. When he faced her, his shoulders softened. "Marcie, you need to understand that I'm not doing this to hurt you." He sounded rather defensive.

She cut him off before he could finish. "I know you're not, and I do understand why you need to do it. What I did was stupid and wrong. I also made you a promise to tell the truth and not withhold anything."

Sam leaned back against the counter, and Marcie stood across the kitchen. She wanted to take a step toward him but feared the strong pull. So she stood there, her gut twisted into knots. Sam crossed his arms in front of his chest. The window of opportunity slipped away. *Stop being such a coward.*

"You have any food? I'm getting hungry," he said. She looked up at him and smiled. There was some effort in his eyes. She couldn't quite put her finger on it, but he hadn't turned away. He shielded her in a way a man would do for a woman he cared about.

"As a matter of fact, I do." She brushed past Sam to the row of pine cupboards below the narrow fir counter, next to the sink. "Your choices are macaroni or homemade soup: Ham and bean or turkey vegetable?"

"You can your own soup?" Sam grinned boyishly. "You continue to surprise me. Hey, guys, want some homemade soup? I've never had homemade soup someone canned. Jesse, has your wife ever made you homemade soup?"

"No, Sam, my wife works like me. We share the cooking. But if you're going to heat some up—I'll eat. Guess there's no chance of grabbing a burger around here." Everyone frowned at Jesse. "Well, how's a grown man supposed to survive on just soup?"

"It'll do you good." Sam glanced down at Jesse's large belly.

Jesse scowled and joined Diane at the old nicked table, her notepad wide open, reviewing something she'd written.

"No soup for me, but I'll take a coffee. Thanks, Marcie." She held up her palm, cutting through the chatter. "Listen, guys, we need to sit down and go over Marcie's involvement with Dan McKenzie. We're getting sidetracked. Also, I need to know everything about his business partner, Richard McCafferty, and what Dan's link is to Lance Silver."

"Richard's a friend of mine. He's not like Dan." A vise-like wave stomped out any hope Marcie had of not involving her friends. "Diane, let's talk about me and what I did. I'll tell you anything, just leave Richard and Maggie out of this."

Diane, Jesse, and Sam focused in on her. They weren't going to back off, so she turned away and focused on making coffee.

"Who's Maggie?" Sam abandoned the soup he was stirring on the stove and leaned heavily against the counter beside her. She was pinned.

"Maggie is Richard's wife. She's not involved in any of this."

"Right. Now, Marcie, nobody's being left out. Let me tell you how this is going to go down. You're going to tell us about everybody: all your friends, Dan's, and everyone who's growing marijuana on this island or on the mainland. Whether you think they're connected or not is irrelevant. I want to know every deep, dark secret about everybody. Don't hold anything back. Do I make myself clear?"

"Sam." Admonishment laced Diane's tone. When Marcie glanced over, Diane's face seemed filled with gentle support. "Honey, listen, we're not going to hurt anyone. We need a clear picture of all the players, including bystanders. What you may not think is relevant could be key in our investigation." Her voice softened with understanding.

Did Marcie trust her? To a point. However, one thing was clear. She needed to remove all suspicion from Maggie, and Richard; neither deserved to be drug into this mess—her mess.

"Okay, but I want your word you'll leave Maggie out of it. Dan's made a mess out of so many innocent people's lives, probably even more than I know. They don't deserve to be tarnished with the same brush."

"Marcie, we're not going to railroad anyone, but there are a lot more people involved than what you've told me, and we know there's a connection to Lance Silver, considering the amount of drugs this guy's moving. He's got a lot of people under him, so I want details on all of them, including Silver being the master of ceremonies at the upcoming Fireman's Ball."

A wary shudder slid up Marcie's spine. She knew Lance, kind of, sort of—enough to stay well away from him. It was a warning Granny and Sally had drilled into her over and over—a warning she heeded to this day.

Lance had a private estate on the west side of Las Seta, overlooking the bay. It was directly across from the private island, the one the timber company had bought, logged and flogged, and burned scrap on; which had smoked out of control for the entire summer five years earlier. Lance had been furious with the timber company, as they all were. But when the charred bodies of two loggers from the timber company were found tied to the dock of that tiny private island, Marcie had known who was responsible. She also knew there'd never be any evidence, or witnesses, to tie Lance to the murders.

Everyone on this island knew Lance and his completely secluded, fenced, and alarmed, lavish estate. He was a philanthropist, at times social with his community. But he was mostly an isolated recluse who flew off, at times, seemingly on a whim, to another estate he owned in another part of the country. She knew he was connected and that he was one of the largest marijuana dealers in the area. And she knew he was no one she ever wanted to cross.

"Look, Lance is always the emcee. He likes to be acknowledged at our community functions, by the residents, so that everyone will believe he gives something back to this community he loves so much."

Diane and Sam roasted her with a hard look. Jesse slid around in his chair and studied her with concern. Maybe he could see the fear she tried to hide.

"Those are his words, not mine. Look, just talking about him makes me ill. I need to sit down." Her knees were shaking. Jesse pulled out a chair, and Sam supported her arm. Sam squatted and rubbed her hands. She could see the concern on his face.

"Granny and Sally would never allow me anywhere near him, neither would some of the other islanders. They always said darkness seeks out the light to destroy it, and Lance is so powerful. Granny and Sally wouldn't even take him on. I've never seen them back away from someone before. They told me that, sometimes, there are battles we aren't meant for. I've done a lot of stupid things, but I've avoided Lance every time he's sought me out. I never did business with him. I'm not that stupid. There's something about Lance that reeks of impure strength. Once in bed with him—you're never out. He's unpredictable. He's dangerous."

"How do you know this much about him if you're not around him?"

"I listen, Sam." She pulled her hands away and crossed her arms. "Even though this island is a haven for me and the others who live here, there are families here, people, doing things they shouldn't—things that aren't right. You have to know the history of this place. In the fifties, marijuana crops were the main agriculture on this island, maybe they still are. People who live here are secretive to outsiders, and if you choose to live here, there's this pact, an understanding, you have. If you want peace—you say nothing. I grew up here. People who live here knew my granny. She had history, roots here. So, through Granny, people here trust me. I listen when they talk. When you're a permanent resident, with history, you hear what's really going on.

"Lance moved here years ago, wealthy even then. He turned this island upside down while building his lavish estate with cutting-edge solar power, establishing his operation. Everything I've told you; I heard third hand, but it's reliable. And no, I won't give you the names of who told me. I don't care what you threaten me with. The information is from honest folks who know what's going on, and if I tell you their names, and you talk to them, they'll get hurt. We live here. We want to live in peace. Do you understand?" She was so agitated by the thought of bringing harm to the people here that Sam must have seen it, because he squeezed her arm, in an understanding kind of way, before standing up and leaning against the deep porcelain sink.

She continued: "What I did this year was find spots to grow marijuana around Gardiner, in the seclusion of the isolated state park land. I'd never do anything on this island. I'd never tarnish Granny's property that way. Mother Mary, if Lance ever found out…" She shook her head and closed her eyes when a chill shot up her spine. "You're right about one thing—he controls who grows here and how much. But I don't know the details. I don't want to know."

"Tell me about the outdoor gardens you planted." Diane scribbled notes as Marcie explained.

"Dan taught me how to find isolated spots close to a water source so that I wouldn't have to haul water. That would be time consuming, difficult, and a definite red flag. In those hidden clearings, with plenty of sun, he showed me ways to hide the garden. He would find an alder tree and use a hatchet to cut a circle around the circumference of the tree. He would spray poison into it, and the alder would die and drop its leaves. That way, the garden would still be sheltered and hidden from the choppers above, but it would get lots of sun. Then I'd till the soil with a shovel, work in some lime, and plant the rooted cuttings."

"How many plants in a garden?" Diane's questions were specific and professional.

"I averaged forty plants, some more, some less."

"We're going to need to know where these gardens are. Do you think you can show me on a map?"

"I can try, if you give me a map of the area."

"What did you do with the plants after you harvested? Who'd you deliver to?"

"Well, that's the thing. The outdoor gardens haven't been harvested. I'm supposed to be doing that soon, but I have no idea where it's supposed to be delivered. I'd think it'd go to Dan's deep Gardiner property, where Sandra lives. I've only harvested marijuana plants once, and that was done on Dan and Richard's property in a big old shed. Dan showed me how to cut the buds, how to harvest the leaves. Those were plants he sold to his friends."

Diane gave her a look as if she should have known better.

"Well, that was what he told me."

"Okay, Dan McKenzie owns two large properties in Gardiner, one where you stayed and looked after the marijuana." Diane held her pen up. "Isn't that owned by Richard McCafferty, too?"

"Richard bought the property a year ago with Dan, to build homes, not do grow-ops. Richard's not into that kind of thing. That property's a, split zoned, commercial property. They applied for a change of zoning on half, and put in a development permit to build twenty-five new homes. That's all Richard's doing."

"Is this the property where the house burned down?" Sam dished up soup, and poured coffee, obviously needing to keep busy while mentally putting the pieces together.

"Yes, Sam, it is."

"You had a dream about a fire? I pulled the fire marshal's report. The old house that burned there had residue from high-grade marijuana in the basement." Diane swallowed as she referred to her notes. "I told you yesterday that both Richard and Dan are under investigation for suspicion of arson."

"When you dreamed about this fire in New Orleans, you said to me that you knew it was arson, and you were sure you did something wrong," Sam said. "If that's the case, tell me the truth, Marcie. Was there a grow-op in the basement?"

Marcie got up and pumped herself a glass of cool water from the hand pump mounted beside the sink. She swallowed the entire glass to steady her nerves. She placed her back to everyone and watched a deer, grazing on overgrown grass and weeds, through the small window over the sink. "When I lost my memory, I dreamed of a fire my first night in New Orleans. That dream brings the events of what happened that night into a different perspective.

"The night of the fire, Dan was in his excavator pushing the house walls down. I guess I started running toward him. I wasn't thinking. Richard shouted from his loader for me to get back. Then I heard the sirens— as the house collapsed under the flames, just as the fire trucks and the sheriff pulled in. The fire guys shut Dan and Richard down. Richard must have walked straight toward me, because he grabbed me by the arm and told me to leave. This was right before the sheriff and deputies separated us. I remembered the shed was full of marijuana plants; so I slipped away from the deputy, who'd turned his back on me, and hurried behind the RV and another fifth wheel on the property, that was when I saw Elise.

"I knew she was dead. She smiled, and a dimple creased only her right cheek. I kept thinking her smile was crooked, and there was no peace in it. I was so cold. She held her index finger and thumb up, mimicking a gun shooting me. Then she leaned her head back and laughed, a deep, throaty, wicked laugh, while her long blond hair blew in the wind. She walked around the corner into darkness. I panicked. I was worried about getting busted for the marijuana. I damn near had a heart attack when I reached the door and the padlock that was always on it was gone. I peeked in, and the shed was completely empty."

Sam slid his hand over her shoulder, a slight touch. His hand fell away when she faced him.

"I didn't know who took it, but I felt set up, lied to, ripped off and relieved, all in the same moment. You know?" She walked away and sat, scooting her chair closer to the table, facing Diane. "Sandra showed up a short time later, after the firefighters managed to get the fire under control. She was devastated about the house. She sought Dan out to comfort her. I've never understood their relationship. She's an extremely overweight substance abuser who goes from one beauty treatment to another, and she has this phony part of her that she wears, like a mask, to hide all her pent-up anger and hurt. But her real talent is being the best grower and dealer in the area. Add to that the fact that she's a professional with a physiotherapy degree, and she works through the state as a care worker for severely handicapped kids. You're probably asking what any of this has to do with the fire."

Three sets of blank eyes stared back.

"Sandra had this brilliant idea of turning one of the houses Dan owned into a group home for unwanted handicapped kids. Apparently, the old house that burned down was supposed to be the group home. Somehow, she had obtained a state contract. I couldn't figure out how they'd planned to do it. You see, that house was so old and rundown. Dan would've had to gut and renovate it, and that would have cost a lot of money. I knew enough about Dan to know he wouldn't have put out that kind of money."

"What does this have to do with him growing marijuana?" Jesse rested his elbows on the table. He'd been unusually quiet until then.

"Nothing, except this was what Sandra wanted, and he needed to keep her happy because, without her, he didn't have a marijuana kingdom. So that put Dan in a dilemma. He couldn't talk Sandra out of it, and he wasn't going to pour that kind of money into a house the state required to be up to code. So wouldn't it be so much easier to just burn it down, then let the insurance company rebuild it?"

Sam and Diane both looked at each other.

"Marcie, are you saying Dan and Richard burned down the house for insurance money?" Diane set her pen down and leaned her forearms on the table.

"Not Richard. There's no way he was in on it. He was furious with Dan about the group home. He wanted no part of Sandra."

"When Dan was questioned by the sheriff, he accused a group of young guys who'd rented the house from him, of burning it down, the same ones he had evicted only a week before the fire," Marcie said. "He screamed it was payback and said he kicked them out because he was sure they were growing marijuana in his basement. That was the first I'd heard about it. Diane, you said traces of marijuana were found in the basement. I don't think you should discount the fact that maybe those young guys *were* growing for Dan. He's too sharp. No one would be doing anything around him unless he knew about it."

"Marcie, you can't be sure Richard isn't involved."

Marcie tapped her chest. "I know it right here. Richard's not deceptive. He's hard and difficult at times, but honest in his way. And after the sheriff and firefighters left, I heard Dan and Richard arguing."

"What did they argue about?" Jesse frowned.

"Richard accused him of being in a hurry to push the walls in, as if he wanted it to burn quickly, and then I heard him yelling, 'So how'd you do it, wiring, gasoline, what?' Then he shoved him hard with both hands, called him a greedy bastard, saying he just couldn't leave well enough alone. Dan didn't fight him or even try. Richard threw his hands up and walked straight over to me. I've never seen him so mad.

He told me that if I was smart, I'd get away from Dan, that he had no intention of ever being faithful or committing to me. He'd screw anything as long as it had two legs, was female and available. Richard couldn't see how much his words hurt me, even though, deep down, I knew they were true. At the time, I didn't want to hear it. He must have realized after he said it, because he hugged me and asked if I knew the kind of monster I was involved with. Then he told me to get on the next ferry and go back to my cottage. Then he left."

"Where'd he go, Marcie?"

"Well, home, of course, to Maggie and the kids."

"So what did you do?"

"I went back to Las Seta."

"You didn't talk to Dan, ask him where the marijuana went or if he burned the house down like Richard said? You just left? You know what, Marcie? From the little bit I know of you, I somehow doubt you just walked away." Sam pulled out a chair across from Jesse. When he sat, he unzipped his jacket, and Marcie saw past the mirage of how badly she had hurt him.

"Sam, deep down I knew Richard was right. Dan's a greedy bastard, but I wouldn't admit it at the time. It was easier to leave, to ignore all of it. I loved him too much, and if I allowed myself to question his true motives, I would've had to be honest with myself, to acknowledge that I was the one who screwed up, that our whole relationship was built on a lie. I wasn't ready to do that. So, yes, I left. And you know what? Right now, I thank God, my angels, and my spirit guide who put me in your path." She didn't realize tears streamed down the side of her face. She gazed over at Diane. "I want Dan in jail. Please tell me what I need to do."

CHAPTER 21

S am pushed his chair back on the coarse hardwood floor. He roughly cleared his throat, uttering from the screen door, "I need some air." The old fir steps creaked. His footsteps crunched through the gravel. Then silence.

"I'm sorry you had to hear that, but I needed to say it," Marcie said.

Diane looked away. All this information sharing was way too personal. Jesse coughed, and the handmade chair squeaked when he stood. He watched her for the first time with, what appeared to be, an appreciative understanding. "I'll join Sam," he said.

For a moment, Marcie wondered if Diane would make an excuse and leave, too. She stared wide eyed back at Marcie and closed her notebook, clipping her pen to the front cover.

"Marcie, Sam and I are friends. I hope you mean what you say, that you want to help, because Sam's not looking too good."

Well, that did it. She had her full attention now. "Is it because of me?"

Diane scooted her chair back, stretched her legs out, and crossed her ankles. "Honestly, yes and no. When you met Sam, he was on his way home. He left the team to get his head together after working for years investigating these grow ops. You know the Washington State

Patrol initiated a federally funded task force four years ago to investigate Lance Silver. That was before the International DEA task force—before Sam arrived."

Marcie nodded, remembering, all too well, that fiasco. The narcotics division had messed up badly, specifically one cowboy named Lieutenant Styne. "Yes, I remember how your Lieutenant Styne terrorized people on this island for weeks. He stopped every vehicle and treated us all as if we were criminals. He disrespected my granny, called her a useless hippy. He even made a public announcement at our Anglican church one Sunday morning. He, personally, was going to clean up and eradicate the marijuana drug problem on the west coast and the San Juan Islands, starting with Las Seta. Then he raided the residents here with twenty-five members of the Washington State Patrol. They appeared in military helicopters from the naval base. Officers rappelled down lines. I think they really enjoyed that approach and honestly believed they were taking us by surprise."

"Marcie, there's a serious marijuana problem on these islands, and I know that the investigation wasn't handled..." Frowning, Diane hesitated. "Okay, it was handled badly."

Marcie flattened both hands on the table when she leaned a little too quickly toward Diane. "Badly, you're kidding, right? Did you know I was out walking when one guy and one girl cop came out of the Thomas' place, pushing a baby stroller loaded with marijuana, which they had apparently confiscated. They stopped me to ask for directions to the dock. They'd gotten lost and separated from their team. So I pointed them in the right direction. Do you know what happened next?"

Diane's face turned beet red. She cringed, covering her face with her hands and moaned.

"On the way back over to the mainland in their boat, the officers decided they didn't need to take all the marijuana back with them—it was way too much. So once again, in their brilliance, they dumped some of it overboard. Who would have known a southeaster would come up and blow the packaged marijuana back to Las Seta? The school kids sure had a heyday picking it all up from along the shoreline."

Diane peered through open fingers of both hands, which still covered her face.

"So, Diane, did the idiot cop who dumped it over ever confess?"

She cleared her throat. "No."

"Would you like me to finish the story of Lance and how that cowboy cop taunted him?"

Diane dropped her hands and stiffened her back. "Marcie, you obviously know how ineffective it was handled. But did you know that over three million dollars, in marijuana alone, passed through Lance's hands last year? He had twenty people growing and cultivating for him, indoors and out."

Marcie slapped her hands on the table. "Let's put all the facts from both sides on the table. You want to stop the grow shows? You need to see it from the people's perspective, too.

Diane crossed her arms.

"Your cowboy knew what Lance was up to, but he refused to wait for a search warrant. He followed Lance home to his other house near Adelma Beach. You know the west coast monstrosity of an oceanfront property where Lance used to keep his office? Cowboy waited until Lance turned out the lights. He broke in, jumped him in bed, put a knee in his back and cuffed him, even roughed him up a bit."

"Okay, Marcie, you're well informed. Lance got off, as you know, and Lieutenant Cowboy was shipped off to Nebraska by the Feds. What we do know is that Lance is into more than just marijuana. Three years ago, the DEA tracked a boat, carrying cocaine, from South America all the way up to the west side of Las Seta, where Lance Silver's estate is. After that, a new international team was assembled with the DEA. A few years ago, Sam joined our team."

Marcie had heard rumors that Lance was under investigation, again, but she didn't know any details.

"Right before Sam left, we obtained a search warrant and arrived at Silver's estate with full backup. A second team arrived at his Gardiner compound, where we know there's an underground truck trailer storing marijuana. The SWAT guys, DEA, Interpol, Washington State Patrol, and even the Coast Guard were involved. Both places were clean except for a scribbled note with Sam's name on it that we found in Lance Silver's desk drawer. At the same time, a tip was phoned in telling the sheriff to check Sam's locker at the gun club. There we'd find a key to Lance Silver's estate, along with marijuana."

"Did you?" Marcie leaned closer.

Diane glanced toward the door as she licked her lips. She met Marcie's gaze straight on. "The deputies from the Sequim detachment checked when we were still on the island. And yes, they did, right where they were told it would be. There were five pounds of marijuana."

Marcie clasped her hands on the table in front of her. Worried, she too watched the door. "Sam told me Lance had screwed him. Drugs were planted in his locker, and then he left, went back to New Orleans, where I met him."

"Marcie, that's not all that happened. We were ordered back by our boss, Dexter. A chopper flew Sam and me straight to the gun club, where Dexter waited. The sheriff had brought in IPB to investigate Sam, and they were interviewing the gun club manager, a short, balding little turd, when we walked in. Apparently, he had phoned the tip in but wouldn't say how he knew. Sam lost his temper and hit the guy. We knew he had lied, and Sam would have beaten this jerk until he confessed if Dexter and I hadn't pulled him off. There was an internal review, and charges of assault were pending, but Dexter made them go away. We knew Lance Silver had the wily prick in his pocket. Dexter leaned on the guy, told him he'd personally go through every part of his life until he found something to put him away, whether it was tax fraud or too many parking tickets. It was enough. That lowlife recanted everything and refused to press assault charges, said he now had reason to believe the drugs may have been planted.

"I knew Sam wasn't sleeping, so that confession, packaged up with all the stress, was the final straw. He threw his badge on Dexter's desk, furious, yelling that those drug dealers were so far above the law that, whatever justice the law preached, they'd find a way to get off. He wouldn't listen to reason. I was afraid he'd do something stupid, so when I found out about you and how you landed in his path—well..." Diane splayed both hands in the air. "Let's just say that, now that I've met you, I do believe you landed there for a reason, and you may have saved him from doing something really dumb. Please, don't screw it up."

Marcie pushed away from the table, telling Diane she needed to clean up. Diane's soft brown eyes regarded her with sympathy, as if she understood Marcie's ache for Sam. She stuffed her notebook in her coat pocket and went in search of Sam and Jesse.

CHAPTER 22

Marcie tilted her head back under the steamy, hot spray, doing her best to wash away all her worry for Sam. Now she understood better something Mama Reine said. Sam had been set up, just like Jerome. There was a strong spiritual connection between them. This was warfare on the divine level, with a dark entity who kept coming back—in a different body, a different life. She knew that if she tried too hard to analyze it, she wouldn't grasp the allusion.

Marcie turned off the water, pulled the pink curtain back, dried off, and wrapped a thick towel around her. She pulled open the door and had no time to think when a familiar, slender hand clamped firmly over her mouth. She shrieked, but the sound didn't carry.

"Sorry to scare you, Marcie, but keep your voice down. You'll scare the birds. Now, what are you doing with the cops, and why didn't you call me? I was worried about you." Dan held her tight, the way a man does a simple possession.

She pushed his hand away and barely caught hold of the towel when it slipped down and exposed her breast. She grabbed the striped towel with both hands and held tight as she pushed past him into her bedroom. She grabbed her robe off a hook behind the door. Keeping her back to Dan, she dropped the towel and pulled it on.

"What are you doing spying on me?"

An easy smile lit up his alluring face. It always amazed her how his looks alone brought a hitch to her breath. His eyes, she always loved his eyes. But now there was something different about his sparkling, hazel gaze. The color had changed, but how? Then his natural charm flowed over her with devastating force. Marcie's knees weakened, completely unprepared for his ability to bypass her defenses.

She kept forgetting to surround herself with the circle of white light —to call in her angels to protect her, to clearly see the gold cord connecting her to the universe. He was already inside her, manipulating her feelings, confusing her. Now she knew how he did it. He touched her, and in that second, he attached one of his dark cords to her.

"I was worried about you when I didn't hear from you. I came out here to look for you."

Then she remembered her earlier, wary, invasive feeling. "How long have you been here? Were you in my house earlier?"

His wicked smile was followed by a cold, mischievous laugh. His face hardened when he crossed his arms in front of him. The wall that he controlled around himself spoke of years of conditioning. Then she felt it, a subtle slip of energy from the top of her head like a breeze in the wind. Her heart pounded. She had to protect herself, to resist him. He was already confusing her. Good Lord, he was powerful. She sucked in a deep breath and halted his invasion by putting up her own circle. She called upon St. Michael, in her head, to cut his cords. It was hard because Dan was good at what he did and very dangerous. Why hadn't she seen this before?

"You still have crops to bring in, Marcie, and my buyer's waiting." His voice was magnetic. She loved listening to him talk.

So much existed between them that they didn't need to speak. He seemed to be aware of what she thought, what she'd done. Whatever his gift, he had a power she hadn't seen before. He must have always known he had it, like a shaman, but not a good one. He could attach to her when her guard was down. He read her aura, her thoughts. To an unsuspecting person, he easily brought chaos, lies, and disorder, and he walked in the shadows. All this knowledge came to her now.

"Whatever you're planning, I'd think again about betraying me," he said.

"I have no idea what you're talking about. I can tell you one thing for sure, Dan; I'm done with you and your crop. If you want it —get it yourself." She tried to hurry past him, but his arm snaked around her waist. The hold wasn't brutal or hard, but it pinned her against his familiar body; a body she craved to, once again, entwine with hers. She breathed him in. He had no body odor, just a surprising earthy fragrance. To her physical self, it was a drug she craved, and that alone crept inside and whispered throughout her. He appeared dominant, in control, when he tried stealing her vibrant life force. But Marcie knew he'd fold if she leaned on him. Dan was a devious man who somehow always landed on his feet, skirting trouble by pinning it on others, mostly women, while he slithered away.

Dan cocked his head at an angle to look closer into her. He slipped in again, and with the invasion came nausea churning right in her center. She swallowed. Psychically, he was way too powerful for her. As Sally, her teacher, would say, she was still a babe in the woods, and she had no idea the power she was up against.

"I don't think so, Marcie. You see, this is how it's going to be. You're going to finish what you started."

"Get your hands off me and listen to me. I'm done. You can't bully me anymore. I'm not that stupid. Now get out of my house." She wrenched his arm away and pushed past him. Just touching him sizzled a lustful desire in her heart. She turned the corner, then another one, through the front room, the kitchen; breaking more contact with each wall between them. She needed to walk out of here, to walk it off around her house—clear it out. Where were Sam and Diane? She willed them to return.

"That key and the pot found in your new lover's locker at the gun club is just the beginning. The next time, he won't be able to talk himself out of it or convince that cowardly manager to change his story. The evidence against him will be indisputable, and the crime will lock him away for life. Don't mess with me, Marcie."

His words stopped her cold. "How did you know?" She whirled

around so fast that she nearly fell over, stumbling a couple steps as she bumped the table.

Clarity came with a warning. He wielded magic with his emotions, focused for his personal gain. She understood now what he did. He gathered inspiration and power from the forces of nature and the natural world around him, relying solely on his instincts. The strength of his belief in what he did was appalling. He manifested his greed no matter the consequences to those around him. Earth-based spirituality focused on one principal—harm none. He was going against nature. What she didn't understand was why no karma had touched him.

His smile lit up his entire face. He looked different. It was his eyes again; they changed in color from golden brown to whisky flecked and amphibian. She knew, all too well, that the eyes were a window to the soul and everything attached to it. As gifted as the lineage Marcie came from was, wariness and fear warned her that he channeled his wants, his desires, and his magic in a way beyond anything she was familiar with—beyond her training with Sally. Her back was to the wall. She realized she had no choice.

"Good girl," Dan said. "Oh, and just one more thing; Maggie's going to help you."

CHAPTER 23

Barefoot in the dirt, Marcie circled her quaint, log cottage counterclockwise again and again. How could she reverse what he had manifested; this ugly destruction he had put into play? She pleaded for help, and each time her head sucked her right back to him. She couldn't read him no matter how hard she tried. He was superior in his skill. What kind of abomination of nature was he? Her skin crawled just thinking about the need to be with him that still slithered inside of her. It was a pure addiction that, she now knew, wasn't entirely of her own doing. He'd created that. He knew her weakness. Now she fought with every nuance she could muster, calling all the good forces beyond her in love, hope, and faith to stop him and whatever else was at play. *Let me go!*

"What the hell are you doing?"

Sam, Jesse, and Diane circled around her cautiously. Their concern for her exploded with looks of horror across their faces, as if she'd suddenly lost her mind.

"Look at you. You're a mess. Your legs are all scratched. They're bleeding." Sam hustled through the salal, huckleberry, and thorny blackberry bushes surrounding Marcie and easily scooped her up. She instinctively wrapped her arms around his neck and held on while he hurried into the cottage. She breathed him in, his own piney scent bringing her back to him.

"Marcie, ease up on the grip. You're choking me."

"I'm sorry." Tears burned her eyes, and she stifled a sob.

Sam used his foot to pull out a kitchen chair and eased her into it. She swiped at her eyes. Dirt smeared her pink housecoat, her feet, and her wet hair was a tangled mess.

"Marcie, what the hell were you doing? What's wrong with you?" Sam hurried back with a washcloth and towel he'd grabbed from the bathroom. Jesse rifled under the kitchen sink for a bucket and pumped in some fresh water. Sam kneeled in front of her, dipping the rag in the bucket and bathing her cuts.

"I..." Her breath seeped out, but the words wouldn't come. She tried again. "I was looking for you." She couldn't look at him. "Ouch." Pain cut like sharp teeth when Sam wiped away blood oozing from several jagged scratches.

"Marcie, I need to put some antiseptic on these cuts or they'll get infected."

"No antiseptic. Over by the sink, there's a bottle of distilled lavender. Bring it here. I'll spray it on. It'll work better and won't hurt as much." Diane was gone but had soon reappeared with thick cotton socks from Marcie's drawer.

Marcie knew Sam was waiting for her to look up. He had a way of maintaining eye contact that went beyond a casual glimpse, but then he'd know, and she couldn't take that chance, because he'd stop her, and this was the only way to protect him.

CHAPTER 24

"We need to get going and make the crossing before dark," Marcie said. She glanced up at Diane, and, for a tiny moment before she turned away, Marcie was positive Diane knew. Of course they suspected something had happened. Look at her. She was a mess. She'd never been any good at hiding things.

"Marcie, you need to get dressed. Brush your hair," Diane instructed her in a motherly way.

Marcie said nothing. She got up out of the chair and went to her bedroom. After she dressed and brushed her snarled hair, she crammed clothes into a black canvas bag, willing the constant trembling in her hands to stop. Her damp, brushed hair hung down her back. Dressed in blue jeans and a dark hoodie, she was ready. She carried the large tote out with her.

Jesse leaned against the kitchen sink, studying her with a cold, hard eye when she walked into the room.

"Where are Sam and Diane?" She didn't know why, but she didn't want to be alone with Jesse. She liked him, but he'd pull her secrets out.

"You're pale, shaking, and scared shitless of something. I sent Sam and Diane out. They took a walk up to the main road, getting a feel for the area." He shrugged. "What gives, Marcie? You ain't the same calm, collected little girl who came back here with us this morning."

She dropped her bag at her feet and wiped away the lone tear. "Jesse, have you ever had to do something you didn't want to do but knew it was the only way to protect someone you love?"

"You want to tell me what's going on?"

No matter how much she wanted to confide in him, she couldn't. She closed her eyes and summoned every ounce of strength to pull herself out of the miserable pit she'd sunk into. "No, it's fine. We'd better go. The sun will be setting soon." She looked up at him, but she couldn't interpret what clouded his eyes: righteous fury, empathy, support, condemnation?

He walked straight at her. His narrowed eyes peeled back each one of her hidden layers and seemed to dig out her secrets. He picked up her bag, walked past her out the door. "Come on then, little girl. It's getting dark, and the big bad wolf's coming out soon."

Her whole body trembled. She fisted her hands so hard her nails dug into the fatty flesh of her palms, desperate to find a way out of this living nightmare. She did the only thing she could; she followed Jesse, breathed, and climbed back into the truck.

***

WHEN THEY ARRIVED BACK AT DIANE'S, MARCIE TOLD SAM, DIANE, AND Jesse she was tired, but what she really needed was space and time to think. She hefted her bag in her cozy room and perched on the edge of the soft bed. She'd taken no time to appreciate this welcoming room's cozy décor. Creamy wainscoting trimmed warm, peach walls. A six-drawer, honey-colored dresser sat opposite the bed, mounted with a large mirror—a mirror that wouldn't hide secrets or the dark circles under her puffy eyes. She could hear Sam, Diane, and Jesse through the closed door, involved in some deep discussion.

The bedside digital clock read 8:10 PM. She'd a lot of time to think, so she looked around for a distraction. Jerome's letters beckoned from the oak nightstand beside the bed. Consumed by all this worry, she didn't know if these letters would be enough to get her through the next few hours. She groaned and picked up the packet. A wider envelope dropped from the stack into her lap. Inside was a thin paper journal with a lovely handwritten inscription, *Isabel Standford Morison.*

Marcie propped up her pillows and leaned back, clicking on the bedside lamp. She gently opened the delicate journal and glanced at the first page.

July 18, 1824.

Rand and I will marry today. I am grateful he is willing to give me his name and be a father to Jemmie, my precious boy. The secret of his father and the shame he'll carry, I pray he'll never find out. Rand promised no one would know. He said only that Jerome was killed and that it would be best if it were never discussed, never brought to light, or he would be unable to protect me and my child from disgrace. Jemmie would be taken from me. Oh, how I fear to even put those words down.

Guests are arriving. Soon I'll have the protection of his name, and Jemmie will have the future he so rightly deserves.

Lies, deception, greed, lust, shame. Those words reminded Marcie of what she'd brought into her own life. Two sheets of paper slipped out from behind the journal. Carefully, she eased apart the thick paper, old and spotted. This one had no date, but as she read on, she was filled with sorrow and pain.

Marcie skimmed through; she managed to decipher the author as Isabel Marie Chamblee, daughter of Emiline and Benjamin Chamblee. She grew up on a plantation in the southern parish of Terrebonne. Her words were cold when she made brief mention of the slaves they owned, as if they were a herd of cattle to be fed and worked.

I met Jerome in the summer of 1813. He came with privateers Jean Lafitte and Barney Swade, who conducted business with my father. I fell in love with him the moment I saw him. My father knew. That was why he forbade me to marry him and threatened to send me away. Daddy hated

Jerome, said he was an Acadian with a questionable business practice. I disobeyed him and snuck away one night with Jerome. We married in a quiet ceremony, in New Orleans, with only Jean Lafitte and Barney Swade attending.

Jean is an amazing man. I always thought of him as being larger than life. I overheard him warn Jerome of the consequences of crossing my father. Jean urged him to move to his compound for protection, only Jerome was adamant we move to Grand Isle, where he had built a comfortable home. My darling husband refused Jean's generosity. Jerome believed it was necessary to keep business at a distance. He's so protective, and it bothers him so to leave me for weeks and months on end. He's hired staff to care for me while he's gone, a cook and a maid. He refused to use slaves. Although both the cook and maid are octoroons, he pays them a wage. They still address him as "Massar." He remains indisputable, with his moral lines drawn, about owning another human being.

I overheard disagreements between Jean and Jerome when Jerome refused to take slaves as cargo even though Jean and other lieutenants brought them in. Instead, he's limited his cargo to the nonhuman, even though what they took was not their own.

THE NEXT PACKET WAS ANOTHER JOURNAL, THIS ONE UNDATED. AFTER A closer look, Marcie realized she'd read out of order.

JEAN ARRIVED WITH MY FATHER'S COUSIN, RAND MORISON, WITH NEWS THAT *Jerome had deceived me. He stole from Jean. The evidence was found in his possession. I don't know what to do. I'm large with child and expect to deliver Jerome's child any day—my child. I've cried until I have nothing left. My shame is so great, and Rand has been so kind to me through all this, assuring me that he cares for me and vows not to rest until he exposes the truth. He said he had suspicions for some time, and when he visited his good friend, he discovered the truth. It was irrefutable evidence. Jerome was a slave, a mulatto. Although he appeared white, even with a mass of golden hair, his skin held a hint of dark complexion that he brushed off to his Acadian ancestry. Rand said that his whole story was fabricated. As it's illegal for a black man to marry a white woman, our marriage will be annulled. Rand said he would take care of it.*

I still could not believe it was true until he showed me the evidence. Jerome's mother was an escaped slave who had been owned by George Harklin twenty-eight years prior. Jerome is twenty-six, his mother now dead, but she was named Letty. Rand showed me the papers. Jean was furious and vowed I'd be looked after. I'm still in shock and ashamed to admit, as I pour my heart into this journal, that my love for Jerome is still there. He was my first breath in the morning. I don't know how I'll survive. I pray this isn't true and that I'll wake up and find out this was just a bad dream, a nightmare. Please, dear God, spare me this pain, for me and for my child. I cannot go home. I have not heard from my father, in over a year, since I left with Jerome. Although he sent word through Rand, he'll never forgive my transgression.

Rand and Jean both assured me my child would be spared. The state legislature laws are clear: With the blood factor and association, the physical appearance, and less than a quarter African mixture, the child is legally white. They vowed no one will know. Oh, dear God, please take this pain from me. How could he do this to me? Damn him to hell.

Weakened and sick from what she had read, Marcie knew the truth had been manipulated for someone's vengeance. Flooded by a wave of hostility at Isabel's ignorance, she wanted to reach through time and shake the woman senseless. How could she believe that Jerome would have stolen from Jean? How could she turn her back on Jerome? A desperate need to somehow balance right compelled her to keep reading.

Isabel had suffered alone and silent, pouring out her heart in her journal. She referred fondly to Rand as an attentive suitor who stayed close to her. She'd done her best to close her mind to Jerome, although she ached for him constantly. Her words on paper fought those feelings, replaced with hatred for his perceived betrayal.

Isabel confessed she'd overheard whispers saying that Jerome was, in fact, in the Cabildo, awaiting hanging. Isabel's words became colder and focused on her child, Jemmie, the spitting image of his father, although he carried the light complexion of his mother. She thanked the Lord for that much. Pain and longing befell her each time she looked upon him. She battled a conscious effort to banish Jerome from her mind. Only Rand, in his tender concern for her, kept her sane.

The journal continued until the last entry.

FEBRUARY *28, 1825.*

I cannot believe what I've discovered. Who was the betrayer? Rand. May God forgive me for what I've done. I lost faith in you, Jerome. My beloved Jerome, please forgive me. I don't know how to protect our child. I still cannot believe what I found in Rand's letter. I put it back, as I'm fearful of what he'll do to our child. He lied about you. You were set up. My dearest Jerome, I pray you're looking down and watching over him. How could I not believe in you? I didn't know the evil that lurks in this man to fabricate what he did. I found my father's letter to Rand, along with forged documents. You were not an escaped slave, and you never stole from Jean. Jerome, you never lied. You were a victim, as was I and our child, separated by the vengeance of two men. My father vowed to destroy you for taking me, and I'd never have believed him capable of such a heinous act. He schemed this whole downfall to keep us apart. Jean's stolen goods were planted, by Rand's orders. My father and Rand, how they managed to deceive Jean, I cannot fathom. My father sent Rand to seek me out, to make me his, part of my father's reprisal.

I don't know where to go. I cannot go home. Jemmie and I live on Grand Terre with Rand. He's now my husband and he'll not allow me to leave. My father's plan all along was for Rand to be my husband.

Jerome, I have betrayed you as if I pulled the trigger myself. I don't know what to do, but I'll confront him tonight when he returns. Jean's gone. I don't know when he'll return. Does he know, or was he deceived, too?

MARCIE CLOSED THE JOURNAL. EMPTINESS AND A HORRIBLE LOSS FILLED every inch of her, but she'd swear this heartache belonged to Isabel. Marcie grabbed the entire stack of letters and rifled through them.

What was her connection to all this? Deep down, she felt the wind stirring as she ripped open the remaining papers, letters. The bed was scattered with stories in chaotic chronological order of what had happened to Isabel, to Jerome. At the bottom of one letter was someone's scribbled note, *Benjamin Chamblee, check the lineage from Gabrielle, sister, mother of Rand Morison? Lost track, found granddaughter merged with the Renards relocated to Washington State in a new farm community 1912.* She didn't recognize the handwriting.

"No, it can't be. The Renards were my daddy's people," Marcie said. She couldn't make out the rest. It appeared like chicken scratch. She rummaged through the papers, journals, but Marcie could find nothing else. What she didn't understand was why Jerome came to her and guided her to these letters. What was he trying to show her?

"What are you doing?" She was so absorbed in what she read that she didn't hear Sam come in.

"Sam, come here. Look what I found." She showed the rough-penned family tree. "Do you have any idea who did this?" He squinted and then went to the wall and flicked on the overhead light. She glanced toward the open window. Night had settled in. It would be a full moon tonight.

"Could be my granddaddy's writing, I've seen it on some of the legal documents I was sent." Sam was a proud man who stood tall and broad shouldered. Right now, she wanted nothing more than to be held by him. She felt secure and protected around him, even with the hardness in his face, as he quietly read. What was he thinking? She needed to see his eyes. She watched his reaction closely when she handed him the next page, the chicken scratch and family name she knew all too well. Barely a second passed before his eyes locked on hers. *Well, well, so he knows my daddy's history, too.*

CHAPTER 25

Marcie slid the window open and popped the screen out, setting it on the floor. She slid a chair under the window and climbed through. Her feet dangled from the main floor window before she jumped, landing in the dirt, barely missing an azalea bush. She paused and listened; no movement, nothing. Thank goodness, everyone must be asleep.

For the past half hour, Marcie had listened from behind her door. Diane and Jesse had turned in a few hours ago. Sam slept on the sofa in the living room, his light shimmered under her door. When he'd finally turned off the lights, she'd waited in agony; it was the longest hour of her life. It left time to think, and that she didn't want to do, so she shut her thoughts down, instead summoning the strength and determination to focus on tonight's strategy. Time was a factor; she needed to get to as many gardens as she could, give Dan his damn weed, and get him the hell out of their lives. And Sam, she'd do everything in her power to make sure Dan didn't hurt him. *Whatever it takes, I'll protect you.*

Dressed in snug Levi's, a long-sleeve T-shirt under her dark fleece hoodie, and laced-up hiking boots, Marcie set out at a jog. The full moon provided enough light on the secluded back road. Thank God, she knew the area well. She glanced at her watch, close to midnight. She broke out in a run. Marcie still couldn't figure out how Dan knew about Diane. Maybe his connections ran deeper than she suspected. Could it be possible that he was in Lance Silver's back pocket? With Sandra involved, it was more than conceivable. She skidded a little when she rounded a bend on a downward slope and saw the outside lights blazing in front of the rural volunteer fire hall, a half-mile from Diane's, where a dark SUV was parked.

The interior light shimmered when the driver's door popped open. Maggie McCafferty, Richard's devoted wife, stepped out and walked around the rear of the SUV. Maggie was a slender, vibrant woman, with rich dark, curly hair that brushed her shoulders. She glowed with such inner beauty that Marcie had always felt warmed in her presence. She loved her husband and children fiercely; a weakness that Dan, no doubt, had used to his advantage.

Marcie's feet ached, but she didn't stop until she stood right in front of Maggie, who glowed under the fluorescent shimmering moon.

"Well, Dan was right. He'd said you'd be waiting for me here at the fire hall. Oh, Maggie, what are you doing involved in this mess?" Marcie wanted to shake her, send her home. Instead, she gathered her in a long, hard hug.

"Richard and I love you and have ever since Dan brought you into our life. You think I didn't know what you were doing with him? Come on, Marcie, I've been watching for a while, sitting by the sidelines. Richard likes to pretend Dan's side business won't affect their partnership, but his marijuana grow-ops—he's gone bigger. He's out of control. Dan made it no secret that you volunteered to help him grow." Maggie's whole body tensed as she stepped back, swiping at the dampness glistening like silver under her eyes.

"Maggie, how did Dan get you involved in this? What did he say to you?"

Maggie's lips trembled, her face a mirage of emotions. She hid nothing from those she loved. She shoved her fingers through her thick, curly hair and tilted her face up at the moon. "His back's to the wall, and he knows things about Richard that could put him in jail."

"What things?"

She shook her head. "It doesn't matter."

"It does matter."

"He said Richard burned down the house on their property."

"What? No way. Dan started it. He had the motive. Did Richard tell you he did it?"

Maggie had the most beautiful dark, toffee-colored eyes, they were glistening as another tear fell. She waved Marcie off, shutting her eyes and then opening them when hardness set her face. "Stop! You think I'm that much of a fool? Richard was furious when he found out that Dan promised that piece of shit house to Sandra just so she could have a group home for some severely disabled kids. The woman's seriously sick; neck deep in the marijuana underworld, and is using a bunch of defenseless kids to give herself a picture-perfect front."

"Look, Maggie, we were all mad, but I can assure you Richard couldn't have…"

"He has proof, Marcie." She crossed her arms over her down vest and shivered. "I'm not standing out here all night arguing with you. Get in the truck. Dan said to meet you here, and I have to deliver everything you cut to Sandra. We have less than six hours. Let's finish this. I don't know what I'm supposed to do, so you need to tell me." Even in the darkness, Maggie's eyes reached out and pleaded.

"Richard doesn't know you're here."

Maggie shook her head. "He's on the mainland at some auction. Dan made sure he'd be gone. I asked Mom to stay over and watch the kids. I told her I was going out with a friend—girls' night out. I have to be back before the sun's up."

This went against everything Marcie believed, involving someone as innocent to the drug scene as Maggie. "Sandra's house is an extension built onto Dan's shop. We need to go there first. That's where Dan stashed my dirt bike. It's my only way in. My gardens are remote, and we can't get your truck close enough. After we go to Sandra's, our first stop's in the state park. You wait for me at the end of the road, by the gravel lot. If at any time you see cops, you cut and run."

"See, that wasn't so hard. Marcie, you cut the marijuana, give it to Dan, and then you and I are going to walk away. And we'll never speak of this again." Maggie walked around her SUV with her shoulders hunched.

Marcie followed and climbed in the passenger side. "Maggie, I hope it'll be that simple...." She started to say more, to tell her that Dan was a monster, that he had a bigger plan, that there would always be something, but she slammed her mouth shut. "You're right, Maggie. This is the end."

CHAPTER 26

"Do we knock on her door?" Maggie parked in front of the darkened shop and the attached new bungalow with tree-green, Hardie Plank siding and cedar trim around the windows. It would have been a cute house, if it were anywhere else. Maggie switched off her headlights. Inside the house, lights blazed through the shuttered blinds of the front window.

"I'm not knocking. There's a key under a rock beside the shop door." Marcie jerked open her door. "I don't know about you, but I prefer to have as little contact with Sandra as possible."

By the time they reached the shop door, the outside security lights were blazing like a two-hundred-watt bulb. The industrial-strength door popped open and Sandra Carter filled the doorway. She was a short, overweight blonde with long, layered hair swept over her shoulders in the style all the divas paraded, and she dangled a wine cooler between the fingers of her right hand.

"Come on in, Marcie. Dan told me you'd be coming by." Her voice cut with a subtle arrogance as she turned her back and waddled into the crammed shop filled with tools, boxes, a pool table, workbenches, and two dirt bikes. The sliding glass door leading into the house was wide open.

"Is Dan around?"

Sandra downed her entire cooler and dumped the empty on the pool table. "No, he's far too busy. He doesn't have time to drive way out here."

Although Marcie was relieved, Sandra's deliberate poke, that Dan had no time for her, still smarted.

"Take the duffel bags and backpacks over on the workbench." Sandra pulled the door on an old yellow fridge open, grabbed another wine cooler, and twisted off the cap. She took a long swig and then pointed her finger at both dirt bikes. "Dan told me to tell you to use either one."

A moan drifted through the open door.

"Is someone here?" Maggie stood so close that her warm breath fluttered Marcie's hair. Marcie had only been to Dan's shop a few times, but each time she was amazed at all the boy toys, trophies, chain saws, and sporting equipment piled on shelves around the shop. This truly was a man's piece of heaven.

Unhurried, Sandra shuffled back into her house. Marcie and Maggie followed across the cement floor.

"Oh, James, you threw up again." Sandra showed no emotion as she thumped her wine cooler on the long cream-colored counter in the kitchen. She wore blue jeans and a plain blouse. She swayed in her walk as if each step was an effort.

She picked up a towel that was draped over a blue easy chair in the open living room. Two teens were strapped to their black wheelchairs. Each of their heads lolled. Only one could make eye contact with Marcie. Sandra wiped the vomit dripping down one boy's chin, soaking his orange shirtfront. "Look at the mess you made. Your tummy's upset. Well, let me wipe it up. It's probably time for your meds."

Revulsion and despair ached in Marcie's bones.

"What are you doing with these kids?" Maggie stepped around Marcie in the open-concept living area, with two overstuffed sofas, all open to a spacious dining area and kitchen. Behind Maggie was a short hallway with two doors. One led to a large bedroom, the other a bathroom. The walls were painted a camel brown, adorned with family photos and Mexican artwork.

Sandra didn't make eye contact. "I'm looking after them. After all, someone has to. These poor kids have no one to advocate for them. No one cares about them. The government cut funding and closed the group homes. I'm the only chance these kids have." Sandra showed no emotion as she carried a feeding tube and medication over to a dark-haired boy whose head now lolled side to side.

Marcie grabbed Maggie's wrist before she could step forward. An odd odor had her lifting her nose and sniffing. "You're making hash brownies?"

Maggie's face paled. The tawny color in her eyes pulsed as her eyes widened. Every muscle in her body was wound so tightly that Marcie thought she'd bounce away.

"They're almost done. When you're finished tonight, I'll send some home with you." Sandra tossed her long mane of hair over her shoulder. Her tiny brown eyes blinked rapidly. "Oh, damn it. I need to take out these contacts. You two better get going. You've got a lot of marijuana to cut and only a few hours to get it back here." She flicked her hand at Marcie and Maggie, shooing them past a glass table dinette, into the shop and closing the sliding door behind them.

Marcie kicked pieces of scrap wood on the cement floor and stormed to the workbench, grabbing duffle bags and backpacks. "Maggie, take these."

"Are you kidding me? Marcie, we can't leave those kids here with her."

Marcie swallowed the bile burning her chest. She grabbed Maggie by both arms. "Take the bags and get in the truck." She pushed Maggie out of the open door and tossed everything in the back of the truck. Marcie leaned close and whispered to Maggie, "I'll phone in a tip to the state police when we're done tonight. If I call now, they won't do anything. She has a contract. She has resources, and our backs are against the wall."

"Marcie, I never thought I'd see the day you'd turn your back on some special needs kids, and the most vulnerable, at that. To leave those kids is a heinous…"

Marcie spun around and cut her off. "Keep your voice down. You and I are both trying to protect someone we love. If you go in there and stir up trouble, it'll be you and me that ends up in jail, and those kids will end up staying with Sandra. She'll look like a hero." Marcie lowered her voice to a mere whisper. "If the sheriff catches her with all the marijuana while looking after those kids, it becomes a different picture."

Maggie slammed the tailgate closed and let out a heavy sigh. "Sorry, Marcie. I didn't mean to accuse you of not caring."

"Get in the truck. I'll be right behind you." *Shake it off, get your bike, and get the hell out of here.*

Maggie started the truck. Marcie lifted the garage door, grabbed a helmet, packed the last backpack with a flashlight and clippers, and then pushed her bike out and fired it up. She didn't look back. She didn't close the door, aware that Sandra watched her every move.

CHAPTER 27

She pushed hard, channelling all of the fear nibbling at her spine into each careful step. The magnificent forest soothed and replenished every tense, out-of-sort, thought that had dogged Marcie during the day.

Except tonight, something creepy whispered within these deep shadows, bringing the illusion that danger lurked and would pounce at any moment. *This doesn't feel right.* Marcie hesitated and struggled to keep her breathing even.

A full moon tonight added to the mystery, which cast an altered reality from the light of day. She shone her flashlight over the dirt path, but shadows lurked in the ground cover, salal, bushes and cedars; all of nature's power awakened and adding to this eerie chill.

Marcie drew a picture in her mind of where she was. The forked path was after the twin cedars and before the brambles opening up into the first garden she'd planted for him.

Not long ago, she'd rejoiced at being a major part of Dan's life and had put all her love into growing these plants for him. However, that was before she had been smacked upside the back of the head. That awakening made her face the truth of her role in this drug-related insanity. Now forgiveness for what she'd done was all she wanted—and to protect Sam.

Left with no other alternative, she pushed on to finish what Dan didn't have the balls to do. It was what he did. Women did his dirty work all the time, except this time, his charm and charisma wouldn't work. She began to see him as the monster he truly was. Had he really planted those drugs on Sam? Whether he did or not, his threat worked.

Something's wrong. Again, the nagging voice prodded. She swept her flashlight beam over the fork in the path to a clump of overgrown blackberry bushes, which beat any security system around. Who'd be stupid enough to climb through it?

And there it was, God dammit, Old Rock. She and Dan had chiseled their initials into the front of the huge stone on the first day he'd brought her out here to teach her the art of outdoor cultivation. Amazing how time shifted. Once proud of her exhibit; now she only prayed it'd disappear.

Behind the big rock, vines lifted, exposing a tiny opening that someone small could crawl through. Sliding on her stomach, Marcie shimmied through dirt and damp ground cover, pushing with the toe of her hiking boot. Halfway under, her backpack snagged on barbed thorns, and a sharp rip split the unnerving silence. Marcie swallowed hard, unable to stifle the terror rocking her insides. What made it worse was that she couldn't shake a dreaded feeling of being watched. She pushed hard with her foot to scramble forward, but it was no use. She was stuck.

"For fuck's sake, I need to be done with him." Marcie whispered the desperate words and rested her forehead in the dirt. She slid back under the vine to where she'd started and squatted behind the rock. The extra time this took spiked up her already frazzled nerves, and that made her paranoid. *Stop it. Maggie's waiting.* She pulled her arms from the thick straps, dropping the backpack. She'd trained for this. She knew what to do. Why was this so hard now? She wanted to cry but refused to give in.

Keep it together. Trapped by a predator who knew what emotional strings to pull, she had no time to wallow. Ready now, she tried again, this time shoving the nylon backpack on the ground in front of her.

"Ouch, shit." A jagged piece of rock dug deep in her knee. She breathed in and out to shake off the sting, forcing herself to keep going to the other side.

On her hands and knees now, Marcie remained motionless in the clearing. Something wasn't quite right, so she clicked off her light, allowing her eyes to adjust to the dark. She could see nothing, but her unease persisted. It was probably just Dan and his threat to Sam. *Stupid, stupid!* Had nothing her granny and Sally taught her sunk in?

Time was not her friend. The cops, the military—they all knew this was the time of year outdoor crops were ready. Helicopters swept overhead throughout the day, searching isolated areas to seize all marijuana crops. She'd soon find out if hers were gone.

"Okay, okay, just do it." This self-talk was a problem tonight. She bit her lip to refocus and snapped on the small flashlight, shining it upon the dead alder and the ring around the base of this once hearty tree, exposing its bitter death. She stood up and tossed her pack over her shoulder, sweeping the light in a wide arc over her mature, budded field. She dropped the backpack, unzipped the pouch, and pulled out a pair of worn handheld garden clippers.

Tucking her flashlight under her chin, she dangled the strap over her left arm and approached the first plant. She snipped the bud, shutting out the little voice in her head and using the tension to drive her as she cut each mature, leafy bud, dropping them one by one into the plastic-lined backpack.

Her mishmash alignment of five-foot-high plants was imbedded in her memory. *Hurry up. Keep your eyes open and listen.* The whispered warning drummed inside her stomach. Louder and louder, her heart hammered, leaving her deaf to the hiss of the night. She was breathing too fast. She forced herself to take even breaths. *Calm down.* If she was caught, the repercussions would destroy a lot people she loved, and she wouldn't allow that to happen.

She reached the last plant, cut, and then tucked the clippers in a side pocket and zipped up her backpack. One final check, she shone her light over the garden just to make sure she didn't miss any. *Okay, girl, make tracks.*

Kicking through the underbrush, she froze. Her throat squeezed shut, threatening to cut off her breathing. Disoriented, she stared at the wild rose bush draping itself over a mature marijuana plant. Her mind scrambled. *Think, think. Did I trim it first, or is it a warning?*

Her stomach clenched when her memory cleared. Another step closer to the compromised plant, and there was the bud, ripped off and deliberately stuck through the top leaf. She jerked her head around; consumed now with a rising panic to flee from this warning of someone's calling card. *Gotcha!* The stories Dan told of what growers often did in the marijuana show to tip people off were imbedded in her brain. Her secret spot, deep in the woods, had been found.

Fight or flight bowled her over like a hurricane tide. She looked right, then left. *Get out now! Run! Someone's watching, waiting. You've been set up.*

Pure terror had Marcie grabbing the backpack and dropping down, scurrying on her stomach under the vine and into darkness, allowing her ears and sense of touch to guide her. Thorny bushes snagged and pulled, even a sharp sting didn't register as a need to stop. Instead, pain fueled her desire to escape. Good or bad, whoever was here and had discovered the crop didn't matter.

Be quiet. The warning had her crouching behind the rock, trembling. Keeping a frantic grip on the darkened flashlight, Marcie willed her eyes to adjust to the night. She needed to find the path and get the hell out of here.

Panic urged her to ditch her backpack and move, but an image of Sam popped in her head, along with Dan laughing in the background. "Oh, Sam," she whispered. A tear leaked out and dripped down her cool cheek. She knew what she had to do, so she closed her eyes, gave herself a good dressing down, and listened to the sounds of night. Time was running out. *Come on, suck it up. You can do this. Use those gifts God gave you. Ground yourself. Listen and feel for someone.*

Marcie rose on legs that, for a second, trembled. Then she quietly slung the backpack over her shoulder, and, for one ridiculous moment, said farewell to what was left—the leaf to be cooked down into resin; not where the money was, and definitely not worth the work. Let Dan send someone else. She had the prize—pure, unadulterated and organic, worth its weight in gold.

A brisk wind rustled the tree branches. She fought an overwhelming urge to bolt down the darkened path but slugged on through this gigantic mistake, carrying this vile bag—her albatross. Not long ago with Dan, she'd delighted in the cover of darkness; except now she knew it was nothing but a bridge to lies, deceit, and everything wicked. *This walk on the dark side, tainted with ample opportunity to toy on the wrong side of the road, and you know that in the light of day it remains too hushed, too dangerous to expose. Do you get it now?* Oh, she definitely did.

She'd stashed her dirt bike in the thick brush lining the old logging road where it waited around the next winding bend. Walking faster through the thick forest, she passed the Scottish pine surrounded by ferns. *You're almost there.* Marcie agonized, suppressing a driving desire to sprint the rest of the way. She stopped, looked over her shoulder, then pulled out the bike from its hiding spot.

Panic closed in when she straddled the machine and quickly fired the engine. With her knapsack looped over both shoulders, she let the clutch out. The motor revved and slashed through the silence. She raced down the path. A quick gear change, and then she cut right onto another trail, which led back to the old highway. She could see safety now, even headlights from an approaching car. The ache lessened, and the eerie pull on her back lifted. But until she finished every garden she had planted, none of them were safe.

CHAPTER 28

Still spooked, she tossed Maggie the pack. Who was watching them? Was it Dan, his friends, or someone else? She killed the idle on her dirt bike. "You see anyone?"

Maggie froze while packing the bag in the back of the SUV. She whipped her head around, searching behind her in the darkness. "What's going on? You think someone's watching us?" She stepped closer, lowering her voice. "Marcie, do you?"

Marcie closed her eyes. Now she was freaking Maggie out. "I don't know, Maggie. I'm a little off tonight. Just be careful, and don't take any chances. You've got the kids to think of. You cut and run if you think anyone's watching."

"Stop it, Marcie. I'm not leaving you out here alone. Look, we don't have much time. Let's just finish this. Where to next? Marcie, come on!"

Marcie knew she was right. Still, she couldn't shake the feeling of cold terror, of something completely off. "I've got ten up by the bridge."

"I wish I could help you more, but I don't know how to cut it."

"You shouldn't even be here!"

Maggie pressed her palm over Marcie's mouth. "Stop it—no more.

We have four hours left, and if it's all the same to you, I'd rather not stand here rehashing everything over and over." Under the moonlight, diamond-studded earrings glistened in Maggie's ears when she swept her hair back.

"Maggie, your earrings, take them out."

"Richard gave me these. I…"

Marcie gripped her wrist. "Just take them out. We can't be seen with what we've got." She pointed to the moon. "They reflect the moonlight quite nicely. Good for romance, not for this."

Maggie did what she asked and then pulled out the local map and a pen from her pocket. "Show me where to go next."

Marcie traced a line and marked off the service road. "Let's go. That road's isolated, but make sure you kill your lights before you get to the end. Be careful." She pulled her helmet on, attached several bags to the back of her bike, and took a shortcut up a trail often used by horses, ATVs, and other bikers in the area.

After Marcie finished at the bridge, Maggie took the first load back to Sandra's. Marcie knew Dan wouldn't be around, although he'd check in from a safe distance. He was smart in a cowardly kind of way. He used women, targeting smart, dysfunctional, educated women, letting them do the work, take the risks and the fall.

Exhausted, Marcie was filled with malice toward a man she'd given everything to. *Well, not everything.* Worry raced through her mind as she wondered what kind of trouble Maggie would run into at Sandra's place. Marcie never knew which one of Sandra's lowlife friends would be hanging around at this time of night. She prayed Maggie could dump the load quickly, leave, and be waiting for her by the time she finished this run.

Gripping the handlebars, Marcie couldn't remember ever having been so tired. Her mind drifted, wanting nothing more than to curl up in her soft bed, and that was when she lost her focus. A downed log appeared out of nowhere. Time stood still, as did any awareness of hitting the log, flying through the air, and landing on the ground so hard she rolled.

She was numb at first, until each of her senses popped back, one by one, completely out of sync. Her dirt bike idled in the distance. A chirping choir of frogs sounded so close she wondered if they were stalking her. On her back, she gazed at the bright moon. A rock stabbed her lower back, and it screamed for relief. Marcie tried to sit up, but a sharp, blinding pain shot upward through her left side. Her right leg burned as if a red hot poker had been jammed into it. Pure agony stole her breath, so she lay back down. If she kept her breathing short and shallow, it wasn't as bad. Marcie needed to finish, and it was Sam's face that flashed in front of her, giving her the strength to try again. She rolled to her side and screamed as hellfire shot up her right leg, but she kept going until she leaned all her weight on her left knee. Something wet dribbled down her left arm. In the moonlight, she could see her ripped sleeve and blood coating her skin. She couldn't tell where else she was hurt. Her head was so heavy. She yanked off her helmet, letting it fall away. Her bike, where was her bike? She lifted her head and listened to the engine sputter and cough, and then nothing but silence.

Marcie could see her bike outlined in the darkness and tried to crawl on one knee, but the forest began to sway. She locked her arms when dizziness stole her vision, trying desperately not to fall. Her stomach heaved, and she vomited before tipping off balance, hitting the ground with her face. Then, one by one, her muscles gave out. She closed her eyes for a minute to stop the spinning, but the battle was lost when everything went black.

CHAPTER 29

Sam jammed the accelerator, swerving past a few early-morning drivers on Highway 101. "Sam, slow down before you kill someone." Diane gripped the handle above the door.

Jesse grabbed the seat behind Sam's head. "Christ, Sam, slow down."

"I fell asleep on the damn couch so I could give her some space and she snuck out through the fucking window! Why! Why would she do it?"

"You're not the only one who feels sucker punched, Sam." Diane flicked on the police scanner.

"When I find her, I'm going to lock her up." Sam pounded the steering wheel with the flat of his hand so hard the black wheel dipped.

"Sam, we don't know why she left. So let's find out the story first before you do something that can't be undone," Diane snapped.

"She's in trouble, someone got to her," Jesse said,

Diane jerked around in her seat and eyeballed him. In the rearview mirror, Sam saw something in his friend that kicked all the air out of his stomach.

"You guys miss what happened yesterday when you saw that lost, vacant girl wandering barefoot through a thorny bush? She was shaking. She could barely hold it together. I knew something was up, but I didn't expect this. I thought after a good night's sleep, she'd open up in the morning."

"And you're just remembering to say this now?"

A siren wailed, blared its horn. Sam could see an ambulance behind him in the rearview mirror. Swearing, he was forced to slow down and pull over. The ambulance blew past.

"Guys, I got an awful feeling. You don't think…?"

Jesse slapped Sam's shoulder. "You mean do we think you're being paranoid? Follow them."

Diane sliced her hand through the air when she cranked up the volume on the police scanner. "Quiet so I can listen and find out what's going on."

Sam followed at a close pace to the flashing ambulance. Despite his anger at Marcie's betrayal, he needed to know that she was safe. He knew something was wrong. Jesse was right. She'd been terrified. But what could have happened in the half hour they'd left her alone?

"It's an injured biker off the trail." She pointed ahead to where the ambulance turned onto a forested side road close to the falls.

Sam intended to turn around, keep looking for Marcie, when a woman standing behind a black SUV ran out and frantically waved at the ambulance. She looked like a soccer mom, completely out of place, wearing black jeans, with her dark, wavy curls swishing against a black hoodie and down vest—the perfect attire for blending into the night—just as the sun cleared the horizon.

Diane leaned forward, closer to the windshield. "Sam, pull up. Let's check it out."

"Yeah." He pressed the accelerator and cranked the wheel until he pulled alongside the ambulance. Dust and gravel flew as he slammed on the brakes. Diane flashed her badge as they all approached the paramedics. The agitated soccer mom stumbled back, her face flushed, before she hurried the paramedics, with their gear, down a narrow trail in the forest.

Diane, Sam, and Jesse followed behind and said nothing, listening to the information the woman rambled off. After a short hike in, Sam saw a dirt bike, with its front wheel bent, lying tangled in a blackberry brush. And he saw the still form of his woman, stretched out, scraped and bleeding, with her right ankle bent at an awkward angle.

Something erupted inside of him. He must have roared, as he bolted past the paramedics and skidded down beside Marcie. Someone grabbed him. He didn't think. He just swung his fist. The next thing he knew, he had been tackled from behind and pinned face down in the dirt, Jesse on top of him.

"Calm down now. Let the paramedics help her."

"Get off me, Jesse. I need to get to her." His arm twisted up higher behind him.

"Are you going to hit me again?" Jesse asked.

His adrenaline still pumped, but his head was now clearer. Where had that angry beast come from? "No, I didn't mean to hit you. Let me up. I need to see how she is."

When Jesse stood, Sam rolled over. Two average white male paramedics hovered over Marcie. Her eyes fluttered, and she screamed and then cried when they attempted to mobilize and place a splint on her lower right leg. Sam yelled again. He hurt for her and needed to stop her pain.

"You control him, or I'm calling in the sheriff." The older, balding paramedic shot a wary glance at Diane and braced himself in case Sam broke out of Jesse's hold.

Diane grabbed Sam's shirtfront and dragged him, with Jesse's help, over to where the frantic dark-haired woman stood a few paces away.

He breathed as if he'd raced up the side of a mountain.

"Pull it together, Sam!" Diane yelled. Then she brushed past him to where the paramedics had strapped an unconscious Marcie onto the portable gurney along with all the supplies they'd hefted in. Sam couldn't hear what Diane said as he lit into the wide-eyed soccer mom who stood her ground in front of him.

"Who the hell are you? What did you do to her?" He wanted to shake the lady as he hovered over her, leaning his weight toward her like a freight train.

She stayed in control, meeting his gaze nose to nose. The brave woman replied, "I'm a friend of Marcie's. My name's Maggie." And then she clammed up, refusing to answer why she was there and what she and Marcie had been doing.

Sam insisted on carrying one end of the gurney so he could watch over Marcie. Her big eyes fluttered open, tinted with agony, and that ripped open the festered scab in his heart that had just begun to heal. Jesse helped the paramedic carry the front of the gurney. Diane, Maggie, and the dark-haired paramedic led the way, lugging the medical supplies.

"Lift her up; keep her level." The back door popped open, and the lift was strapped to the stretcher. The IV bag hooked up in the field was hung on a hook inside of the ambulance beside the older paramedic as he shoved on a pair of glasses. Sam climbed in.

"I'm going with her."

"Diane and I'll follow." Jesse closed the doors and banged the side. "All secure; get going now," Jesse shouted.

Sam couldn't think or make sense of how this woman twisted up his guts. He rested his hand on her forehead and then skimmed around the cuts and scrapes on her cheek, and the reopened gash on her head. This time, there was sure to be a scar.

The paramedic roughly cleared his throat.

Sam looked up into a flash of anger.

"Just stay out of the way," the paramedic said.

"Look, I'm sorry, but she scared the hell out of me, I didn't mean to…"

"You didn't mean to threaten that you would see to it that the only job I could get was delivering newspapers if I hurt her? You mean that one?"

A wave of guilt crushed Sam's pride. His faced warmed. "Yeah, sorry, I didn't know what I was saying."

The paramedic adjusted Marcie's IV and checked her blood pressure. He answered with a sharp glare. That made the ride to Jefferson Memorial Hospital in Port Townsend unbearably long.

Marcie was in and out from the pain, but she came around near Discovery Bay. She looked straight at Sam with tears glistening, turning the soft blue in her eyes translucent. Her lip trembled. The killer was that what she said next threw him for a loop. "I love you. That's why I did it."

"Not here, okay?" Then he just held her hand, even with the scrapes and nicks. He just held on while she cried.

Diane, Jesse, and Maggie caught up with Sam when the stretcher was wheeled into the emergency room. The tall, broad-shouldered, militant ER nurse turned all of them around and directed them to the waiting room, where they were told to sit and wait until the doctor had a chance to examine Marcie.

Sam tried to push past the head nurse, a tall, solid, older woman who reminded him of a German nanny.

"You go park your butt in the waiting room with your friends now and control yourself. If you cause any disruption, and I don't care if you're the king of England, I'll have security toss you out."

Jesse grabbed Sam's shoulder, placing himself between Sam and the nurse. "He'll do just that, ma'am. Sorry, but he's darn worried about his girl, is all."

"Humph" was all she said before crossing her arms and striding behind the wide emergency room desk.

Jesse physically turned Sam and pushed. "Move it and go sit down, or I'll help security toss you out."

Diane and Maggie sat against the far wall. Side by side, each claimed an orange plastic chair. Thankfully, the small waiting room was virtually empty. Jesse and Sam faced the women. Sam made no attempt to be discreet in the way he studied Maggie. She was a small, curvy woman with a round face, dark, curly hair, and large tawny eyes sparkling with vulnerability. Overtop, she wore a mask filled with a determined strength; a woman who wouldn't give up. She then turned to Diane in the way people do when needing support. Sam realized then what really bothered him. This woman and Diane appeared comfortable together.

"Odd man out, am I?"

"What're you rambling on about?" Diane said.

He jabbed his index finger straight at Maggie. "You two, you develop some kind of chick bond? Or what is this?"

"Jesus, Sam, you can be an ass sometimes." Diane leaned forward, clasping her hands between her knees.

Maggie sat erect and unmoving. It was weird; even the furnishings appeared to vibrate with the same electricity that was pumping through Maggie. Her hostile stare met his head on, declaring that she was prepared to kick his ass.

"Maggie is Richard's wife. You know Richard—Dan's partner." Diane turned toward Maggie. "You two haven't formally met, but you already know this is Sam."

Maggie leaned forward and crossed her arms over her stomach. "If I didn't know you cared for Marcie, I wouldn't hesitate to tell you what a prick I think you are. But I'm going to let it go for now and chalk it up to stress and the worry of seeing someone who means so much to you lying there hurt." When Sam tried to interrupt, she held up her flat, authoritative hand with a fiery punch. "I'm not done. Maybe you should pull your head out of your ass long enough to see that you don't hold the corner on caring for Marcie. She was out there for me, for you, and for Richard. She cares more for…"

"Maggie, stop. Don't say any more. Both of you, keep your voice down. This is not the place." Diane turned her head to the nurse's station. "We have an audience."

Jesse smacked Sam on the back of his head. "Cool it, hoss. Maybe we should take a walk."

"No, I'm not going anywhere." He must have spoken too loud, because Brigitta, his nickname for the head nurse who itched to toss him out, coughed and narrowed her eyes.

"Both of you," Diane kept her sharp, silky voice just above a whisper and leveled all the fingers of her right hand first at Sam and then Maggie, "I'm going to do the talking."

"What did she mean by that crack about Marcie being out there for me?" Sam realized he was pissing Diane off, and he slid one seat away from Jesse so his hand couldn't smack him again. Diane became quiet when she was mad, and he could feel warning vibes now.

Looking a little worse for wear, Diane's cop cut stuck up in clumps after she ran her fingers through the short, thick strands. Still wearing her black windbreaker and jeans, she got up from the dingy plastic chair and stalked to the seat beside Sam and sat, sliding around to face him. "I realize you're upset." Her face, her eyebrows were a mass of control when she spoke in a clear whisper. "There's more going on than you know, and I asked you to cool it. We'll talk outside, because one thing I believe is that the walls have ears. Keep in mind that the people involved are around. So for everyone's sake, including our safety, shut up. Don't speak, don't interrogate her. We'll talk later, when we're out of here." She stood while continuing to speak to Sam and moved straight to the young, thin intern, wearing blue scrubs, who approached fast.

"Is there a Maggie here?" The young woman, who looked barely older than eighteen, cleared her throat and spoke in a crisp, matter-of-fact way; as if she had no time to waste.

"That's me." Maggie stepped around Diane.

"Marcie's awake and asking for you."

"Whoa, Doc, just a sec. How is she?" Sam pushed his way in front of Maggie, facing the baby-faced intern.

"She has a right tibia plafond fracture—a broken ankle. There appears to be no soft tissue damage, so it's set with a splint. Are you related to Marcie?" Her voice sounded more like a sixteen-year-old's.

He didn't know how to answer. He was furious. How could she not ask for him? "You can say I'm her significant other, the one who's trying to keep her from doing anything stupid. Listen, Doc, she had a concussion over a week ago. Did you run any tests, or scans, for a head injury?"

She cocked her head, swinging her blond ponytail over her shoulder. "We've already taken care of it, and we're waiting on the results now."

"Can we all see Marcie?" Maggie spoke with urgency. "Please?"

The intern carefully looked at the group of four. "Just for a few minutes. We need to get her admitted and moved to a room after the neurologist examines her."

Jesse hovered behind Maggie. Sam didn't know how, but, between Maggie and Jesse, they were ushered past the nurse's station.

What he saw when he walked in was not a woman of deceit and lies. This was someone who had been hurt deeply. Her lip quivered as she struggled to hold it together. Draped in a blue hospital gown and covered with a thin cotton blanket, she appeared vulnerable on the narrow bed. The right side of Marcie's face resembled an artist's palate; all scraped and smudged. The gash on her head had been re-taped and was swollen and an ugly purple. Her cast was not plaster but the newfangled walking splint. Sam's hand shook when he hesitantly fingered the strands of hair that slid over her forehead. Tears filled her eyes.

"Oh, Marcie, what have you done to yourself?" Maggie moved around to the other side of the bed and rubbed her arm. They exchanged a sisterly protective look, one Sam knew all too well. They watched each other's back.

"I'm sorry, Maggie."

"For what?" she snapped.

"I didn't finish."

Maggie leaned down and hugged her, and Marcie groaned. Maggie pulled back. "Where does it hurt?"

"My shoulder, my side. I hurt all over."

Sam wanted to shake her, to hug her, to yell at her. But more than anything, he willed her pain to stop. "Did they give you something for the pain?"

She merely shook her head. "No."

"I'll get you something," Maggie said.

Marcie reached out and grabbed Maggie's wrist. "I don't want to take any drugs. I need to keep my head clear."

Sam caressed her cheek. "Taking something for the pain isn't going to kill you, but it will take the edge off."

Jesse stepped forward and squeezed the silver bedrail. "Marcie, take something."

She looked at Jesse and her whole face quivered. A tear fell before she nodded. "Okay."

Jesse slapped Sam's back. "I'll go find the doc."

A nurse followed shortly with some pain medication, which Marcie reluctantly took. She closed her eyes for a minute and sobbed. Sam passed her a Kleenex, and she wiped her plugged nose.

She had failed to complete the job. That was all she could think about other than the fact that her leg throbbed like nothing she could remember. Diane stood at the foot of the bed. She had dark, puffy circles under her eyes, and she said nothing.

"I told Jesse and Diane everything, Marcie," Maggie said. "We're in over our heads."

Diane's stance never faltered. Her lips thinned as she inclined her head. "You should have told me, Marcie." Diane spoke with such quiet control.

"How much trouble am I in?"

"First, I need to find out how soon we can get you out of here."

As if on cue, the intern, followed by the neurologist, strode in. Surprisingly, Sam, Diane, Jesse, and Maggie were allowed to stay. Maybe it was because of the respectful way they moved back and stood quietly out of the way.

The neurologist spoke briefly to Marcie, pulled a penlight from the pocket of his white doctor's coat, and checked her pupils. Then he tapped a spot on her elbow and uninjured knee. The results from a rushed head CT were evidently in the metal chart the intern clutched against her chest. The neurologist reached for the chart and flipped it open. "Your CT's negative, no trauma or concussion."

The dark-haired neurologist pushed his gold-rimmed glasses up when they slid down his nose. He leaned over the silver bedrail, questioned Marcie about her choice of a recreational vehicle, and advised her to stay off the bike. When he asked for details of what had happened, she recounted a censored version with clarity while maintaining eye contact with Maggie, Diane, Sam, Jesse, and then the doctor.

"When can she be released?" Diane asked as she stepped beside the short and boxy, middle-aged neurologist.

"I want to keep her overnight for observation; so tomorrow at the earliest."

Marcie blew out a heavy sigh and pressed her head into the pillow. She wanted out, but the throbbing in her leg was enough of a catalyst for her to agree for now.

"I know what you're thinking, but as soon as you're settled in a room, we're talking," Sam said as he lowered his face a mere inch from hers. "Okay, Doc, how soon can we get her moved?"

CHAPTER 30

Diane used her resources with the Port Townsend sheriff's detachment to secure a private room for Marcie. Within an hour, Marcie was moved to a small, bright room on the fourth floor with a large window overlooking the parking lot. Marcie pressed an electric button on the side rail to elevate her head. The kind, motherly floor nurse raised her foot, which thankfully relieved pressure from the miserable ache in her leg.

Marcie wished for a few moments alone with Maggie to find out what she had said. For some reason, her instincts were stuck behind a foggy wall, which was most likely from the drugs.

Maggie, Sam, Diane, and Jesse lingered in the background until the nurse left. She sighed; her brief reprieve was gone. The door had barely closed when it popped back open, this time filled with a tall, dark-haired Richard, whose wild icy blue eyes fired at Maggie. He absorbed everything and everyone in the room with such razor-sharp control that any hope for a quiet, peaceful resolution was extinguished. The heavy, dark stubble and unusually messy, short-cropped hair had changed his hard, handsome, rustic looks to those of a man out of control. He grabbed Maggie's arm, hauling her fast and hard into his arms and holding tight. His lips pulled back as his jaw tightened. A man fiercely protective of his family, he looked as if he wanted to punch someone in the room and didn't much care who. Then he closed his eyes and rested his chin on top of Maggie's head; his chest heaving as if he'd run the entire way there.

"What the fuck were you two doing?" Then he held Maggie away from him, like a recalcitrant child, far enough to look straight down into her eyes. "Where are the kids?"

Until now, Maggie had appeared so strong and unbreakable. Marcie hadn't realized how much Richard was her rock. That force of knowledge hit Marcie square in the gut. She watched something crumble inside Maggie. Her face scrunched and her lips trembled in a losing battle.

"My mom—she's at the house."

Sam moved closer to Marcie. "There are a whole lot of secrets going on here, Richard. I'm Sam. That's Diane at the foot of the bed, Jesse behind you, and you know Marcie, of course. But let's start with what Marcie and Maggie were up to last night, shall we?" The air in the room froze.

"Sam, Diane, Jesse, exactly who are you, and why are you here?" Richard asked.

"Now that's a fair question. I'm with the DEA, with kind of a weird twist in this. You see, Marcie here landed in my path in New Orleans, and, ever since, I've been trying to get her out of whatever hole she's dug herself into, but she's making it damn near impossible. Now Jesse's with the NOPD, my former partner and friend, and Diane is my friend and current partner with the task force. Both are trying to help. We seem to be in an unusual situation here."

It didn't take a genius to see Richard shut down as if clamping an iron wall around him.

"Sam, there's a lot you don't know," Jesse said as he wandered into the center of the small, bright room.

"What?"

"Dan stashed the drugs in your locker."

"What?" Sam's face paled.

Jesse moved to the foot of the bed so he could eyeball Marcie. "Remember the mess we found this girl in yesterday? Scared. Freaked out. Remember what you said, Marcie? 'You ever have to do something, and it's the only way to protect the one you love?'"

Marcie scrunched her eyes, turning her face away.

Jesse walked around Diane to the other side of the bed, forcing Marcie to look at him. "Apparently, Dan McKenzie was hiding in the cottage. Remember Marcie's off feeling? Someone was in her house. Well, he was there, and he caught her alone, after her shower, when we were hiking around the property."

"For fuck's sake, Marcie, why the hell didn't you tell me?" Sam hovered, bracing a hand into her pillow on each side of her face.

She couldn't hide from him. "Because he said if I didn't go to every garden I'd planted, and get him his marijuana, he'd make sure that this time, so much evidence, of some unspeakable crime, would be planted on you that even your boss would be convinced you worked for Lance Silver. You'd not only lose your job but your freedom."

"You believed him? Come on, Marcie."

She touched Sam's arm. "No, Sam, I told him to get lost, that I wouldn't help him. That was when he told me intimate details of what was found in your locker, where, when, and how. Only someone who masterminded the setup could know those details. Am I right?"

Sam pulled away.

"Richard, I'm sorry." Maggie spoke quickly. Her voice rose to an anxious pitch while she paced in front of the man she loved. "Dan came to see me yesterday. He said you'd be away on business, and he was right. I never asked you about your business before you left."

"What the hell does that have to do with what you were doing last night?"

As gifted as Sam was at concealing emotions, he had nothing on Richard.

This time, Richard shut his eyes as if remembering something. When he opened them, his jaw hardened, and his voice held a hint of steel. "I was at an auction in Seattle that Dan arranged. For some reason, at the last minute, he couldn't go. Supposedly, equipment from a bankrupt contractor was featured. I didn't buy anything. What we needed wasn't there. Then he messaged me to meet with an investor, but he never showed. I missed the last ferry, so I drove around the peninsula. When I couldn't keep my eyes open, I stopped around two in the morning at a rest area to sleep for a few hours. Son of a bitch."

"Richard, he has proof that you started the fire and burned the house down." Maggie touched Richard's sleeve.

Richard just looked at her. He didn't blink. "What the hell are you talking about? I didn't burn any house down."

Diane dropped down into a typical padded hospital chair that had been shoved in the corner. "Richard, an anonymous tip was called in to Crime Stoppers a while ago. You were there at the fire, and a good arson investigator can recreate a fire from the ashes. There's enough evidence from the burn patterns to prove that it was electrical, and there's evidence the wiring was tampered with. Also, marijuana residue was discovered in the basement. From what was left of the house, they were able to determine that there had been no forced entry. They suspect whoever set the fire had access to the house, and, let's add a piece of information the investigators didn't know, motive. There was the state contract for a group home and the fact that the house needed extensive renovations." Diane, as usual, was blunt and to the point.

Maggie reached up pale, slender fingers to touch Richard's darkened cheek. "Dan said there's an eye witness who puts you coming out of the house at almost the same time the fire broke out."

"And you believed him?" He shook her off. "You think I'd do that? Answer me. You believed I'd burn down some, piece of shit, run-down house for what? Insurance money, renovations? What, are you crazy?"

"No. I didn't believe him at first, but he brought the witness with him."

CHAPTER 31

Two nurses from the floor arrived within moments of Richard's explosive outburst.

"What's going on in here?" one of the nurses demanded.

Diane stepped forward and flashed her badge. "I'm so sorry. Richard was so upset to see how badly his friend's hurt and to hear how she was injured. He panicked and imagined the worst. She could've been killed, and it got the better of him, but I can assure you, as an officer, that there'll be no more noise."

One of the nurses remained by the open door. She waved someone away. "It's okay, George. Go back to your room."

The other short, plump nurse faced Diane, pursing her thin lips. "I think it's best if everyone leaves. The patient needs rest, and I won't tolerate any further commotion."

Diane didn't move but softened her shoulders and her voice. "You're absolutely right. The hospital is a place of peace. I promise you there'll only be calm words spoken, and we'll be leaving soon. Would it be all right if we take a few moments to say goodbye and make arrangements for Marcie's care before she's released tomorrow?"

Both nurses appeared satisfied when they glanced at each other.

One shrugged. The large one with the short, permed hair responded, "Just make it quick," and then they left.

"Diane, you're a born diplomat. Your negotiating skills could be put to good use with hostage negotiation. Ever thought of transferring?" Jesse leaned against the wide window ledge.

Marcie's heart raced. Why hadn't Maggie told her that Dan had brought someone with him? A sick rumble pummeled her already shaken insides. She searched Sam out, wanting to ask. He leaned closer, snaking his arm around her pillow. Their eyes met, and his odd expression kept her from asking.

"Richard, you need to take Maggie home," Marcie said. She couldn't get a read on the situation. Her foggy brain jammed all her senses, and she was worried about what Dan might do to Sam. She needed time and quiet to digest all she'd heard.

"She's right, Sam. Let's go. We'll pick this up later." Diane slipped around the bed, brushing past Jesse. She gazed thoughtfully down on Marcie and laid a calm hand on her shoulder. "We'll go. Get some rest. We'll be back to get you."

"Thanks."

For the first time since Marcie had met Jesse, he picked up her hand, lifted it to his mouth, and kissed it.

She fought the tears. "Thank you, Jesse."

"Thanks for caring enough for Sam that you'd risk doing something absolutely stupid. If there's ever a next time, Marcie, talk to me first."

She nodded as a smile wavered in among her crying jag.

Sam didn't move. "I'm staying."

Warmth poured into Marcie's center. Regardless of why he wanted to stay, he was here.

Diane tossed her keys to Sam, which he caught midair. "We'll catch a ride with Maggie and Richard. Call me."

Richard wrapped his arm around Maggie and pulled her with him to the foot of the hospital bed.

"Oh, Marcie, I'm sorry, honey." Tears pooled in Maggie's wide eyes as she swallowed. There was a whole lot they both needed to say, but when Marcie looked up at Richard, who stood stone still, there was something else passed down to her—rage. They turned and left.

"Marcie." Sam touched her forehead.

"Hmm?"

He said nothing for a few seconds. "Never mind. Get some sleep. I'll be right back."

She wondered what he wanted to say, but she was so tired. She closed her eyes when the room emptied, breathing deep, past the ache in her battered body. She tried to sleep, because she knew that with a clearer head, she'd have a better chance at figuring out how to bring an end to Dan's madness.

CHAPTER 32

Sam caught up with Diane, Jesse, Maggie, and Richard in the parking lot beside Richard's dark blue, one-ton, pickup truck. "Diane, wait." He pulled her aside, behind a black BMW, just out of hearing. Jesse took Maggie's keys from Richard, making plans to follow behind in Maggie's SUV.

"You haven't told me what Maggie said. I somehow believe it has to do with those marijuana gardens Marcie was growing for Dan."

Diane placed her hand on Sam's shoulder and led him away from Richard and Maggie. "Yup, they were cutting all the marijuana. Marcie took a dirt bike in, and Maggie delivered to Sandra Carter. Maggie wants me to call the sheriff and send them to Sandra's house. She's really upset. Sandra has two special needs kids she's looking after while packaging the marijuana."

Sam ran his hand roughly over his face. "You're kidding, right?"

"No."

"What are you waiting for? Call the sheriff. Get him over there."

"No."

"Diane, what the fuck…"

She cut him off. "We call the sheriff and Dan finds out; we'll lose him and our link to Lance Silver."

Sam looked at Diane, unable to understand how she'd sacrifice the most vulnerable kids—the ones with no voice.

"Don't look at me like that," Diane said. "I'm not unfeeling. I already made a call to a friend of mine, a social worker, and asked her to find a way to get those kids pulled out of there now without tipping Sandra off." Diane placed a steady hand on Sam's arm. "Go back in and stay with Marcie. Dan could show up. I suspect he has eyes everywhere, and we don't want him getting near her again. Jesse and I are going to Maggie and Richard's. We'll talk to them without you. The way you and Richard appear to butt heads, I think he'll be more apt to open up for us."

Richard approached, shoulders hunched, fists clenched. He looked miserable, tired, and he appeared to seethe. "Diane, we're leaving now. Are you coming or staying? Decide now, or I pull out with or without you." When he spoke, he transferred his gaze from Diane to Sam in a combative challenge, the one guys do when one treads on the other's turf.

Sam shoved his hands in his pockets. He didn't move.

"I'm coming. Sam's going back in." Diane placed a gentle hand on Sam's shoulder—one preventing him from moving any closer to Richard.

Sam didn't trust Richard, no matter what Marcie said about him. He wanted one-on-one time with him. He was convinced Richard had his hand in some part of what Dan was involved in.

Diane walked away with Richard and climbed in the back of his truck. When Richard drove past, the steely warning he launched at Sam flared in the hard set of his jaw.

CHAPTER 33

All achy and banged up, Marcie slumped in a typical black wheelchair, pushed by one of the floor nurses out of the hospital. She had no idea how Sam had arranged her discharge so quickly, but when she awoke after a few hours sleep, the nurse had checked her vitals and release papers arrived.

Sam parked Diane's SUV in the loading zone at the front door. Although it was warm today, heavy clouds swept in with a slight breeze, stealing away any chance of sun; which added a further gloom to Marcie's already heavy head.

While the nurse held the wheelchair, Sam eased Marcie into the narrow backseat of Diane's SUV. She knew he tried to be careful, but when he accidentally banged her cast against the door's edge, the searing pain shot up her leg, and she swore a few curses that would have curled her granny's hair. Beads of sweat trickled down her back and into the thin, blue cotton of the borrowed, baggy, hospital scrubs, now stuck to her back.

Sam leaned over Marcie, careful not to bump her foot. His eyes were bloodshot, and he needed to shave. "You're going to bed as soon as we get back to Diane's." Then he took off his black windbreaker and draped it over her.

While Sam drove, Marcie remained lucid, hovering on a level somewhere between cotton-filled grogginess and hurried anxiety, ready to resolve this mess. She leaned against the door and closed her eyes, allowing the engine's hum and vehicle motion to lull her body past the state of a limp rag doll.

Jerome appeared to her as she remembered, with a halo of golden hair, except now she knew who he was.

They stood together in a clearing, by a pool of tranquil water, vibrant greenery from bushes and trees surrounded them.

"I found your letters."

"She never got them. Her father intervened."

"What happened to you?"

"I think you know. I survived twenty years in the Cabildo, hell on earth, and watched a monster take what was mine."

"Rand Morison, he's the one who betrayed you. But why?"

"I was in the way. Her father had plans. Rand and Isabel were his blood. Her father was pure darkness and could not exist in love."

"I found something in the attic about Sam. His father was killed. His stepfather raised him. I don't understand."

Jerome wore a white shirt that shimmered over his arm. His light touch was filled with love and hope. "Marcie, you need to look here now. We learn from the past. I needed you to understand what had happened to Sam, how he grew up. Darkness feeds down to the next generation if you allow it. You already saw, in the notes, that your heritage comes from Rand Morison. They're nothing but pirates who feed on the darkness of greed, take whatever's not theirs, by whatever means. The piracy continues, instinctively handed down. But for you it exists in Rand's great-great-grandchild, who's here in the community where you live. It's not so different, Marcie, what we stole in my time and what you illegally sell now. Boats still come, but the cargo's different. There's one on the way up now from South America, bringing cocaine, and Richard knows. It's pure evil, now the drug of choice.

"Each generation of Rand's surviving offspring has descended further into darkness. They're powerful and still evade detection. Dan's not a middle guy, Marcie. You have it all wrong. He's vying for the top. You were the target all along. It was no coincidence when you met Dan at that market after your granny died. That was arranged. Lance Silver's wanted you as a toy for years.

He sent Dan. You were his assignment. He was supposed to get your land. But Dan discovered he needed your light, too, and it became a game for him to eliminate all your goodness and fill you with his darkness as he slowly dragged you into that vile, sticky black tar of his underworld. Didn't you feel the spiritual connection? You two have been together in another life. There was a lot of pain between you in that lifetime, and you died of a broken heart."

"There's something about him I've never felt with anyone," Marcie said. "I couldn't get past this desperate need to be with him, to connect with him. I needed his love, and it felt like he dangled it like a carrot. I'd almost have it. Then he'd snatch it away again. What's wrong with me that I still want him so much? It's like I'm being pulled toward him, and I can't help myself."

"Marcie, he's powerful, and he knew how to surpass your weak aura. He connected to you, attached his cords to you. You weren't strong enough to fight him after your granny died."

"Did he ever love me?"

"This isn't about love, Marcie. Darkness holds no love. Haven't you figured that out yet? He wants and needs your light; he feeds off it. It makes him stronger. The only way he can get his power is to take yours. He's taking it from you bit by bit, and if you continue with him, he'll suck the life force right out of you. You'll end up with some autoimmune disease, and then you'll be dead. Your physical body can't take much more. Didn't you notice that your energy depleted around Dan?"

"Yes, but I made excuses."

Jerome touched her hand. "Marcie, don't be confused by what I'm telling you. The universe is not black and white. It's filled with mysteries that'll take a lifetime to tap into. And then, you'll still know very little. Not all of Rand's offspring have followed the darkness. Some broke away. You have that chance, too. And not all were born with dark entities. It's like a game within the shadows, to turn those of the light dark. And if they can't, they're eliminated in many different ways.

"Just remember that the future's not set; it's what you make of it. You, Maggie, and Sam, are all pawns, easily disposed of and inconsequential. Don't you get it yet? Dan and Lance care for no one but themselves. To them, this is about destruction, greed, control, and power."

"What about Richard? I know he's not bad. He can't be part of this."

"Richard's involved more than you know. He's the warrior who's

balancing on the line of light and darkness. He ventured into the muck, but it hasn't stuck to him yet. He, too, is at a crossroad, and only he can make that choice. You need to trust and have faith. You need to look closer and not on a linear level. What you see in the material world is an illusion; it's not as it is. When you get past that, you'll see what you came from and what you are now.

"I've been sent to help you get back on the right path. I need you to learn from what I did and what happened to Isabel and me. You have a choice to make. Start by looking back at your childhood. Your Granny saved you, remember? When you were a child, your father's land oozed in immorality. It was who he was. He liked them young, didn't much care where they came from. Your mother lived in the other house with you, chose not to see. You're still deeply scarred from that cesspool. Your granny took you when you were twelve, and she broke that circle for you. Dan came from that circle, a spawn of your father's seed."

"He's my brother?" she cried, feeling the violation of her intimacy.

"No, your father wasn't blood. He was your stepfather, and Dan wasn't raised by him. Dan's mother was one of his victims. But Dan is Rand, who's come back into this life bringing his karma and powerful gift of sight, destruction, and power, but even more so, he sees through the veil and is far more gifted in sight than you'll ever be. You need to go back to your teacher. She's still waiting to hear from you."

"Who's my real father?"

"You're not ready to know that, Marcie. Your teacher will help you find him after you cut ties with Dan and put an end to his destruction. You have the power to do it and end his battle with Sam. Stop giving Dan control. Take it back, turn the tables on him, but do it in love, not hate."

"Why's he trying to hurt Sam?"

"Sam's from me, my generation. Sam's goodness is a threat to Dan because he holds him back from gaining all he desires—power and control. To you, it's just drugs, marijuana, and money. It's more than that for Dan. He made a choice, and he knows, more than you, who the threat is: Sam, you and your light."

"How do I turn the tables on Dan?"

A cell phone rang in the distance. Marcie jerked away from the peaceful pool to the cramped vinyl backseat of Diane's SUV. She teetered on the brink of her dream world and conscious reality. Her back ached, and she had a kink in her neck. She shoved Sam's coat behind her to cushion the armrest digging into her spine. Sam closed his cell phone and dumped it on the empty passenger seat.

"Change of plans; we're going to Richard and Maggie's." He watched her in the rearview mirror. "You okay?"

"Sam, I don't know how to stop Dan. We have to find a way. He's going to destroy you, all of us, and he's powerful."

His eyes narrowed as he first glanced at the road and then at her in the rearview mirror. "Marcie, you made me a promise. Do you remember? You said you wouldn't withhold anything, and yet you did, when Dan cornered you in the cabin. Why?"

Would he ever forgive her? Maybe she should've told him. "I was scared, Sam. He caught me off guard when I got out of the shower. I don't know where he was hiding in the cabin. He wanted his marijuana from all the gardens I'd planted. He can't get it himself because he doesn't know where they're all planted. I believed him then, as I do now. He'll hurt you, Sam."

"Marcie, I could've stopped him."

"No, Sam, you couldn't. And he still may set you up. What I didn't believe until he cornered me is that Dan is very much involved with Lance Silver's drug empire."

"And you do now?"

"Well, of course. When he mentioned Lance in the same breath as his threat to set you up, I knew. You should be worried, Sam. Lance Silver has the kind of power that controls politicians. People disappear. One thing's clear, Sam; whatever they decide to set you up with, it'll be unexpected, and there will be rock-solid evidence that'll most likely put you in prison for life."

"You still lied to me, Marcie—so how am I supposed to trust you again?"

She shut her eyes and looked away. He didn't understand. But how could he?

"Well, I don't know what to tell you, because I'd probably do the same thing again." Her throat thickened, making her words sound strained.

"Ah, shit, don't do that."

Marcie refused to answer him. Her eyes burned and her throat throbbed. She felt an icy wall deepening the gulf between them.

"Well, that's just great. As if I need this crap now, too." He banged the steering wheel with the palm of his hand.

He turned off the Olympic highway. Thank goodness they were almost there, because the rest of the drive passed in bitter silence.

Richard owned twenty acres, ten miles from Diane's spread, in rural Gardiner. Sam pressed the brakes and turned down the paved driveway. Only a few fir trees remained, dividing the front stretch of the property from the nearly deserted gravel road. Marcie let out a sigh, forcing out all the awful, pent-up anxiety. The barn, the fenced pasture, the weeping willow by the pond, and the five acres of cleared green land, surrounding a beautiful, two-story, west coast house, appeared out of the thick fir trees. A labor of love, Richard had built it for Maggie.

A long cedar porch ran the width of the house, framed by custom-built Victorian spindles and posts. Richard leaned over the smooth white railing, dressed in the same black jeans and long-sleeved, coffee-colored T-shirt, the sleeves pushed up to his elbows.

Marcie curled her fingers around the back of Sam's seat as he parked beside Richard's big truck. The way Richard glared, and the way he gripped the railing; she wondered if he'd launch over it the moment Sam opened his door. All that burning male pride—she couldn't remember having seen Richard in such a state, even amid his fights with Dan.

Sam popped open her door on the side where her feet dangled. He reached in to help her out, but she slapped his hand away. It was so like him to think he knew what was best and how it was to be done. Marcie slid forward and lowered her leg out the door.

"Don't be like that." Sam scooped her up in his arms and lifted her with a speed that had Marcie's mouth falling open.

"Put me down. I don't need your help. I don't want it. I can do this myself." Damn, it felt so good to be in his arms, but she was still mad and wanted to wallow a bit longer, ignore him, and give him the cold shoulder. So she hit his arm, anywhere, to inflict the same hurt, then burst into tears because her heart wasn't in it.

"Put her down now!"

She didn't see Richard race down from the porch. She saw a madman who appeared wound so tightly that he itched to take something on.

"Back off, Richard. This doesn't concern you."

But Richard didn't. Instead, he jabbed a finger at Sam, into the crest of the sea lions pasted on Sam's dark blue shirtfront. Marcie flinched from the fury erupting from every part of Richard.

"Well, actually, yes, it does. Put her down now." He stepped in closer, provoking Sam the way a man does when he's searching for a fight. Marcie reached out and touched Richard's shoulder. For a moment, she thought he'd knock her hand away. She could feel the ire vibrating inside him. He was beyond reason, and Sam acted like a possessive child, refusing to put her down. In fact, his steel arms, one clamped under her knees, the other around her back, held her like a vise. She looked from Richard to Sam, fully aware she was caught in the middle. What bled from their eyes was truly barbaric—two overtired, irritable alpha males fighting over a woman, establishing turf rules; neither willing to back down.

"Hey!" Jesse yelled from the back door as he started toward them. His jacket was long gone, and his bulky black shirt hung over his baggy blue jeans. Who knew such a large man could move so fast? Maggie and Diane, dressed just as casually, were right behind Jesse, running into the middle of the ruckus, trying to pull the two venting men apart. That was when things really came unglued. Richard was so wrapped up in his anger that when Maggie grabbed his arm to pull him back, he shook her off, and she stumbled back a few steps, losing her footing.

"Hey, hey, guys, knock it off!" Diane yelled as she caught Maggie before she landed in the dirt. Jesse stepped between Richard and Sam just as Sam set Marcie down to lunge at Richard. Jesse butted Sam back with his shoulder and then placed the flat of his hand on each of their chests. Although they jostled him and reached around to grab at each other's shirts, Jesse's large arms flexed as he stood his ground.

A wretched high-pitched scream stopped everyone cold. Nine-year-old Ryley, jean clad and wearing scuffed-up sneakers and a SpongeBob

T-shirt, stood on the top step, holding five-year-old Lily's hand. Lily was a tiny girl with dark, springy curls, barefoot, wearing a simple, yellow, cotton dress. But when Marcie looked closer, Ryley held Lily's limp hand while she stared vacantly into space. Then she shrieked again—this time louder. Maggie ran to her, stumbling in the dirt before she reached the steps.

Ryley, at first glance, appeared a typical little boy. But a typical nine-year-old boy wouldn't have held on to fear and frozen on the stairs when his dad lost it. He wouldn't have held worry in his innocent eyes. Even when he dropped his sister's hand, because his mother took charge by picking her up and carrying her inside the house, kicking and screaming, Ryley, for one split second, appeared lost.

A film of tears glossed over Ryley's fragile, sky-blue eyes. He raced down the steps and launched himself at Richard. Richard's face tinged pink. He kneeled down and clutched a very scared and shaken little boy. His eyes shuttered closed—he was appalled by what he had done.

"Dad, you scared me." Ryley couldn't hold back the high-pitched sob.

"I'm sorry." All the hardness in Richard's voice had dissolved.

Marcie gazed up at Sam. She stood with all her weight on her uninjured foot, beside him, leaning against the SUV. All her physical aches were pushed aside as she drowned in the aftermath of her part in this shameful and childish exhibit.

Sam had the most amazing focus. He planted his hands on his hips and watched Maggie and her child, through the screen door, as if really seeing this deeply caring woman for the first time. Not even the breeze that kicked up, fluttering his short sleeves, distracted him. When he glanced over at Marcie, the quiet sympathy filling his warm blue eyes became an unasked question, one he didn't need to voice.

"Lily has autism. She would've picked up on all of our emotions, and she reacted the only way she could," Marcie said, listening to the muffled screams of the tiny child echo deep inside the house. What Marcie knew about Lily, something Richard and Maggie didn't, was that their child lived on both sides—the spirit and the physical world; stuck in a void that mixed as well as oil and water. Marcie, at times, could see past the veil, but Lily had no veil and struggled to fit in her physical body, which was why she reacted so violently to touch, sound, and emotions. A simple pair of wool socks touching her skin could throw her into hysterics, as could the doorbell, the smoke alarm, or two angry men out of control.

Jesse stood between Sam and Richard.

Diane's chest heaved as if she'd sprinted up the driveway. Her short-cropped hair still stuck up on one side. "Richard, Sam, Marcie, we've got some things to go over. Hey, Ryley, do us a favor. Go tell your mom we'll order dinner in, and you get to decide what." Diane ruffled Ryley's short, dark hair as he wiped his tear-stained eyes while clutching his father's large, working man's hand.

Richard, in a playful, lighthearted way, stood up. Dirt caked his pants as he winced, putting his hand over his heart. "I vote Chinese—not pizza."

"Dad, I want pizza," a now-composed Ryley said before he took off toward the house, but he stopped at the door and turned to his dad. With big eyes and a slight shake in his voice, he asked, "You're not going to fight again, are you?"

"No, bud. No one's going to fight. I promise we're going to stay out here and talk real nice. You can go on the computer in my study and play the new game you're so hot about."

"Mystic Warriors!" He jumped, throwing his arms up in victory, and then yanked open the screen door, letting it bounce off the dark cedar as he raced inside.

"Let's talk down by the willow. We'll be far enough away so the kids won't overhear. Marcie, can I help you?" All Richard's pent up fury had been zapped away liked a popped balloon when he saw what it did to his kid.

"Thanks, Richard, but I have crutches. I can hobble along."

Sam must've taken that as his cue, as he produced a pair of crutches from the back of the SUV. This time, he kept a respectful distance as he handed them to Marcie. He wouldn't look at her, and Marcie couldn't shake the awkward ache adding a few more inches to the gulf between them.

Jesse held out his muscular arms the way a padded-down football player does and walked between Sam and Richard. Smart man, he didn't trust this shaky truce; even though it was for the children's benefit.

They wandered to the freshly stained picnic table and four patio chairs nestled beside a huge weeping willow tree, a safe distance from the front of the house. Marcie let out an ungraceful moan as she sat in one of the blue, plastic chairs. Sam slid a second chair in front of her so she could elevate her leg.

"Thank you," she said. They felt like nothing more than polite strangers. Her foot throbbed and tingled, leaving her groggy and not as clear-headed as she'd like to be, but she was lucid enough to see the stress and anguish lining Richard's face; the same as was reflected on Diane's. Jesse looked pissed as he dropped into the chair beside Marcie.

Sam spoke from behind her. "What's going on?"

"When Maggie took the first load of marijuana to Sandra's house. Sandra emptied the duffle bags around the two handicapped boys, hanging the bud to dry in the same room where the boys slept. They inhaled the odor all night. Marcie, we understand you planned to call the sheriff after Sandra had all the marijuana."

Marcie shut her eyes as she remembered those helpless teens. "I screwed up, and those poor kids are going to suffer because I didn't finish."

Sam pressed a supportive hand on her shoulder.

"It was a good idea, Marcie, and you were right," Diane said. "She has a contract for respite care with the Department of Health and Social Services. Getting caught with all that marijuana would've brought charges of trafficking." Diane perched on the bench seat of the picnic table across from Marcie. Richard lounged in the remaining chair beside Diane.

Diane clasped her hands and dangled them between her legs as she leaned forward. "I called a friend of mine who's a social worker to see if she could pull those kids out of there. Fortunately, she didn't have to. They went home this morning. Apparently, she's had them for the last couple of days. My friend checked on the type of contract Sandra has. It's not the group home contract, but when she has a suitable house that's large enough, she will get it. In the meantime, she'll be doing respite care for severely disabled teens and mentally challenged adults. She's making good money."

"How could a drug dealer get a contract?" Jesse asked. It was a question they were all thinking.

Diane shrugged out of her dark jacket. It was warmer out of the breeze. "Well, no one knows about her sideline. She has a university background as a child and youth care worker as well as a physiotherapy degree. She's worked for the state and local hospitals, for many years, caring for the severely disabled. They see a different side of her, a respectable side doing work very few want to. She's smart. She can go virtually undetected as a grower and dealer. The authorities won't believe us, and my friend got her hand slapped for digging too much. The program manager's a friend of Sandra's. Several state employees speak highly of her skill as a care worker. What I'm going to tell you guys stays between us until I can figure out what to do. The state agency doesn't want to push too hard to know what she's doing because they'd look bad."

"So how much money does Sandra get paid for looking after these kids?" Sam asked, never leaving his spot behind Marcie.

Diane's face tinged pink. "Seven thousand per kid, per month." She ground her jaw as she spoke.

"Holy shit, what the hell's wrong with the DHSS? Aren't they supposed to be protecting those with special needs?" Sam really was out of the loop.

"Sam, our kids are just a number. The government people don't give a crap about what happens to them." Richard's deep voice dripped with sarcasm while he squeezed the arms of the chair to the point Marcie wondered if they'd snap off.

"Richard, that's not fair. Most social workers do care, a lot, but their hands are tied. They're told what to do, what to say, and when to look the other way. This government gives contracts to friends and abuses power. It's severely flawed. If there's a problem, they hide it. But I promise you, I won't let this go. We'll expose what she's doing, but we need to stay smart."

"So when does that happen, Diane? Is that before or after one of those kids gets hurt or maybe dies?" Richard's temper smoldered in his eyes.

Sam wiped his hand over his face. "Wait, I still don't understand. I get the part where she's friends with this manager, but I thought the application process was strict. There are safety issues, right? What about the background check? Isn't the social worker supposed to talk to the neighbors? And how could the state even go along with having the disabled stuffed way out in the middle of nowhere, cut off from the rest of the world?"

"Sam, social workers initiate referrals to a program manager, who issues the contract. The program manager is apparently very supportive of Sandra, and, according to my friend, has personally visited the property and met with Dan as the property owner. Your questions would be valid if we were dealing with logical people, but you need to know there's an arrangement between, Dan, Sandra, and the program manager."

"I'd like to know if maybe this program manager isn't, in fact, involved in the grow-ops with Sandra," Marcie said. "It'd make sense. Most of her friends work for the DHSS. She has tons of out-of-control parties, and her friends are always there. When Sandra harvested the first grow show in one of the houses on Dan's property, she used the state handicap van to transport the weed. One of her co-workers helped." Marcie spoke so calmly, caging the rage bubbling inside at this injustice.

"Oh my God, Marcie. Are you serious?" Diane, who had remained so controlled and cool, now paced in front of her.

Marcie folded her hands in prayer, immersed deep in thought.

"What I'd like to know is how you, Richard, could even consider being a partner with Dan, who's involved with the likes of Sandra. You have a special needs kid. You make absolutely no sense," Jesse said, stretching out his legs and crossing his arms, hammering Richard with his coal-dark gaze.

Richard vented a disgusted laugh. "I went into partnership with Dan long before Sandra came on the scene. I've known Dan a good many years. We worked construction together before I met Maggie. I knew he smoked marijuana, grew his own, big deal. Lots of people do.

Doesn't make them drug dealers. Dan had a good idea with this land when we bought it together. The real estate market was good then, too. We'd provide affordable housing while creating our own little nest egg. These big grow shows of his started after.

"Sandra comes from a totally dysfunctional family in Port Angeles, but she never used to be this bad. I know she had some trouble a few years back, was raped, but then she hung around a really bad crowd. Can't say it was any surprise after Dan told me. I suppose that's part of what changed her. Still don't understand this need of hers to look after special needs kids."

"You still haven't answered why you're in business together." Jesse cut Richard no slack.

Richard jumped to his feet, shoving his chair so hard a clump of grass flew. He stomped a couple steps, glancing at the house before facing Jesse. "Because the real estate market's in the toilet. I've got all my money tied up in it, and Dan won't buy me out." He thumped his chest hard. "That property's worth less now than when we bought it, so I'm stuck in business with him. But our part together, I guarantee you, is legit."

"The grow-op in the basement of that, piece of shit, house you burned down, and the marijuana plants in the shed Marcie looked after, how can you have no part of that if it's happening right under your nose?" Jesse asked, tit for tat. He gestured his hand in the air, a man who questioned everything.

Richard ground his teeth. His icy, blue eyes sought out Marcie. His tone was sharp and overtired. "He just did it. I wasn't consulted. I found out after it was up and running. Yes, he had a grow-op in that basement. I told him to get rid of it, and the one in the shed, too. I looked away for quite a while when I thought he was growing for just friends. But, suddenly, he had too many plants. He was getting greedy, and that made him dangerous. Right after that, the house burned. Marcie, I ignored what you were doing with that weed, because I like you. Since Maggie and I met you, we've felt protective of you. Why did you do it for him?" Richard kicked his empty chair.

"Because I was so in love with him, I thought I could change him." Their eyes met and held. She knew Richard understood what she was trying to say by the way his eyes filled with pity. She'd been a fool in love.

"So what happens now? Dan wants the marijuana you grew for him. He's involved my wife, who has no business being part of this. Is he going to make good on his threat?" Richard shrugged and scrubbed the top of his head a little too hard.

Sam cleared his throat. "Richard, I think it's time to call Dan."

CHAPTER 34

Marcie changed into a pair of Maggie's light gray sweat pants and a bright red sweatshirt. She was bone tired, and when she tried to lie down on the leather sofa in the large, open front room, her mind raced—her adrenaline pounded. So she lay there, allowing the knots to build in her stomach until the dinner bell rang. It was four large pizzas, delivered to the back door.

Six adults and two children crowded around a large, country oak table, crammed in like sardines. Everyone minded their Ps and Qs, especially around the children, and because Ryley continued to cast wary glances between his dad and Sam.

After dinner, Diane helped Maggie wash the dishes in the large, open brick and marble kitchen. They chatted warmly about family, friends, and her children as Marcie watched them over the long, creamy counter dividing the eating area from the main cooking part of the kitchen.

Richard put the kids to bed and then whistled while he sauntered his six-foot frame, complete with solid pecs and tight, narrow hips, back into the kitchen. He was a definite catch, but he only had eyes for Maggie. He walked up behind his wife and pulled her against him as he nuzzled her ear. Their fingers intertwined briefly before he pulled away, but not before their eyes connected in their own private moment. He was head over heels in love with her and had been ever since she had served him in a bar as a twenty-two-year-old waitress. He had asked her out within five minutes and married her three months later. After ten years, the chemistry still sizzled between them.

Jesse was on the phone in Richard's study, talking to his wife.

Sam sat at the table across from Marcie, his eyes glued to her, sipping his coffee from a pink flowered mug. Marcie could feel his heat and fought to look anywhere but at him.

Richard crossed his arms and rested his hip against the tiled counter by the sink. "Dan's going to meet me tonight for a beer."

"No, Richard, don't." Maggie pulled her hands out of the soapy water she'd just dunked them into and spun around. "Stay away from him. Hasn't he caused enough trouble?"

"It was my idea, Maggie." Sam got up and claimed the seat beside Marcie, resting his arm around the back of her chair. He didn't notice how still she went.

"I've got to meet him," Richard said. "Besides, nothing's going to happen. Remember, we're friends." He said it with a hint of sarcasm, which brought Marcie's head around. What she saw on Richard's face was sheer male fear.

"You hate him." Marcie didn't realize she had spoken aloud. Everyone focused on Richard, but they didn't see the confusion that she did. "He messed with Maggie, and you won't forgive him for that, will you?"

Richard glared at Marcie. His pale skin was tinged a hint of pink, and his long, narrow nose flared when he spoke. "You're fucking right, I hate him. Who the hell does he think he is, showing up at my door, talking to my wife, forcing her into something…" He held his hands up in the air, shaking his head as his firmed lips trembled and formed a fine white line. "If she was caught, she'd spend how many years locked away in prison?"

"This guy's either a confident fool, extremely cocky, or brilliant," Jesse said as he entered the room. "He has no loyalty to friends and is desperate enough to use underhanded tactics to get what he wants. I haven't met the guy, but looking at you, Richard; I'd be wary about pissing you off." Jesse wandered over to the corner wood stove behind the table, shoving his hands in his pockets before turning around. "I'd say he's not done yet. So what's he going to do next to get the rest of the marijuana? You had how many gardens yet to do?" He leaned forward enough to pin his bullshit-free eyes on Marcie.

This was no time to be embarrassed, but she was. "Nineteen."

Jesse nodded as if satisfied. The way his eyes worked, he had obviously devised some plan.

"What happens when he gets cornered or in a jam? How does he react?" Jesse glanced first at Richard and then at Marcie.

Marcie met Richard's reluctant gaze, then dropped her eyes to a piece of nail hanging from her thumb.

"He's complex, something like this; he'll scheme, but he could also throw a temper tantrum like a little boy," Richard answered. "He's almost two different people. At night, he hangs around with a pretty bad crowd. During the day, he seeks out respectable folks, puts on a mask. One thing about Dan, he's afraid of getting in a fight, because he knows he'll lose. So he creates a mess, points the finger at someone else, and runs away." Richard gestured his finger toward the door. "You'd think it would teach him to wise up, but he keeps doing it. He drinks heavily, screws women and doesn't stop to ask their names, always getting women to clean up his messes. How does he do it, Marcie? Why are you so willing to do anything for him?"

Her face flamed red. "The side he shows me is cavalier, dashing, radiant, and charming. There's something about him that was addicting, the way he focused all of his attention and caring on me." She dropped her eyes again to that irritating piece of nail. "He knows all the right things to say, as if he can read you. I think he does. There are many parts to his personality. He's intriguing and fun to be around. I've never experienced it with anyone else. I'm sure you've noticed his special link with children. He appears to care deeply for their welfare. I've watched him around Ryley and Lily. Ryley worships him. And Lily, he was quite concerned with how to help her, how he should best approach her, what you're doing for her therapy, what he could do to help. Richard, I know he's asked you, too. Whatever motivated him to do that…?" She stopped, held her hands up, and shrugged.

"He talked to you about how to help my kid?" Richard snapped.

Marcie saw the instant a black haze of fury took hold of his senses. He pushed away from the counter and stalked around the kitchen island, squeezing his fists.

"Richard, it was a year ago. What I'm trying to get at is that he's unpredictable. He throws you off by making you think he cares. These many sides of him are like different personalities stuffed inside one body. It's in his makeup—what he is. He's my father's son."

CHAPTER 35

"Dan's your brother?" Sam scooted his chair back and hovered over Marcie. She was forced to look up.

"No, he's not my brother. He's my stepfather's son, but he wasn't raised by him."

Richard leaned on the table, on the other side of Marcie, and raised the flat of his hand. "Where are you getting this from, Marcie? Dan's mom lives in Port Angeles. He has five brothers and sisters. His dad walked out on them when he was a little boy. I don't think he's seen him since. So was this your stepdad?"

"No, Dan's mom was another victim of my dad, Scotty Renard. He liked unwilling prey—mostly young girls." That got everyone's attention. The Renard property was forty acres at the front of Gardiner, filled with a history of criminal shenanigans. She noticed everyone's eyes were agog; they obviously hadn't known he was also a sexual predator. She knew Sam remembered the name scribbled at the bottom of the journal she showed him last night. Many coincidences, but were they?

Diane abandoned the dishes she had loaded into the dishwasher and moved in her stocking feet closer to Marcie. "Isn't he doing time for heroin trafficking?"

"Yeah, that's what they eventually got him on."

"Jesus, Marcie, I thought you were raised by your granny on Las Seta. I didn't know you were a Renard." Richard backed away and leaned in the doorway.

"I was twelve, living with Mom in a second house on Scotty's huge property. My brother, Simon, lived with dad. Dad was a substance abuser, just like Mom, drunk by noon and took whatever choice drug was available."

Sam and Diane glanced at each other but said nothing.

"Scotty's a convicted heroin and gun dealer, but his hand was always in some pot—anything he could steal and sell. When I was twelve, a heroin junkie shot my brother in the face. That was when Granny came and took me. I was lucky. Scotty Renard was a predator. I've never told anyone this, but he'd begun to show an inappropriate interest in me. I was the age he preferred."

Diane reached down and squeezed her hand. "Don't, Marcie. We all know where you're going with this."

She just nodded. "I'm cold."

Maggie hurried to the back door and lifted an earth-brown sweater off a hook. She draped the thick wool knit around Marcie's shoulders. Her nurturing hands squeezing in a supportive way.

"Dan is Scotty's son. He carries the same gifts and is nothing but a predator of greed, destruction, and power. The only difference? Dan's a dangerous coward, and, another thing, he's not the middle guy. There's a ship coming up from South America, and it's filled with cocaine. Dan arranged it. Richard, you're also involved more than you let on."

Every eye focused in on Richard. Jesse took a step toward him.

"What the fuck do you know?" Richard slammed his fist on the kitchen table. Sam's mug bounced, spilling coffee onto the shiny oak. Marcie jerked back, horrified by what she'd said and terrified of falling victim to Richard's wrath. Could it really be true?

Sam moved around Marcie, her shining knight, and shoved Richard. "Back off, now."

"Richard, what've you done?" Maggie spoke with anguish as tears glistened in her silky brown eyes.

"Where did you get this information from, Marcie, and how did you know about this ship?" Diane asked. Seeing no other choice, she gripped Richard's solid forearm and hauled him back, stepping between both him and Sam. Diane was the only one who didn't appear surprised by this news. In fact, by the way she looked over Richard's shoulder and then over to the back door, it was clear she wanted to change the subject.

"Well, this is interesting, Diane. It seems you already know, but I just found out. Jerome told me," Marcie said.

The fire crackled in the wood stove in the kitchen, cutting through the silence and the chilly fall air.

"No more secrets," Sam said. Everyone stared at him.

Richard walked around Diane and placed both hands on the table, facing Marcie. "So who's Jerome, and how does he know about me?"

Marcie watched Sam closely while she spoke. "Jerome appeared in my dreams. He's my guide, but he's also much more."

Sam pursed his lips, and, to his credit, said nothing.

"Are you telling me some guy from a dream told you this?"

"Yes, Richard, I am," she answered. She knew by the way his eyes widened that he had to be wondering whether she was sane.

Richard threw his hands up in the air and then combed them through his short, dark hair. Sam was probably the only one who didn't know anything. Or did he?

"I know Dan expanded his operation," Richard finally said. "Whatever he's doing on the side, I'm not part of it. He put up a huge chunk of cash to bring some coke up. All I know is that he's in it with someone else, and I don't know who for sure." Richard scooted past Diane and paced the kitchen. "There's a guy named Graham. He owns a large piece of real estate in Port Townsend. He's met with Dan several times on our property. I was asked to front some cash and was assured of a big return on my investment."

"Oh my God, Richard, you didn't." Maggie hurried to the long counter where Richard paced and pressed her shaky hand to her mouth.

Richard walked around the counter until he hovered over his wife. "No, Maggie, I didn't. There are some lines I'm not going to cross.

These are dangerous players he's involved with, and they don't care who they hurt."

Diane cleared her throat. "We've been tracking a boat coming up from South America that, we suspect, is carrying cocaine. We also know the boat's owned by Dan's brother, Greg McKenzie."

If everyone was shocked by Marcie's revelation; it had nothing on Diane's little secret.

"Diane, how long have you known about this, and why didn't you tell me?" Sam ran his hand over his unshaven face.

"We found out the day you left to go back to New Orleans." Diane gestured defensively with both hands.

"So, who's monitoring it?" Sam asked.

"DEA, Coast Guard, Interpol—it's a joint effort. We suspect there's also going to be some trade of high-grade marijuana, and that's where Marcie and Maggie come in."

Marcie glanced at Maggie. Her mouth hung open. Obviously, she also realized they were pawns in a bigger plan.

"So let me get this straight: What I grew and cut, and what Maggie delivered to Sandra, is going toward this deal?" Marcie spoke directly to Diane.

"It sure looks that way, Marcie."

"Diane, who's pulling the strings behind this deal?" Jesse leaned against the brick wall beside the wood stove.

"Lance Silver," she answered.

CHAPTER 36

Maggie, Diane, and Marcie stayed behind while Sam, Jesse, and Richard went to the Island Seekers bar; a quiet pub overlooking the ocean in downtown Gardiner. Richard would meet Dan for a beer, and Jesse and Sam would linger in a dark corner, out of sight, to watch.

Maggie paced the open kitchen. She fed another log into the wood stove and closed the damper. She pulled out the mop and washed the creamy golden tiled floor until it gleamed. Marcie brooded in silence, watching the wall clock tick by at a snail's pace. It was after eleven, and the men had been gone for nearly two hours. Maggie, now ass deep in the refrigerator, was pulling out food, spraying down the shelves, and giving them a good scrub.

Diane retreated to the living room. Marcie could hear her rummaging in her briefcase, the one she'd retrieved from home, along with Marcie's own duffle bag, after the men left for the bar.

Marcie pushed her chair back and grabbed a single crutch, hobbling into the bright living room. It featured a twenty-foot ceiling and a spindled fir stairwell that led up to the second floor, where four bedrooms overlooked this spacious room. The leather furniture surrounded a river rock fireplace, and there sat Marcie's duffle bag, dumped on a rich mahogany loveseat. She unzipped the side pocket and pulled out her silk-wrapped tarot cards.

With her stocking feet resting on the square coffee table, Diane peered over her open file, her reading glasses perched on the end of her nose. "What's that?"

"My tarot cards. I play with tarot cards. There, I said it." Marcie waved the bundle. Maybe because she was so tired, drugged, battered, and bruised, she didn't care to hide it.

Diane closed her file and slid off the leather sofa, dumping her glasses on the coffee table. Marcie hobbled back to the kitchen, with Diane dogging her heels.

"Wow, Marcie, pretty cool," she said.

Marcie stopped and really looked at Diane, then continued back to her chair, placing her cards in front of her and resting her crutch against the wall. Diane pulled out a chair, sat down, and tucked in closer to Marcie.

"These were my granny's cards." Marcie shuffled, which brought Maggie's head out of the fridge.

"I didn't know you read tarot cards." Maggie stood up, a spray bottle and sponge dangling from her hands.

"I guess it's not something I share with just anyone. I pick up on people's feelings, even see things in my dreams sometimes. My granny taught me how to stay close to nature and ground myself in the natural world. The tarot's a tool I use for clarity to help when I'm seeking answers. As you know, our paths aren't set, but if we can see what obstacles lie before us, we know what we need to do to overcome and change that path." Marcie continued to shuffle as Maggie tossed all the food back in the fridge and then pulled out a chair.

"Do you mind if I ask you something?" Diane clasped her hands on the table in front of her.

"No, go ahead."

"If you can see all this, and have the answers; why did you get involved with Dan?"

Marcie stopped shuffling and met the honest curiosity in Diane's big eyes. The words should have hurt, but there was no cruel intent in her question.

"I was so in love with Dan. The signs were all around me, but I chose not to see. When he cornered me at Granny's yesterday, I realized then that my obsession with him was partly his doing. He's a wizard. He found my weakness, my pain, and he used it to make me want him. This is nothing but a game to him. He's dangerous."

She shuffled the worn, crinkled cards one last time. "In New Orleans, I met the most amazing woman, Mama Reine, a surrogate mother to Sam. She smacked me upside the back of my head with the words of my deeds; something my granny would have done if she was alive."

Diane and Maggie scooted their chairs closer.

"Oh, this sounds interesting. Mama Reine—tell me about her," Maggie said.

Marcie thumped the cards once with the knuckles of her right hand and then held them to her chest. She looked at Diane and then Maggie, considering how much she should say. "She's a witch in Terrebonne Parish who reminds me of Granny. Mama Reine helped me see again right after I got my memory back. You know those who practice magic must be completely honest in all aspects of their personal life. You use energy to strengthen the power within you, not to use over someone else. What I took for granted, and forgot, was a very simple rule taught to me. When I practice my gift, no matter what anyone says, this is a gift from God. The spiritual laws are clear. Don't ever abuse your gift. Never is it to be used for personal gain to harm another. It's what I did when I helped Dan. I refused to see all the roadblocks right in front of me, the cycle of abuse. I chose to be a victim by allowing him to treat me so abominably."

Marcie picked up the cards and shut her eyes, visualizing herself grounded to the earth. *Please, dear God, bring in your angels and spirit guides to protect me. Surround me in a circle of white light, and please provide me with really clear answers for this mess with Dan and how to get out of it.* Marcie opened her eyes to two women who were studying her so closely she felt like a frog they'd just dissected in a petri dish. Marcie cut the deck, put it back together, and laid out three cards in front of her: the Knight of Pentacles, the Lovers, and Judgment. "Well, this is interesting. Pentacles are earth, material possession. The knight brings the message, presenting an offer. This man's already here. He's hardworking and takes care of details in pursuit of a goal. This is Sam. He stands firm from opposition, will not quit, and is true to his personal convictions.

"The Lovers are a physical addiction, a man and a woman, similar to the story of Adam and Eve in the garden, fighting to resist temptation; a choice between right and wrong. It represents the need to find out what you care about and face that ethical or moral choice. Which one will you decide? And Judgment—this is a good card, in a way; with the archangel above, all the dead rising up from their coffins, held accountable for their actions. Judgment day's coming, and burdens will be lifted and released for those who take a stand in the right. A transformation, a day of reckoning, being cleansed, refreshed. What it's saying is I need to learn this lesson so it's not repeated. Have I released my past mistakes? I need to so that they'll be behind me and I'll be ready to start new."

"So what does all this mean?" Diane whispered.

Marcie laid her hands over the cards. "Past, present, and future gave me a glimpse into me, except I'm not seeing the whole picture. I'm rusty, and I know there's more. I've always had trouble reading me, but sometimes there are instances where we're not supposed to know."

"Now I'm confused. What does that mean?" Diane asked.

Marcie leaned back and winced before looking thoughtfully at her. Her leg throbbed. "I need to go back to my teacher. It's time, because what I suspect is at play, and what I can't see, is beyond time and hours. It's had history and generations to build. First thing in the morning, we need to go back to Las Seta and see my teacher, Sally Wilcox. She's waiting for me to return."

Maggie arched her dark, shapely brows, jerking her head a few inches forward as if a rope had just yanked her. "She's a witch," she said.

CHAPTER 37

"The whole night was a waste of time." Richard tossed his keys on the long kitchen counter, where they slid under a stack of bills. His hard mouth was set in a firm line as he opened the light oak cabinet by the sink, reached for a glass, and filled it with water, guzzling it down. "Dan knew something was up. You know how cagey he is. He wouldn't sit still, kept looking around the dark pub; said his vibes were at a peak and he was positive someone was watching him. There's no way he saw Sam and Jesse. I couldn't see them." Richard toyed with the glass, stared out the kitchen window into the black night, and then let out a heavy sigh before putting it in the sink and turning around.

Now, after midnight, Marcie struggled to keep her weighted eyelids open. Her head bobbed, and every part of her ached. She wanted nothing more than to go to bed.

"He even had the nerve to apologize for involving Maggie, but you know Dan and his remarkable way of shifting blame. He said, and I quote: 'I was in a bind, and I panicked. You have every right to be angry.'" Richard pivoted and jabbed his finger at Marcie. "Also, he made sure to blame you, Marcie. He said you didn't finish what you were supposed to—bad girl." Richard sarcastically waggled his index finger.

Jesse and Sam leaned up against the wall. They looked so tired compared to Richard. Obviously, their adrenaline was not as pumped.

"Richard, what about the auction he sent you to? We know he wanted you out of the way, but did he offer any explanation?" Diane cleared her throat and combed her fingers through her messy hair.

"Let me tell you something about Dan; he always has an answer. Not much trips him up, and unless you're trained to read body language, you wouldn't know he's lying. I guess I didn't see it before. Now, I honestly believe he doesn't know how to tell the truth. He said he must have screwed up his facts. He was positive the guy at Commercial Irrigation said the auction featured a bankrupt contractor's tools. Even in the message he left about the investor I was to meet, he said the guy wasn't returning his calls. Apparently Dan's been hounding him, leaving messages as to why he didn't show."

"This guy sounds like a sociopath, except I've never heard of a man using women to do his dirty work in order to protect him because he's too scared. Really, this is a new twist." Diane appeared fascinated.

"Don't get too enchanted, Diane. Ever hear of a guy named Charles Manson? That's exactly how Dan sucks the women in."

Diane's lips thinned, and her cheeks heated. "I'm not stupid, Richard. If this guy's anything like Manson, he's fucking dangerous. I'm trying to get into his head so I know how he ticks. And that helps us catch him."

Marcie broke the standoff. "Would you two stop bickering? I'd like to hear it all, and no, Diane, you're not stupid, but I was. Now, if it's all the same to you, move on. I'm tired, and my leg hurts. Sam, Jesse, what did you pick up from where you sat?"

Sam didn't move from his spot by the door, where he leaned against the wall. He watched her with such tender caring that her heart fluttered and she had to remind herself to breathe. "Marcie, you're tired. You look as if you're going to keel over."

"I am tired, Sam, but I'd like to hear everything."

"There's nothing else, Marcie. Dan's cell phone rang, and he left." Richard stood behind Maggie, resting his hands on her shoulders.

"Marcie, you need to go to bed. Let's figure out where we go with this in the morning," Jesse said as he leaned against the counter. His dark eyes appeared unusually brooding.

Maggie yawned and reached for her husband's hand. "You know what? We're all tired. Everyone stays here tonight. We have enough room, and then we can start tomorrow with clearer heads. Sam, help Marcie upstairs to the guest room. I'll leave some blankets on the sofa for you, Jesse. Sam, if you want to sleep on the second sofa in the living room, you're welcome to. Diane, I'll get you settled on the pullout in the den."

Maggie was subtle. The choice was theirs to stay together or not. Chairs slid back, and goodnights were exchanged. Then Sam appeared at her side, scooping Marcie out of the chair, his strong arm encircling her waist, and he all but carried her upstairs to bed.

Sam left the door open when he set her on the edge of the bed. He backed up a few steps. Marcie wanted to clear her throat; it seemed to be coated with something thick and warm. She must have stared like a fool. Time slowed, and Sam didn't move. She ordered herself to take a breath and then another, to be reasonable and clear in what she wanted. She needed Sam, but she realized, as he lowered his head and looked away, that it wouldn't be tonight.

"Goodnight, Marcie." That was all he said before he left and pulled the door closed behind him.

MARCIE'S LEG ACHED FIERCELY WHEN SHE WOKE IN THE GUEST ROOM LATE the next morning. The first thing she saw was the ceramic cross with cherubs and angels mounted on the warm peach wall over the white dresser. She ran her hand over the fluffy pillow beside her and let out a groan from the twinge in her shoulder and the persistent ache that climbed up her leg. If she hadn't had to pee, she would probably have laid there and wallowed in discomfort. Left with no choice, she tossed back the golden floral duvet and scooted like an old woman out of bed; still wearing Maggie's sweats.

Marcie opened the door and hobbled down the hall to the main bathroom. Feeling gross and gritty, she climbed into the shower, allowing the hot spray to ease her aches, careful of the scabbed-over scrapes and cuts. She scrubbed away what she could of the dried blood and dirt from the crash. When Marcie returned to the guest room with her long, wet hair brushed back, her duffel bag rested in the middle of the already made bed.

She dressed in tan capris wide enough at the leg to fit her cast. A mocha T-shirt, a white sweater overtop, and one sock and running shoe completed her ensemble.

It was slow going, maneuvering the stairs while she listened to the chatter, the distinct morning rattles of dishes, pots and pans and all manner of the breakfast things. No wonder no one heard her stagger awkwardly on her crutches into the kitchen. But maybe they did; Diane handed her a piece of toast coated with thick strawberry jam, which she gobbled while being ushered out the door by Maggie before she could say good morning to the kids and Maggie's mom, who was already tending the children.

Sam, Richard, and Jesse waited outside. Everyone was dressed casually in blue jeans, T-shirts, and windbreakers as they piled into Maggie's eight-passenger SUV, but not before Sam lifted Marcie into his arms and carried her down the steps while she swallowed the last of her toast. Richard drove them straight to the Sequim marina.

Everything fell right into place. She didn't know how Maggie and Diane had managed to convince the men to go and see Sally. What she expected was absolute refusal from the men, saying they wouldn't even consider wasting their time on some voodoo nutcase. Marcie expected to be going alone, or, at the very least, just with Sam.

Richard owned a cabin cruiser that he kept docked at the Sequim marina. Marcie sat up top, and Sam faced her. She could see the hurt in his eyes each time he glanced her way, adding to the mass of confusion clouding her powerful feelings for him. She allowed Sam to help her out of the boat once it docked. He passed her the crutches and followed behind. Her pride wouldn't allow her to accept more right now. She hobbled up the pier to her parked Toyota. Everyone slowed to a snail's pace so that Marcie wasn't left in the dust.

"Okay, so which way to this guy who's got the information on Dan?"

Marcie froze, gripped her crutches, and whirled around to look first at Maggie and then Diane. Neither would meet her gaze as Sam, who was now breathing down Marcie's neck, waited for someone to reply. She blinked, realizing that, while she had wallowed in angst over the barrier between her and Sam, not once had anyone mentioned Sally.

"I'd still like to know where you found out about this guy who has all this inside information. Was it a phone call you got last night when we were out?" Richard questioned both Maggie and Diane and then frowned when he looked down at Marcie. She knew darn well that her panicky eyes had to be as big as saucers.

Marcie stuttered, "It was my idea. I told Diane and Maggie last night that it's time to go back to my teacher. She's a friend of my granny's and a prolific, gifted reader who was teaching me the path to enlightenment when Dan snared me with his charms. Before I got on the plane to New Orleans, she begged me not to go, to come home so she could finish teaching me. She knew what I was doing, and she knows what Dan is. Jerome's come to me several times in my dreams, and he's told me to go back to Sally. And you know what? None of us knows what Dan's going to do next. If he needs all the marijuana, he's going to try something, and, if it's all the same to you, I'd like to be prepared so that he doesn't catch me off guard again. He's unpredictable. He's threatened you, Sam. You too, Richard. He's dragged Maggie into my mess. And you both know that, with his connection to Lance Silver, he has power behind him. Don't forget, Richard, what you said last night. If he really is like Charles Manson, we need to expect the unexpected, and Sally can help." Marcie knew she was rambling.

That did it. Sam flung his hands in the air while Richard pinned Maggie with his famous unimpressed look. Jesse crossed his arms, smiling smugly. The light danced in his eyes as if he alone understood what she was trying to do.

"Great, that's just great. How long's it going to take us to get back? We just wasted over an hour getting here when we could have been formulating a concrete plan to establish some solid, credible evidence against Dan and his connection to Lance Silver." Sam smacked the back of his hand into the palm of his other hand and then jabbed his finger at Marcie. "This voodoo bullshit—I got it all the time with Mama, and I'm done with it. Listen up, Marcie. A dead guy comes to you in your dreams, telling you to go back to your teacher, and you listen?" Sam walked away, down the dirt hill, back to the dock. He must have realized no one followed when he stopped halfway down. Marcie continued to the truck. She pulled the back door open at the same time as Diane and Maggie did on the other side of her clunky SUV.

"Whoa, wait a second. We're going back. Stop. We're not getting in the truck. Jesse, Richard, help me out here," Sam said.

Marcie slid her crutches onto the floor and dangled her injured ankle out the door. "Sam, we're here, so if you feel it's a waste of time, you go back. I'm going to see Sally. I need help, and she can provide answers, whether you believe it or not." She lifted her leg in and closed the door, grinning at the speed of his hurried return.

Marcie cranked the window down to air out the stuffy vehicle.

Sam leaned in, shaking his head; a man resigned to his fate. "We're staying one hour—that's it." Indignant, Sam climbed in on the driver's side.

Marcie leaned forward, patted his shoulder, and smiled brightly. "It's going to be a little crowded."

Packed like a can of sardines, Jesse pulled his door closed after he and Diane crammed in the backseat with Marcie. Marcie gave hurried directions to Sally's place; through one hundred acres of preserved forest, meadows, and green space, off of a quiet cove and by the state park located at the far end of the island. She coveted her privacy and isolation, and people on the island respected her for it.

"I hope she's there." Maggie was perched on Richard's lap in the front. Her large, dark eyes glanced at her husband.

"She'll be there, even though we're barging in on her with no warning." Marcie felt confidence pour through her.

"Well, of course she'll be there. She's a psychic. She should know we're coming. And didn't you say Jerome told you it was time to see her?" Sam's sarcastic remark earned him a flick to the back of his ear from Marcie.

"Don't be a smartass. Oh, there's the driveway—on the right." She gripped the back of his seat, pointing a finger past his face.

"You mean the trail that's not passable? That's not a driveway."

"Come on, Sam, just drive in. It's fine."

The ruts jolted the SUV, and bushes scraped both sides of the vehicle, but Sam steered down the narrow trail, which seemed as if no vehicles had ever passed through. It opened into a beautiful grassy clearing full of fruit trees, mature gardens, a pond, and several outbuildings. Right in the center of this lush property was a large, square-fenced garden filled with vivacious pinks, purples, reds, yellows, and whites. Spectacular flora, fall perennials, and wildflowers danced in the sunlight. A short, compact woman stood in the middle of it, wearing a straw hat, watching them approach.

Marcie opened the back door when Sam parked in front of the light brown cottage. Before she could step down, Sam appeared at her door, lifted her out, and gently lowered her beside him. She looked up. Her heart pounded when panic licked away her confidence, leaving her feeling shy and awkward. She swallowed hard. "Thanks, Sam. Crutches, please." Tension still lingered between them, except each show of kindness dissipated her hurt a little more. And he was still here. Maybe he was more intuitive than he let on.

Gently, he touched her cheek. "We still need to have a talk; just you and me."

She froze when she saw something past all the hurt. He suffered, too, and that thought brought a wave of alarm causing her to choke up.

"Marcie, girl, is that you?"

She placed the flat of her hand on his chest, feeling the rapid patter of his heart, right before she hobbled around him, toward the warm, gray-haired woman who approached like a fairy godmother with wings.

"Sally, I'm so sorry to barge in." She felt a little guilty for intruding as she extended the palm of her hand out to the others, who came around the front of her old, rusty vehicle. Sam flanking her. "These are my friends: Sam, Richard, Maggie, Jesse, and Diane." Marcie dropped her eyes to the ground before sucking up her courage to face the one person she'd truly let down. "You were right, Sally. I'm so sorry I didn't listen. I didn't want to know." Marcie's chin wobbled.

Sally was a small, plump woman. Her straw hat brushed Marcie's chin when she hugged her. How long had it been since she'd seen Sally? She hadn't changed. The same lines on her face seemed to draw Marcie into a storybook life filled with wisdom and experience. Sally was one who followed the guidance of Spirit, never questioning what she was told.

Marcie blinked back the tears. "So much has happened. I need your help."

Sally rested her hand on Marcie's shoulder. "I can see that. You were snared good, and it hurt to peel you out of that web of conflicted confusion. You made some wrong choices, and you're all banged up. Well, come on in. I'll put some tea on, and we'll get started, see what we can do to fix this mess."

Richard and Sam faced each other, raising their eyebrows, obviously puzzled, but, to their credit, they said nothing. Marcie responded to them by rolling her eyes. Jesse popped on his dark shades and leaned against the hood of the truck.

Everyone followed as Sally marched, head high, to a large cedar deck at the back of the cottage; which had a latticed trellis on one side, draping a mature wisteria over the center of the deck. Pink and white roses, in full bloom, extended down the other side, with fresh mulch piled around each of the beauties. To complete this paradise, flower baskets hung from tall metal posts mounted in the four corners of the spacious deck. The fragrance alone was one step from heaven. Well, it should have been; except Marcie couldn't shake the building anxiety and the knots cramping her stomach with worries, and, what ifs, dogging her over what answers Sally would provide. Sometimes, the answers weren't what she expected. Then what would she do?

Sam and Richard appeared bored while they claimed old wooden chairs around the square patio table. Sally slid the screen door open and went in the house. Marcie listened to Sally rummage inside, the whistle of the kettle, clangs and rattles as she prepared for her guests.

"She's going to be more help than you think," Marcie said.

Richard cleared his throat roughly.

The wood deck creaked when Sally approached. Her wrinkled round face was void of any emotion. "I've heard it all dear. You may as well just say, 'Be quiet, the witch is coming.'"

"Sorry, Sally. We're a little on edge. I appreciate you allowing us to barge in." Marcie felt as if something had changed between them. Her teacher, who had taken her under her wing to help her develop her ability to channel and hear Spirit, who helped her rise to a higher level and shake off all the darkness that had still lingered in her aura—now Marcie felt there was an uneasy separation.

Sally smiled distantly and then put down the tray with stacked cups and a pot of tea. She reached across the table, patting Marcie's fisted hand. "Relax. Breathe. Give yourself some credit. You've overcome a huge obstacle just ripping those blinders off and seeing that man for who he really is. Now, everyone, help yourself to tea." She nudged the tray to the center of the table.

Sally pulled out a stool directly across from Marcie. Everyone scooted their chairs closer while Sally lit a white candle, pulled a cloth bundle from her pocket, and unwrapped tarot cards from a paisley silk scarf. Sally passed Marcie the deck of cards. "Shuffle and cut. You know how, but this time, place three piles away from you and then re-stack with the last cut on top. Ask your question."

Marcie followed Sally's instructions and handed the deck back.

"Which is top?" Sally asked.

Marcie touched the deck and then watched as Sally laid out three cards directly in front of her: the Fool reversed, the Tower, and the Eight of Pentacles.

"Oh dear, it's worse than I thought. Well, let's just dive in, and then we'll figure out what we can fix from this mess," Sally said.

Marcie leaned forward in anticipation and glanced at the others. Everyone remained quiet. Richard looked at his watch and sighed, then shrugged when Maggie smacked his shoulder.

"You seem to think you have more important things to do, like chasing your tail in a circle, instead of getting a clear read from Spirit as to where you all stand. This may be Marcie's reading, but you're all part of this, by choice or not." Sally never looked up as she spoke. Her tone was clipped, and, wisely, Richard didn't respond. He crossed his arms and appeared to mope.

"Young man, if you really want to have a good look at me, take off those shades. It's dim back here. I've been around skeptics my entire life. Just be respectful." She jabbed a bony finger at Jesse.

Jesse yanked off his shades and popped them in his jacket pocket. "Meant no disrespect, ma'am. Just curious, is all, to meet someone of your talent."

"Hmm" was all Sally muttered as she continued to study the colorful, worn cards. "This is you, my dear." She tapped the Fool, pictured above the cliff, with her index finger and connected her light golden eyes directly with Marcie. "This is about choices, not seeing what's before you but walking blindly, without care for the consequences. Your eyes are tiny and cannot see the pitfalls right in front of you. It's been a carefree go for you, with no established roots. Do you see the knapsack tossed carelessly over the shoulder? It's not even held with any conviction. There's no firm grasp. Others followed your light, see? At the heels. You've led innocents along with you, believing no harm would come. Your eroded foundation has blocked your light. See the cliff reversed? It's above you. The solid rocks, the icy blue, has clouded your sight. The light is below you. You can't see because of the choice you made to follow blindly. Even the feather in your cap, the red is about power and volatile passion. The shirt looks like coins, pentacles, spokes of a wheel, but it's false, not right or true. Easy money. For you, it wasn't about the money. For him, it was."

Guilt warmed Marcie's face. Did everyone know how right Sally was?

"Now don't you go feeling ashamed and sorry for yourself. I knew what you were doing. It's about right choices and balance. What you take, you must give back. There's no room for greed in the universe. You know that. You can lie to yourself and say it was for love, but, for you, it was an obsession. You got to look after his plants, to be near him. All of Dan McKenzie's promises, you lapped them up. You were willing to do anything for him. There's no honesty between you two. There can't be honesty in darkness, and that's all this is. He has so many dark entities attached to him, that the 'real' him doesn't exist. The only way they survive is to feed off your goodness, and the goodness of others like you, until you're destroyed. Your granny's here, standing right behind you, hopping around, excited. You couldn't hear her no matter how hard she tried. Dan McKenzie stalked you. When you met, it was no coincidence. It was planned.

"Lance Silver always wanted a piece of you to toy with. Your granny kept him away. We scared sense into you about that evil man." Sally glanced kindly at Marcie. "It was partly my fault; when my best friend, your granny, died—I got distracted, and I never saw Dan coming. He slipped past my radar and tracked you. Until I saw you two together, I didn't realize the danger attached to you. By then, it was too late; you wouldn't listen to me."

Sally closed her eyes, propped her left elbow on the table, and bowed her head, putting her hand on her forehead. She stayed silent for a few minutes and seemed to take in the conflict within the card. When she lowered her hand, she placed both in her lap, clasping them together. When she looked up, her smile was filled with love and gentle support. "It's time this came out. This card is all about conflict and problems; from your family, their background—your background. But look at this." She tapped the card with her index finger. "It's the castle crumbling. The dictator's crown is blown off, but the other retains his crown as he tumbles backward into darkness.

"The lightning bolt and arrowhead are purposeful. They hit their target. Fire leaps out, burning through the windows. But you look at the golden leaves on each side of this tower, two sides of a family tree. The one side retains its crown. The other's destroyed, a family predestined to destruction. See the three windows? Three is about change. The one with the crown falls backward, hands extended out in faith, falling into darkness. He can't see. The blue gown trails behind. This blue speaks of healing, a gift. The one without the crown flounders, falling forward into the clouds, vision obscured."

She looked from Sam to Marcie. "The lightning bolt represents the power behind this destructive force. This card speaks of going back generations. This power's incarnate. The magic and control he wields is strong." She blew out a quick huff of breath. "This is about an abrupt ending, a sudden change. If you continue on as you have, you will be destroyed, both of you." Sally waved her hands in the air. She didn't extend compassion. She dug right in, speaking about all she saw while she cupped her ear and nodded each time she heard from Spirit.

"Ah, this is better, the Eight of Pentacles, a card of an apprentice, starting over. This is something new and good." She tapped three times with her index finger into the center of this positive card. "All's not lost. You do have something to get you in the right direction—diligent, hard work."

She reached beside her and patted Sam's hand resting on the table. "Sam, you're the target, always have been. Whatever you build's marked. None of you here are powerless. Look around you at this table. Each one of you is here for a reason. And each one of you, together, is a powerful ally. Pool your resources… your strengths. Work together. Be honest with each other." Sally looked at each of them, focusing hard on Richard until he squirmed in his chair, pulling on his jean jacket.

"And the most important thing to remember is that times have changed. You have rights and resources you didn't have before. This played out before in another life with Jerome." She winked at Marcie, who felt as though a sledgehammer had struck her. Everyone whispered and fidgeted in their chairs. "I asked for help for you, and it was sent by the legion of angels around us. Jerome's your spirit guide, and he'll lead you away from Dan and his trap. Those letters are to teach you how a dark entity manipulated and destroyed two lives. What each of you needs to do now is use the resources available to you, legal and spiritual. Document your facts, keep a paper trail, and work together."

"Sally, how do we stop Dan?" Marcie asked. "He tried to set Sam up by planting drugs in his locker, and he went to Maggie and said he had a witness that Richard burned down a house. He said he would expose Richard if she didn't help me get his marijuana."

Sally reached over and touched Marcie's hand. "Listen. Dan's a monster. He'd have killed you by sucking your energy from you until you withered away. He's not done with you yet. He has plans. That's what he does. He preys on the innocent. He's a wizard, and he's known since he was a child that he was different, that he had gifts, but he has so much darkness inside of him. It was attached to him when he was born. He knows how to use the elements to benefit him, and, yes, even to harm others. You send love." Sally jabbed her whole hand at Marcie. "You know this. Flood him like a fire hydrant spraying a hose of love at him. Those dark elements will scurry and hide. Love overcomes darkness. Have you forgotten that? Stay in the present and start listening to your angels around you. They're bouncing behind you, with your granny, but you're still not listening to them. Get all that clutter out of your head. Start meditating again, every day."

Sally shuffled her deck of cards. "Now, tell me about these special needs kids you found when you delivered the marijuana."

Maggie's eyes widened, and her jaw dropped. "How'd you know?"

Sally pulled back her lips in a tight smile, flashing unusually clean teeth for an eighty-five-year-old woman. "Spirit told me." She pulled a card from the center of the splayed deck, holding it close to her face. "Well, interesting. What are you up to, Dan? He's hidden the truth and distanced himself. Smart, but cowardly. It's all about money. He has no feelings. Ask for help for those kids from your angels. You turn it over to them. Something's happened to one of them already." She shoved the card back in the deck before any of them could see.

"You've got enough to do. Go back to your granny's place. It's time for you to stay here on Las Seta. It's where your battle will be fought. Surround yourself in light, and you'll be protected. Do this the right way, with love, and bring an end to this man. Then you turn your evidence over to the right authorities, and you walk away. You let them deal with Dan. There are others like him; bigger, more powerful."

She focused stern eyes on Sam. "Young man, you start listening to this girl beside you. Listen to the answers she gets from Jerome, to what comes in her dreams. That's all I can help you with today, my dear. This battle's yours. Dan will come again. Follow your instincts. You've got one more shot to get it right." Sally's voice trembled. She cleared her throat and pasted on a stiff smile.

"Just remember, difficult times present themselves for things we have no control over, but this," she sketched a line with her finger past each of them to form a circle, "the snare Dan's caught you in, it's time to turn the tables and change the outcome. Whether you know it or not, by coming together, as you have, you've already begun."

"Just remember that time's not on your side. You're running out. Keep your heads together, your faith strong. Absolute trust and honesty is important from each of you. Now, I've a garden to water." She rose from her chair, busying her hands with her bundle.

Marcie knew Sally had held something vital back. She'd become reclusive and touchy, not focusing on anyone. Marcie whispered to Sam, "Can you take everyone to the truck? I want to talk to Sally alone for a minute."

She caught the possessive male light in those brilliant, blue eyes, and they warmed her like a tropical beach down south. It was unsettling, to say the very least, to have a man letting her know, with a simple look, that she mattered.

"You're trembling. I can feel it." He placed his hand over her shoulder, and the touch sent her blood humming.

"You do that to me."

He cupped her cheek and gave her a soft look, sending her pulse scrambling, and he said, "Call me when you're done. I'll come and get you."

Marcie leaned into his hand and shut her eyes, absorbing his touch right down to her toes. "I will."

"Come on, guys. Let's go," he said.

Everyone offered a brief goodbye right before being ushered off the deck by Sam, and around the side of the cottage. His voice purred like warm whiskey, causing a tug in the center of Marcie's belly, as he made some distracting comments on the vast array of early autumn color filling the gardens around the tranquil property.

Marcie hobbled around the table, her crutches lying on the deck behind her.

Sally frowned, pursed her lips, and crossed her arms, resembling an irritated witch. Marcie felt as if a stern lecture was sure to follow. "Marcie, I've known you and watched over you since your granny, my best friend, rescued you from the cesspool you grew up in, so I've the right to say some things to you."

Her eyes bore into Marcie's. "You screwed up. And it took an act of

God to turn the tide. You lied to me on the phone. You think I didn't know you carried something illegal? Drugs! You've been asking your entire life for your knight in shining armor to come in and sweep you off your feet. You were fooled by Dan. You'd make excuses, and you compromised your values—yourself. I hope you know that good man who's waiting for you now is who you asked for. He's the right one. You need to stay strong. Don't allow Dan's ability to get past your defenses to seduce you into doing anything for him. His shadow still lurks around you."

Marcie bit her lower lip, feeling herself slip toward a good sulk. She knew there was a lot she needed to atone for, but having it cast out in her face wasn't helping.

Sally continued: "Lose the pity party. You did it. It's done. But I need to be harsh because you have no idea of the power that's coming down on you. He got his hooks clean into you. I've seen innocents carried out on a stretcher when they've done battle with a dark entity like Dan. He knows how to tap into you, when to do it, and you let him in." The top of Sally's head came no higher than Marcie's chin. She reached her wrinkled bony hand up and squeezed Marcie's arm. Dirt coated her fingernails, a familiar sight that was so Sally.

"You weren't ready to go out into the world without protection, but you're going to start here and now. Every day from here on out, you bathe in salt and carry it in your pocket. Take this silver hematite and keep it with you. You pull that gold cord down from the universe and wrap yourself in it. Do it now, and keep it there, and you fill your heart with love and hold on to it. Answers will be given to you. Ask your angels. Jerome is with you. Call on him for help each step of the way, and you listen to the peaceful feeling in your gut and the wariness that comes over you when something's not right, because that's him. Then you'll know which choice to make. Keep everyone focused. Temper your attitude, and believe what you hear and see in the messages that come to you."

Marcie felt her stomach pitch as a chill shot up her spine. She hugged Sally tight. "It's going to be bad, isn't it?"

Sally held her away, just as a mother does to a child she's about to scold. "You know better than to allow fear in. Darkness feeds on it. Surround all that fear, anger, hate, and doubt with love and light."

Marcie winced when she heard the crunch of gravel. She didn't have to turn to know it was Sam. "The letters, I need help with the letters and Jerome. He keeps coming to me in my dreams."

Sally cut Marcie off quite briskly. "What's this? I just told you, and you're not listening. When you walk the right road, the answers will be given to you. Hold up the palm of your hands. Close your eyes. Call on St. Michael, call on Jerome, listen, believe, and follow the messages they give you. Jerome's here with you now. He'll guide you one step at a time. You're being tested in your faith right now, Marcie. Whether you believe it or not, you're making steady progress. Ask yourself: When you're alone, do you believe? Yes, or no, Marcie?

"Do not be lured by darkness. Jerome was snared. His wife became a victim. Those letters are to help you see from another angle. He needs you to understand how dangerous this entity is. You'll be given the answers as you need them, no more and no less. Listen and act upon them. If you do not follow through with what Spirit's telling you, the repercussions will be severe. I know you understand that much. There's no black and white. Everything's an illusion. I can't tell you what steps to take. I can only help you hear what you're ignoring. Jerome's letters are his story, a history linking you and Sam. Haven't you listened to what he's told you so far? Work together with your friends, honestly. Be just, and don't do anything alone. Light overcomes darkness. Love overcomes hate. Now go with your man and spend some quiet time in nature. If you need more help, let me know. I'll come."

How could she miss the slight falter in Sally's eyes? For her to offer to leave her sanctuary was a huge concession on her part. Even when Granny died, she hadn't left. She had said her friend would understand.

Sam picked up Marcie's crutches and slid his arm around her waist. The heat of his body nurtured her right down to her toes.

"Let's go back to my cottage," Marcie told him. "I think that's where we need to formulate whatever we're going to do to stop Dan. Besides, I'm starving." She rested her head against him as she wrapped her arm around his waist. He didn't pull back. He nudged her closer, walking with her, and that was when a locked cavern, stashed in some secret compartment inside of her heart, opened just a crack, releasing the ultimate trust that she'd never given anyone before.

"Well, let's do it." Sam lifted Marcie, crutches and all, and carried her to the open truck door, easing her into the backseat. "We're staying on Las Seta." That was all he said when he closed Marcie's door, climbed in the driver's side, and started the truck.

"So is this where we go rehash whatever that was we heard?" Richard was being crass, with a silent Maggie, chewing her fingernails, perched on his lap.

"No, this is where we go to formulate a plan, Richard, with all the secret information each one of us knows about Dan, Lance Silver, and their drug operation," Marcie answered. "And then we're going to put it all together and figure out what the hell we're going to do."

CHAPTER 38

Marcie's eyes flickered open, warmed by the late afternoon sun splashing a pool of soothing light over her. Even though she had slept deeply on her double bed, she stretched past the blossoming weary ache infiltrating all her muscles.

Her soothed stomach was content from the bowl of homemade bean soup Sam had heated on the propane stove. Everyone had crowded around the table, rehashing their outrageous morning, what they'd heard, while eating lunch, but Marcie hadn't listened. Her eyes struggled to stay open with each bite, and when she was done, Sam slid her bowl aside, caring and attentive as he gently lifted her and carried her to bed, laying her granny's quilt over her while she drifted off to sleep.

Marcie breathed in the peace and tranquility, a constant here on this property. Maybe the visit to Sally had sparked awareness to the importance of respecting and honoring her given gifts.

She could hear muffled voices drift with relative calm from the kitchen. It was comforting. She closed her eyes and pictured the five of them, sitting around the kitchen table, plotting out their plan of action. They were five honorable people she loved, respected, and felt deeply connected to.

What an odd mix they were. She took a moment to offer gratitude for each one of them before tossing back the quilt and tumbling out of bed. She clunked her way down the hall and stopped outside the kitchen. Her friends were gathered around the kitchen table with maps and papers askew, deep in discussion. Maggie was the first to look up.

"Maggie, you've been dragged into the middle of a mess I'm responsible for," Marcie began. "Whatever plan we come up with, you need to stay out of it. Lily and Ryley need you, and you need to be with them."

She had everyone's attention. Even Richard had dropped his elusive hard-ass demeanor to something that reflected deep concern.

Sam slid his chair back and strode to her side. "I didn't know you were awake."

"You mean I didn't wake the dead with the ruckus I made hobbling in here?"

"Nope, but our heads are elsewhere."

She allowed Sam to lead her over to his empty chair. Without argument, she gave him the right to help her sit. His gentle touch glided up her back and sent a warm buzz tingling from her head to toe. His hand lingered on her shoulder, a protective gesture that spoke of the link blossoming between them. When her eyes met his uneasy gaze, she saw something else hidden in the shadows.

"We've already discussed the matter while you slept. Lily and Ryley will be moved here tomorrow. Just so you know, Marcie, you, Maggie, and the kids are out of it from this day forward. Jesse, Diane, Richard, and I'll be doing what needs doing. We'll be taking the risks, making the decisions."

She couldn't believe it. Leave it to a man, a whole pack of alpha males and one alpha female, to believe they knew best. When she looked at Richard, Jesse, and Diane, they appeared to flank Sam, unified leaders who lorded over the group. A plan had been developed, outlined, and executed all while she'd slept. When she glanced over to a silent, tormented Maggie, her stomach kicked up a pang of suffering, filled with fear and uncertainty. Her skin prickled with awareness, and for the first time in years, she sensed the turmoil that belonged to someone else. Then Marcie did something unexpected while reaching for Sam's hand. "I think that's a good idea."

BEFORE DARK SET IN, JESSE DROVE DIANE, RICHARD, AND MAGGIE TO THE dock. They'd agreed to return with the kids in the morning. Besides, they needed supplies, not just food but also the kind only Diane could get: ammunition, radios, and gear for surveillance.

When Jesse returned, he didn't linger in the kitchen. He dumped his coat on the back of a kitchen chair and said goodnight, taking the bed in Granny's room. Marcie felt clumsy and foolish, facing Sam alone in her cozy kitchen. She wanted to reach out, but the fear of rejection hammered her in place. Sam shoved his hands in his pockets and then took them out again. He too apparently shared her case of nerves.

"There's only my bed left, unless you want the sofa that's too short for you or to crowd Jesse in that small double bed." There, she said it. But then she winced and started to backpedal before he rejected her. "What I meant to say…"

"I told myself when you snuck out that you'd deliberately lied right to my face, that you told me what I wanted to hear and you'd been waiting for the first opportunity to slip away and go back to Dan and your marijuana. I felt betrayed. If you had stuck a knife in my gut, it would've been kinder. I wasn't going to be used again. I questioned my good sense."

She lingered in the archway, wearing the baggy sweats she'd pulled on earlier. "I can see how you'd come to that conclusion, except my mind doesn't work that way."

Sam angled his head. "No, you're an up-front, extremely naive woman who's a little out there."

"A little? Isn't that like saying the moon's a little round?" She leaned against the wall.

Sam stepped closer. His arms were still crossed in front of him, but a glint of humor now rested on his face. "You're not ashamed of who you are, and I don't remember ever knowing a person to hold themselves accountable for the bad things they've done even before truly knowing they'd done something wrong, to say they're sorry countless times and mean it. It's unsettling."

She pushed away from the wall and would have taken an evasive step back but was hampered by her cast. Sam solved the problem of keeping her still by placing his hands on the wall, one on each side, by her head.

Her heart hammered so hard that her thoughts scattered. "I needed to apologize to you, to make it right. You're a good man. You've never left me, even when you were angry, and you had every right to be."

He raised his eyebrows. "There you go again." His face was so close, full, tempting lips she knew all too well—ones so skilled in knowing how to kiss a woman.

"Your heart's pounding. Listen, can you hear it?" He moved closer, his voice a smoky whisper. He placed his hand on her chest. Her breath trembled from her loss of control, becoming sharp and shallow. He spread his fingers and smoothed over her breast. Her knees weakened. She must have weaved, because his hand slid behind and gripped her hip, holding her steady.

"So I guess the couch is out?" she asked.

He lowered his head and nipped her bottom lip. Her fingers reached into his hair, pulling him closer until he finally covered her mouth with his. He toyed with her nipple, straining the cotton shirt. She let her tongue dance with his, but he set the pace, and when he pulled back, she nearly moaned until he scooped her up and carried her to the bedroom.

He kicked the door closed with his black boot and laid Marcie gently in the middle of the bed. Something broke loose deep inside her, a control she'd always had, except with Sam. Her thoughts scattered when his warm mouth found hers again. She shivered. He was driving her mad with the way he worked his mouth down her jaw to her neck. His magical hands, with long, wide fingers, slid under her shirt, skimming the curve of her breast. She pulled at his shirt, fumbled with his belt buckle, but he pulled away.

"Sam, I don't need all this seduction."

"I do, and I plan to have you naked under me. You'll be glad I took the time to do it right when I'm done."

Her whole body trembled as he knelt down and removed her one shoe and then the sock. He took care not to bump her injured ankle even when he slid her pants off. His fingers practically melted her shirt and bra off. He pulled the covers back and helped her under. The air was chilly, but neither appeared to notice.

Sam stepped back and watched her with dreamy blue eyes. He wanted to touch every part of her, to taste her and the bright innocence that openly welcomed him. He took his time, pulling his shirt off, removing his clothes, and then he climbed in beside her. Skin to skin, he tasted and touched her every curve, his hands moving faster, maybe a little rough. But, by God, the woman responded in a way that was driving him half blind.

She was small—but strong. His mouth on hers became hotter, and more demanding when he moved between her legs. She wrapped one around his waist, and he was mindful not to touch her injured ankle.

She buried her face against his throat. Her tiny hands skimmed down his back, grabbed his hips, and pulled him toward her. "Sam, now, please, for God's sake." Her voice wavered as she struggled to catch her breath. He took both of her hands and rested them above her head, linking his with hers, and sank into her; deep, in one smooth motion. He muffled her cry of shock and pleasure with his mouth as he moved inside her. He watched her in the moonlight. Her eyes darkened, changing color to a deeper and darker hue of blue. Her eyes widened, fluttered, as her breath deepened. Her grip tightened when he increased his rhythm—harder, faster. He watched her eyes open and felt her come apart around him; no secrets between them, only pure, honest love. He buried himself deeper and held on until she peaked and bucked under him, then he let himself go while he buried his face in her scads of glorious hair.

She'd drifted off; for how long she didn't know, as she lay sprawled across the bed, blankets strewn everywhere, and Sam still on top of her. He must have sensed her stirring, because he rolled off, tucking his arm under her, pulling her with him until she rested her arms on his chest. Sam reached down and pulled the covers around them. She touched a soft, wayward strand of hair dangling across his forehead and absorbed the soft rhythm of his breathing.

"What's wrong?" His sleepy voice scratched with gravel. He twirled strands of her thick hair through his fingers.

"I was just thinking of how I keep screwing up, and you don't leave." This time, she didn't shut her eyes to block out the intensity of his watchful gaze. "I was thanking God and my angels and Jerome for every stupid thing I did that brought me to you. Sam, maybe we should just leave, go somewhere far away where you'll be out of Dan's reach—Lance's, too."

He pressed his firm lips to hers. "We're going to fix this here, Marcie. We're not running away, and we'll bring Dan and Lance Silver's little empire down. You need to trust me."

"I do trust you, with my life. Who I don't trust are Dan and Lance."

He pulled her head down to rest on his chest, surrounding her with his arms. "Go to sleep. Tomorrow, we're going to fix this."

Marcie basked in a solid sense of protection; for the first time ever, in the new beginning of something good, of being part of a magical life filled with more goodness, hope, grace, joy, and love than she thought was possible. She was with her Mr. Right. She rolled over a little awkwardly, hindered by her cast, and snuggled her back against his chest, allowing his arm to drape over her. His fingers linked with hers, a sizzling connection that comforted and soothed her to sleep.

He waited in the light. This time, her awareness was acute in this dreamlike state. Brilliant radiance poured around them with gigantic waves crashing in the background. Marcie continued to move forward on the wooden deck of a tall ship surrounded by the vast, rippling blue-green ocean. Jerome and his golden locks stood behind the helm. His eyes were on the horizon, and he was wearing a gleaming white shirt and tan canvas pants tucked into tall, black boots.

Marcie instinctively moved toward her tall, gentle guide. Her long white gown flowed around her. She moved up each smooth wooden step while the sloop swayed beneath her bare feet. He never turned his head but stayed straight on course, eyes forward, as his powerful hands maintained a steady hold on the wheel.

"Marcie, you're starting to understand. What you're up against is reversing a course of events set in motion before your time. It's like this wheel. The direction isn't cast in stone. The forces of nature have the ability to throw you off course and change direction. You've already started, all of you, and what you need to do is step back and let Sam, Jesse, Diane, and Richard go forth with their plan."

"So it'll be all right? I don't need to do anything?"

"I didn't say that. You need to stay with Maggie and the children when they arrive tomorrow. You also need to be ready and listen to the signs around you. Dan will come again. You'll know what to do when he does. But one word of caution, do not give voice to the doubts that'll flood you, or they'll take root. That's what he's counting on. Remember, the choice you make will be the one that turns the tide and breaks the chain of the dark entities' continuing cycle. This dark element has grown stronger with each incarnation, and it rose from little more than the sludge of oil spills contaminating Mother Earth."

Marcie saw sadness lurk in the shadows around him. He was long dead and gone. "He took your wife and raised your son."

His eyes bore into her. "He plans to take you from Sam and destroy you both."

"Isabel didn't believe you until the end."

"Marcie, it was a different time and place. She had no rights, no say, and no resources. You have legal rights now that didn't exist for her, even though corruption has woven a thread through your legal system. Remember, there are those watching from the sidelines who'll help you, all of you. You already know what he is."

"Dan's a wizard."

"He's more than that, Marcie. He's a master of deception. Dark entities flood him. He can no longer exist without them. Your teacher knows. You're still learning. In human form, he's a true sociopath, mimicking emotions without feeling them. His explosive charm is what allowed him to seduce you. He becomes an addiction, keeps you completely off balance. He sought you out. He carefully chooses each of his victims; going after the weak, those who lack self-esteem and those filled with self-doubt. Then he reads your thoughts.

And he knew just how to feed your ego with compliments, flooding you with bewitching attention."

"Remember how he seemed to understand you, and his thoughts were completely in sync with yours? He could see into your weak aura. You've never healed from your parents abuse, and that raw hole is how he got in. He saw it. He reeled you into his web of lies, and you did anything for him. But the choice was still yours. You weren't listening to the spirits around you. They screamed at you, posting signs and roadblocks, while you stumbled blindly over them and chose to ignore what sat right in front of you. I've come to guide you now. You have help on this side. More angels will come as you need them. You have help on the physical plane, too, from your teacher, Sam, and your friends."

"This is your lesson: Be strong, seek out hope and innocence. Block out Dan. Gather your love and fire that powerful energy back at him. Keep your circle of protection around you and your friends. Keep your thoughts guarded. When your aura has healed, you'll see him as he truly is, and you'll be repelled. You'll see the scam he projects as a teacher to help those around him and a leader to those who follow him. He has cords appearing like black hoses in his aura, attaching to the weak and vulnerable. It's what gives him power. It's how he feeds. You keep the cords cut, or he'll drain all your energy."

"In New Orleans, your memory loss was a gift. I cut his cords for you. He knows they're cut, and he's scrambling to reattach to you. Dan practices his craft alone and portrays himself as someone who picks up vibes. But he's much more. Remember, after he sucked you in, all the emotional pain he hammered into you? Then, after, he was genuinely sorry he hurt you, but this was only to keep you off balance, from seeing what he truly is—a monster with no remorse, no conscience, and no sense of responsibility. He takes the credit but never the blame. And how many times has he done this? When he hurt you emotionally, it was your fault, or you made him do it. He truly believes you're fortunate to be given his time and attention."

"Think back to when you met him, the attraction and starry-eyed illusion that he was your Mr. Right. Remember the feigned interest in everything you did; merely an illusion he created. It really was an outstanding performance, and the act dropped when he was convinced his control over you was secure. Even though I know you see it, all that good in you cannot grasp the concept of this being pure deception. Instead of walking away, you stayed and tried

desperately to rescue the wonderful person you were sure was buried deep inside. What's hard for you to grasp is that this ideal man never existed."

"Dan lives by self-serving rules, and he will change without warning. Here's your warning, Marcie: He knows you're on to him. He fooled you again when you got on that plane, and he's preparing himself now to repeat a desperate performance to win you back. His goal is to destroy you emotionally; it is the only way for his darkness to survive—to become stronger. Your prayers are setting him back, and he's fighting you. His purpose, and pleasure, is to create as much emotional turmoil, guilt, self-doubt, and depression as possible and ultimately eliminate your power."

"He's a human being. Can't he be saved?" Marcie asked.

"Listen to you. Understand this. It goes against your every natural instinct to turn your back on one of God's children, but you can't change him. A dark entity cannot be turned light. Flood him like a fire hydrant filled with the unconditional energy of love, and that darkness will scurry away. Then you let go, and you leave. Finish with him and get him out of your head."

"Was he always like this? Was he born this way? I don't understand."

"These are the mysteries of the universe. You have a lifetime of learning ahead of you. He was born with the darkness attached to him, with his veil thinned. He is the same dark entity who destroyed Isabel and me on the physical plane. You all have a battle ahead of you. You work together in the light and you'll be victorious. Just don't fall prey to his trickery. His charm is thick, and he still has the ability to surpass your defenses. You need to resist and be strong, or he'll win. Use the gifts your granny and Sally taught you, and listen to what the spirits are telling you. You'll be guided as long as you remain open to the light. You mustn't doubt." The mist filled around him. She reached her pale hand out. She had more questions, but he moved away.

A gentle pull on her shoulder brought her spiraling back into the dim room. The early morning light crept up on the horizon, and Sam stood dressed beside the bed.

CHAPTER 39

"Jesse's down at the dock, picking everyone up." Sam, dressed in a long-sleeved, black shirt and his usual jeans, leaned down and took his time kissing her good morning—the way a man was supposed to. Marcie ran her fingers through his damp hair as he deepened the kiss. "Good morning," he said in a sexy voice before pulling away, smelling fresh and clean.

He left her to dress, which she did, pulling on dark capris and a matching T-shirt, and then she shuffled barefoot into the kitchen without her crutches. Sam handed her a steaming mug of coffee just as Richard, Maggie, and the children burst through the door. Diane and Jesse brought up the rear. Both hefted two large backpacks along with two boxes of food, which they dumped onto the cluttered kitchen table, pushing aside an empty plate.

Marcie sipped her strong black coffee, but her nerves were frayed as if she'd already downed a pot.

"You okay, babe?" Sam didn't miss much. He slid closer, gently massaging her back.

"Sam, move it. It's show time," Richard said before he kissed Maggie on the cheek, shooed the casually dressed children into the front room, and then glanced at Marcie. When he did, his eyes widened right before he smirked. Marcie looked down at the floor. She couldn't hide anything from Richard.

Diane tugged her black jacket down to cover the bulge of her weapon. She pulled a folded piece of paper from her back pocket and dangled it for everyone to see. "Search warrant so that whatever we find to jam this bastard up won't get tossed out. No one else on the team knows about it except the judge, Dexter, and the six of us in this room." Diane folded the paper and stuffed it back in her pocket.

"Good job, Diane." Sam was all business.

Jesse checked his ankle holster. Diane handed out microphones and earpieces. Marcie knew they were hiking over to Lance Silver's to plant some kind of listening device in the house, or as close as possible, so they could hear when Dan made contact with Mr. Silver himself.

"Let's go," Sam said, leaning down to kiss Marcie on the top of her head. He didn't linger but followed Jesse, Richard, and Diane out the door to her truck, which they'd confiscated. Then, as an afterthought, he turned back and yanked open the screen door. "I want both of you to stay inside until we get back. No wandering off." His alpha male side had taken over again.

"We'll be here, Sam, but we're not staying cooped up indoors on this beautiful day. The sun's out, and there's not a cloud in the sky," Marcie said.

"I'd feel better if you didn't go out, period." Sam glanced over Marcie's head at the kids and then sighed. "Could you at least keep everyone close to the house?"

Marcie hobbled to the door and touched his hand. "I can do that."

Sam kissed her again, this time on the lips, and then he was gone. She waved as her truck disappeared up the narrow driveway.

Marcie moved to the propane stove, lit the burner, and put on a kettle of water. Maggie sat in the front room with Lily in the overstuffed easy chair. Ryley kneeled on the hardwood floor and rifled his Game Boy out of his dark blue backpack. What struck Marcie when she hobbled in toward them were the dark circles that had appeared overnight beneath Maggie's brilliant eyes. Even her alabaster skin appeared pale in the bright light against her dark blue sweatshirt.

Lily wore a bright pink Dora the Explorer shirt and pants. When she pulled away from Maggie, she wandered unfettered with the body of a headless Barbie doll. She bounced from the chair to the table to the old, worn couch in front of the window, in socks and shoes, which was something of an anomaly, and then back to the floor to repeat her circle.

Marcie leaned against the bookshelf and gazed out the large picture window. The birds danced in circles, flapping their wings, skittering in and out of the trees. The happy chirps carried through the window as if they were beckoning their friend to join them under the peaceful blue sky.

The dark green leaves were beginning to turn, and they'd soon begin to fall in the autumn chill, another cycle ending. Marcie glanced at the front deck she rarely used and the large Sitka spruce with her rope swing tied to a sturdy branch. As a shell-shocked twelve-year-old girl, she'd swung for hours under that tree. She'd dreamed she could soar with the birds fluttering above her, taking her into a dream world free of shame. Right now, she felt compelled to wander out in the sunshine with the children. This property was her safe haven, and she believed nothing could harm her here.

"Maggie, let's take the kids out front. I think Lily would love to swing."

Marcie watched Lily bounce on the chair and wondered if, in fact, she understood even as she dangled lost between worlds. Maggie didn't answer, biting her lower lip and staring vacantly out the window. Lily dropped her naked doll and raced to the door, and Marcie went after her. By the time she staggered with one good foot down the stairs without her crutches, Lily had hopped on the wooden swing.

Ryley's voice echoed through the open window. "Mom, I want to play with my Game Boy."

"Bring it with you. It's nice out, and you're not staying inside with your head stuck in that computer game," Maggie snapped. She must really have been tired.

By the time Marcie reached her granny's worn picnic table near the swing, the explosive pressure in her broken ankle ached terribly. It was her fault, as she kept leaving her crutches propped against some wall in the cottage.

"Where are your crutches?" Maggie hovered as Marcie sank onto the plank bench and groaned.

"I forgot them, so sue me. I'll just make you wait on me, and I'll stay right here and watch the kids for you." As if on cue, the kettle whistled. "That would be my water boiling for tea."

Maggie rolled her eyes and marched into the house.

Marcie laughed lightly. Still grinning, she turned back to the kids. Her stomach tightened when panic chilled her blood and plugged the easy flow through her veins. Her heart lurched and jammed her throat with something thick and gooey, cutting off all sound and means of speech. Dan McKenzie towered over Lily with a wicked smile while he gently pushed the tiny girl on the swing. Her thoughts scrambled while glued to the bench. *Breathe.* But it was damn impossible, as her pulse burned down from the crown of her head, pinning both feet to the ground. How'd he gotten past her circle, onto this land, without her knowing?

"Hey, Marcie, how's your leg?"

He never missed a beat while pushing Lily with a skillful, loving touch. This was in direct conflict with what she knew he was. She felt herself slip, mesmerized by this split in his personality, and wondered if, in fact, two different people resided in him. Lily appeared happy and comfortable, and that confused Marcie.

"Hey, Lily, that's a good girl. You just keep swinging. Uncle Dan's going to have a little talk to Marcie and your mom. Hey, Ryley, I didn't see you hiding over there. How's it going, bud?" He crossed his nicely tanned arms over his light T-shirt and sauntered, with an intense interest, over to Ryley, who sat under the old cedar, cross-legged, playing his Game Boy. For just a moment, Marcie was swept away in the warm charm he focused on children, one of the things that had first captivated her. What a magnificent father he'd be, or so she had thought. It was a ploy, the explosive charm that had sucked her in each time. Innocent children couldn't see past his deception.

Dan squatted in his light khaki pants beside Ryley, draping one arm across the boy's shoulder while he watched him engage the buttons on his handheld game. Dan chuckled and warmly jabbed his finger at the screen, and both he and Ryley cheered.

"Right on board, give me five." Dan held out his hand, and Ryley slapped it. Marcie couldn't remember the last time Ryley had beamed with such joy.

"Ryley, come here!" On the porch, Maggie dropped the ceramic mug of hot tea and bolted over to Ryley.

It wasn't until Maggie had crossed in front of her that Marcie felt the snap, breaking the link Dan had focused on her with such ease. A chill climbed up her spine. How could she be caught again so easy?

Dan and Ryley glanced up, and Marcie didn't miss the sudden change in Dan. His shoulders stiffened. The light in his face faded into something cold and dark. His hazel eyes blazed the color of cheapened rye and locked onto Maggie, irritated and full of fire.

"See, Dan? Isn't this cool? Look what happens when I fire this," Ryley said.

"Wow, man, that's awesome. You're really good." His eyes never left Maggie as he slid his hand down Ryley's arm. "Hey, Maggie, it's good to see you. You've got quite the champion Game Boy player here. He knows how to kick some serious butt."

Ryley gazed starry eyed at his hero. Lily began to squeal and kick as she twisted and rocked the rope swing, making eye contact with no one.

"Ah, I think she wants me to push her again." Dan stood up, but this time Marcie watched an agitated Maggie skirt around him, block his path, and push him with both hands splayed hard against his chest.

"No."

"Whoa, Maggie, sorry. If you don't want me to, that's fine. I'm just trying to help. I like Lily. I think she's a great kid, and look, she liked it. She was having a great time."

"Stay away from my kids." Maggie's sharp voice shook.

Dan held both hands up in a show of surrender. His face took on the remarkable image of a man seriously wronged. What a performance. But his eyes; Marcie could see from where she sat, sparkled and glowed with something mischievous and lizard-like. She looked closer. His eyes had changed. They were darker, heavier than she remembered.

Her gut ached watching Maggie stand her ground, breathing as if she'd sprinted a mile, but Marcie knew she was close to losing it. To make it worse, Ryley was sidling closer to Dan. What did he want with them?

"Hey, Ryley, go inside and help your mom make me some toast? I'm starving and didn't have a chance to eat, and Maggie, would you mind making a pot of green tea?" Marcie asked.

"Mom can do it by herself. I want to show Dan how this works."

"Ryley, I'd really like you to go in with your mom and Lily now. Dan came to see me, and he wants to go over some adult stuff in private. Isn't that right, Dan?" Her smooth voice was determined even when she turned her entire focus on Dan—whose focal point shifted back to her with the lopsided grin he used to snare vulnerable women.

"Ryley, listen to Marcie. Go inside with your mom," he said. His eyes never left Marcie's while Maggie hurried Lily and Ryley past Dan and into the cottage.

"So, Marcie, you didn't answer me. How's the leg?"

"I didn't think you cared. But it'll heal."

He moved with such grace and confidence, sitting right beside her. His leg brushed her brown capris as the bench shifted to support his weight. He scanned the circumference of the yard, looking over her head, which barely topped his shoulders, into the distant brush that covered her granny's property.

"Wow, look at this place. We should've grown one large garden here. Look at all this space. The salal over there? There's no better camouflage. How many acres again? Thirty, right? That's a lot of ground cover in one spot, safer for you. Look what happened riding your dirt bike on the back trail."

Being with him confused her, and she struggled to separate reality from illusion. She was riveted to his words when he gently touched her leg.

"And then there's us, Marcie. You know."

"What, Dan, what about us? There's no us. That was you fitting me in when it was convenient for you."

His face softened. He clasped his hands in front of him, but not before she caught the slight tremble in his hand. Even his cheeks tinged a subtle shade of pink. He leaned forward, tilting his head to the side a little sheepishly. "I screwed up, and I know I hurt you badly. What I did wasn't fair, and I can't make excuses for sending you off alone, letting you take all the risk. I'm under so much pressure with what I've taken on. I took you for granted. I thought you'd always be there and that you clearly understood how much you mean to me. It was my fault for not telling you every day how special you are, what a good, loving woman you are. You're the only one who's slipped in." Dan placed his hand over his heart. "I vowed I'd never let anyone in, but you're here, and, no matter what I do, I can't get you out."

His voice softened in a way that made her want to cuddle the vulnerable little boy inside of him. A familiar pull and giddy feeling inside her stomach had her spiraling back into that lost world. Suddenly, she was jerked back, as if drowning in a pool of water. "Did you set me up in New Orleans?"

His face hardened. "Is that what you thought? That I'd do something like that to you? What kind of monster do you think I am? Fuck, I was worried sick about you. I called you over and over. Your cell phone kept going to voicemail. You have no idea what I went through when I tried to track you down. I finally came out here, and, by sheer luck, I found you. But you pulled the rug right out from under me when I discovered that you had three cops with you. And, yes, I threatened to set up that boy wonder you latched onto because I was jealous… angry… hurt. Pick any one of the above. I thought you had turned on me and betrayed me; I thought that was the only way to get you back. I should never have made you go out there to get the weed, and I shouldn't have involved Maggie. I wasn't thinking. You took ten years off of my life when I found out you'd crashed." He stopped, and her heart was shattered by the sheen of tears in his eyes.

She looked away when doubts crept in. Maybe he wasn't responsible for her attack.

"Look, Marcie, you've had some fun with this cop guy, but I love you so much. I can get past this if you'll come back to me and be mine." He reached out and touched her forearm, then slid the back of his fingers up her arm in a gentle caress, stroked under the curve of her chin and gently tucked her long, wavy hair behind her ear. "You and me, we'll make a good life together. Marcie, I have plans, and you're part of them and everything good that'll come with it. We'll travel, spend a few months down in South America."

Fear, or something like it, pounded inside of her head, her heart, her gut; screaming to wake up and shake off the magnetic physical pull toward him. She no longer felt a desperate need, as if her heart would blister into a million tiny pieces if he didn't belong to her. Awareness blinked on, similar to a hundred-watt bulb. This physical attraction was at a cellular level, like an alcoholic's craving for liquor. Marcie shut her eyes to break the cord and his contact, sending a silent plea to her angels for help. When she opened her eyes, he studied her deeply, but the expression and blank look were nothing familiar. She couldn't read him. Somehow, he had this ability to hide and block all access while still being a master at tapping into people, reading their most personal thoughts. Marcie struggled to keep hers safely locked away.

"I can't shake this want of you, Dan. I need peace, and I need to be loved. What do you want from me?"

He appeared to glow when he leaned toward her. "I told you; I want you back, and I'll do anything to get you." He reached for Marcie's hand, linking their fingers.

She struggled emotionally to pull away, but he was like a powerful magnet, yanking her back again and again. A single tear slid down the side of her bruised face.

"I promise you, it's going to be better. Marcie, trust me. I'll protect you." He took both of her hands in his. "As soon as all the marijuana's cut, you and I'll take off and rest for a bit on a tropical beach down south. I'll get someone else in to finish the rest of the gardens. You're hurt, and you shouldn't have been out there anyway."

Marcie lifted her head and caught something in his eyes that made her pause.

"So how many gardens were missed?" he asked.

Marcie hesitated. "Nineteen. So is the bud I cut ready to go?"

"All trimmed and dried, but I need all of it."

"Did Sandra trim it while looking after those disabled kids?"

"Look, Marcie, I was as mad as you when I found out those kids were there. I laid into her pretty good. It won't happen again, or she's out of there." He sliced his hand through the air. "I'm totally on your side, but let's stay focused and finish. Forget Sandra, all right?" He smiled a devilishly lopsided grin in his unique way that lit up his entire face, snagging another hook inside her. He pulled a folded rural map of the Gardiner area out of his back pocket and flattened it on the slatted wood table behind her. "I need to get someone out there now."

"Do you think the gardens are still there?"

"They'd better be. My buyer's waiting. After we get back from our little vacation, we can move on, get another one started indoors. But, you know, for next year, let's do it all here. We can fence it off, make it secure, and we'll have more control. Don't forget it's closer and easier for you, too, Marcie. With all the military sweeps around the state park, it's getting way too dangerous on the mainland. And just think of all the cash we'll make."

Marcie sucked in her lower lip and nodded. "So, if we start it here, you'll help?"

"Oh, for sure."

"Because, you know, that's a lot of water to haul every day. Does that mean you're going to move in?"

He touched her cheek with his thumb and forefinger, and his face softened. "That's what I've been saying to you. You and me, Marcie— it's time."

"So we're going to make a lot of money?"

"We will, especially from the trade."

"What trade?"

"Well, this time, my buyer's trading straight across for something even better. And it's already been sold."

CHAPTER 40

"You did what?"

Marcie limped back and forth through the kitchen, stopping by the stack of shoes by the front door and slipping on a sandal. She felt completely off kilter, as if she'd gone two rounds on one of those rides at the fair that was filled with spins, twists, and turns and then dangled you upside down. She couldn't stand still and gave no thought to the persistent ache in her ankle.

"Maybe they can catch him getting the marijuana from your gardens," Maggie said.

Marcie shook her head as she continued to pace. "I don't think so, Maggie. Dan won't get his hands dirty. He'll get someone to do it for him."

"Mom, can I go outside?" Ryley walked in with a challenging nine-year-old attitude.

"No, you can't. Go back in the front room and read that bone book you brought." Maggie jabbed her finger in the air.

"Where's Dan? Can't I hang out with him?" Ryley didn't move.

Maggie's face pinched as if she'd lose it at any moment. But, to her credit, she shut her eyes for a second and swept her shoulder-length hair back while tapping her foot in one of her nice new runners. Marcie could tell she was counting down. "No, you can't go and see him. He's gone. Right, Marcie?"

Maggie's fingers were still locked in her hair, but Marcie could see the slight shake and recognized the fear behind this sharp reaction with Ryley.

"Your mom's right. Dan left. Listen, bud, go in the hallway closet and grab one of those jigsaw puzzles. Work on it in the front room—just for a little bit. I know you're bored, but we'll have some lunch and then after we'll head outside and check out the lake."

He was ready to argue but must have sensed his mother's rising temper. He frowned and left in an unresponsive huff, irritated and mumbling. Marcie smiled a little when she heard a few clunks and clatters in the hall closet.

"Maggie, it's going to be okay...." The distinct churn of gravel sent Maggie and Ryley bolting to the door. Marcie struggled with her cast as she glimpsed her truck pulling in. By the time she reached the doorway, Sam was on the porch, walking through the screen door with Ryley dogging his heels, boisterously announcing that Dan had just left.

"Dan was here? What did he want?"

"He wants me back."

"You're kidding." Sam ground his teeth and scowled at Marcie. "And when does he want you to get the rest of the marijuana?" His response was unusually abrupt.

"He doesn't. Someone else is going to handle it for him."

Sam lifted her chin with his finger. "Well, too bad for Dan, because we found out his brother, Greg, will be here tonight with the cocaine. By this time tomorrow, it'll all be over, and that scumbag will be locked behind bars."

CHAPTER 41

"When he makes the exchange, you need to be in position," Diane ordered her handpicked team: Green, Winters, Mercer, and Craig. They mobilized at the old fire hall, now used for storage at the north end of Las Seta. Donaldson was noticeably absent.

Their boss, Dexter, and the rest of the team arrived with the Coast Guard after sundown and were in position at Scotty Bay, waiting for Greg to arrive with the cocaine and Dan to arrive with the marijuana. Dexter radioed once in place. This was expected to be the largest cocaine and marijuana bust in Washington history. These dealers were organized and well financed, and, until now, luck had been on their side. Then, this morning, Diane had snuck into Lance's compound and planted a listening device outside of his study. Sam, Richard, and Jesse had camped outside of the estate, in the rugged forest, using the thick foliage as their hideout while they listened. That was when they had hit the pot of gold. Tonight, they'd nail all of the players with enough evidence to put them all away and seriously dent this west coast trail of drugs and all the way down Interstate 5.

Sam closed his eyes to curb his worry for Marcie when her sweet, bruised face snuck into his thoughts. He couldn't relax. He was too wired, and it didn't help that adrenaline pumped through his system at a ferocious pace. His hands started to shake, more like a twitch, as if he'd drunk a gallon of coffee, all because he'd left Marcie alone. He sucked in a deep breath and blew it out hard, helping to steady his hands, but this did little to comfort his unspeakable need to keep her close. Every morsel of decency stabbed him in the gut—how could he have left her unprotected around this predator? If anything happened to her, he'd never forgive himself.

"Sam, Jesse, we have a problem." Diane raised the palm of her hand to gain their attention as she pushed through the few agents, dressed in full Kevlar vests, to where Sam and Jesse leaned against the back wall. A radio buzzed and crackled behind her.

"I said to keep radio silence," Diane shouted, letting loose her constantly controlled temper.

Sam pushed off the concrete wall. Every nerve ending jumped as beads of sweat danced down his spine. "What's going on?"

"We got a situation off the main dock. Some locals have taken to policing the island and took matters into their own hands. They have some young thug in a boat about a mile off shore. An arsonist, he's apparently been lighting fires, vandalizing property. They radioed ahead to the Sequim detachment to come and get him. As soon as they reach the halfway point, they're going to dump him in the ocean whether the sheriff's there or not. They won't wait. Sequim doesn't have a boat tonight. They tried to rent one, but…"

"Fuck, you got to be kidding. No, don't you dare say it," Sam roared, pounding his fist into the creamy paint-chipped wall.

Jesse narrowed his dark eyes. His heavy brows appeared to knit together. He said nothing, crossed his arms, and looked around as if trying to figure out what was really going on.

The agents in the room cleared out. "The Coast Guard has the closest boat available. They've been dispatched," Diane said as Sam fell in beside her. The pit of his stomach dropped, shooting an icy chill down through both legs, pinning his heavy feet to the ground, making it an effort to move.

"Diane, we need to be in place now." His blood churned to a pulse that echoed deep and slow.

"Sam, we don't have a choice. These people will dump this kid and leave him to drown. The Coast Guard needs to be there before they drop him in. I'm sorry. The boat's already been pulled. I've been instructed to send three of my agents along in case there's trouble with the locals."

"Diane, the Coast Guard's going to be seen pulling out. This is un-fucking-believable. How could this have happened tonight, of all nights? They knew, God fucking dammit. That son of a bitch knew!" Sam followed Diane out through the double doors.

"Look, Sam, I know, but we need to go. As soon as the team's grabbed this punk from the locals, they'll be back."

Jesse hurried past them in the same blue jeans and black windbreaker he'd worn for the past couple of days. "It's a setup to pull our people out so the exchange can still happen. Should have smelled this coming."

Sam knew to trust his gut, and by ignoring it, as he'd done, Marcie could be in danger. A well-honed man like him was rarely cold. Right now, he shivered under his warm, dark jacket as if his blood had turned to ice. He bolted behind Diane and Jesse in his thick-soled black boots. Three agents appeared as a shadowy outline, hurrying to the obscure dock behind the fire hall. Lights blazed from the forty-five-foot response boat as it swooped over the rough waves to the dock, where the agents waited.

"Sir, I've got a truck waiting." Sam jumped and reached for his gun.

"Green, fuck…" Sam splayed his hands toward the remaining agent.

"Sam, get in here. Move it. I have a really bad feeling," Jesse yelled as he climbed in the back of the pickup truck.

"In about thirty seconds, we're going to find out if our cover's been completely blown." Sam jumped in the front, shoving Diane in the middle, while baby-face Green fired up the engine.

"How quick can you get us there?" Sam asked.

"With or without being noticed?"

Sam groaned. "Just get us there."

"Ten minutes, tops," Green said, and he floored it.

CHAPTER 42

Marcie killed the lights on her truck when she turned onto Glynn Road, a half mile from Scotty Bay. Her damp palms slipped, so she tightened her grip around the wheel. This isolated part of the island was camouflaged with heavy brush and many old trees so even tonight's bright moon couldn't penetrate the pitch black. Branches and overgrown brush scraped the side of her truck. Bumps and ruts in the packed dirt road squealed and rattled her suspension, bouncing her old Land Cruiser up and down. It was awkward driving with a cast. Her plastic splint had stuck under the gas pedal twice while she used her left foot to stomp on the brake. It was a wild challenge and not one of the brightest things she'd ever done.

The back road trail opened into a large clearing. Marcie yanked the wheel left until a faint outline of an old slanted shack appeared. "Close enough." She shoved the truck in park. "Okay, okay, calm down." Her insides shook so hard she had trouble breathing.

Marcie opened her door. She could hear the waves crashing against the big rocks below. The moon was waning. The lunation tide would be extremely high. What a great night for bringing a boat in the cove. Wearing one hiking boot, dark pants, and a black sweatshirt, she stepped down with her left foot, crunching the leaves and grass, keeping all weight off her injured ankle.

Shadows and darkness made her feel vulnerable, and so did soft, distinct footsteps whispering through the brush. She turned when a tall, shadowy outline, cloaked in a dark hood, approached under a glistening silver moon.

"Right on time. I could always count on you," Dan said.

"I'm here. Did you find the gardens I marked?"

"It's done."

"So now what?"

"We need to make the trade. The barge is in."

"Barge? I thought it was a boat?"

"Change of plans."

Her breath fled as if someone had jammed a fist in her gut. "You told me a boat would be here at eleven. You'd have all the marijuana, and we're trading it for cocaine. Are we still delivering it to your friend on the island? And what about leaving? You said we're leaving tonight for some exotic beach. Has that changed, too?" She rapped her knuckles against the open door. *Now what?*

Dan stepped closer, shoving her door closed, resting his hand on top of the truck. "Stop worrying. We're still leaving, just doing things a little bit differently. Come on, trust me, Marcie."

Why hadn't she expected this? He was famous for last-minute changes, keeping her out of the loop and constantly off guard. How many times had he done this?

"Something wrong, Marcie?"

She willed the shaking inside her to stop, then reached out and touched his arm. "No, nothing's wrong. So where's this barge?"

"It's waiting for us down at our yacht club's prestigious pier." If this were another time, she'd have warmed to his sense of humor. Las Seta yacht club was an eight-by-eight clubhouse made with rotted wood and a door with two rusty hinges thrown together by a group of renegade Las Setans ten years ago. From there, a dirt path led down to a rickety pier, hammered together by homesteaders who had inhabited Las Seta in the early fifties.

"So what about the marijuana, is it ready to go?" Her leg ached and her stomach cramped, so she rested against the truck. Dan leaned just out of reach. Something about him pulled away. *Why?*

"It's all taken care of—packaged and ready."

"Where is it?"

"It's in the yacht club."

"What's going on, Dan? Come on, let's finish this," someone said. A voice Marcie didn't recognize sent a cold chill purring up her spine. A shadowy character appeared out of the darkness and stood just below Dan's shoulder. Next to Dan, he resembled a short, squat man, but then most men didn't reach Dan's height of six foot four.

"Okay, let's get this over with. Marcie, you need a hand?"

"Huh? No, I'll just follow right behind you." Marcie reached out, grabbed Dan's sweatshirt, and pulled him back.

"Who's that?" she whispered, panicked.

"That's Donny. He's helping out."

"Are you crazy? You can't bring in new people. Who else is involved? What are we walking into?" This wasn't how it was supposed to go down. A twinge of fear escalated, and so did the fight or flight instinct pummeling up her back.

"Marcie, you've got to stop this. I told you to trust me. I've known Donny for years. He's good. I thought we worked all this out. Do we go and finish this, or are you going to bail? Come on, Marcie, trust me." He cupped her cheek with his entire palm. There was something different about his touch.

She knew then what she needed to do. She reached up and touched his freshly shaven cheek. "All right, but I think I need your help. Can you walk slowly so I can hold on to you?"

He leaned down and kissed her hard; his breath minty fresh. "You got it, babe."

Dan's strong confidence reeked with cocky sureness. He held his arm out, and Marcie slid her hand under it. She could feel the muscles turn to steel as he led her down a steep path. He paused for a moment, looking around. She was positive he smiled in victory when he covered the hand gripping his arm and squeezed lightly. Something rustled up ahead. She couldn't see anything in the bushes lining this part of the path. She could only sense someone moving in front of them.

They stepped onto a small, shaky pier nicely lit by the soft glow of the moon.

"Hey, Donny, you got it?" Dan stopped beside the sixty-foot steel barge.

"Yeah, we're done." Donny stood on the flat deck, with a second person of medium build, wearing a baseball cap and smoking a cigarette.

"Dan, how's things?"

"Couldn't be better. So I heard there was some activity earlier in the cove, the Coast Guard loitering about."

Dread turned her blood to ice, and it spiraled like tiny threads through her veins. Oh, shit.

"You okay, Marcie? You're shaking."

"I'm fine. Cold, is all."

"You wouldn't happen to know why the Coast Guard was here?"

Where's Sam? "No, why would I?"

He flashed a harsh smile, his bright white teeth reflecting nicely under the hint of moonlight. He looked away. *He knows.*

A beam of light flashed. Pandemonium reigned all at once. The roar of a boat surged toward them. "Freeze! DEA! Everybody, get your hands up!" The deep voice boomed over the loud speaker, and then a horn blasted. Caught up in the chaos, Marcie didn't know where to look, where to stand.

"You bitch, you think I didn't know that you backstabbed me?" He ripped his arm away and backhanded her across the cheek, knocking her into the cold, inky darkness of the ocean. She hit something hard, lost her footing, and went down deep into the freezing water.

A bright, golden light rose above, surrounding Marcie like a soft blanket protecting a baby. A slender pale hand extended out of the light, followed by a willowy, graceful face. The woman's silky blond hair swam all around them. When she spoke, it was with sweet determination, crossing through the thin veil of worlds that separated them.

"Over here. Come on. You're safe, Marcie. Sam's waiting for you. He

needs you. Do you finally understand? You're the victim of a vicious, ugly cycle. You broke free from the darkness by refusing to be a victim. You stood tall, taking back your power, and you stood for truth. Dan won't have you now. You destroyed his plan, and you embarrassed him with the one man who controls him. No woman has ever done that to him before. The darkness he covets is part of him. Because you're strong. You ended his familiar hold on you."

CHAPTER 43

Sam, for the first time in his life, felt rage and then terror slice so deeply that it penetrated his bones. The instant Dan struck Marcie and knocked her into the water, he'd swear that agony crippled his heart, and for a moment, he'd left his body. Pure instinct had him racing out of control from their deep cover in the trees, a hundred feet from the yacht club's rickety shack. He lost sight of the objective—bringing down Dan McKenzie and Lance Silver.

Marcie, sweet Marcie, had become his Achilles heel. Sam pounded down the hill, tripping over roots and sliding in the dirt. She meant more to him than this case—a case that had consumed him for so long.

Onto the dock, he ran, diving blindly into the ocean, reaching around until he hit boulders, rocks, and the bottom before pushing back up. His chest burned when his head broke the surface. "Marcie!" Gasping, fear almost paralyzing him, he treaded in the frigid water. He couldn't see her in the darkness, even with the lights around him, but he knew this was where she had gone in. Sam sucked in a lungful of air and dove down again, reaching into the shadows.

A spotlight illuminated the dock and shoreline when he broke through the water again, this time gulping down the cold, dank air.

Diane raced along the rocky shore, stumbling over boulders and rocks. "Sam, she's on the rocks!"

Sam trembled while he clawed his way out of the water. Jesse dropped to his knees on the shaky dock, grabbing Sam's arm and leg, pulling him out of the water onto the narrow pier. Drenched, Sam slid on his stomach and pushed himself up on shaky legs, panting as if he'd just run a marathon. Pure adrenaline had him stumbling over boulders, guided by Diane's flashlight, to a huddled form lying still on the sand and gravel shore. A thick, foamy tide brushed over the twisted fabric pasted around her legs and cast and then retreated. By the time Sam reached Marcie, she still hadn't moved. He pushed past Diane, who was down on her knees, whispering to Marcie as she rolled her over. A low moan gurgled from her wet, sandy lips. Sam cradled her in his arms, and her eyes fluttered open. She reached up and grabbed his sopping wet jacket. Sam pulled her closer, wiping the grit and tangled strands of hair from her face.

She coughed. Her voice was raspy. "Where were you?"

He pressed his lips to her forehead, rocking her while he fought back tears.

"She's going to be okay." Jesse patted his back and then removed his coat, draping it over Marcie.

Sam didn't know how he found the strength, but he lifted Marcie on legs that had turned to rubber and carried her. He couldn't let go. Marcie's head lolled on his shoulder while he struggled up the hill, slipping on the steep incline, refusing Jesse's help. His legs should have given out by the time he'd stuck her in the backseat of the big four-door sedan that was parked in front of her truck, and surrounded by agents; a renewed fury over what he could have lost kept him going.

Sam didn't need to question anyone about what had happened. The whole night had been a complete fuckup. Where was Greg's boat bringing the cocaine, and why had the Coast Guard arrived in such grand force without warning them of their arrival?

The seventeen-member task force was supposed to wait until the drugs had actually changed hands—until Dan and Marcie were on the boat. But then there was no boat, and a mysterious call had pulled the team out. This fuckup had amateur hour posted all over it, as everyone appeared to scramble.

MARCIE SHIVERED IN THE BACKSEAT OF THE BORROWED LATE-MODEL OLDS belonging to Kent, the owner of the Las Seta Hotel.

The interior light lit up a dusty vinyl interior and magnified the deepened lines around Sam's startling cobalt eyes. He dripped from his coat, his hair, but he insisted on peeling off Marcie's sopping wet sweatshirt. He dumped it on the dirty floor mat and helped her pull Jesse's oversized coat on. She couldn't remember ever having been so cold. The water temperature this time of year would have been around fifty degrees. Sam hovered nearby, soaked but unwilling to change his clothes. He leaned over Marcie as worry lines creased his forehead. "I'd rather be safe and have you checked out by a doctor. You've been hurt more times in the last few weeks than most people have in a lifetime."

Marcie was shaken by what had transpired and was most likely in shock. "Sam, I'm just cold, and I want to go home. Call Sally. She's a natural healer, and I trust her opinion more than any doctor."

"Does she have a phone?" He ground his teeth after blowing out his breath in a huff.

Her throat closed, jamming up the words she tried to speak. She couldn't hold back the floodgate burning her chest, causing tears to run down her face. "Yes, Sam, she has a phone."

"Hey, hey, babe, you're not okay. That's it. I'm taking you to the hospital in Port Townsend, end of argument."

She reached out with a trembling hand and held his arm until he climbed in beside her and pulled her tight against his drenched coat. Leaning against him gave her the strength to talk. "Sam, I'm okay. I matter to you. You've never left me, and you have no idea how much I treasure that. I love how protective you are, but call Sally—please. She had a phone line installed inside of her house."

He let out a sigh. "Just one word—one hesitation from her, and you're going to the hospital. Is that clear?"

Tears spurted again, locking up her throat so she could only nod.

"Let me wrap it up here, and then we'll go." Sam slid out of the car.

Marcie grabbed his arm before he could move away. "Sam, what happened? There was no boat. What about Dan and the drugs? Do we have enough to expose him? Is it over?"

Sam leaned over Marcie. He pushed her long, drenched hair over her shoulder. "We had some trouble. A group of your island residents picked the same that time the Coast Guard was in place to deal with a problem."

"What problem?" She focused on what he wasn't saying.

He glanced out the back window at the three agents standing behind the car. "Some kid has apparently been lighting fires. Five men grabbed him, threw him in a boat, called the Sequim detachment, and issued a demand to meet them halfway across and pick up the 'little prick'—their words, not mine. At the halfway point, they were going to dump him into the ocean whether the troopers arrived or not. Sequim didn't have their boat tonight, so they scrambled and pulled the Coast Guard, who was already in place, as well as some of our agents, leaving only Jesse, Diane, Green, and me. We would've been in place before you got here, but two abandoned trucks were blocking the only intersection on this island. Diane, Jesse, Green, and I had to run the last mile."

How did Dan find out? She trembled with damp eyes that reached out to Sam. "He knew, Sam. He knew about the Coast Guard—he knew everything. I don't understand how he always knows. Lance Silver would've been behind the blocked road, those men in the boat, and the call to the Sequim detachment. Only he has the power to control some of the residents here. Dan wouldn't." Hope that had become such a vital force slid away. Unable to find the words, she skimmed his damp hair and his strong jaw with her trembling hand. "Will we ever be rid of Dan?"

"You and I are done with him, Marcie. Whatever happens next, we're out of it. You played your part, and it damn near killed me to let you go to him."

"Sam, what about the cocaine and marijuana, and where was the boat? Sam, please, what's going on?" He didn't need to answer. She already knew. "There were no drugs, were there?"

The deep richness that emblazoned his eyes captured hers. "There's no cocaine and no marijuana on the barge. There was a small sealed bag of bud found overboard, along with a garbage bag filled with salal leaves. But you're right—Dan knew."

"You can't charge him with anything, can you?" His face took on an odd expression that had Marcie pulling away. "What's going on, Sam?"

"Greg McKenzie's boat dropped off the radar. The guy who owns the barge down there is a caretaker on Lance Silver's estate. His story is that the barge was just purchased, and he was out testing the engine. In the morning, they're going to be doing some work on it, and Dan's pointing the finger at you for the small amount of marijuana found. He said you grew it. It's your dope, and, remember, he carried nothing."

CHAPTER 44

The last time Marcie's cottage held this many people had been when she buried her granny. Strange voices filtered through the quaint log home like an out-of-sync symphony, with stress and tension disrupting the peaceful space. Marcie lay on her bed, studying Sally. In her bulky, black and white, wool woodcutter's coat, the older woman meticulously closed up the black doctor's bag that had belonged to her father. Marcie's granny's glass kerosene lamp burned brightly on the bedside table, casting a wide circle of light in the small, rustic room.

"You're fit as a fiddle, my girl, but you already knew that. You did an amazing and courageous thing. You listened some. There were some twists and turns, but you held true and stayed honest. You made a stand, cut his cord. I know it was hard. He's powerful. But so are you, and you did it right even though I know you were tempted by his promises. So who got you out of the water, Jerome or Sam's wife?"

Marcie was drawn into the reflective wisdom transforming Sally's light eyes. Waving her hand, Sally dismissed the question and picked up her floppy straw hat from the foot of Marcie's bed. "Ah, posh, girl, I already know. Get some sleep. I'll go and talk to your man out there."

"Sally, how did you know Elise saved me?"

Sally didn't face her when she spoke. She settled her hat on her head, clutched the old doctor's bag, and gripped the doorknob. "I've been at this since long before you were born, seen things I'll never talk of. I listen to Spirit, practice my craft, and I've seen pure evil that made me question everything: God, goodness, the universe. Just know this. There are things you aren't meant to know, and some you are. As far as Dan's concerned, it's not over yet. Remember, the bad will be there, but don't listen to it, and don't listen to the gossip. Rise above it. There'll be an investigation, too, but keep your head high. Your man will protect you. Remember what I told you: 'When you react to something instead of taking a step back to listen to Spirit, that's when you make mistakes.'"

Sally pulled the door open and then stared back at Marcie. She opened her mouth to say something but then clamped it tight. It was her darkened eyes, the way they watched her, that had Marcie wondering why her heart hammered in her throat. Then Sally was gone, pulling the door closed with a soft click.

Marcie rolled awkwardly on her side, snuggled in her soft pink fleece pajamas, with her granny's Irish chain quilt draped over her.

The door squeaked open.

"You asleep?" Sam filled the doorway, dressed in navy jeans and a black FBI sweatshirt.

"No." Marcie patted the bed beside her. "I'm fit as a fiddle, Sally said."

"So she told me, but you're still not getting out of bed until you have a doctor's note." Sam slid his hands into his dry jeans pockets and approached cautiously. He hesitated for a second before he sat down beside her, leaned over, and touched her lips with his lightly. He pulled back a fraction. He was being careful—too careful.

"I won't break, Sam. I'm okay, really."

He just nodded as he looked away.

"Sam, what's going to happen now?"

He slid around on the bed and let out a sigh. "I don't know. The marijuana and cocaine are long gone. We'll never find it."

"The missing marijuana from all your gardens alone should be in the ballpark of a couple million, so, just out of curiosity, what would your share have been?"

The dim room hid the gray shadows from his eyes, but she sensed there was no accusation or distrust.

"You know what? Nowhere near that, so Dan managed to win in the end. When we were together, I wondered how he'd move it. I heard rumors of hockey bags dumped from a small plane to a sheep farm or of people kayaking the freezing waters to a remote northwest Washington location. Dan's into wood. Don't forget, he was a contractor and ex-forester in his youth. I know he loved the story of hollowed-out logs stuffed with BC bud, so I was curious how creative he'd get."

Anger filled her at the injustice. Why was he not being held accountable for all the hurt he'd caused? She knew this was where her faith was weak. "Sam, when I was with Dan, I did what you're supposed to do; I looked the other way. I expected to make a few thousand and be his one and only. How's that for pathetic?"

"Are you feeling sorry for yourself, maybe still hung up on him? Don't forget, I did see you kiss him." Sam pulled his hands back and gestured wildly in the air.

"No, God, no. You need to get your eyes checked. He kissed me, and if you recall, the plan was for him to believe we were getting back together. As much as I wanted to, I didn't pull back. Just so you know, I feel redeemed, as if, for the first time, I'm on the right road with you. I'm angry with myself for not seeing the monster he was sooner, and I'm mad because he keeps getting away with this."

Sam frowned and moved closer, resting his hands on each side of her.

"I want a life with you, and I want Dan out of our lives forever," Marcie said. "More than anything, I want the threat against you gone, and Richard and Maggie..." An awful feeling tightened in her stomach. Richard was supposed to be out there with Sam. Even now, in the commotion, she realized Maggie and the kids were gone. *Oh dear God, what happened?* She grabbed Sam's arm and tried to sit up. "Sam, where are Richard, Maggie, and the kids?"

"Lay down." He rubbed her shoulder through the thick pink fleece. They're safe. Richard pulled them out after you left. We didn't tell you because you had enough to pull off. You didn't need something else to worry about."

"Why did they leave, Sam? Did something happen." Although it was dark, she didn't miss the way he tensed. *What's he hiding?* "Sam?" She touched his arm lightly.

"Richard found out that Dan's involved with a group of three. Lance Silver's one, while the other is Dan's brother, Greg."

Marcie slid her hand under Sam's and linked her fingers with his. "Well, you might as well tell me all of it. Who's the third guy?" Marcie couldn't help the unease sweeping through her.

"We don't know for sure; it's just a rumor, but Richard said it's a cop."

"How does Richard know all this?" Marcie bolted upright. "Sam, are Richard and Maggie in danger?"

"Someone called his cell phone when he was out wandering by the road. Richard refused to tell me the name of his contact. He said if we want to continue getting information, his contact stays anonymous. Jesse made sure Diane agreed. As far as we know, Dan has no idea Richard's been helping us. He's just an angry husband pissed at his unscrupulous partner who tried to use his wife to commit a crime for him. I'm sure Dan will keep his distance from both of them."

"Sam, don't let anything happen to them." Marcie felt the spiral spin of the wheel of fortune; a fate set in stone that couldn't be undone. The hurt in her stomach expanded. She had no idea how long she leaned against him, but soon he lowered her down and covered her with the cozy quilt. Her eyes burned; she was so tired, but she feared the repercussions in this unknown, twisted game, that was beyond time and her control.

He pulled her against his chest. What he didn't say, as he rested his chin on the top of her head, was how angry Dan had been at her for betraying him, how he had raged at the DEA agents who slapped the steel cuffs on him. If Lance Silver had his way, Marcie would become a target.

"Shh, get some sleep. Nothing's going to happen to anybody, okay?"

CHAPTER 45

"Is Marcie sleeping?" Diane peeled off her coat and tossed it over a kitchen chair. She pushed up the sleeves of her black sweatshirt, her gun still holstered. Underneath her bloodshot eyes, puffy bags with a hint of gray seeped through her normally pale complexion. She poured herself another cup of coffee from the banged-up, ceramic percolator and dumped in a spoonful of sugar. Every mug that Marcie owned was littered across the narrow counter, and coffee was splattered on the stove, the floor, and the table.

Two agents swept the front room with a handheld bug tracer. Sam had left that to Jesse, who'd demanded and coerced until the tracer finally arrived. Jesse was like a dog with a bone, convinced there had to be some type of audio transmitter planted. Sam crossed his arms and leaned against the stove. He didn't know what to think, so he watched.

"She fought it, but she's finally asleep. These guys find anything yet?"

"Nothing." Diane dumped her spoon in the cluttered sink. "Somebody had better clean up before Marcie sees this."

"Later. Do you have any news on our pirate?"

"Dan's being held right now on assault and possession with intent to sell."

"Intent to sell is quite a stretch. I can't believe the DA went for it."

"Well, it doesn't really matter, since Dan's lawyer, 'Big Frank' Hawking, appeared in Port Angeles before they could question him."

"You've got to be kidding. Big Frank, the marijuana lawyer? He's Lance Silver's attorney. Any hope for a link between them?"

Diane shook her head and blew on the steaming coffee. "No, sir. Same with the connection to Greg. Nothing. They covered their tracks well."

"So, right now, the DA's leaning on Donny, trying to get him to talk and tell us where the drugs are, but he won't talk. I didn't see him throw the marijuana floating in the water." Diane shrugged.

"Dan said it's Marcie's, and he's doing a damn fine job of shining the light on her. After this fuckup tonight, nothing will stick, except maybe the assault on Marcie," Sam said, shaking his head and turning away.

"Come on, Sam, maybe if we can get Donny to tell us where the all the marijuana went, we can locate it and get Donny to testify that Dan had arranged to exchange all the bud for cocaine. That has some real teeth."

"That's quite a leap, Diane, especially since no cocaine was discovered. So where's the crime?" Sam pushed his heavy sleeves up.

"We'll get him on the cocaine when it's found, and we'll find it."

Sam sensed the fierce determination that transformed Diane, though it was wishful thinking on her part. She wanted Dan and Lance Silver behind bars as much as he did, but one thing was apparent—for now, these two were untouchable.

"We found something. Excuse me, sir," one of the agents shouted as he pulled out the stove and lifted a tiny piece of metal, similar to a small watch battery, from the back of the stove.

Jesse stomped in, ripped it out of the young agent's hand, and held it up. "Probably optical. This is high-end stuff and definitely costs money. My bet, it works on radio frequency. Here's your leak and how Dan McKenzie knew all about our plan. What do you want to bet, Lance Silver's behind this?"

Sam wiped his hand over his eyes. "Of course he is. He's close enough to pick up the radio signal, so while we were at his house bugging it, someone had already planted one here. They expected us. Obviously, what we heard was staged. I knew it was too easy getting in there with his security."

Sam threw his hands in the air but let them drop just as quickly, his heart pounding in his throat the moment he fully comprehended what had just happened. "Guys, they would have heard Richard. They'd know he was part of the setup. Shit, I just told Marcie that Richard and Maggie are safe, but they won't be."

Diane yanked out her cell phone and hurried outside to get a better signal. A few minutes later, she was back. "Dexter's sending two agents over to Richard's right now."

"So now what?" Sam asked.

Jesse yanked his windbreaker off the back of the chair. "I hate to say this, hoss, but I think you're done. Cut your losses. The drugs are gone. You ain't going to find them. These guys are untouchable for you." Jesse jabbed his finger at Sam. "Dan's got all Marcie's marijuana. The cocaine never arrived. He needs nothing from her—not anymore. Read the writing on the wall. It's time for you to make a deal to protect your own before someone gets hurt. Then, go on a vacation."

"And let him win? What, are you kidding?"

Jesse grabbed Sam by the shirtfront. "Open your eyes. You know dirt when you see it. This case is done for you. Let the DEA build another one against Dan and Lance without you. If you didn't notice, Dan McKenzie didn't win. You got the girl." Jesse slapped Sam on the chest and headed for the door. He gestured to one of the agents who lingered in the doorway. "Come on. Get me to the dock where the DEA guys and Coast Guard are still hanging out. I'll hitch a ride back with them to the mainland. Then I'm going home to my wife."

Fire blazed off of Jesse as he jabbed a finger at Diane. "You make sure he listens. This is done. Take a break. There are times you've got to cut your losses, admit defeat. This is one of them." He opened the door, his deep chocolate eyes latching on to Sam before a big sloppy grin plumped out those priceless dimples. "My wife and I expect an invite to the wedding." Then Jesse left, chuckling while he watched Sam stagger back a few steps as if he'd been bashed over the head.

CHAPTER 46

Marcie stood behind the fifth wheel in darkness. It was the night of the fire on Dan and Richard's Gardiner property. Only this time, she lingered in the shadows, watching as Dan and Sandra loaded two hundred pots of marijuana in a horse trailer. She recognized the time; it was before the house burned. She watched her own presence like a doppelganger. In a scene taking place on the other side of the shed, inside Dan's fifth wheel trailer, she undressed and climbed up into the bunk. She remembered vividly the red T-shirt, carelessly tossed on the worn bench seat before she climbed into bed.

Dan closed up the horse trailer, and Sandra opened the driver's door while Dan said something behind her. Their arrogant manners were filled with cocky sureness. Marcie couldn't make out their words. It played out like an old-time movie. Sandra started the truck and slipped out the back way, while Dan closed up the shed and strode to the RV. She remembered now. That night, when he climbed in beside her, his desire for her had been strong, unusually attentive to her needs while he satisfied his. Disconnected, she observed the person she used to be through a veiled connection with Dan—physical only. No emotional or spiritual bond of any goodness lingered there. A murky gray cloud shrouded her third eye. No wonder she couldn't see through the thick block. But now, as she watched from a safe distance, an awareness formed inside Marcie. Every time he touched her, she allowed him to take her energy.

This was her doing. Lying in that RV beside Dan, she coveted the block, and she clung to him while her life force weakened.

She was asleep when Dan crawled out of bed and dressed. He became stronger every time he used her. He softly stepped out and latched the door behind him. Time seemed irrelevant, but Marcie sensed several hours had passed.

Headlights turned off on a black pickup truck, which slipped in from the back of the property. The truck appeared to slither down the rutted dirt road and stopped just before the shed. Whoever was inside killed the inner light before they popped open the door. The pale moon illuminated the figure from the surrounding darkness, Richard.

With his hands fisted, he stepped forward and faced off with Dan. Dan was smug when he reached out and patted Richard's shoulder, but there was no mistaking the searing fury when Richard knocked his hand away.

Their words appeared heated. From a distance, she bounced in place, up and down, yelling at Richard not to do it. But her voice was silent, and her lips were stuck as if they'd been glued.

Richard nearly knocked Dan over when he brushed around him. The darkness swallowed him up. The air visibly shifted when he entered the rundown, vacant house. When she looked back at Dan, he viewed the house with a coldness she'd never seen portrayed on his face before. Moments later, smoke spiraled from the windows, filling the house, engulfing the entire structure at an accelerated speed. She couldn't see Richard. She turned in a circle in the darkness. When she turned back to the house, she saw the end of the devastation: the fire department, the sheriff, Richard and Dan, followed by a familiar scene where Richard rigidly walked over to her, physically turned her, and pushed her away. She remembered now the clear warning: "Get out of here." This time, though, she watched his reaction when she walked away. His face hardened with animosity when he glanced over at Dan. When he looked at her, his eyes softened, as one's did when you cared deeply for someone.

Time stood still when Elise, Sam's dead wife, emerged from nowhere, dressed in blue jeans, a white T-shirt and a jean jacket, with a sidearm strapped to her side. Her long blond hair flowed over her shoulders.

This time, confusion filled Elise's eyes as she held out the palm of her hand. In it was a key to the shop where two hundred potted marijuana plants were stored.

Elise held up her hand, pointing her finger like a gun, taking aim and firing. Except this time, Marcie looked behind her, and she saw the dead grandson of Mama Reine.

She knew now that she had misunderstood. Elise had been part of Dan and Lance Silver's sideline—making sure the marijuana arrived and distributing it in New Orleans. She had recruited Leon, and when he got greedy, she eliminated him.

CHAPTER 47

The early morning sun was just clearing the horizon when Marcie hobbled into the kitchen. Diane and Sam lingered around the kitchen table with a cup of coffee, both wide eyed as if pumped full of a week's worth of caffeine.

"Where's Jesse?"

Sam lifted his foot off the kitchen chair and slid it out with the toe of his black boot. "On his way home. I just got off the phone with him. He's in Seattle. Plane just landed. His flight to New Orleans will be leaving in a few hours."

Marcie felt some added layer of protection fall away. She lowered herself in the chair beside Sam. "I don't understand. I thought he was helping you build a case against Lance Silver and Dan?"

Sam and Diane shared a knowing look. Sam let out a heavy sigh. He leaned closer to Marcie and linked their fingers. "It's over, babe. The task force will evaluate whether they want to start again. This case's blown. The weed's gone, and who knows where the cocaine ended up."

"You're just going to walk away, let Dan get away with this, let him screw some more innocent people? What about Lance Silver? Both he and Dan tried to set you up, Sam."

"It was a message, Marcie, to back off. And you know what? You and I are out of it. But it doesn't mean they win. I promise you, neither one will come after me or you again."

"You can't be sure of that, Sam."

He stood up, leaned down and kissed her. "I've got to go out for a bit." Sam grabbed his black windbreaker off a hook by the door and left.

Marcie held out her hands, gaping at the closed door and then at Diane. "What the hell's that about?"

"He needs some fresh air. Adrenaline's still pumping. He damn near lost you last night, and I think he's come to realize what's really important."

Marcie's telephone rang from the front room. Diane jumped up. "I'll get it."

Marcie was exhausted and lost in her head as she stared at the door. Sam was her man, a fighter like none she'd ever seen. Her head was still coming to grips with everything that had happened. She felt physically and emotionally derailed from this battle, yet, at the same time, an amazing peace existed inside of her when she realized the link between her and Dan was forever severed. Was Sam out of danger? For the first time since this mess had started, maybe he was. Marcie leapt when Diane touched her hand.

"Didn't you hear me? Maggie and Richard are on the phone."

Because it was an old landline, and she still used her granny's old rotary phone, she had to go into the front room to talk. Marcie shuffled to the phone and picked up the receiver lying on the end table beside the easy chair. "Hi, guys."

"Are you all right? We heard you went for a swim."

"I'm fine. Richard, nothing went as planned. Dan knew everything. There's someone on the inside, isn't there?" Marcie could hear Diane rattling around in the kitchen.

Richard let out a heavy sigh. "Look, Marcie, there always has been."

"Sam said we're done. He doesn't want to investigate Lance and Dan anymore."

"Smart man. Maggie and I are out of it, too. That underworld isn't so black and white, Marcie. Some ties run so deep and powerful—they're not going to get caught. There's dark stuff, and many people involved are leading picture-perfect lives. What you see and what is real are two different things."

"But Dan's going to get off?"

"Marcie, they have nothing on him. Let it go. He'll get what's coming to him, most likely from the same underworld he's screwing now. Retribution doesn't always come in the way we expect, so make peace with what happened. My instincts are pretty good, and I think you've found yourself a good man in Sam. Focus on the life you started with him, and forget Dan."

"Marcie, Richard's right. Sam risked everything for you, and not once did he turn his back. That alone should tell you how important you are to him. Dan will get his, maybe not now, but someday. Hold on to that while you focus on making yourself happy."

Marcie sighed. "Richard, what about this contact? Who told you Dan was involved with a cop?"

"Marcie, there are contacts made with dirty cops, airport employees—look, let's be honest. This is what Dan did. Although he fronted other things, the development project with me and his other rental properties, they're a disguise for his sideline, which isn't a sideline. Do you understand? He needs the illusion of respectability to target the innocent. I allowed him to do this, and I chose to ignore it. I'm as guilty as you."

Richard paused as if struggling for the right words to explain. "Dan knew people with the right contacts. Don't forget how charismatic he is. I know there's a state trooper he has some connection with now. This could be the leak on Sam's team. I don't know for sure. In New Orleans, he used to have a contact, but we're going back in time now. All I know is what he told me. She was shot after she eliminated a problem. I didn't want to know then, and, Marcie, I don't want to know now. Dan's been growing marijuana for years, long before you arrived on the scene. You may believe this expansion is new, but that's just another one of his illusions. You don't want to play games with him."

Marcie's stomach burned with nausea. She shut her eyes, knowing the contact had been Elise and the problem was Mama Reine's misguided grandson, Leon. "Richard, you're still partners with Dan. What if he tries to get back at you?"

Maggie's voice trembled on the other end. "Two agents arrived here last night and stayed. Richard, are we in trouble? Is Dan going to come after us? I told you last night that I have an awful feeling he may try something."

The phone squealed, two cordless phones too close together. One clicked off. Richard came back on the line. "Sorry, Marcie, this has been an emotional roller coaster for Maggie. She worries too much, and so do you. Everything will be fine. Dan won't try anything with me. He thinks he's got one pissed-off partner because he pressured my wife into helping with his illegal drug operation. I'm pretty sure he'll be the one avoiding me."

After Marcie said goodbye, she sat in silence and reflected. The last thing she wanted was to upset Maggie. Richard had been right to downplay it. She wondered if Richard might be ignoring a potential problem in Dan or an even worse one in Lance.

Diane cleared her throat. She hovered in the archway. "You okay?"

"You feel like getting some air?"

CHAPTER 48

The high wrought-iron gates were propped wide open. Sam drove Marcie's truck down the long, freshly pebbled driveway. A man wearing a tan, wide-brimmed hat, baggy pants, and a gray wool sweater paused while holding a rake over a pile of leaves on the massive front lawn. The neatly manicured gardens surrounding the house boasted creamy pink and purple hydrangeas, and a prize rose garden filled with blood red and white roses climbing a trellis up the side of the lavish house. Thin smoke plumed from the chimney of what appeared to be the great room, and a creamy gossamer curtain swayed and fell against the large plate-glass window.

Sam parked in the circular driveway right in front of the house. He breathed in deep, coming to peace with what he needed to do. Jesse was right, and Sam missed his wise friend already. This was their chance, Sam and Marcie's, so he didn't hesitate for a second as he climbed the stone steps, holding his head high, to the brand new front door. He was positive that this time, the solid white door came equipped with metal reinforcements. It'd be harder to kick in. Sam raised his fist to pound, but the door slid open. He let his hand fall before jamming both hands into his front pockets.

Lance Silver looked more like an aristocrat than the lowlife drug dealer he was. His sandy blond hair was slightly graying, styled and gelled, not a hair out of place. He wore rimless reading glasses, which he pulled off and dangled from his right hand. He wore tan slacks and a cashmere sweater that probably cost more than Sam made in a year. He stepped back, allowing Sam to enter.

The man showed no fear as he closed the door behind Sam, but why should he, with all his well-paid goons surrounding him? Sam's hands were damp when he unzipped his coat. One of Lance's men, a tall, dark guy who looked like he pumped steroids, removed Sam's Glock from its holster.

"Agent Carre, I presume. What can I do for you?" Lance Silver was a man who controlled his emotions, a master really, and Sam couldn't get a read on what this confident man was thinking.

"I came to make you a deal, one you can't refuse."

Lance Silver grinned and ran his tongue over his white, perfectly straight, teeth. "I'm intrigued. First, my man's going to check you for a wire and more weapons. Then he'll show you into my study."

Sam put his hands on his head while Lance's man searched him. The man was a mutant, and his face resembled a sheet of steel. His emotions were so carefully controlled. He never spoke but directed Sam down the familiar hallway, the one resembling an art gallery, and into Lance's warm, eclectic study. It was a room filled with books, floor-to-ceiling windows, and an energy-efficient wood stove.

Lance sat behind his mahogany desk in a high-back, black leather executive chair. He motioned to a shorter padded leather chair on the other side of the desk. Sam could feel the heat from Lance's man dogging his heels.

"No, I'll stand, thanks. This won't take long. You bugged Marcie's cottage. You knew we'd be waiting for Dan McKenzie and his brother while they exchanged the marijuana for cocaine, so the exchange didn't happen, and we have no idea where the drugs are. It's over. You win."

"I've no idea what you're talking about. Who's Dan McKenzie?"

Sam yanked up his black T-shirt, showing his bare, solid chest. "Don't. There's no wire. No one's listening. It's just you and me coming to an understanding."

"So what is this understanding, Mr. Carre?"

"I walk away, no more investigating you and your little operation. You leave Marcie alone, and Richard and Maggie, too. Richard's still Dan's partner, but I want your word you'll keep a tight leash on Dan, no more shenanigans. He got the marijuana and the cocaine. We won't come after him or you again. No more trying to set up Richard, Maggie, Marcie, or even me. You get Dan to stay away from Marcie and to stop pointing the finger at her. Rein Dan in. You and I both know you can do it."

"What guarantee do I have that you won't suddenly decide to start a brand-new investigation on me next month or six months from now?"

"I'm handing in my resignation with the DEA today."

Lance nodded. His hard eyes appeared to contemplate what Sam offered. "Maybe you'd consider coming to work for me. After all, a man with your talent would be a great asset to me. Financially, I'd make it worth your while."

Sam chuckled, amused by the man's balls. "I don't think so. You seem to forget I'm the one who pushed so hard to investigate you. Do we have a deal?"

"Well, hang on a second. What's to protect me when another cowboy from your team decides to pick up where you left off? You and I both know that'll happen."

"Nothing. But that's not my problem. I'm backing off, resigning, and with that, all my knowledge of you and Dan McKenzie disappears. This current investigation is now down the toilet."

"Marcie. Such a sweet, lovely girl. I could never get past her granny. Tried a few times. That woman, I swear she'd go to battle with the devil himself to protect her Marcie. You must really love her." Lance rocked forward and leaned on his desk. "I'm in a generous mood today. Mr. Thomas, please return Agent Carre's weapon and escort him to the door." Lance's man handed Sam his Glock and then directed him to leave. Lance Silver never looked up. "Mr. Carre, enjoy your retirement."

CHAPTER 49

Marcie sat on the edge of a moss-covered bank, admiring the sculpted rocks sloping down toward Scotty Bay. Puffy white clouds filled the clear blue sky; they were really moving. The wind had picked up. Maple and fir trees rustled and swayed their lovely pastel shades of green, orange, and yellow. *What a fine fall day to take in Mother Nature's glorious changes—to really clear away the confusion and bring some clarity to my busy mind,* thought Marcie. She breathed deeply as she looked down on the bubbling water splashing over the rocky shore.

Diane didn't join her. She must have sensed Marcie's need for space, so she lingered by the borrowed sedan. Sam had taken her truck when he went out earlier. Maybe he too needed some clarity. Who wouldn't after the drama they'd lived through the last few days—hell, for that matter, since she landed in his path in New Orleans?

Gravel rustled behind her, and a truck door closed. She didn't need to look back. She could feel his warm approach from anywhere.

"The mist is rolling in." He hunched down, wrapping his arms around her.

Marcie touched his arm and felt his possessive, loving hold sink right into her. "Diane called you?"

"She knew I'd worry, finding you both gone from the cabin."

She leaned her head back against Sam's shoulder, struck by the peaceful feeling that everything was going to be all right. "I'm glad she did. We better go before we can't see anything."

Sam all but lifted her. His solid arm surrounded her waist, pulling her so close that not even a breeze could find space to separate them. She wouldn't remember what the small detail was that made her look, but when she glanced out onto the bay, the view was impaired by the thickening mist. Then a window opened, with blue sky and Jerome's golden hair blowing in the wind. He smiled, on the deck of his ship, with his darling Isabel beside him. Then he was gone.

She looked up at Sam. He watched the same spot on the bay.

"Wow, look at how thick the fog is," he said.

And she knew, for her and Sam, they'd won.

CHAPTER 50

Marcie watched Sam through the front window as he threw a tennis ball to the fluffy golden retriever, who frolicked and raced to fetch the fuzzy ball. They needed to leave soon. Sam had booked them a beachfront resort down in Mazatlan.

"Here's your tea. Sit down, child, before you fall over." Sally placed a steaming mug on the driftwood coffee table, which she'd made from scraps that floated in from the ocean. She gripped Marcie's hand and led her to the sofa, giving her arm a gentle shake. "Marcie, you listen to me. I can see you fretting over what's past, but you need to let it go. You've been handed a precious gift. Take it. Go on vacation with your new man. Come back and build a life together. And never forget your gift.

"Now that you're listening and following the light, you already know your gift has returned. It's getting stronger, and when you come back all rested and tanned, it'll be time to resume your teaching. I'm happy for you, and you should know that your granny's smiling down on you. You got a good man there, the right man—the man you asked for. You accomplished quite a feat, whether or not you realize it. You broke a destructive cycle that had been repeating for generations. That dark entity didn't get you or Sam; although it tried. New guides and angels come to us all the time, as we need them, to teach us and guide us on our divine path. You won. You both did. Now finish your tea—you have a boat to catch."

"Sally, who's my real father? Jerome said you'd help me find him."

Sally pulled on her cream sweater and strode to the window, watching Sam and her fluffy companion bouncing through the piles of fallen leaves. "When you get back, child, and settled with your man. After you resume your teaching, it'll be time. Then I'll help you find him. Now, go with God and remember the words of our native forefathers about the battle that wages inside each of us. Do you remember, Marcie? One is evil. It's fear, anger, envy, jealousy, sorrow, regret, greed, arrogance, self-pity, guilt, resentment, inferiority, lies, false pride, superiority, competition, and ego. The other is good. It is joy, peace, love, hope, serenity, humility, friendship, respect, sharing, kindness, benevolence, empathy, generosity, truth, compassion, and faith. Do you remember who wins?"

"Yes, I do. The one you feed."

Marcie left the warm, cozy cottage without another word. Her heart felt at peace for the first time ever. Sam turned to her when she stepped off the porch and watched her in his soft, loving way that turned her knees to jelly. Words weren't necessary when a man could say it all with a look. She was everything, the sun, the moon, the stars, and the whole world to him. His face lit up in the easy way she'd come to recognize, over the past few days, since he'd tendered his resignation to the DEA. His walk was lighter, as if he'd shed every one of his burdens. He skimmed his fingers up and around her jaw, and his eyes sparkled with humor.

Sam helped her into the truck. Before he could close her door, she cupped his cheek and traced her finger over the pink nick on his chin, a casualty from shaving that morning.

"What is it?"

"Do you ever wonder what cost we pay for the choices we make, if it's fate or something we created?"

He frowned. "I'm not sure how to answer that, hon."

"You don't need to. I think the answer will come."

Sam leaned down and kissed her cheek and then her lips. "I have faith that it will. Now, let's go to Mexico."

Turn the page for a sneak peek of
LOST AND FOUND the next book in WALK THE RIGHT ROAD
Available in print, eBook & audio

'A 2013 Readers' Favorite Award Winner'

A hit and run
A deserted country road.
A parents worst nightmare.

On a warm fall morning in Gardiner, Washington, Richard and Maggie celebrate happy couple Sam and Marcie's return. What happens next changes their lives forever. A hit and run driver on a deserted country road, and Richard and Maggie suffer a parents worst nightmare.

Now a year later Maggie McCafferty struggles to put her life back together…hiding her pain with outrageous behavior and her own secret she's unwilling to share. Until her friends step in and her strong willed soon to be ex-husband sets out to bring Maggie home— the only way he knows. Just as Maggie begins to trust again, Dan McKenzie calls after disappearing for over a year. But now he's back. And instead of Richard coming clean with the truth of their involvement, Richard digs himself in deeper, with mounting debts, a partner who refuses to buy him out—secrets shared only with Dan. Until one night a mysterious 911 caller witnesses a fight and Richard shooting Dan. But when the police arrive at the deserted construction site the only evidence of a crime is a pool of blood, and a surveillance video.

Under mounting pressure from the police Richard's arrested and interrogated—except fiery secretive Richard is adamant he was home all night. In this bizarre twist of fate, Sam, Marcie and Diane work against the clock and wonder how well they really know their evasive friend. With Maggie by his side, Richard stands by his innocence. Trouble is, if Richard didn't do it, where is Dan? And who is the mysterious 911 caller?

LOST AND FOUND
PROLOGUE

"Hey, you two look great." Richard McCafferty propped his axe against the woodshed and strode away from the large stack of chopped firewood, wiping beads of sweat from his forehead with the back of his heavy work glove.

Marcie shivered underneath her purple down vest, her fingers linked with those of Sam, the love of her life. She leaned against him, into him, and couldn't erase the smile she'd swear was now etched permanently into her face. She couldn't explain the joyful sense of lightness that filled every part of her. Maybe that was why she needed to touch Sam and be with him, near him.

Richard gripped Sam's hand the way good friends do. He winked at Marcie as if he could read her every secret. She dropped her eyes; after all, when had she ever been successful at keeping something from Richard?

"Your cast is gone, Marcie; you're all tanned and healed. Those beaches down in Mexico look like they agreed with you. So when did you guys get back?"

Sam wrapped his arm around Marcie's shoulders and rested his chin on the crown of her head. "Last night. Rented a car in Seattle and drove around the peninsula. Thought we'd stop in, check on you and Maggie before heading over to Marcie's granny's place."

The screen door squeaked.

"Hey, you two! Didn't know you were back." Maggie dashed down the stairs, yanking on a thick green sweater. She skidded around the pile of leaves, nearly tripping over a garden rake before she hugged Marcie and then kissed Sam on the cheek. "You've got quite the glow happening there, Marcie." Maggie shoved in between the couple. "The way you two are glued together, you'd think you hadn't seen each other in, like, forever."

Sam smiled broadly and leaned against the black SUV he'd rented. His blue eyes, brighter than before he had left for Mexico, watching Marcie in a way that let her know how much he loved her. His look would have told her even if he hadn't said the words a few hours ago and every day since she'd told him the big news. Maggie was watching Marcie, and her toffee-colored eyes lit up as if she'd guessed her secret.

"Should we tell them, Sam?" Marcie said. She was teasing, and Richard stared first at Sam and then her.

"Okay, guys, what gives?" he asked.

Sam blurted out, "Marcie's pregnant."

Richard grinned and high-fived Sam. "Congrats, guys."

Maggie squealed and hugged Marcie, patting her still flat stomach. "So, how far along?" Maggie was almost bouncing with excitement as she tucked her shoulder-length, dark curly hair behind her ears. Her pale cheeks glowed a natural rosy pink from the chill in the late fall air.

"Not far, just a few weeks." Marcie could swear her joy shimmered in the air between her friends.

"Mom!" Ryley called from the door.

"Oops. Come on in, guys," Maggie said, hurrying to the steps. Ryley burst out the door, his sneakers undone, wearing only a dark long-sleeved T-shirt hanging outside jeans with patched-up knees. "Put your coat on, young man," Maggie said with a laugh, "and go finish raking those leaves before I kill myself. And this time, put the rake away when you're done."

"Hey, Ryley. No school today?" Sam bent down and retrieved the rake while Ryley pulled on his red jacket.

"Nah, it's a conference day, and Mom won't let me play on the computer. She's making me work," Ryley said, skulking down the steps. Marcie couldn't hear what Sam said when Ryley took the rake, but he laughed so hard he wiped what she assumed were tears from his eyes.

"Sam looks pretty happy, Marcie," said Richard. "He wants kids. See how he is with Ryley?"

Marcie looked up. Richard was so tall, and his dark hair was a little on the shaggy side. "Yes, he does." Marcie swallowed. Her head felt a little thick this morning, but she'd heard that was normal.

"How are you feeling? Maggie was sick the first few months with Ryley. With Lily, she was just tired all the time," Richard said. The lines around his eyes made him appear older, wiser and damn handsome. He knew darn well he still had every woman taking a second look when he entered a room.

"Tired. Feeling like I'm coming down with something. But it's good."

He shook his head; a grim line stretched taut across his lips. "You know, Marcie, I'm glad you and Sam had time to get away. Does Sam regret leaving the DEA?"

"He hasn't said. But being with him in Mexico, just us and nothing hanging over our heads … I've got to tell you, Richard, I didn't want to come back. It was magical, as if I was inserted into my fairytale ending where everything was perfect and nothing could touch us. I worried coming back on the plane if maybe there would be some repercussions when setting foot back here. I can't say this to Sam, but I can't shake this feeling there's something brewing in the wind with Dan and his crew. You know … payback."

Richard pulled off his work gloves and stuffed them into his back pocket. He stared up at the house for a moment before turning and looking at her in a meaningful way. She was sure he knew more than he was telling. "Marcie, this game, this business … even the people who aren't involved but know about what Dan, Lance and that whole underworld do, they don't talk."

"Richard, are we in danger?" Marcie shivered as a light breeze swirled her hair. She swept her fingers through the strands, distracted for a minute by how silky, wavy, and long her hair had recently become.

"You need to know something—and I haven't told Maggie this. I found out one of the disabled kids Sandra Carter had at her home the night you and Maggie delivered all the marijuana … well, he died last week. Whoever his full-time aide was had a way of communicating with the boy, and she said the kid was scared of Sandra. Before he died, he told her … Sandra hurt him."

"Are you sure? I thought those kids couldn't talk. Why does Sandra still have a contract to care for them?"

Richard just shrugged his shoulders. "I don't know everything, just what Diane told me. But they've suspended Sandra's contract pending an internal review."

"Well, how did the kid die, and how's Sandra responsible?"

"I don't know that, either, except they're presuming a mix-up in his meds. Both kids were on so many. Look, Marcie, the reason I'm telling you this is that Sandra's out for blood. She's made drunken threats to some friends against Maggie, and you too. Both of you broke the cardinal rule and ratted them out, her and Dan, and that's her quote. But you understand that world. You knew this was going to happen— we all did when we set them up. This underworld has a way of looking after things in its own way. We all need to be careful. Lance Silver is one dangerous and powerful bastard, and Sandra and her family are unscrupulous. Remember, Dan won't cross Sandra. Not once during that whole mess did he ever point the finger at her."

Marcie glanced over just as Sam dumped a handful of leaves over Ryley's head and then tossed him on the pile. "Why would he protect her, Richard?"

"You still don't get him. He and Sandra go way back. He's cagey, and he knows who he can screw over and who he can't. She encouraged his behavior, and he controls her to a point. If he crosses her, he knows he'll be dead. Have no doubt he'll protect Sandra, because that will protect him, too.

"He casts illusions, even with me, keeping me off guard. He was scared I'd kill him for involving Maggie. What goes through his mind after he screws people is … what he can say to keep from getting the shit pounded out of him. Lance Silver, Sandra, that whole underworld Dan slithered his way into, it's … let's just say that Dan doesn't play by their rules. He's not part of them; he's an outsider who slithered in. Sandra's a part of that world because she grew up in it. I still can't figure out Lance and Dan's connection, or why's Dan's still walking around. I know he's screwed one too many of them."

Marcie frowned, looking back at him, and tried to read past the sudden hardness encasing Richard. "How do you know this, Richard?"

He didn't look at her; instead, he watched his son. "Marcie, you're a big girl. If you're going to live out here, you need to be aware of what's going on around you. There's some ugly stuff, and the people involved lead outwardly picture-perfect lives. You and my wife got dragged into something.…" Richard yanked his gloves from his back pocket and swatted the leather across his jean-clad thigh. He lowered his voice and said, "What you *see* and what is real are two different things."

Marcie looked away, toward the bare towering willow that would shade the front lawn nicely all summer. "Have you spoken with Dan?"

"Nope. I'm just saying you need to constantly watch your back. Retribution doesn't always come in ways we expect."

"Richard, Sam said he took care of everything so we'd be safe.…"

His jaw stiffened, and he scratched his head as he watched Sam and Ryley turn a big pile of leaves into a spread-out mess as Ryley dove in over and over. "There comes a time when you need to look after home first. Sam did that for you. He did what he needed to. For me, that's Maggie and the kids. But make no mistake, whatever Sam and I do, anything can still come out of left field. We all need to be aware and not just trust that we're safe, because that's when mistakes happen … and someone gets hurt." He continued to watch Ryley.

Marcie hadn't noticed before, but tinges of gray now threaded through the strands of hair by his ear. It was thicker than before. Richard turned and smiled at her, but the light didn't reach those steely blue eyes. "Come on, O Pregnant One. Let's go on in and have some coffee."

"Tea for me, please," Marcie said.

This time, Richard laughed, and it wasn't so forced.

———

MARCIE LEANED AGAINST SAM IN THE WARM, CLUTTERED KITCHEN. Richard shoved a log into the wood stove while Maggie picked up the spoon Lily had tossed under the table—for the second time since they'd walked in. Five-year-old Lily, severely autistic, swayed in her booster seat at the table, lining up Cheerios instead of eating.

"Maggie, leave her. I'll take over," Richard offered.

Maggie handed Richard a clean spoon. "Good luck. She's driving me nuts this morning; she's already dumped her first bowl on the floor."

Richard gently squeezed Maggie's shoulder and then moved to the messy table, kissing the top of Lily's curly dark bed hair. "Come on, my girl. What's this about giving your mama a hard time?"

Marcie would swear Lily smiled in amusement. She was definitely a daddy's girl. Marcie needed to speak with Maggie about adding some natural remedies to aid in Lily's therapy. Focused on diet and vitamins, the holistic approach was controversial, with no track record or data, but it was an approach Marcie was convinced would help Lily be more responsive. Maybe before they left today, she'd broach the subject.

Richard spoon-fed Lily, who leaned in for her daddy and took each bite.

"You know, Marcie," Maggie said, "I remember the first few months with Ryley, just the smell of coffee would send me racing to the nearest bathroom."

Marcie clutched her warm mug of green tea. She could feel how relaxed Sam was behind her. He hadn't worried, like she had, about coming home. Marcie had asked him twice what he meant by "taking care of things" so they would be protected from Lance and Dan, but he wouldn't elaborate. And, try as she might, she couldn't figure out what he'd done.

"Thanks for the coffee, Maggie." Sam's southern charm whispered like honey when he spoke. Marcie would never tire of listening to him talk, because he meant what he said, and he spoke from his heart—always. She knew by the way Maggie smiled at him that her friend, too, loved listening to his smooth southern accent.

"All done, my girl." Richard helped Lily down from her chair. She still wore her fuzzy pink pajamas and fluffy elephant slippers, and she bolted straight for the screen door and pushed it open. Richard grabbed her before she went any farther.

She screamed "Sa, sa!" and reached for the door.

"Let's put your coat on. It's cold outside, silly girl," Richard said. He had just zipped up her purple down jacket when she dashed out the door that he held open. Ryley was raking leaves as Lily dashed past him. "Ryley! Watch your sister. Take her over to the swing and keep an eye on her. I'm going to grab a coffee, and I'll be right out."

"Aw, Dad, why do *I* have to watch her again? You wanted me to rake the *leaves*. Why do I have to do both?" he whined, like any young boy tired of being responsible for his sister.

"Go … now," Richard said. His voice was direct while he pointed toward Lily, now running in circles on the grass. Ryley dropped the rake and stomped after her.

"Richard, did you put her shoes on, or is she still in her slippers?" Maggie asked.

Richard leaned past her and poured himself a coffee. "She's fine, Maggie. Stop fussing so much about what she's wearing. At least she's got something on her feet."

Bile suddenly, burned the back of Marcie's throat and rose up like a sharp wind. She grabbed Sam's arm and nearly dropped her tea as she was flooded by a wave of dizziness. A harsh chill rushed through her. "Oh no," she mumbled.

"Marcie, are you okay, babe?" Sam grabbed her mug and set it on the counter.

Marcie pulled away from Sam just as she heard Ryley's irritated yell: "Lily, come back. Lily, stop!" Richard and Maggie pushed past Marcie and bolted out the door, and Sam and Marcie followed.

"Marcie, what's going on?" Sam asked.

"Something's wrong, Sam."

"You're scaring me. Is something wrong with the baby?"

"No. I don't *know* … something …" She stared off toward the road as Sam's hands fell away from her shoulders.

Time slowed. Sam started running and raced past Maggie, yelling something that stretched out long and loud, waving frantically at Lily, who stood in the middle of the desolate gravel road. Ryley stood only a few feet from her. Marcie blinked through the blur as a black car sped around the bend and hit Lily. A sleek sports car with dark tinted windows, it skidded on the gravel but didn't stop or even slow, speeding away.

Marcie's head ached, and she struggled to breathe, feeling as if her chest had been ripped open by a sorrow she couldn't put into words. Screaming pierced her dreamlike state. A sharp wind rustled the trees as Sam, Richard, and Maggie huddled around Lily, and Marcie moved down the steps, across the grass, and reached Ryley, who hovered frozen behind Sam.

"Marcie, call 911. Now, Marcie, now!" Sam shouted as he crouched over Lily.

Marcie grabbed Ryley's arm and ran. Her ankle, not quite healed from her recent break, throbbed. Ryley said nothing as she all but dragged him back to the house. She grabbed the kitchen phone and dialed. Ryley leaned against the wall, his face white, his big eyes nothing but empty pools. She knew he couldn't grasp what had just happened.

"Oh, God. Please let her be all right," she begged as she closed her eyes.

"Nine one one. What's your emergency?"

"Lily's been hit by a car," Marcie said. "She's five years old. She's lying on the road."

"Is she still breathing?"

"I—I don't know. Her parents are with her. She's covered in blood."

"We've got paramedics and police on their way. I need you to stay on the line with me."

Marcie gripped the cordless phone and glanced back at Ryley, who didn't move. "Ryley, I need you to stay here."

He didn't move—he didn't even look at her. She dashed out the door and could see Maggie on her knees, sobbing. Sam appeared to be giving Lily CPR. Richard was beside him. Marcie relayed everything to the 911 operator until she heard sirens wailing in the distance. She hung up when she saw the first red flashing lights.

She hurried back to the road, limping as she held the disconnected phone. Emergency vehicles arrived—an ambulance, the sheriff, and volunteers from the Gardiner and Sequim fire departments blocked the narrow gravel road. Two paramedics raced over and dropped down beside Sam and Richard as emergency personnel crowded around, leaning in. Lily was still alive, but barely. Marcie pressed her hand against her chest. "Hurry," she whispered.

"We need a medevac here now!" one of the men shouted.

"They're en route. They have to land at the fire hall. Let's move it!" another replied.

Richard pushed past Maggie, ignoring her as if she were of no importance. "Is she going to make it?" he cried desperately.

Sam glanced at the female paramedic, who shook her head. Sam stepped in front of Richard as Lily was loaded on the stretcher.

"I'm going with her!" Maggie screamed.

"There's no room!" someone yelled as three paramedics climbed into the ambulance beside Lily. She appeared so tiny, hooked up to an IV, with splints and a neck collar, strapped to the gurney. A state trooper grabbed Maggie by the waist and held her back when she tried to jump in the ambulance. Richard stalked over to the sheriff and state troopers, who leaned against their cars at the side of the road, lights still flashing.

"What the hell are you still doing here? Get your asses out there and find that murdering coward who hit my little girl!" he yelled.

Sam stepped in and took Maggie from the trooper. She collapsed in his arms, clutching his shirt. "Marcie," Sam yelled, "come here!"

So many people hurried around as the ambulance sped away, lights flashing and siren blaring, just as an SUV raced in and slammed its brakes, sending dust flying. Whoever was driving, Marcie couldn't see, but an angry deputy stormed toward the person who jumped out.

"Sam, Richard!" Diane called, flashing her badge. She pushed past the deputy. Marcie took a step—but then stopped, as Richard abruptly punched one of the deputies before being tackled by the sheriff and another officer. One pinned his knee in

Richard's back, laying him face down on the car's trunk as the other cuffed him.

Marcie touched her head. She didn't know what to do as Diane and Sam hurried over. Everyone was yelling, but the sheriff didn't care. He shook his head and stuffed Richard in the back of his car.

Marcie watched Maggie standing alone, sobbing. The spot she stared at was coated in blood. One fuzzy slipper lay there—alone. She needed to go to her but was stopped when a hand touched her sleeve.

"Ma'am, you need to sit down. Are you family?" It was one of the local firemen, his kind hazel eyes appearing through a film of her tears.

"Ryley. I left Ryley at the house," Marcie said.

"Who's Ryley?"

Her vision blurred even more when she looked up at him, unable to make out any of his features. Her nose was plugged, and she swiped her hands over her eyes and wiped her nose with a sleeve.

"He's their son, Lily's older brother. He watched this. He saw Lily get hit. Oh, God." She couldn't hear him reply as he led her over to the fire truck and helped her sit on the back bumper.

"We asked him his name, but he won't talk. One of the volunteers found him on the road, over there, watching the ambulance leave."

Marcie nodded. "Please keep him away. How bad is it?" she asked. She knew by the way he grimaced that he didn't want to say. "You … you don't think…"

The volunteer had an honest face. "Miss? You'd best be getting the parents to the hospital. Prepare them for the worst."

"What hospital?"

"She's being airlifted to Seattle."

Marcie didn't know how she did it, but she stood up and hurried to

Maggie, pulling her into her arms as crime scene technicians arrived and taped off the area. "Maggie, we need to go."

Maggie pushed her away and swept her trembling hands through her hair as tears fell. "Where are they taking her? Is she all right? She was still breathing, Marcie."

"Marcie!" Sam approached at a jog. The lines around his eyes had deepened, and his face was pale. Marcie wanted to fall into his arms, but Maggie was there first, her arms around Sam. He stared at Marcie and rubbed Maggie's back. "They're airlifting her from the fire hall to Harborview Trauma. She's still alive, but it's touch and go. Diane arranged for another chopper, waiting for us in Sequim." Sam hurried Maggie along, and Marcie fell in step beside them but stopped after a few strides.

"Ryley. I forgot about Ryley. We can't leave him," she said. "And Richard, where is he?"

As the sheriff pulled away with Richard in the back, Diane jogged over. The sheriff could be a hard-ass and didn't take kindly to his officers being hit—even by a distraught parent.

"Diane, please bring Marcie and Ryley with you," Sam said as he hustled Maggie to his SUV and helped her in. Marcie stood at the side of the road, alone, and watched as Sam drove away while Diane hurried off to find Ryley.

ABOUT THE AUTHOR

"Lorhainne Eckhart is one of my go to authors when I want a guaranteed good book. So many twists and turns, but also so much love and such a strong sense of family."

(LORA W., REVIEWER)

New York Times & USA Today bestseller Lorhainne Eckhart is best known for writing Raw Relatable Real Romance where "Morals and family are running themes." As one fan calls her, she is the "Queen of the family saga." (aherman) writing "the ups and downs of what goes on within a family but also with some suspense, angst and of course a bit of romance thrown in for good measure." Follow Lorhainne on Bookbub to receive alerts on New Releases and Sales and join her mailing list at LorhainneEckhart.com for her Monday Blog, all book news, giveaways and FREE reads. With over 120 books, audiobooks, and multiple series published and available at all, retailers now translated into six languages. She is a multiple recipient of the Readers' Favorite Award for Suspense and Romance, and lives in the Pacific Northwest on an island, is the mother of three, her oldest has autism and she is an advocate for never giving up on your dreams.

"Lorhainne Eckhart has this uncanny way of just hitting the spot every time with her books."

(CAROLINE L., REVIEWER)

The O'Connells: *The O'Connells of Livingston, Montana are not your typical family. A riveting collection of stories surrounding the ups and downs of what goes on within a family but also with some suspense, angst and of course a bit of romance thrown in for good measure. "I thought I loved the Friessens, but I absolutely adore the O'Connell's. Each and every book has different genres of stories, but the one thing in common is how she is able to wrap it around the family, which is the heart of each story." (C. Logue)*

The Friessens: *An emotional big family romance series, the Friessen family siblings find their relationships tested, lay their hearts on the line, and discover lasting love! "Lorhainne Eckhart is one of my go to authors when I want a guaranteed good book. So many twists and turns, but also so much love and such a strong sense of family." (Lora W., Reviewer)*

The Parker Sisters: *The Parker Sisters are a close-knit family, and like any other family they have their ups and downs. Eckhart has crafted another intense family drama… "The character development is outstanding, and the emotional investment is high…" (Aherman, Reviewer)*

The McCabe Brothers: *Join the five McCabe siblings on their journeys to the dark and dangerous side of love! An intense, exhilarating collection of romantic thrillers you won't want to miss. — "Eckhart has a new series that is definitely worth the read. The queen of the family saga started this series with a spin-off of her wildly successful Friessen series." From a Readers' Favorite award — winning author and "queen of the family saga" (Aherman)*

Lorhainne loves to hear from her readers! You can connect with me at:
www.LorhainneEckhart.com
lorhainneeckhart.le@gmail.com

ALSO BY LORHAINNE ECKHART

The Outsider Series
The Forgotten Child (Brad and Emily)
A Baby and a Wedding *(An Outsider Series Short)*
Fallen Hero (Andy, Jed, and Diana)
The Awakening (Andy and Laura)
Secrets (Jed and Diana)
Runaway (Andy and Laura)
Overdue *(An Outsider Series Short)*
The Unexpected Storm (Neil and Candy)
The Wedding (Neil and Candy)

The Friessens: A New Beginning
The Deadline (Andy and Laura)
The Price to Love (Neil and Candy)
A Different Kind of Love (Brad and Emily)
A Vow of Love, A Friessen Family Christmas

The Friessens
The Reunion
The Bloodline (Andy & Laura)
The Promise (Diana & Jed)
The Business Plan (Neil & Candy)
The Decision (Brad & Emily)
First Love (Katy)
Family First
Leave the Light On
In the Moment
In the Family
In the Silence
In the Charm
Unexpected Consequences

It Was Always You
The First Time I Saw You
Welcome to My Arms
Welcome to Boston
I'll Always Love You
Ground Rules
A Reason to Breathe
You Are My Everything
Anything For You
The Homecoming
Stay Away From My Daughter
The Bad Boy
A Place of Our Own
The Visitor
All About Devon
Long Past Dawn
How to Heal a Heart
Keep Me In Your Heart

The O'Connells
The Neighbor
The Third Call
The Secret Husband
The Quiet Day
The Commitment
The Missing Father
The Hometown Hero
Justice
The Family Secret
The Fallen O'Connell
The Return of the O'Connells
And The She Was Gone
The Stalker
The O'Connell Family Christmas
The Girl Next Door
Broken Promises

The Gatekeeper
The Hunted

The McCabe Brothers
Don't Stop Me (Vic)
Don't Catch Me (Chase)
Don't Run From Me (Aaron)
Don't Hide From Me (Luc)
Don't Leave Me (Claudia)
Out of Time

A Billy Jo McCabe Mystery
Nothing As it Seems
Hiding in Plain Sight
The Cold Case
The Trap
Above the Law
The Stranger at the Door
The Children
The Last Stand
The Charity
The Sacrifice

The Wilde Brothers
The One (Joe and Margaret)
The Honeymoon, A Wilde Brothers Short
Friendly Fire (Logan and Julia)
Not Quite Married, A Wilde Brothers Short
A Matter of Trust (Ben and Carrie)
The Reckoning, A Wilde Brothers Christmas
Traded (Jake)
Unforgiven (Samuel)
The Holiday Bride

Married in Montana
His Promise

Love's Promise
A Promise of Forever

The Parker Sisters
Thrill of the Chase
The Dating Game
Play Hard to Get
What We Can't Have
Go Your Own Way
A June Wedding

Kate & Walker
One Night
Edge of Night
Last Night

Walk the Right Road Series
The Choice
Lost and Found
Merkaba
Bounty
Blown Away: The Final Chapter
He Came Back

The Saved Series
Saved
Vanished
Captured

Single Titles
Loving Christine